BOOK 1

HiLo

THE BOY WHO CRASHED TO EARTH

BY **JUDD WINICK**

WITH COLOR BY GUY MAJOR

RANDOM HOUSE 🏠 NEW YORK

Copyright © 2015 by Judd Winick
All rights reserved. Published in the United States by Random House Children's Books,
a division of Penguin Random House LLC, New York.

Random House and the colophon are registered trademarks of Penguin Random House LLC.

Visit us on the Web! randomhousekids.com

Educators and librarians, for a variety of teaching tools, visit us at RHTeachersLibrarians.com

Library of Congress Cataloging-in-Publication Data

Winick, Judd.
Hilo: the boy who crashed to Earth / Judd Winick. — First edition.
p. cm. — (Hilo ; book 1)
Summary: "When a mysterious boy falls from the sky, friends D.J. and Gina must discover
the secrets of his identity and help him save the world." —Provided by publisher.
ISBN 978-0-385-38617-3 (trade) — ISBN 978-0-385-38618-0 (lib. bdg.) — ISBN 978-0-385-38619-7 (ebook)
1. Graphic novels. [1. Graphic novels. 2. Amnesia—Fiction. 3. Identity—Fiction. 4. Robots—Fiction.
5. Extraterrestrial beings—Fiction. 6. Friendship—Fiction. 7. Science fiction.] I. Title.
PZ7.7.W57Boy 2015 [Fic]—dc23 2014030736

MANUFACTURED IN CHINA
10 9 8 7 6
Book design by John Sazaklis
First Edition

Random House Children's Books supports the First Amendment and celebrates the right to read.

FOR

the Catman

and

the tuFF Little kitten

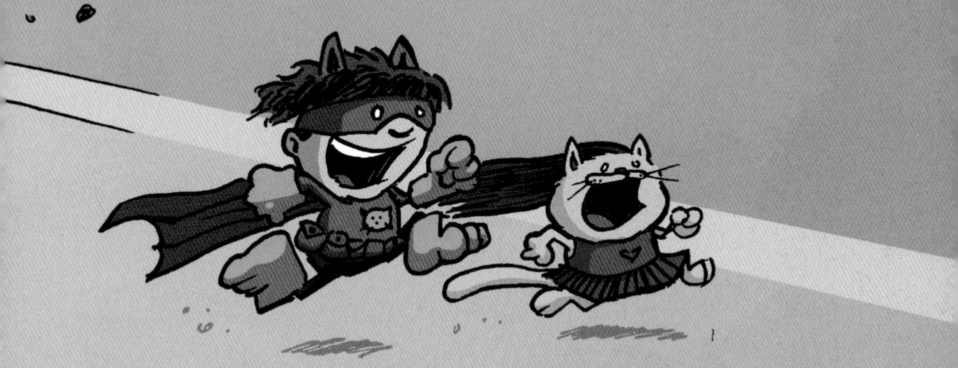

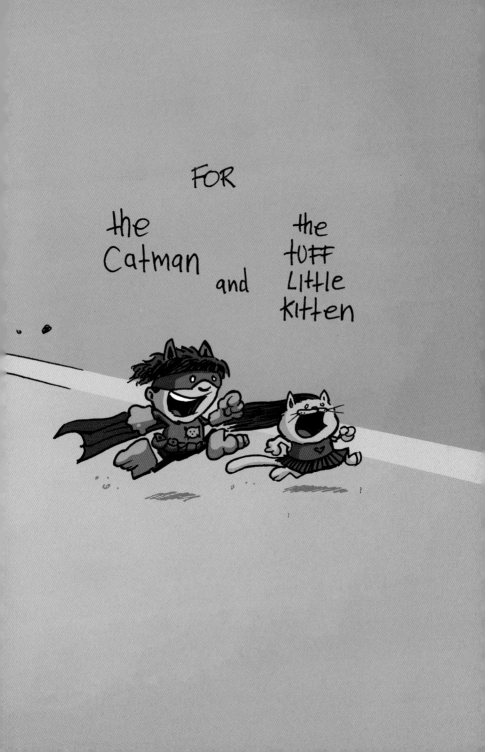

CHAPTER 1

AAAAAAH!

HELLO.
AAAH!!

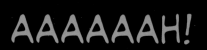

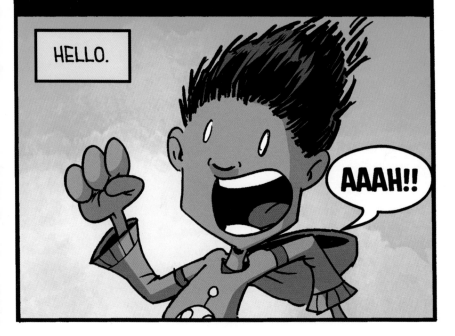

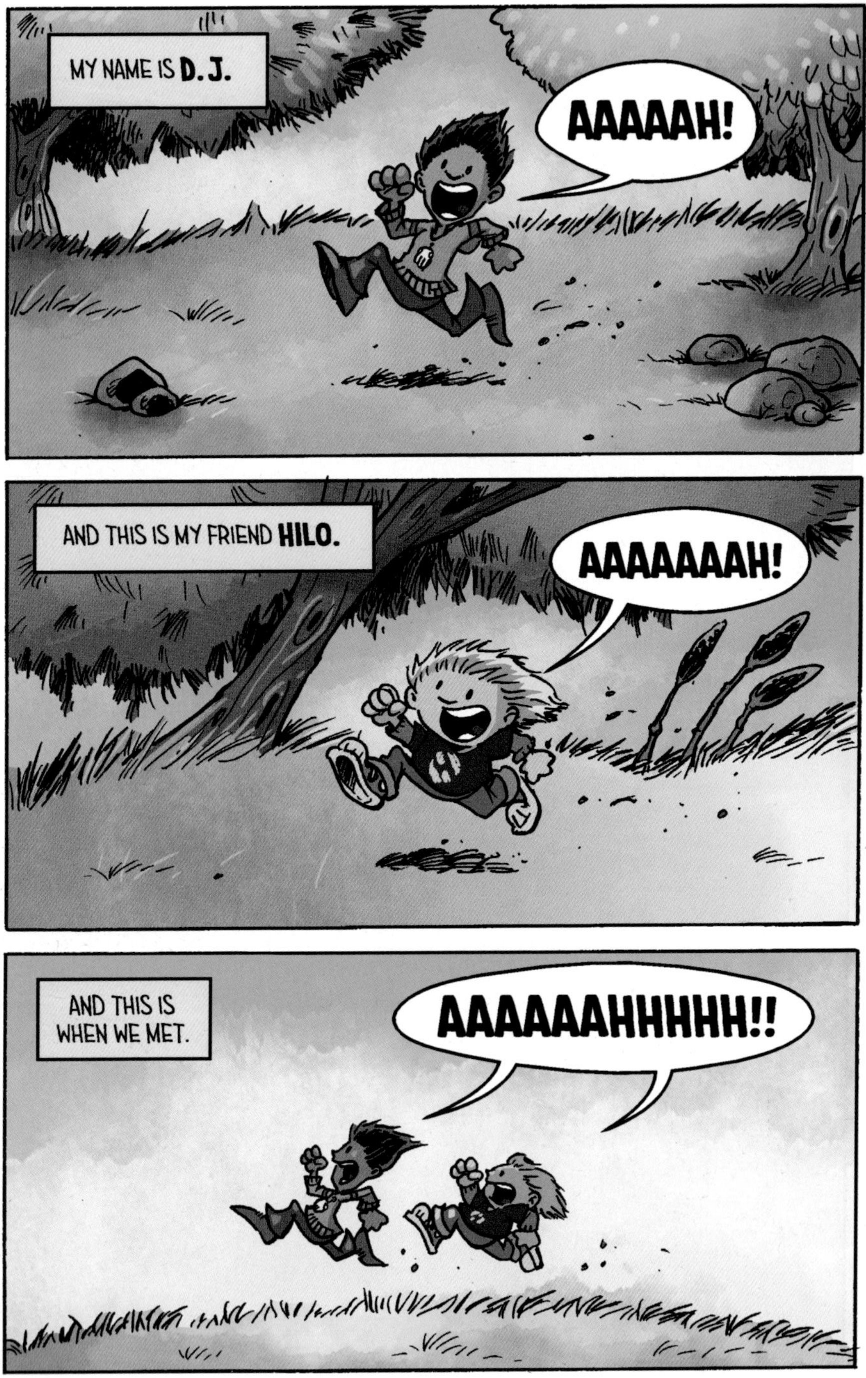
MY NAME IS D.J.
AAAAAH!
AND THIS IS MY FRIEND HILO.
AAAAAAAH!
AND THIS IS WHEN WE MET.
AAAAAAHHHHH!!

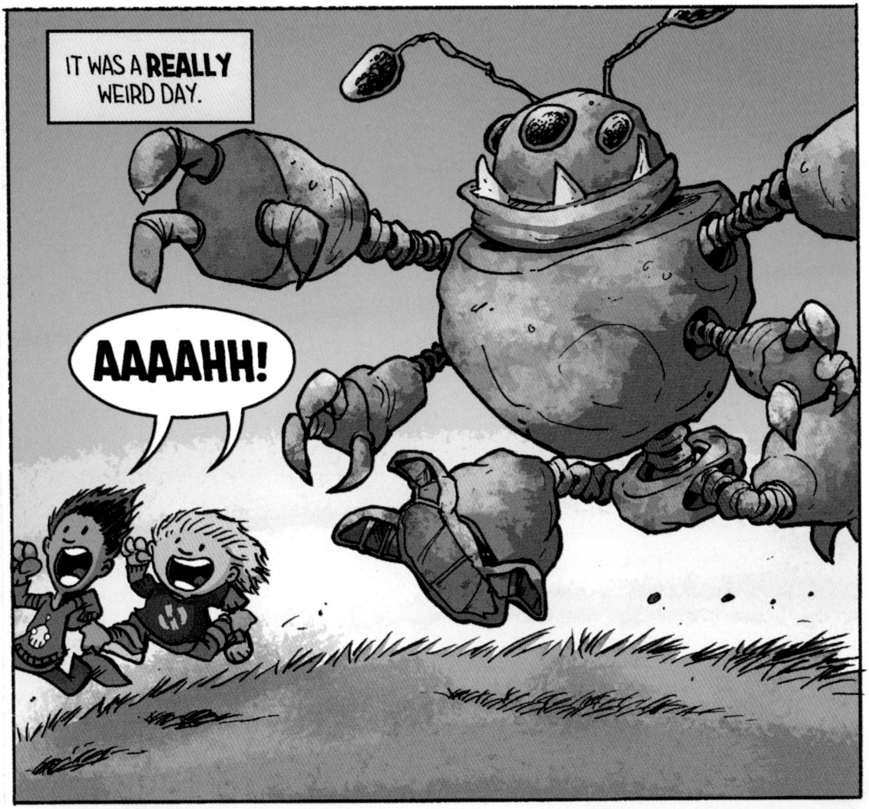
IT WAS A **REALLY** WEIRD DAY.
AAAAHH!

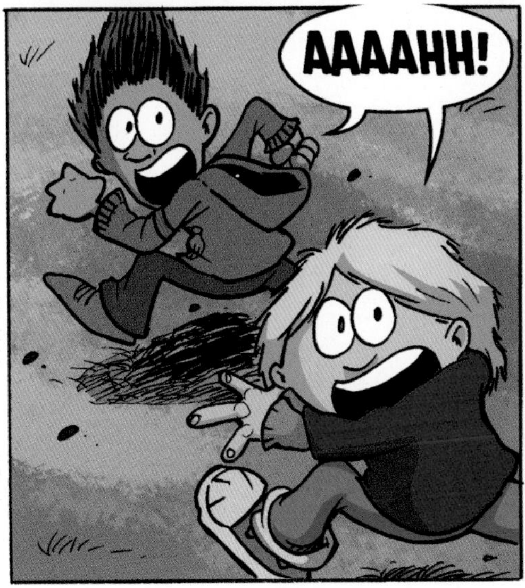
AAAAHH!

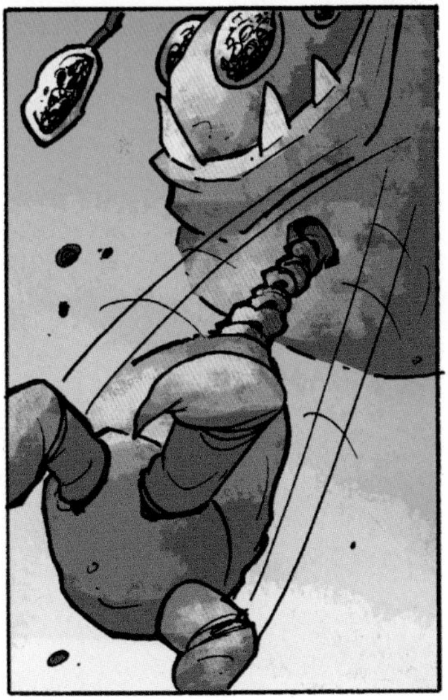

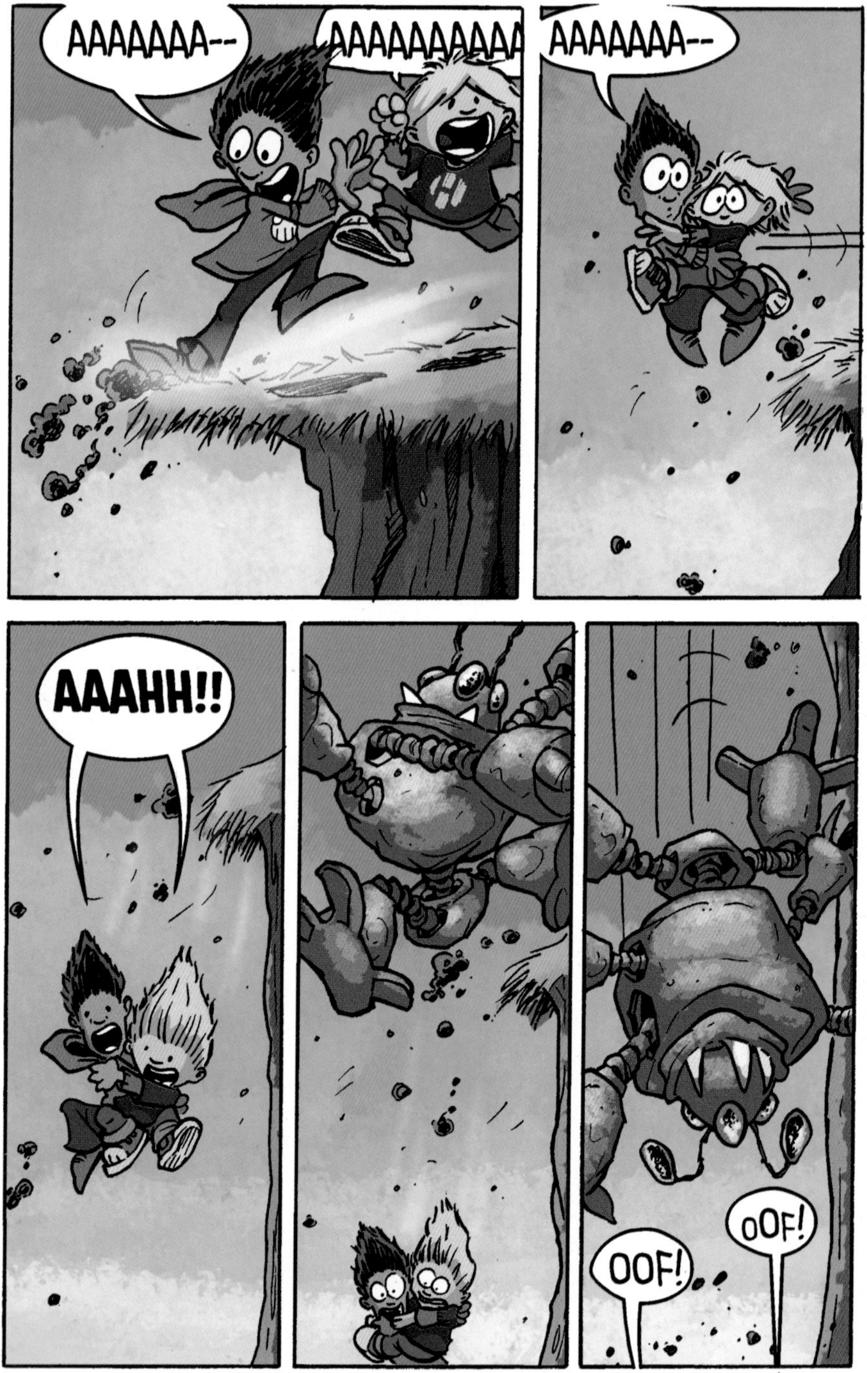
AAAAAAA--
AAAAAAAAAA
AAAAAAA--
AAAHH!!
OOF!
OOF!

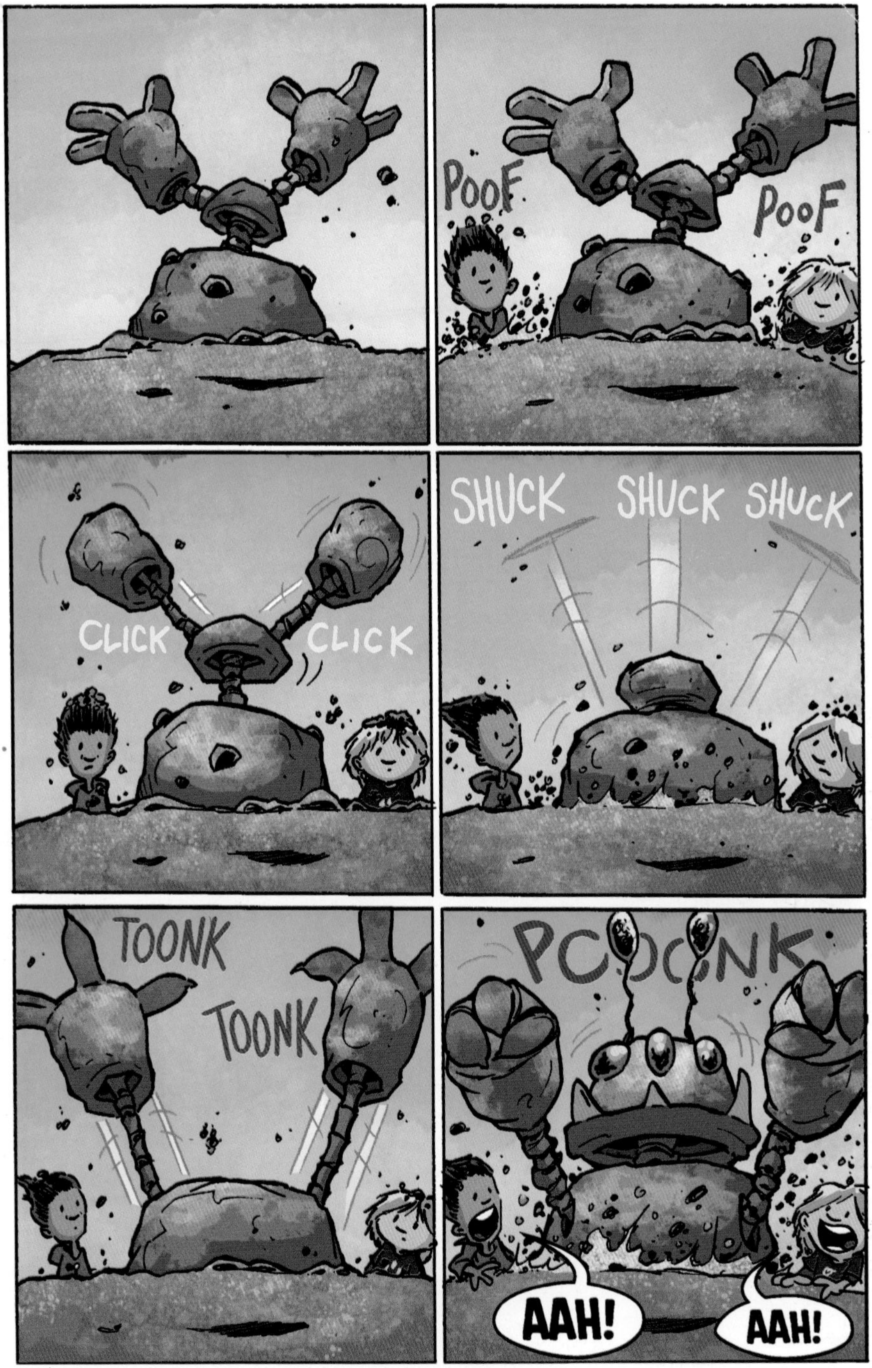
POOF
POOF
CLICK
CLICK
SHUCK
SHUCK
SHUCK
TOONK
TOONK
POONK
AAH!
AAH!

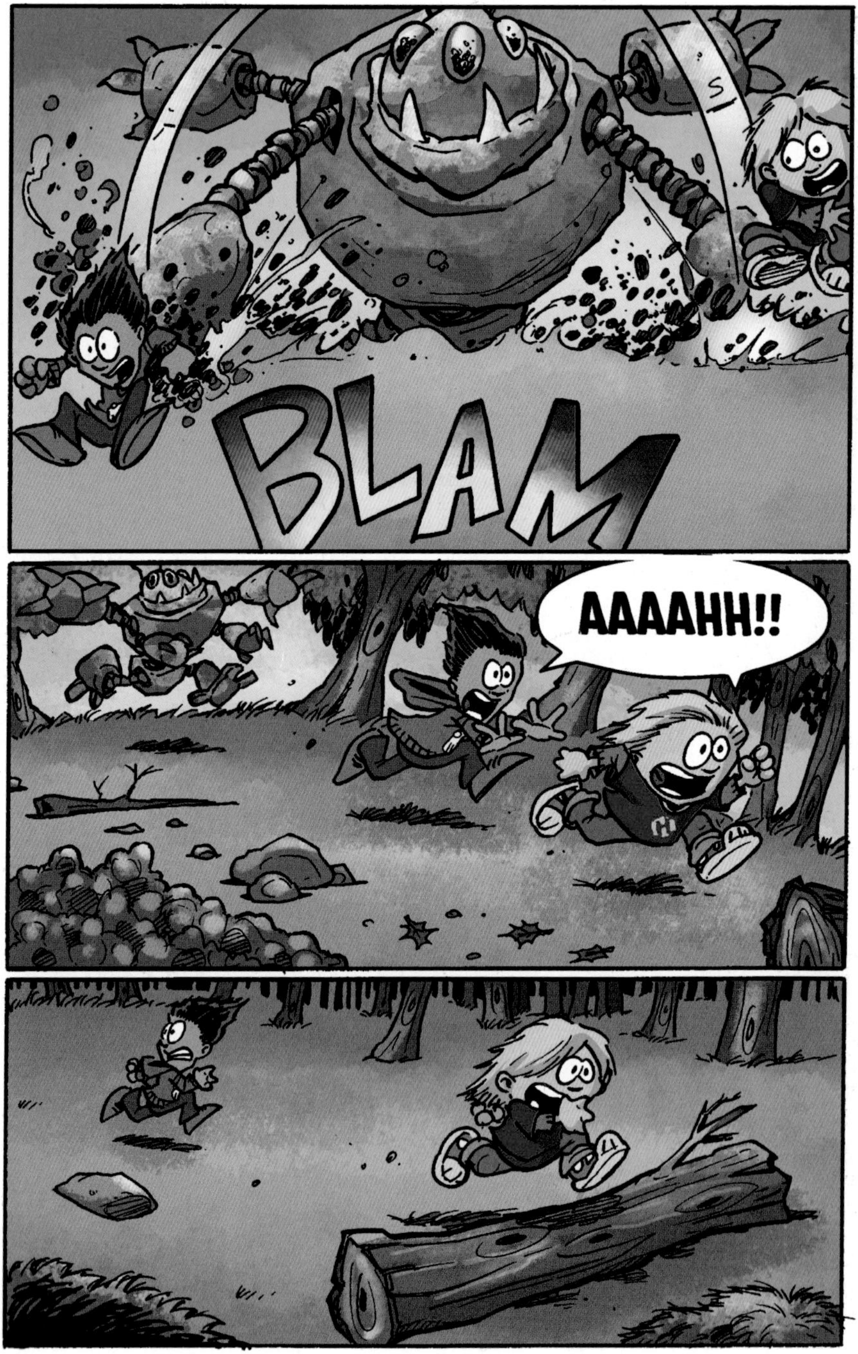
BLAM
AAAAHH!!

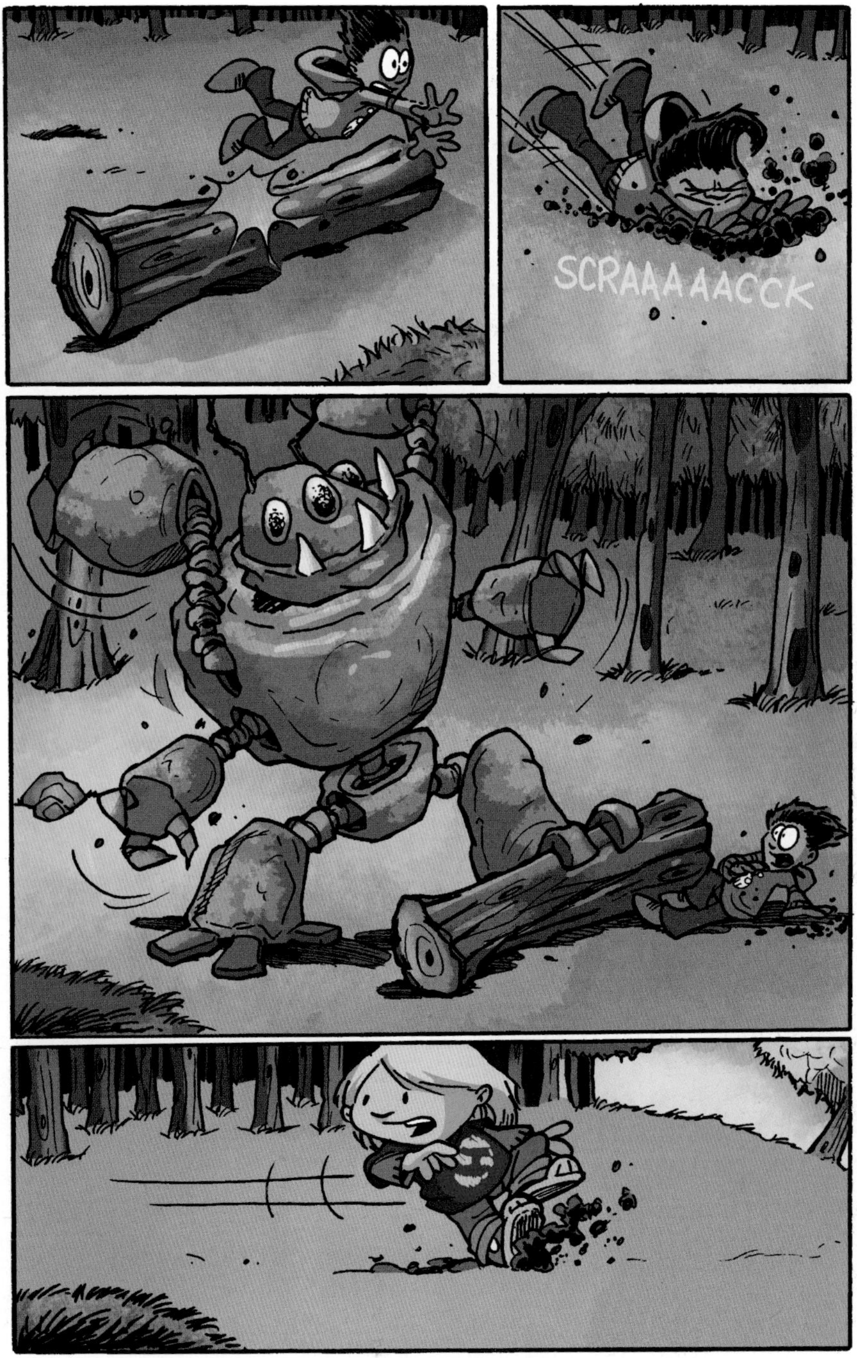
SCRAAAAACCK

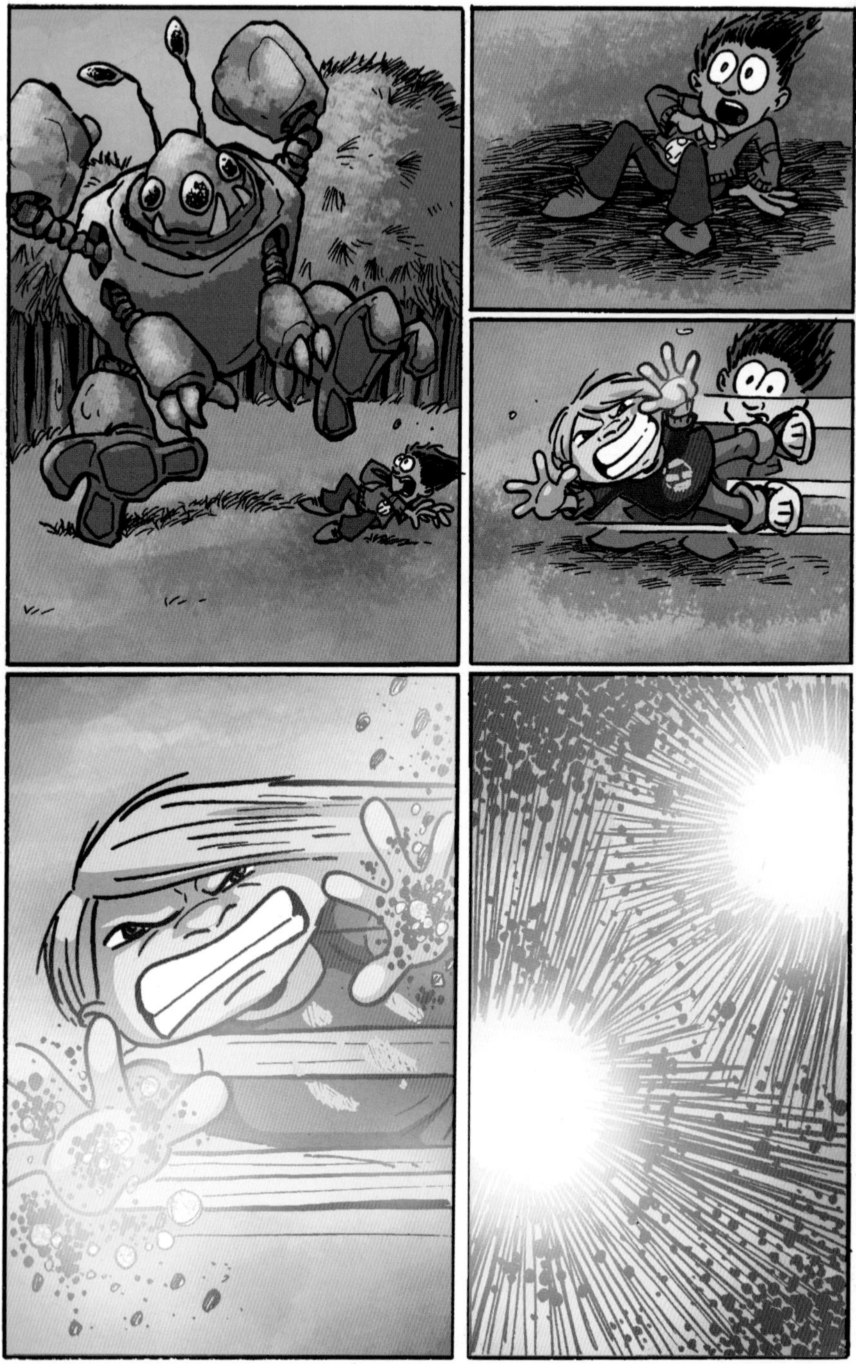

2

GOOD AT ONE THING

MY NAME IS **DANIEL JACKSON LIM.** EVERYONE CALLS ME **D.J.**
AND I'M NOT GOOD AT ANYTHING.
I'M NOT SAYING THAT I'M A **TOTAL** DORK. THERE'S JUST NOTHING THAT I'M REALLY SUPER GOOD AT.

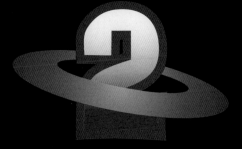

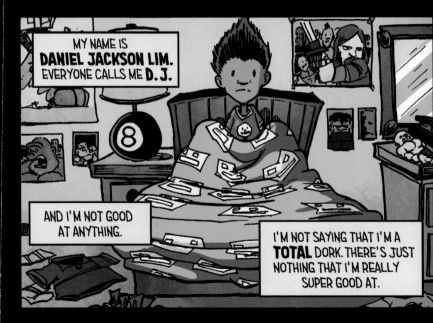

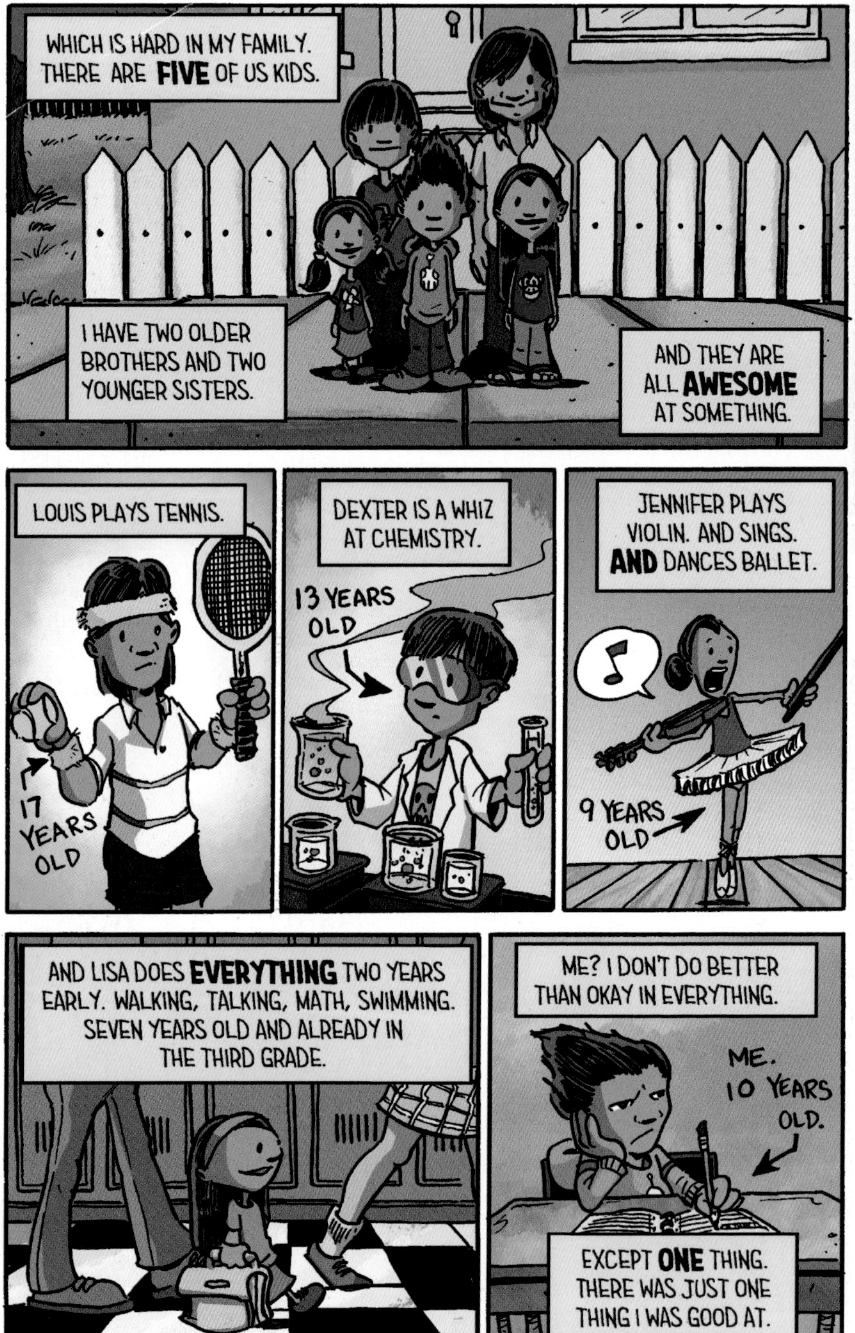
WHICH IS HARD IN MY FAMILY. THERE ARE FIVE OF US KIDS.
I HAVE TWO OLDER BROTHERS AND TWO YOUNGER SISTERS.
AND THEY ARE ALL AWESOME AT SOMETHING.
LOUIS PLAYS TENNIS.
17 YEARS OLD
DEXTER IS A WHIZ AT CHEMISTRY.
13 YEARS OLD
JENNIFER PLAYS VIOLIN. AND SINGS. AND DANCES BALLET.
9 YEARS OLD
AND LISA DOES EVERYTHING TWO YEARS EARLY. WALKING, TALKING, MATH, SWIMMING. SEVEN YEARS OLD AND ALREADY IN THE THIRD GRADE.
ME? I DON'T DO BETTER THAN OKAY IN EVERYTHING.
ME. 10 YEARS OLD.
EXCEPT ONE THING. THERE WAS JUST ONE THING I WAS GOOD AT.

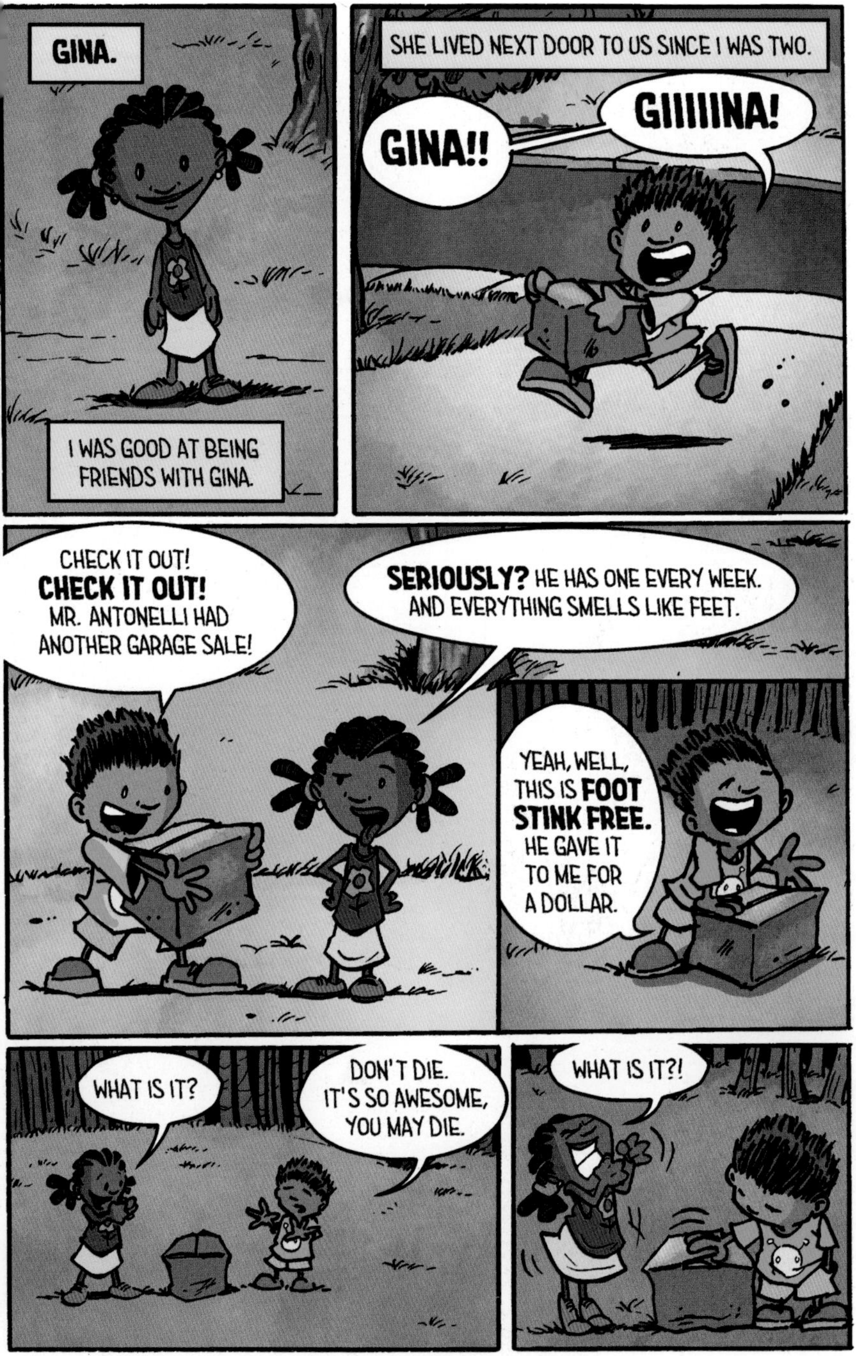
GINA.
I WAS GOOD AT BEING FRIENDS WITH GINA.
SHE LIVED NEXT DOOR TO US SINCE I WAS TWO.
GINA!!
GIIIIINA!
CHECK IT OUT! CHECK IT OUT! MR. ANTONELLI HAD ANOTHER GARAGE SALE!
SERIOUSLY? HE HAS ONE EVERY WEEK. AND EVERYTHING SMELLS LIKE FEET.
YEAH, WELL, THIS IS FOOT STINK FREE. HE GAVE IT TO ME FOR A DOLLAR.
WHAT IS IT?
DON'T DIE. IT'S SO AWESOME, YOU MAY DIE.
WHAT IS IT?!

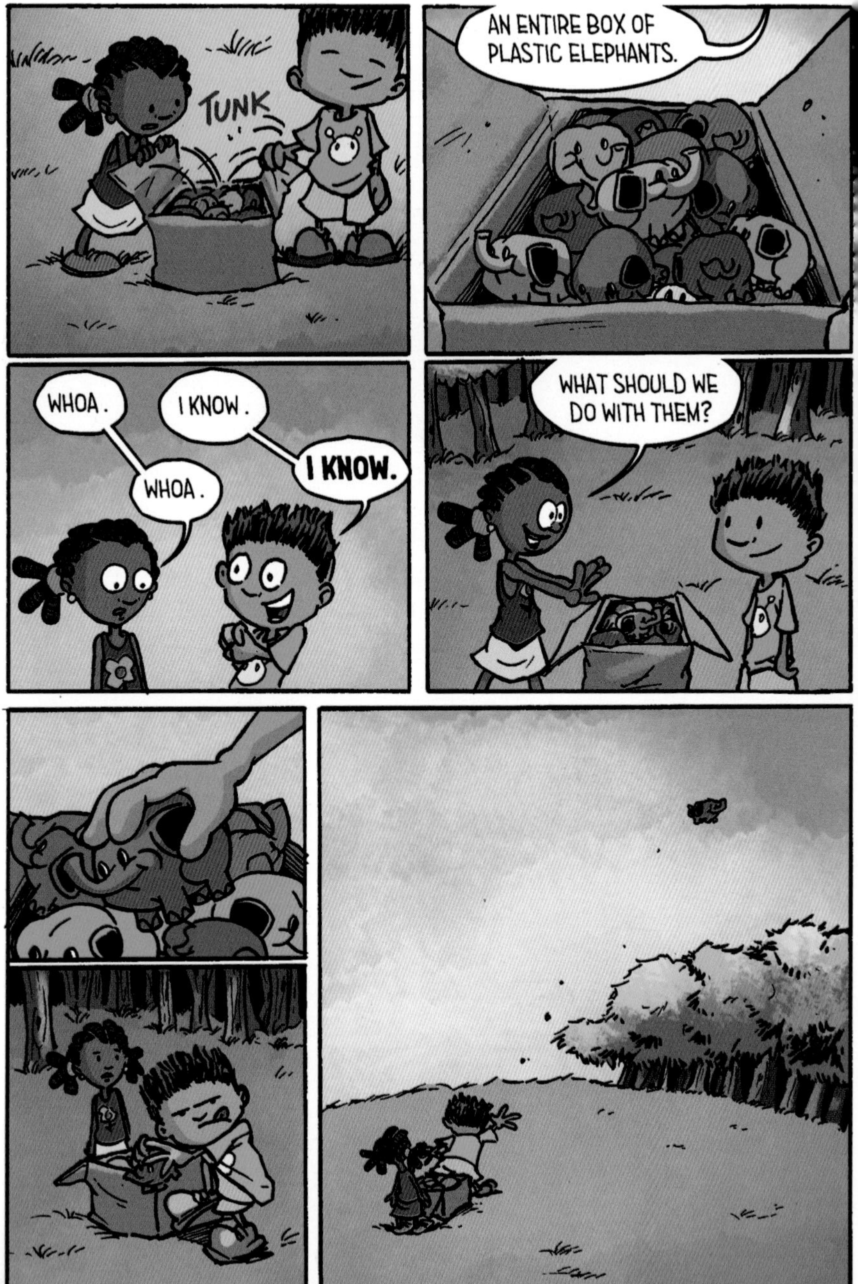
TUNK
AN ENTIRE BOX OF PLASTIC ELEPHANTS.
WHOA.
I KNOW.
WHOA.
I KNOW.
WHAT SHOULD WE DO WITH THEM?

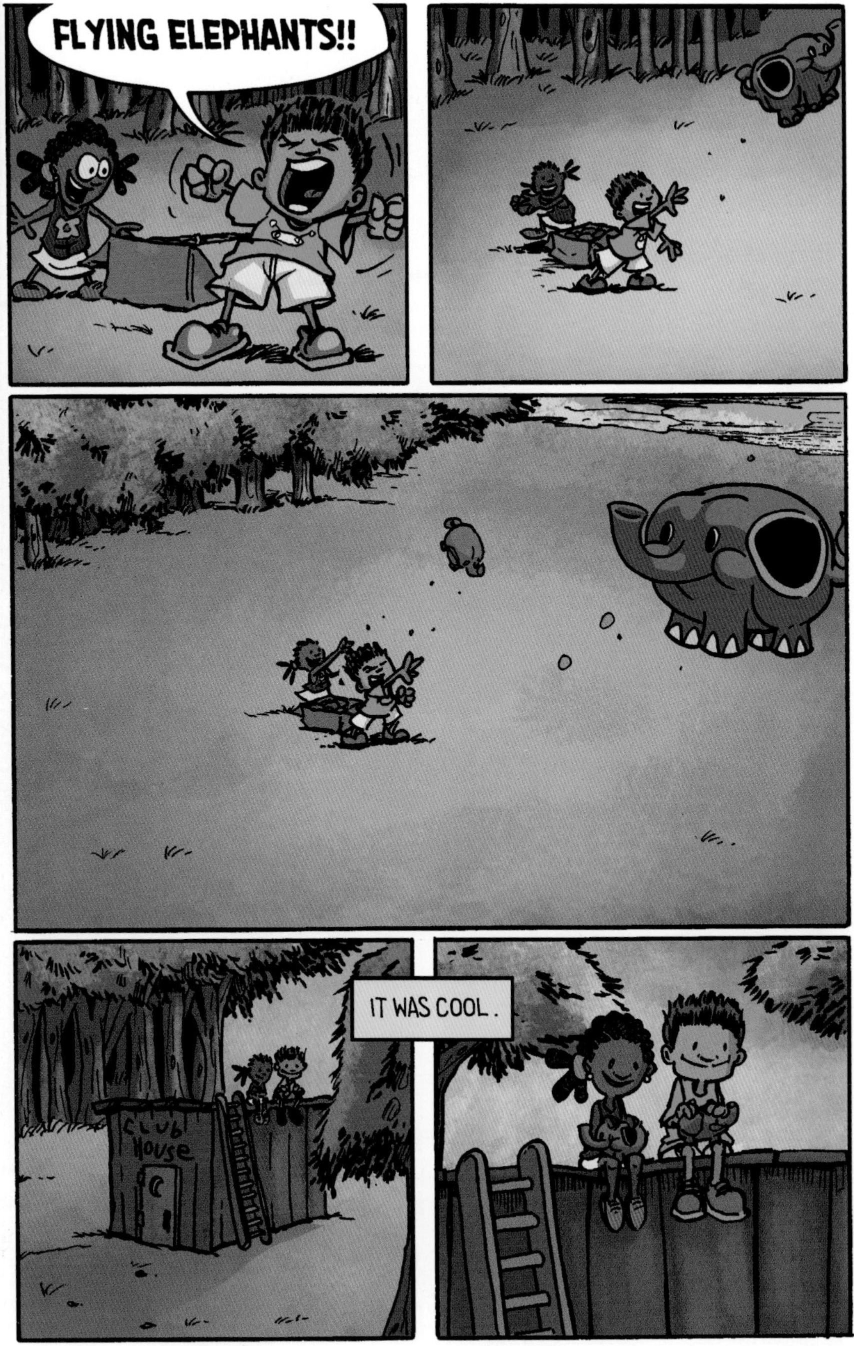
FLYING ELEPHANTS!!
IT WAS COOL.

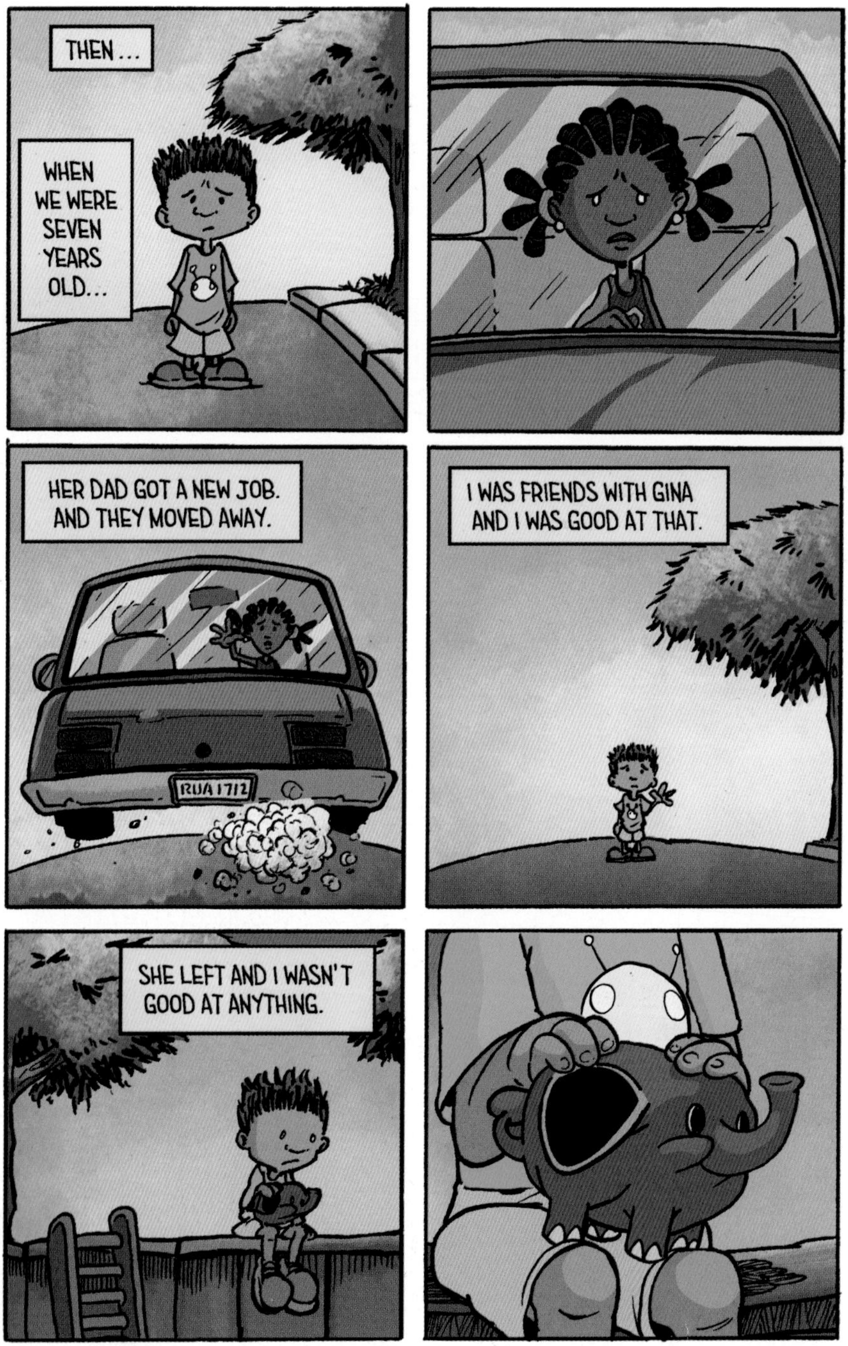
THEN...
WHEN WE WERE SEVEN YEARS OLD...
HER DAD GOT A NEW JOB. AND THEY MOVED AWAY.
RUA 1712
I WAS FRIENDS WITH GINA AND I WAS GOOD AT THAT.
SHE LEFT AND I WASN'T GOOD AT ANYTHING.

THREE YEARS LATER

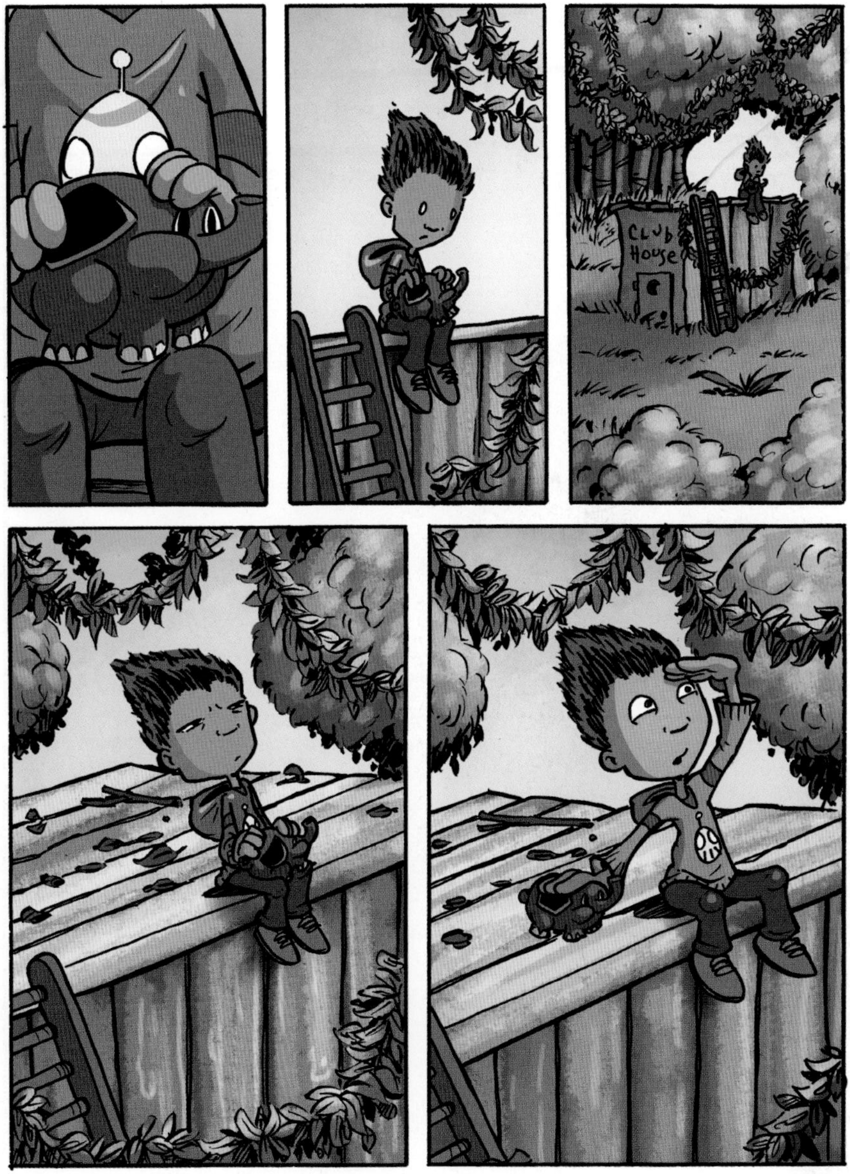
CLUB
House

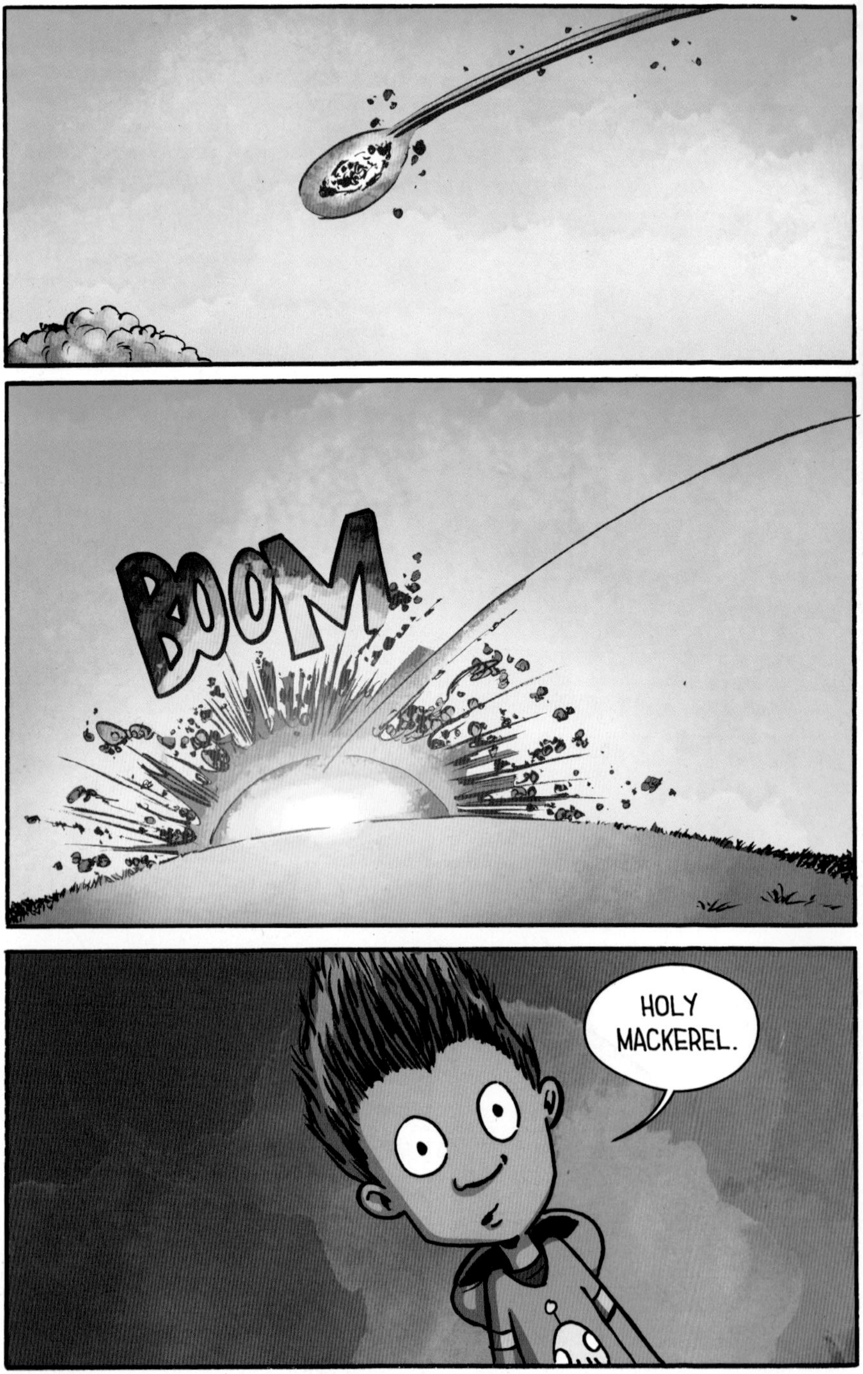
BOOM
HOLY MACKEREL.

CHAPTER

BOOM

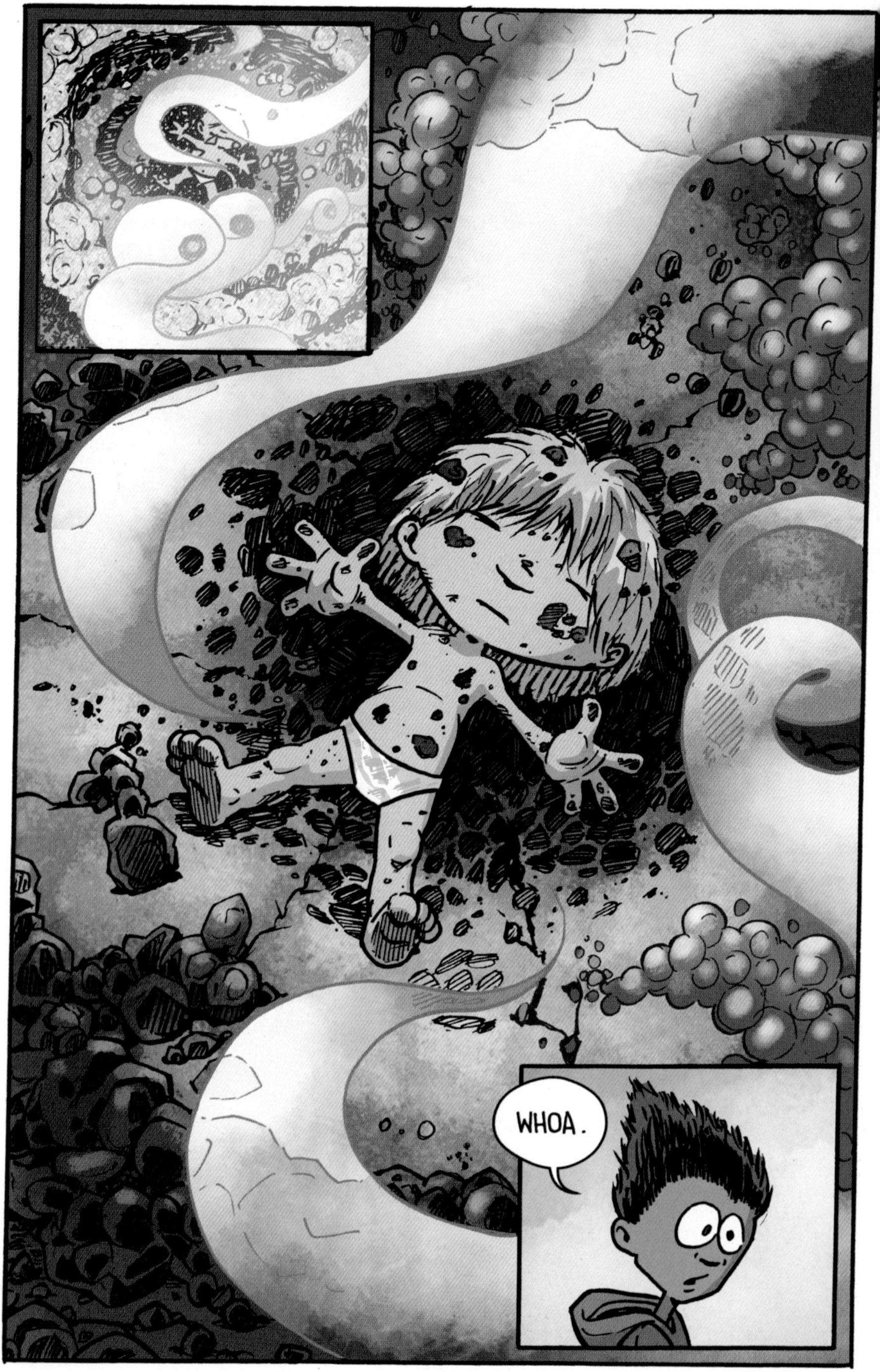
WHOA.

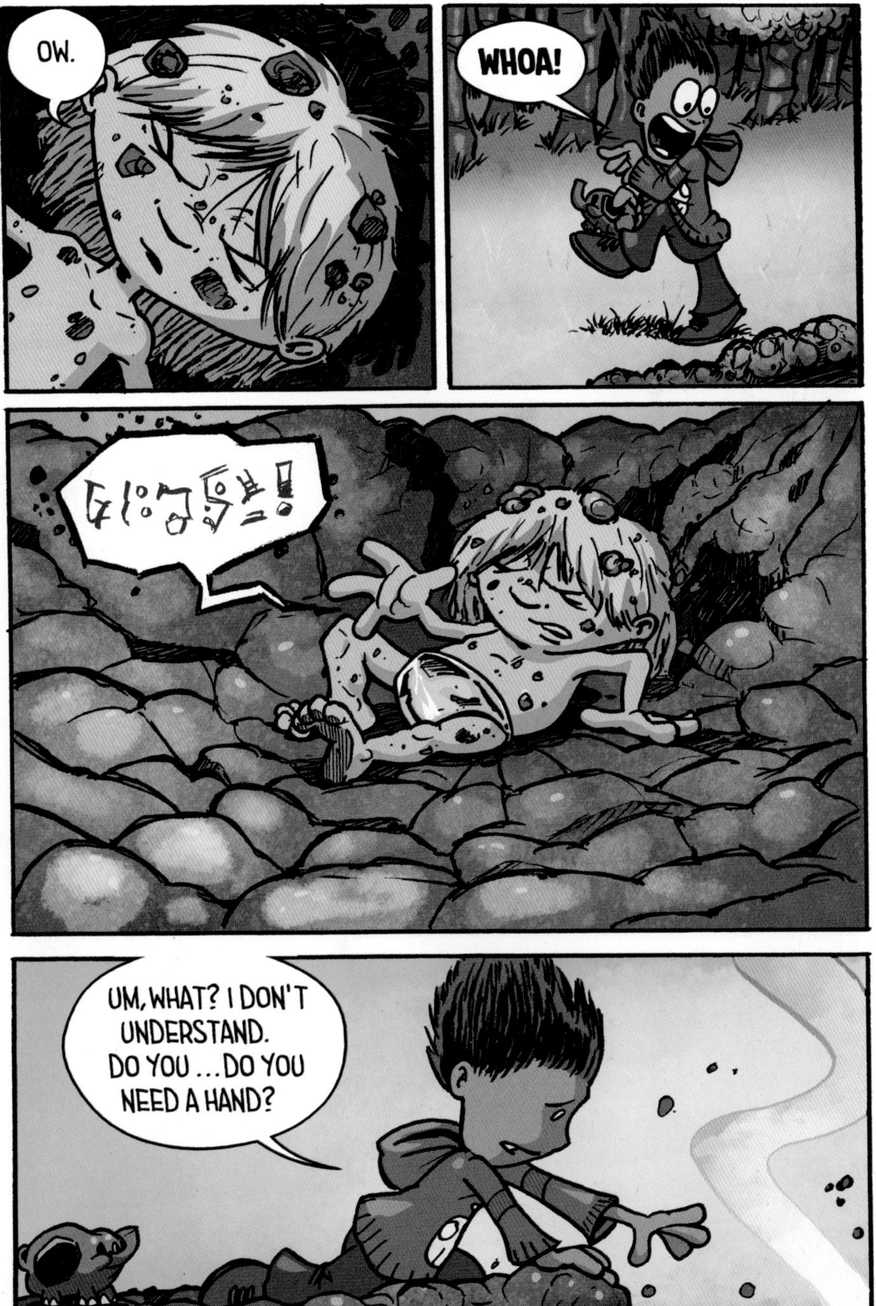
OW.
WHOA!
UM, WHAT? I DON'T UNDERSTAND. DO YOU ... DO YOU NEED A HAND?

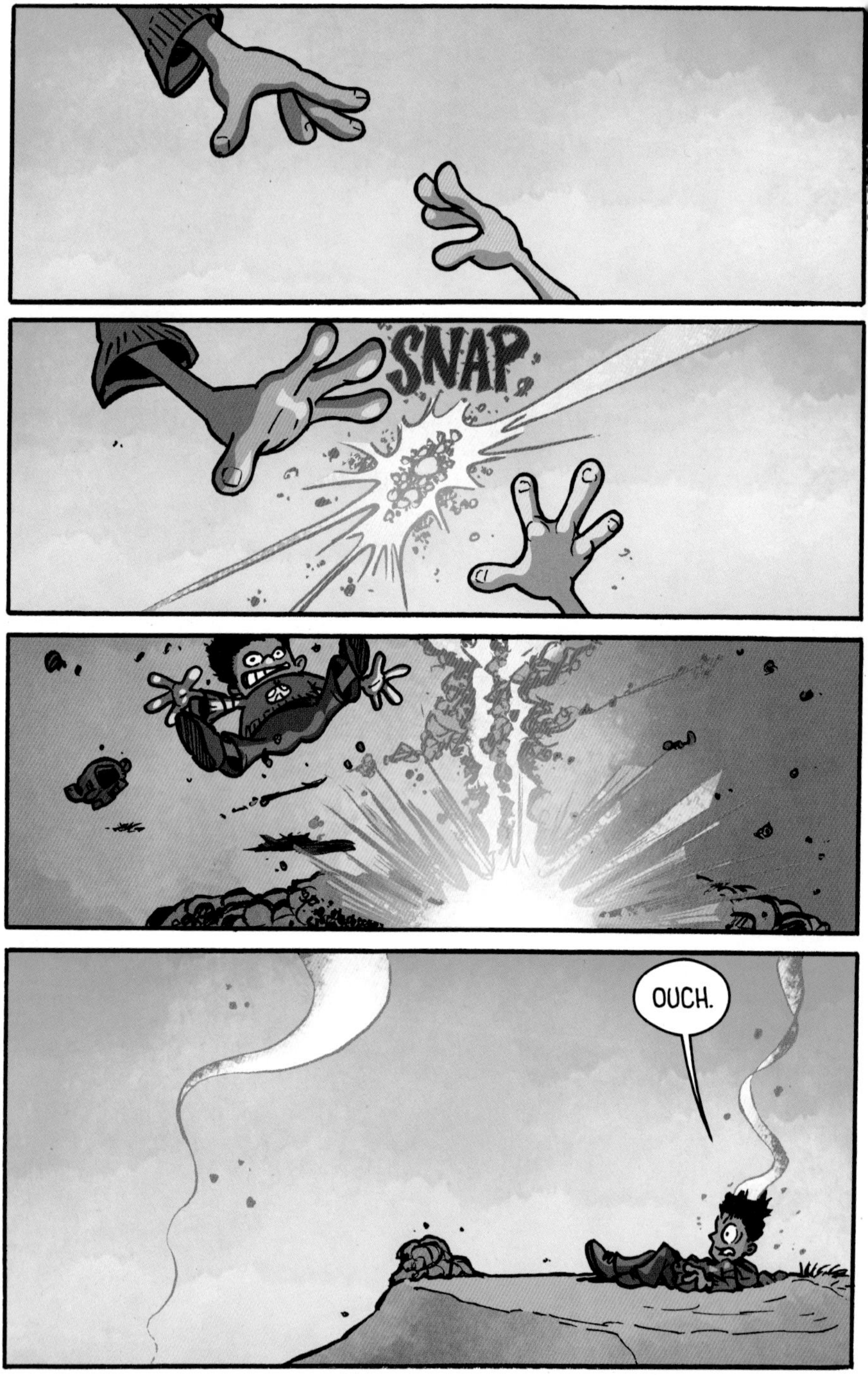
SNAP
OUCH.

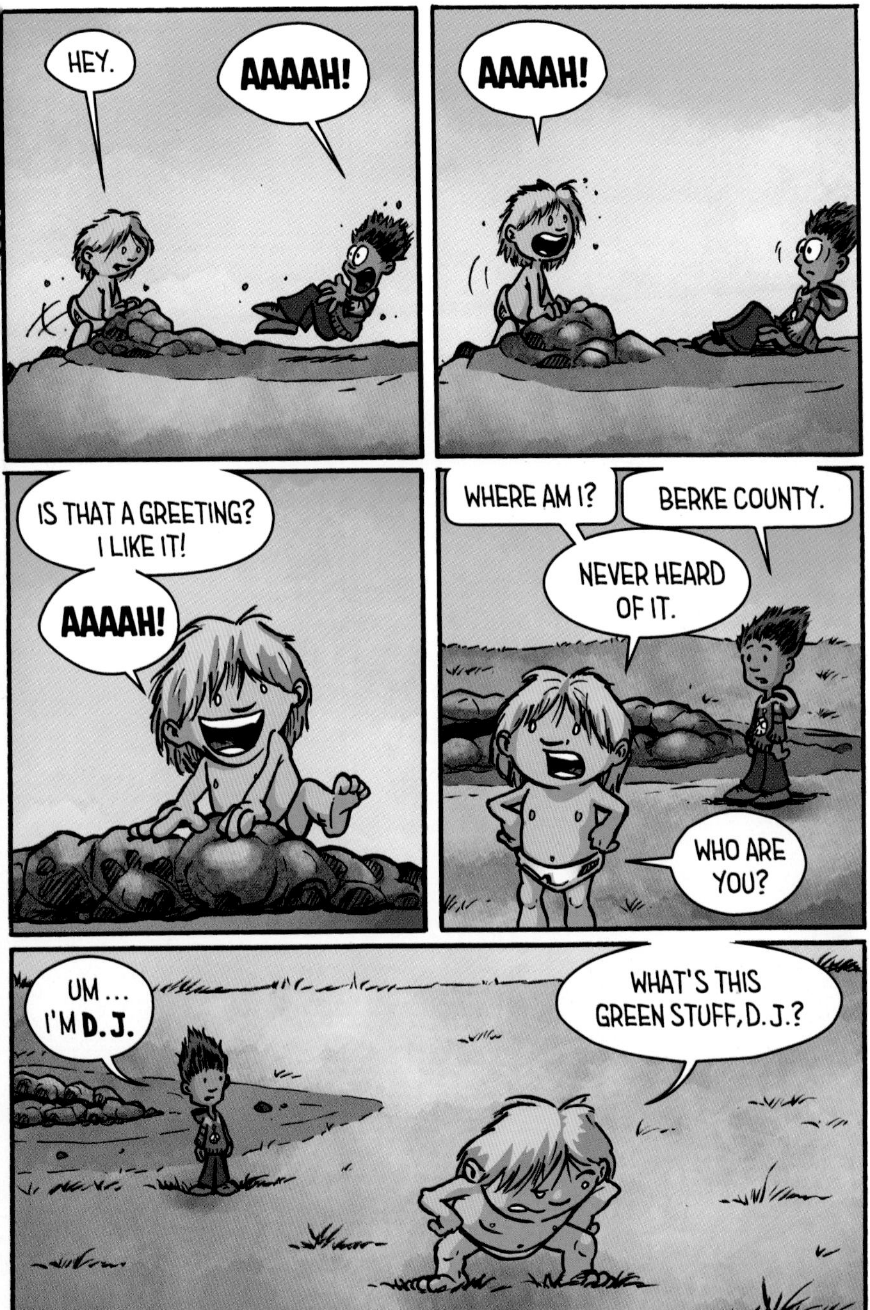
HEY.
AAAAH!
AAAAH!
IS THAT A GREETING? I LIKE IT!
AAAAH!
WHERE AM I?
BERKE COUNTY.
NEVER HEARD OF IT.
WHO ARE YOU?
UM ... I'M D. J.
WHAT'S THIS GREEN STUFF, D. J.?

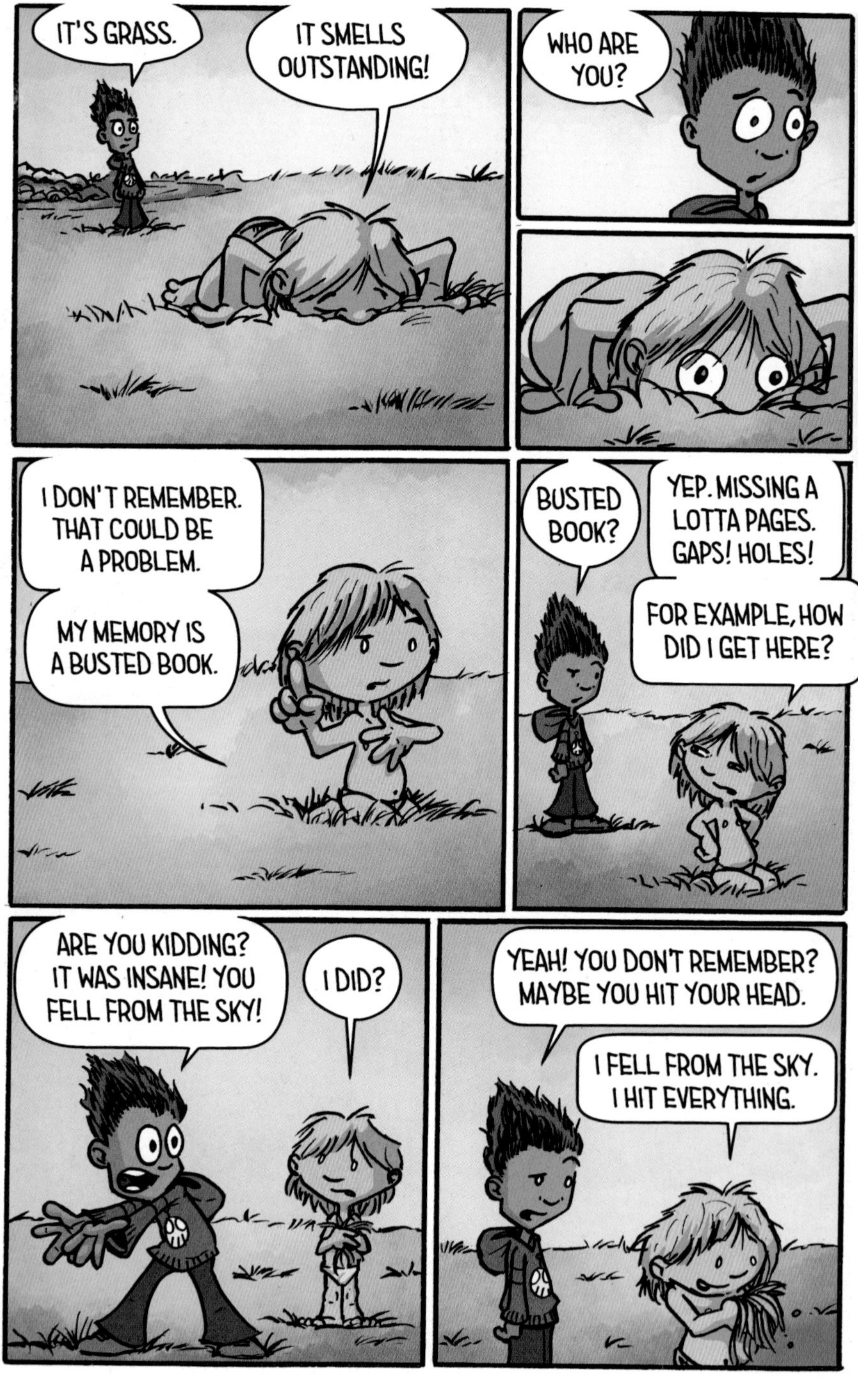
IT'S GRASS.
IT SMELLS OUTSTANDING!
WHO ARE YOU?
I DON'T REMEMBER. THAT COULD BE A PROBLEM.
MY MEMORY IS A BUSTED BOOK.
BUSTED BOOK?
YEP. MISSING A LOTTA PAGES. GAPS! HOLES!
FOR EXAMPLE, HOW DID I GET HERE?
ARE YOU KIDDING? IT WAS INSANE! YOU FELL FROM THE SKY!
I DID?
YEAH! YOU DON'T REMEMBER? MAYBE YOU HIT YOUR HEAD.
I FELL FROM THE SKY. I HIT EVERYTHING.

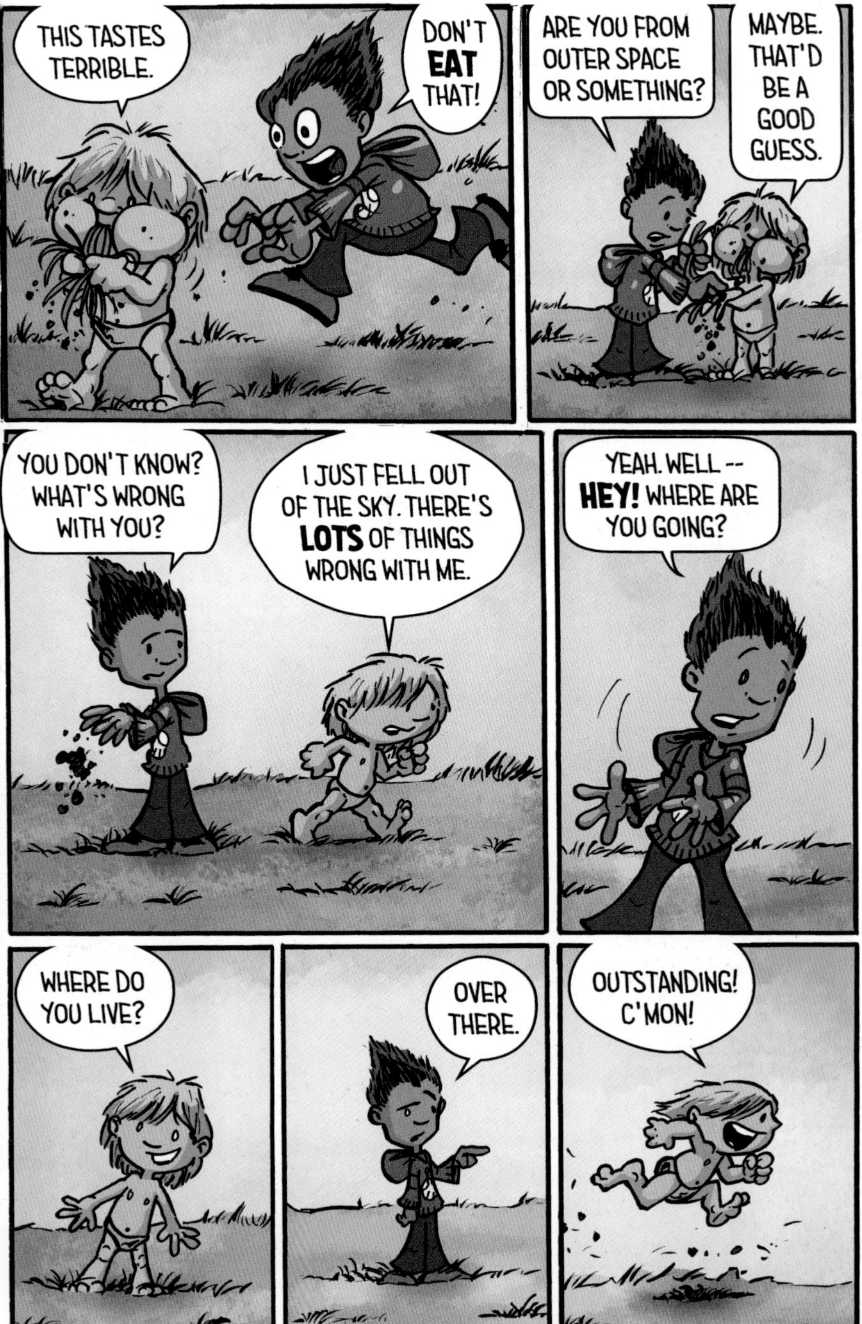
THIS TASTES TERRIBLE.
DON'T **EAT** THAT!
ARE YOU FROM OUTER SPACE OR SOMETHING?
MAYBE. THAT'D BE A GOOD GUESS.
YOU DON'T KNOW? WHAT'S WRONG WITH YOU?
I JUST FELL OUT OF THE SKY. THERE'S **LOTS** OF THINGS WRONG WITH ME.
YEAH. WELL -- **HEY!** WHERE ARE YOU GOING?
WHERE DO YOU LIVE?
OVER THERE.
OUTSTANDING! C'MON!

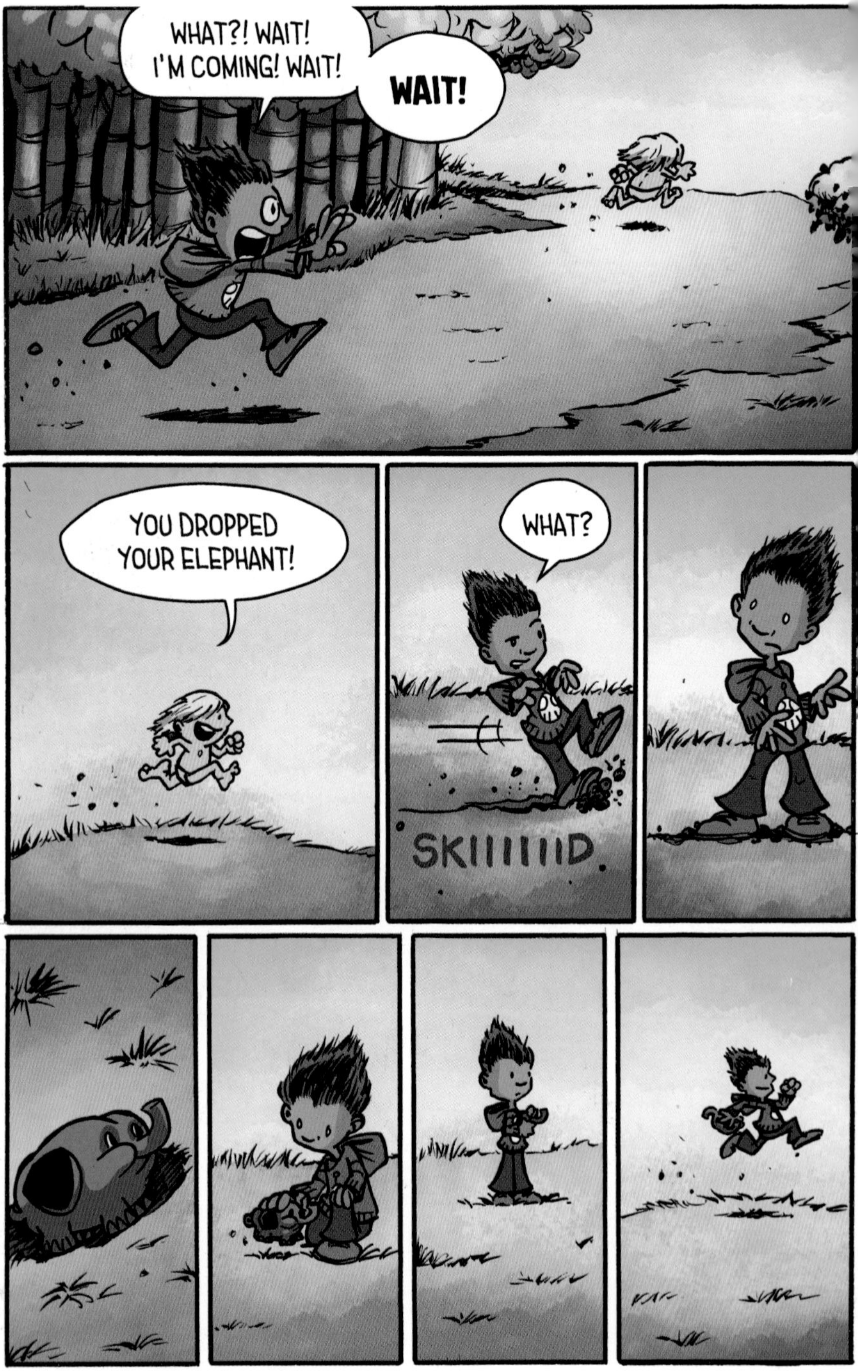
WHAT?! WAIT!
I'M COMING! WAIT!
WAIT!
YOU DROPPED
YOUR ELEPHANT!
WHAT?
SKIIIIIID

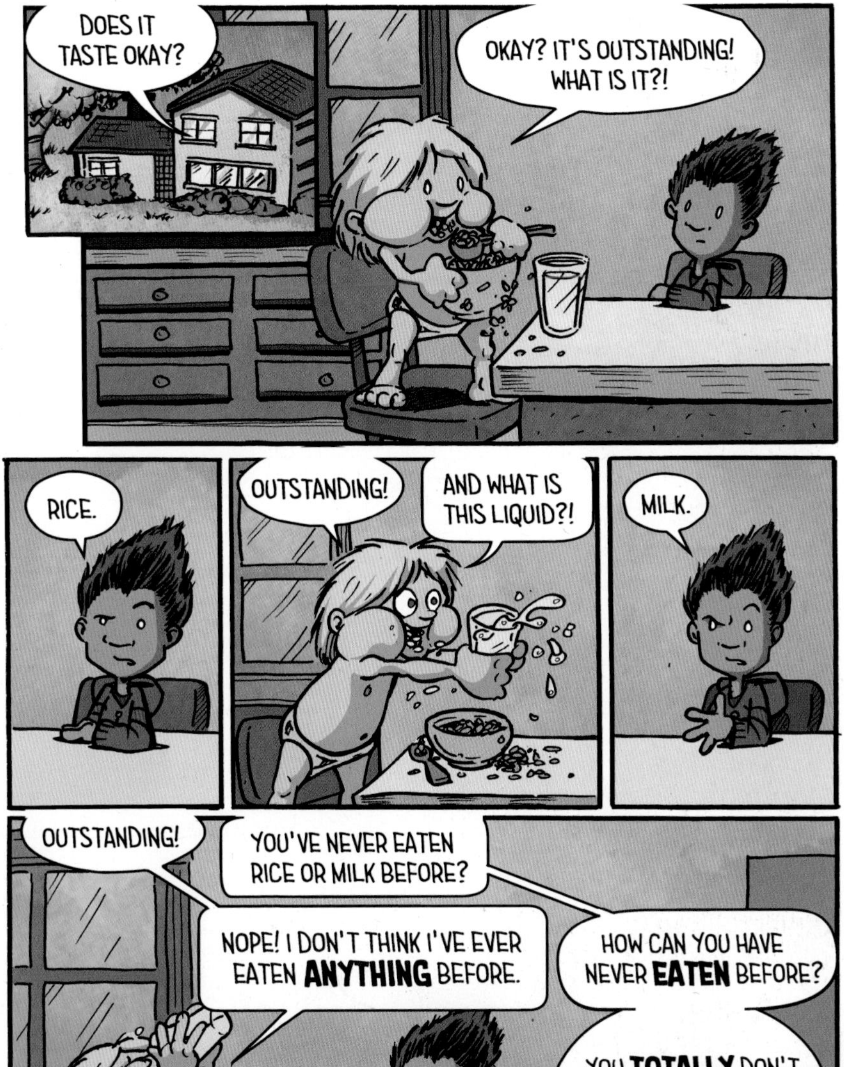
DOES IT TASTE OKAY?
OKAY? IT'S OUTSTANDING! WHAT IS IT?!
RICE.
OUTSTANDING!
AND WHAT IS THIS LIQUID?!
MILK.
OUTSTANDING!
YOU'VE NEVER EATEN RICE OR MILK BEFORE?
NOPE! I DON'T THINK I'VE EVER EATEN **ANYTHING** BEFORE.
HOW CAN YOU HAVE NEVER **EATEN** BEFORE?
YOU **TOTALLY** DON'T REMEMBER ANYTHING ABOUT, WELL, WHERE YOU'RE FROM?

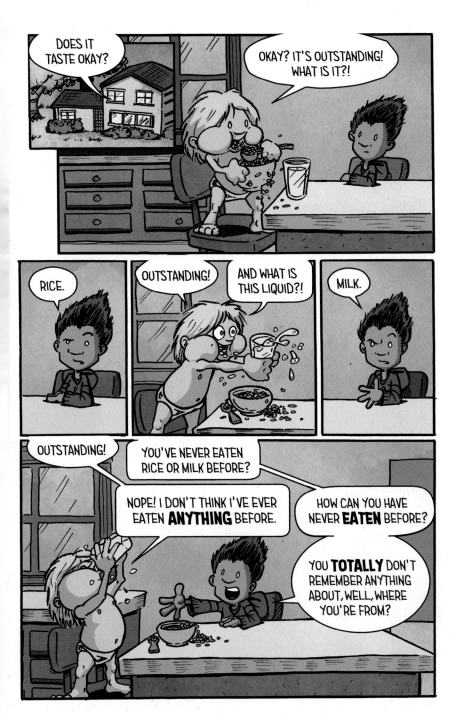

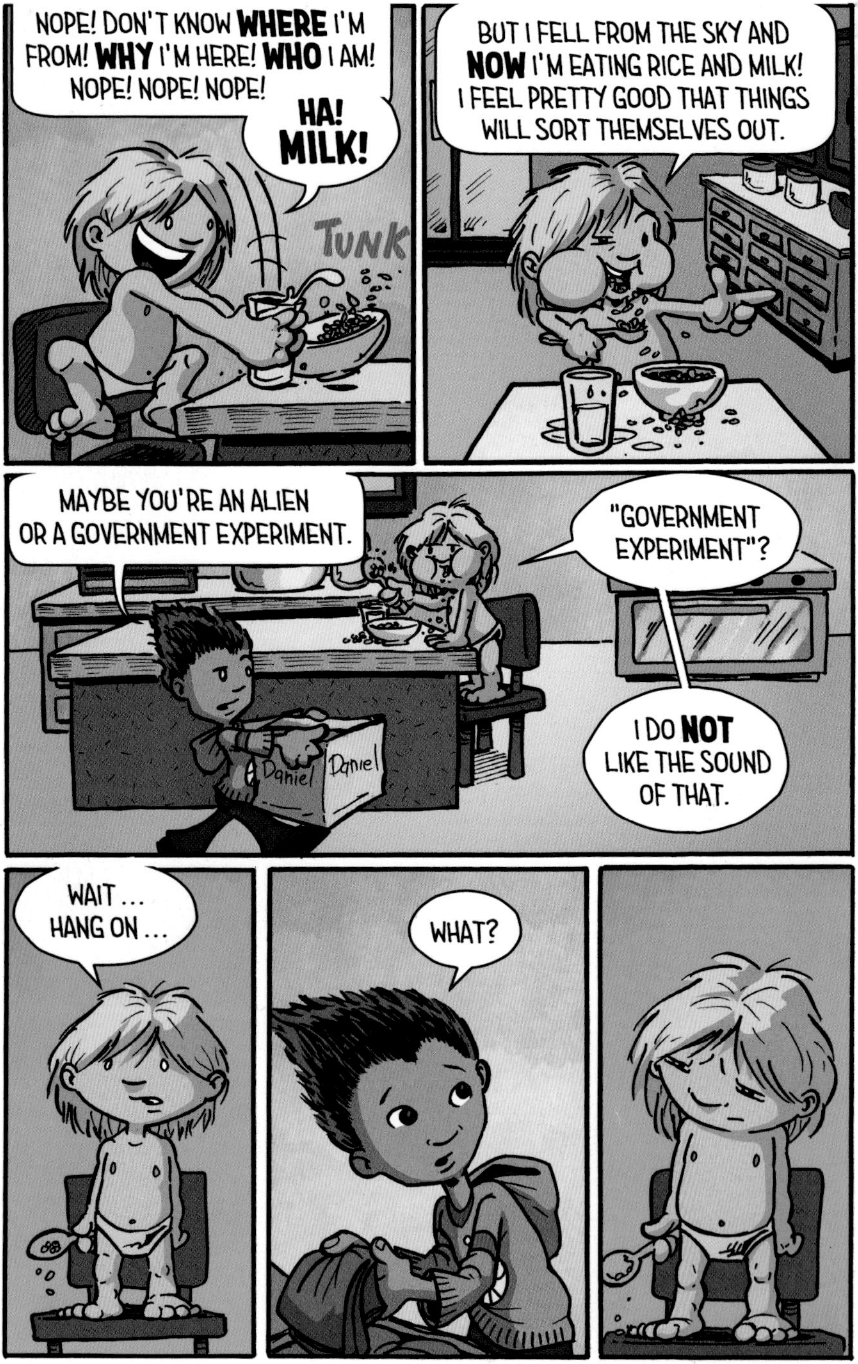
NOPE! DON'T KNOW WHERE I'M FROM! WHY I'M HERE! WHO I AM! NOPE! NOPE! NOPE!
HA! MILK!
TUNK
BUT I FELL FROM THE SKY AND NOW I'M EATING RICE AND MILK! I FEEL PRETTY GOOD THAT THINGS WILL SORT THEMSELVES OUT.
MAYBE YOU'RE AN ALIEN OR A GOVERNMENT EXPERIMENT.
"GOVERNMENT EXPERIMENT"?
I DO NOT LIKE THE SOUND OF THAT.
Daniel
Daniel
WAIT ... HANG ON ...
WHAT?

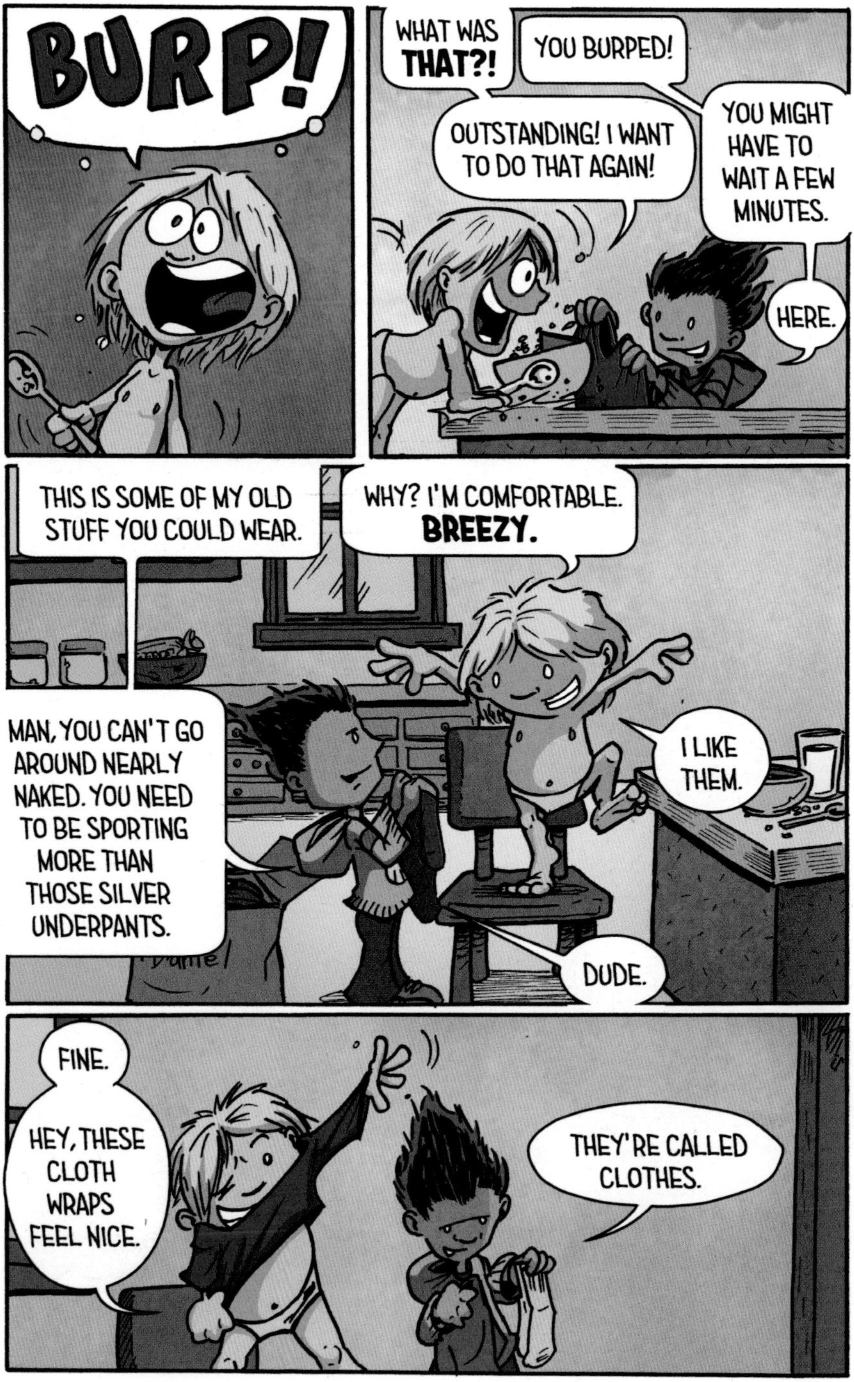
BURP!
WHAT WAS THAT?!
YOU BURPED!
OUTSTANDING! I WANT TO DO THAT AGAIN!
YOU MIGHT HAVE TO WAIT A FEW MINUTES.
HERE.
THIS IS SOME OF MY OLD STUFF YOU COULD WEAR.
WHY? I'M COMFORTABLE. BREEZY.
MAN, YOU CAN'T GO AROUND NEARLY NAKED. YOU NEED TO BE SPORTING MORE THAN THOSE SILVER UNDERPANTS.
I LIKE THEM.
DUDE.
FINE.
HEY, THESE CLOTH WRAPS FEEL NICE.
THEY'RE CALLED CLOTHES.

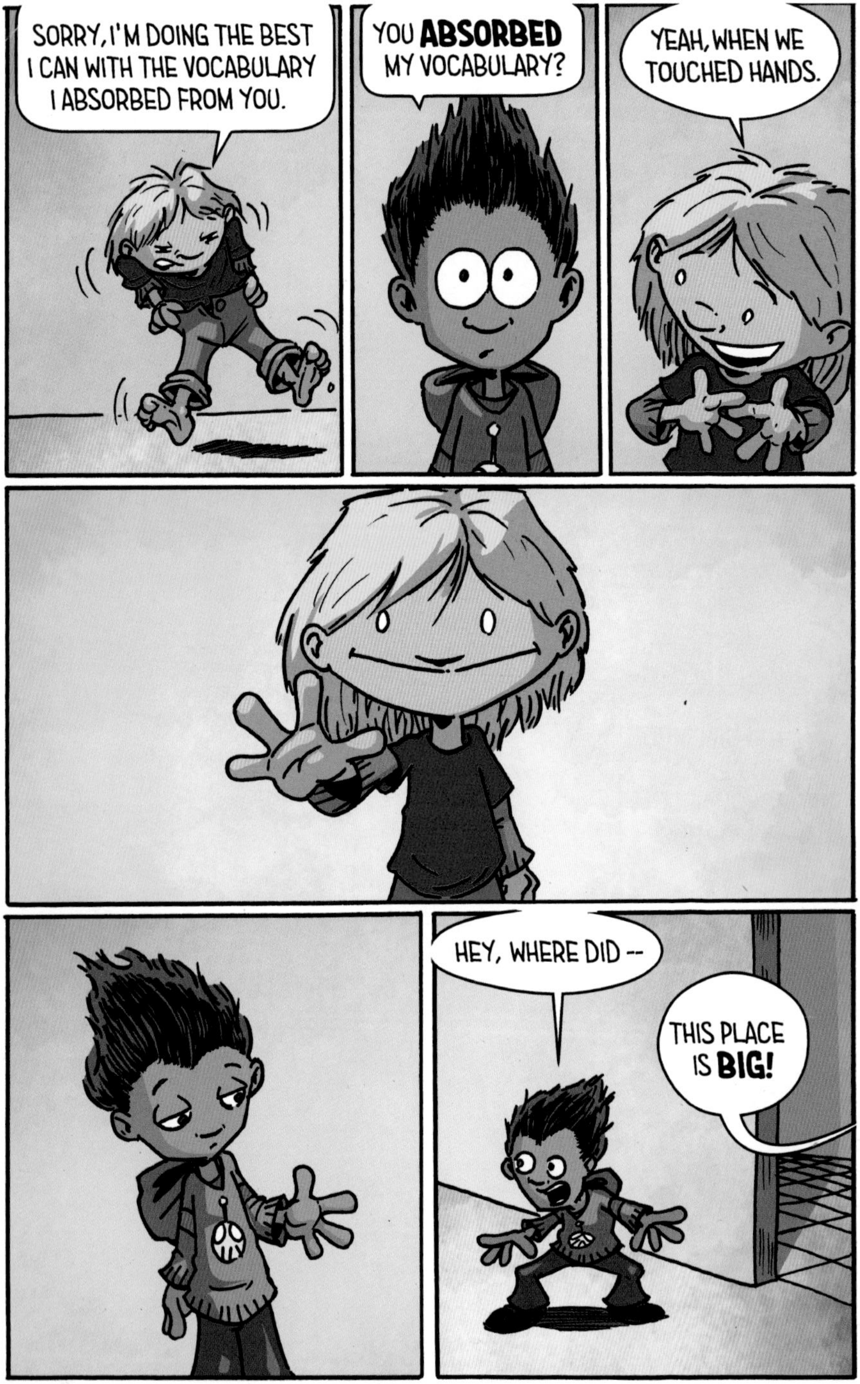

SORRY, I'M DOING THE BEST I CAN WITH THE VOCABULARY I ABSORBED FROM YOU.
YOU **ABSORBED** MY VOCABULARY?
YEAH, WHEN WE TOUCHED HANDS.
HEY, WHERE DID --
THIS PLACE IS **BIG!**

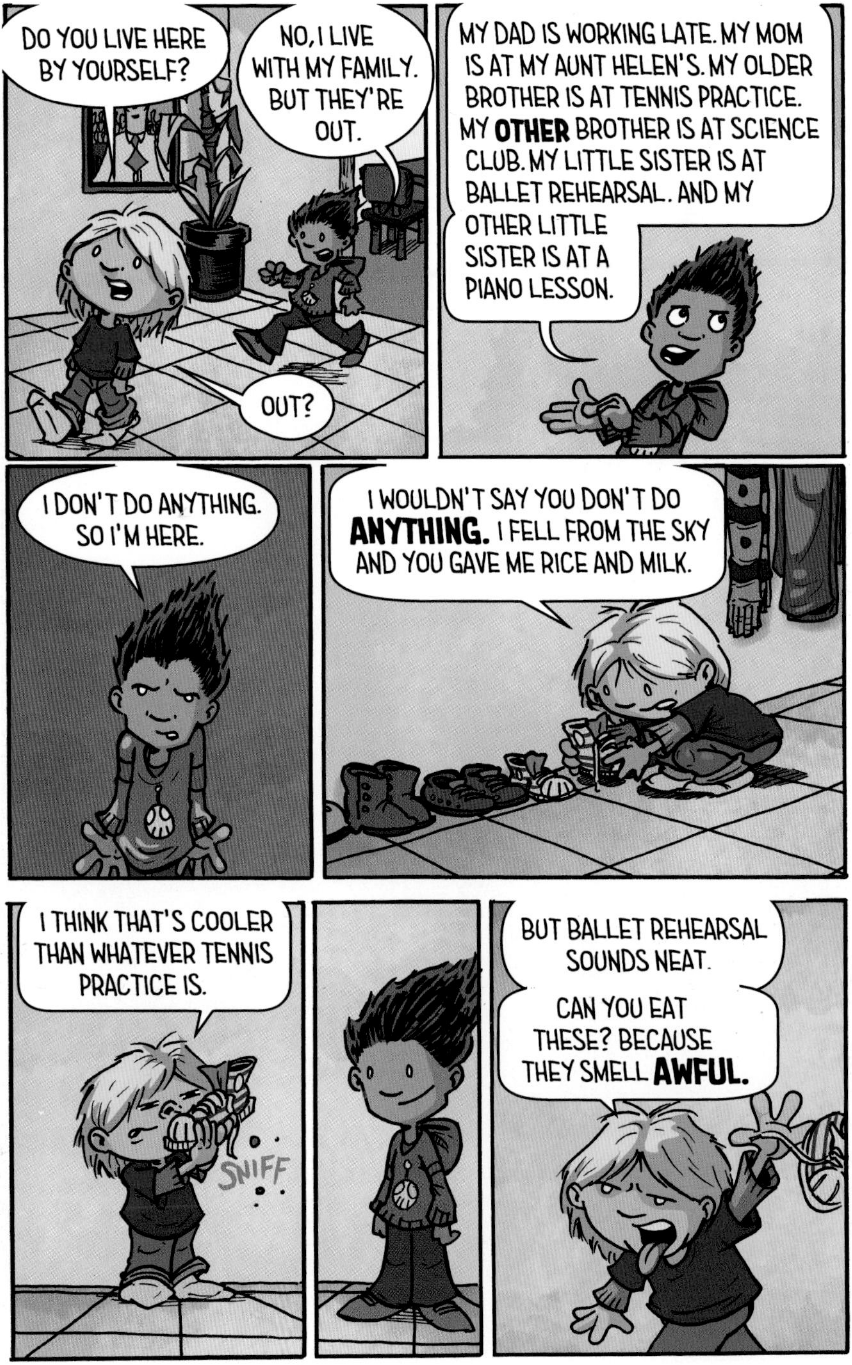
DO YOU LIVE HERE BY YOURSELF?
NO, I LIVE WITH MY FAMILY. BUT THEY'RE OUT.
OUT?
MY DAD IS WORKING LATE. MY MOM IS AT MY AUNT HELEN'S. MY OLDER BROTHER IS AT TENNIS PRACTICE. MY **OTHER** BROTHER IS AT SCIENCE CLUB. MY LITTLE SISTER IS AT BALLET REHEARSAL. AND MY OTHER LITTLE SISTER IS AT A PIANO LESSON.
I DON'T DO ANYTHING. SO I'M HERE.
I WOULDN'T SAY YOU DON'T DO **ANYTHING.** I FELL FROM THE SKY AND YOU GAVE ME RICE AND MILK.
I THINK THAT'S COOLER THAN WHATEVER TENNIS PRACTICE IS.
SNIFF
BUT BALLET REHEARSAL SOUNDS NEAT.
CAN YOU EAT THESE? BECAUSE THEY SMELL **AWFUL.**

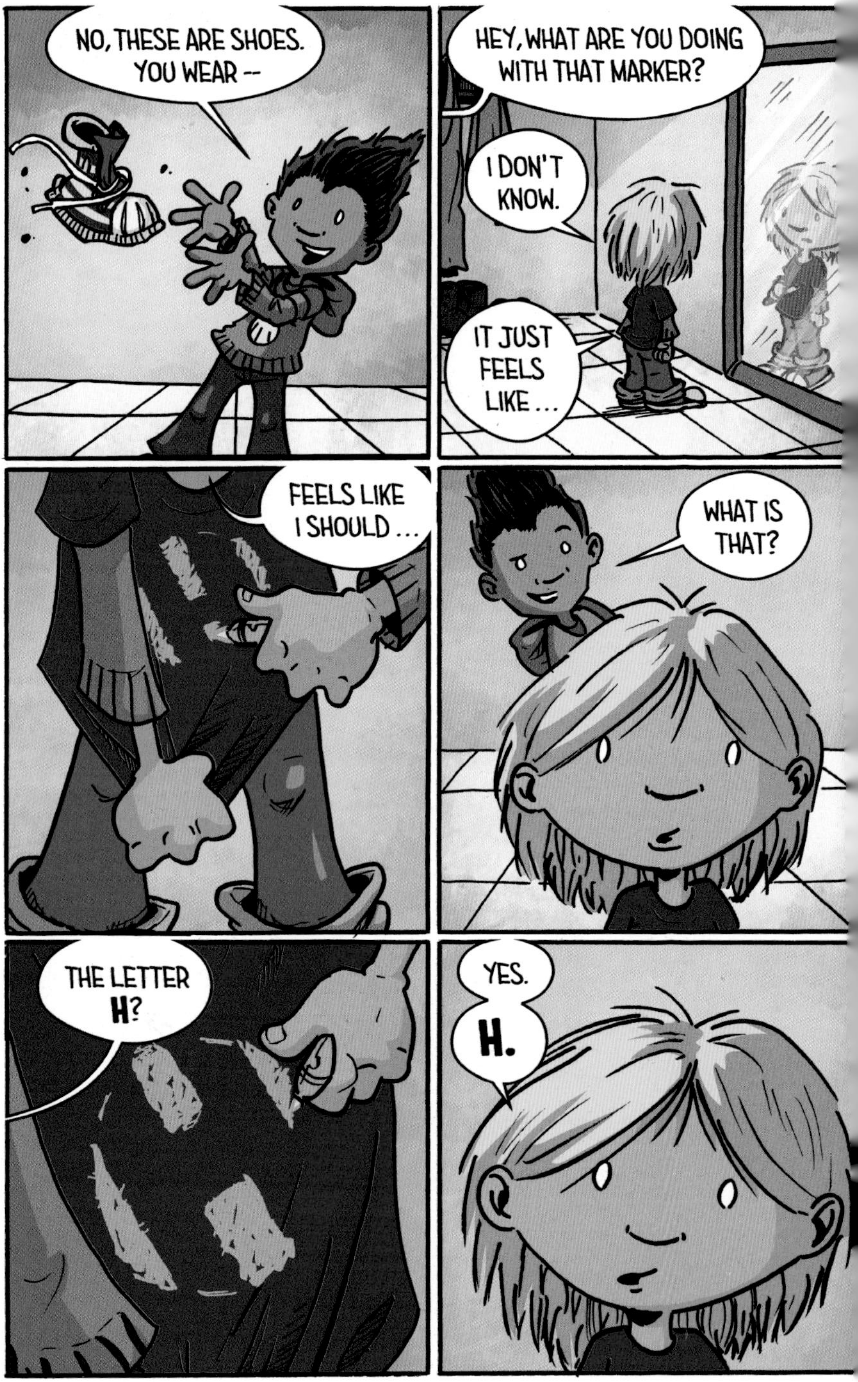
NO, THESE ARE SHOES. YOU WEAR --
HEY, WHAT ARE YOU DOING WITH THAT MARKER?
I DON'T KNOW.
IT JUST FEELS LIKE . . .
FEELS LIKE I SHOULD . . .
WHAT IS THAT?
THE LETTER H?
YES.
H.

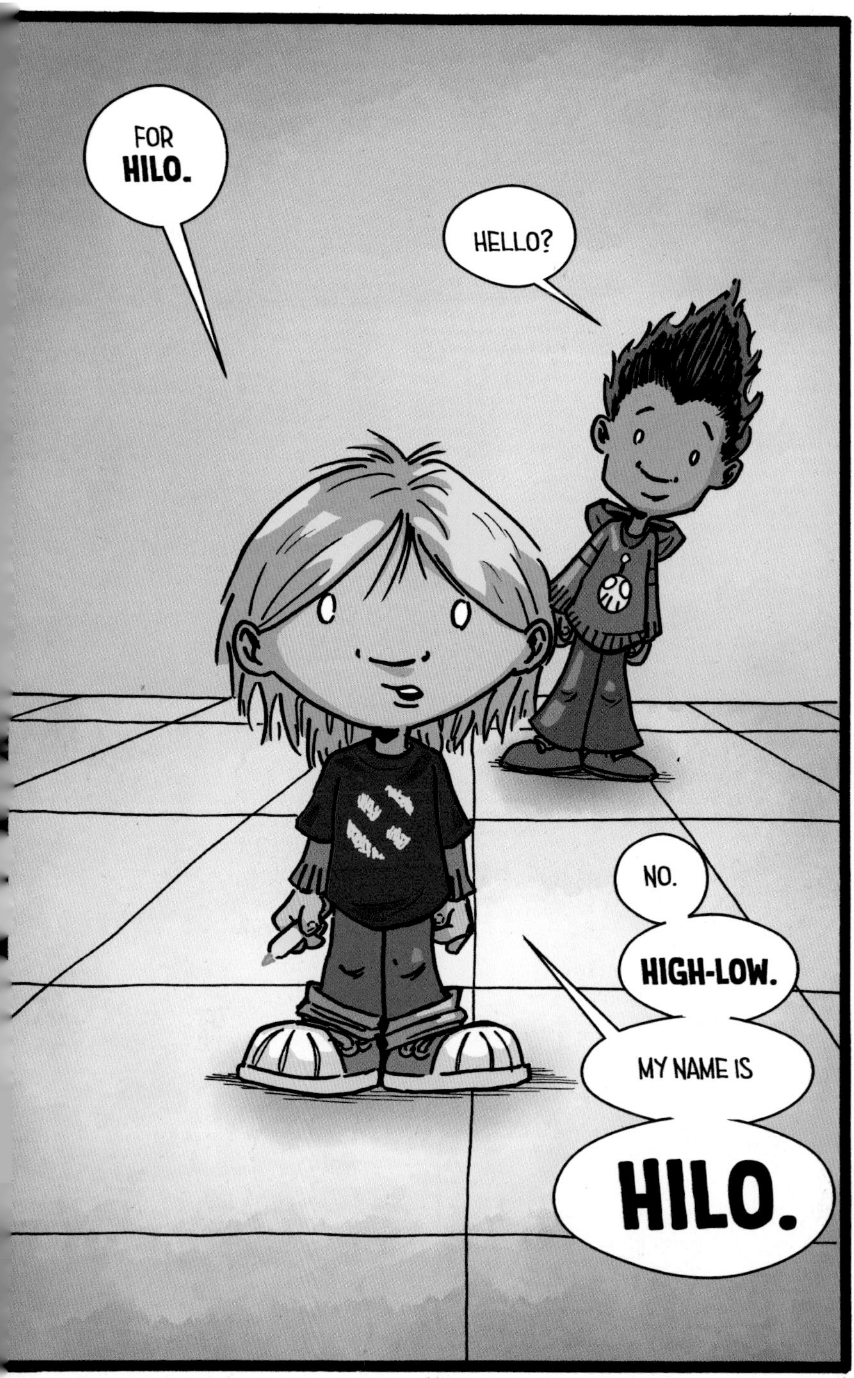
FOR **HILO.**
HELLO?
NO.
HIGH-LOW.
MY NAME IS
HILO.

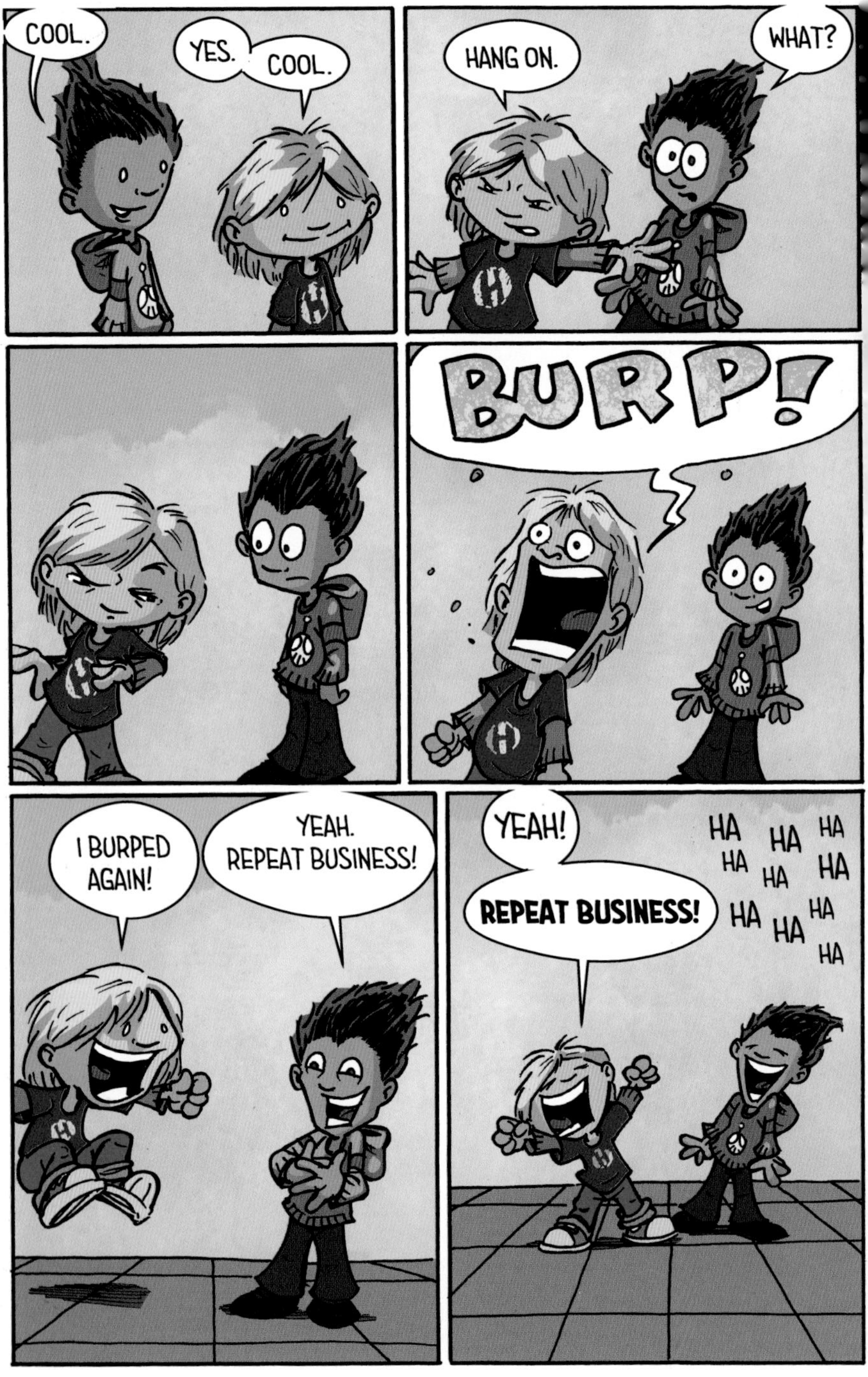
COOL.
YES.
COOL.
HANG ON.
WHAT?
BURP!
I BURPED AGAIN!
YEAH. REPEAT BUSINESS!
YEAH!
REPEAT BUSINESS!
HA HA HA HA HA HA HA HA HA HA HA

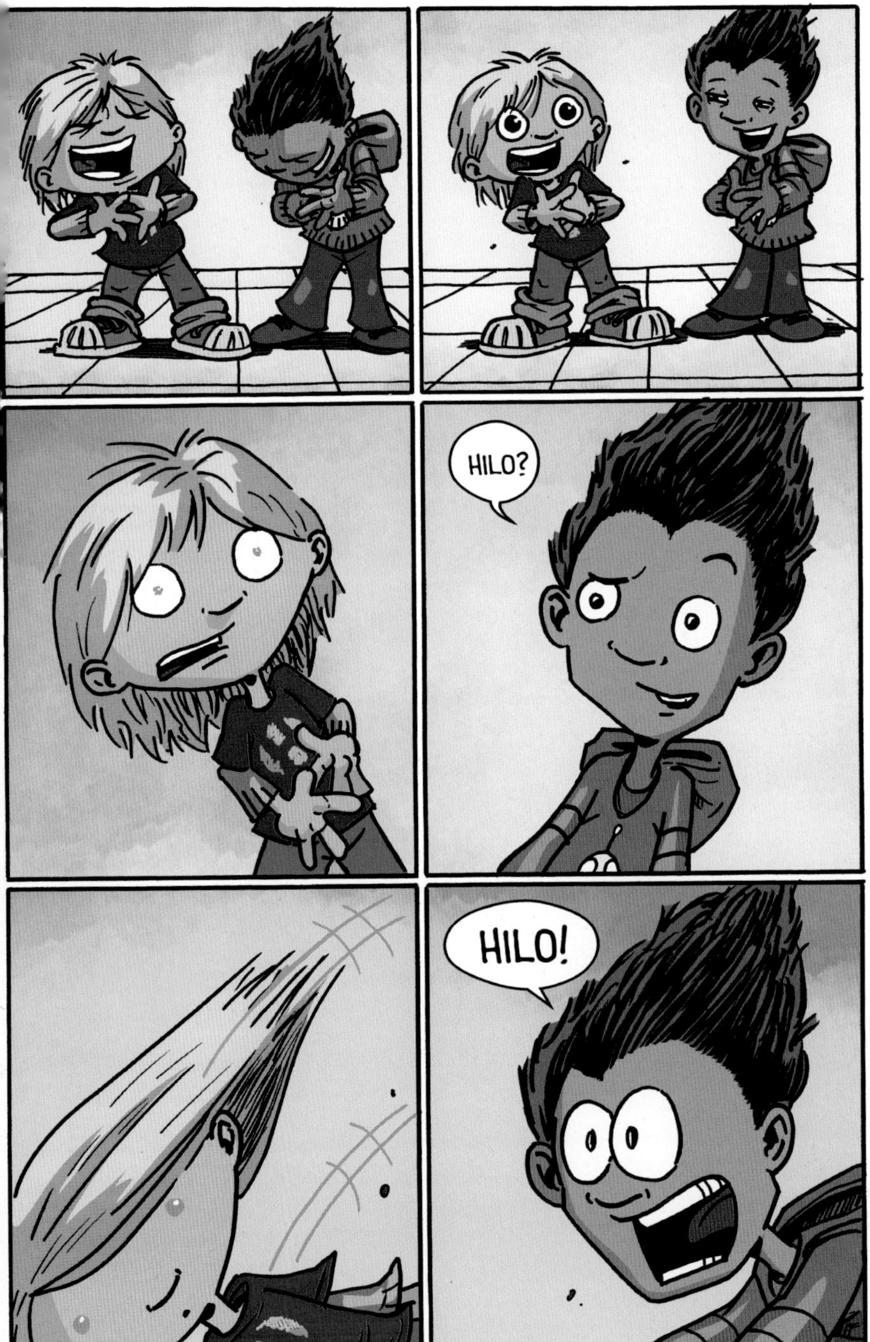
HILO?
HILO!

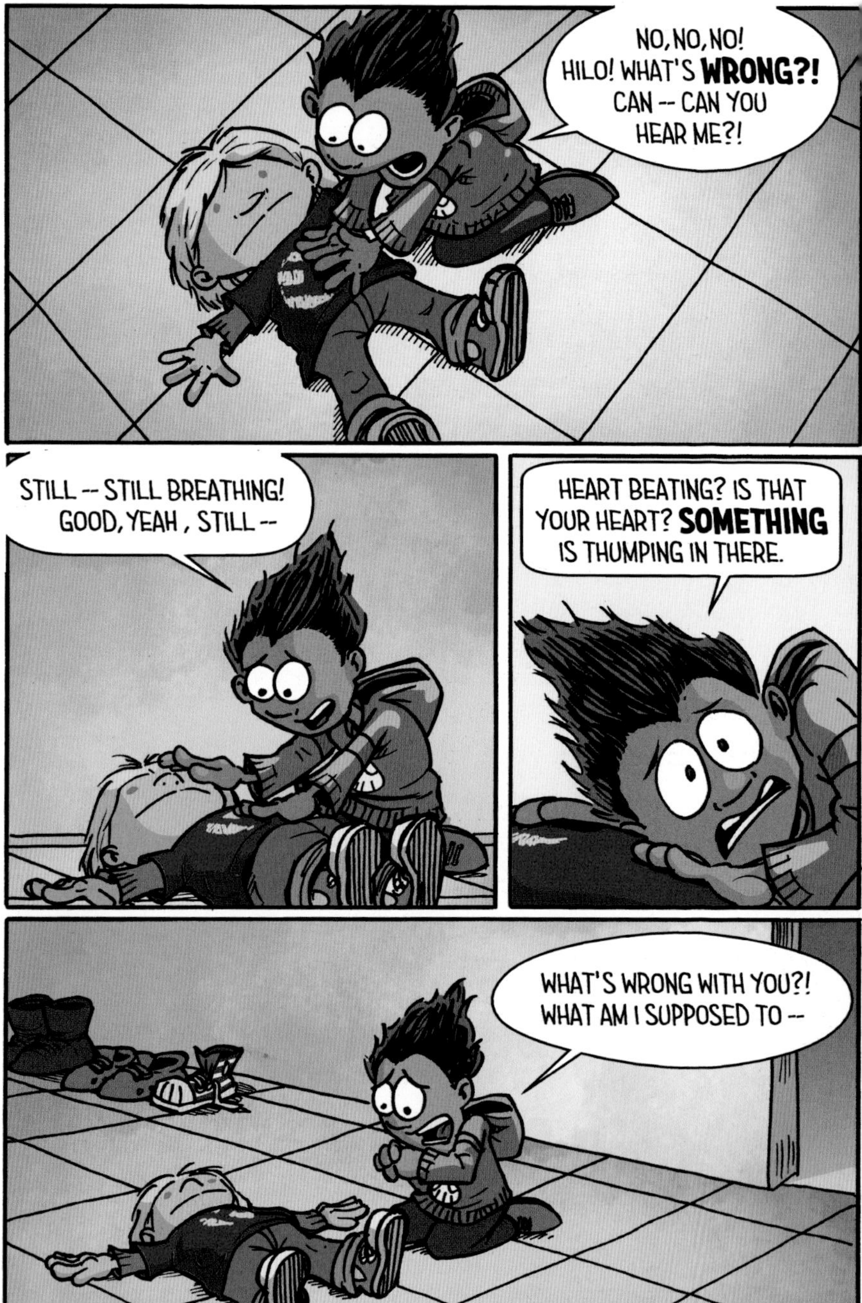
NO, NO, NO! HILO! WHAT'S **WRONG?!** CAN -- CAN YOU HEAR ME?!
STILL -- STILL BREATHING! GOOD, YEAH , STILL --
HEART BEATING? IS THAT YOUR HEART? **SOMETHING** IS THUMPING IN THERE.
WHAT'S WRONG WITH YOU?! WHAT AM I SUPPOSED TO --

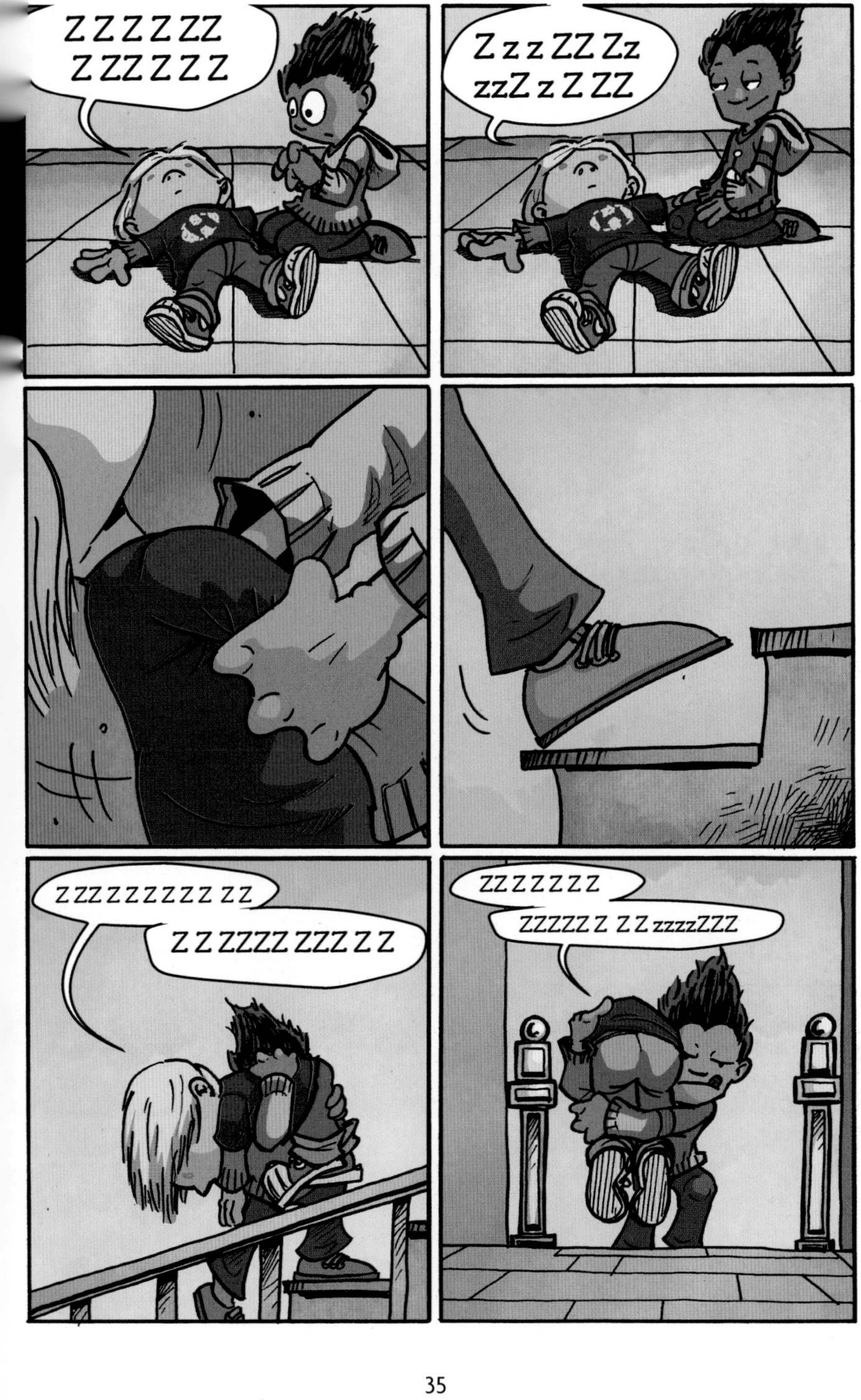
ZZZZZZ
ZZZZZZ
Zzz ZZ Zz
zzZ z Z ZZ
ZZZZZZZZZ ZZ
ZZ ZZZZ ZZZ ZZ
ZZZZZZZ
ZZZZZ Z ZZ zzzzZZZ

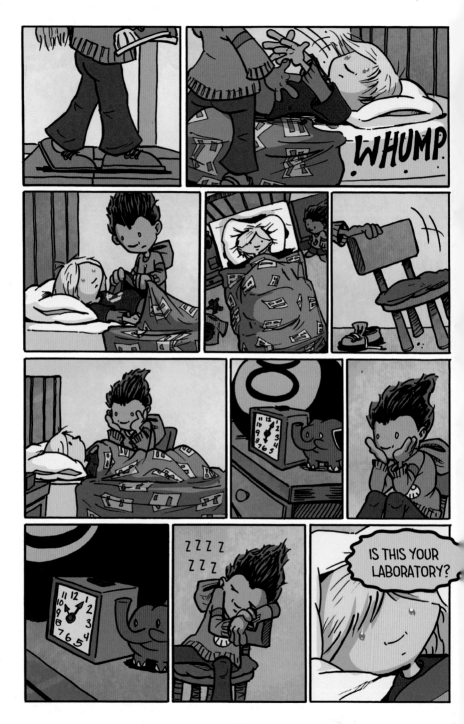

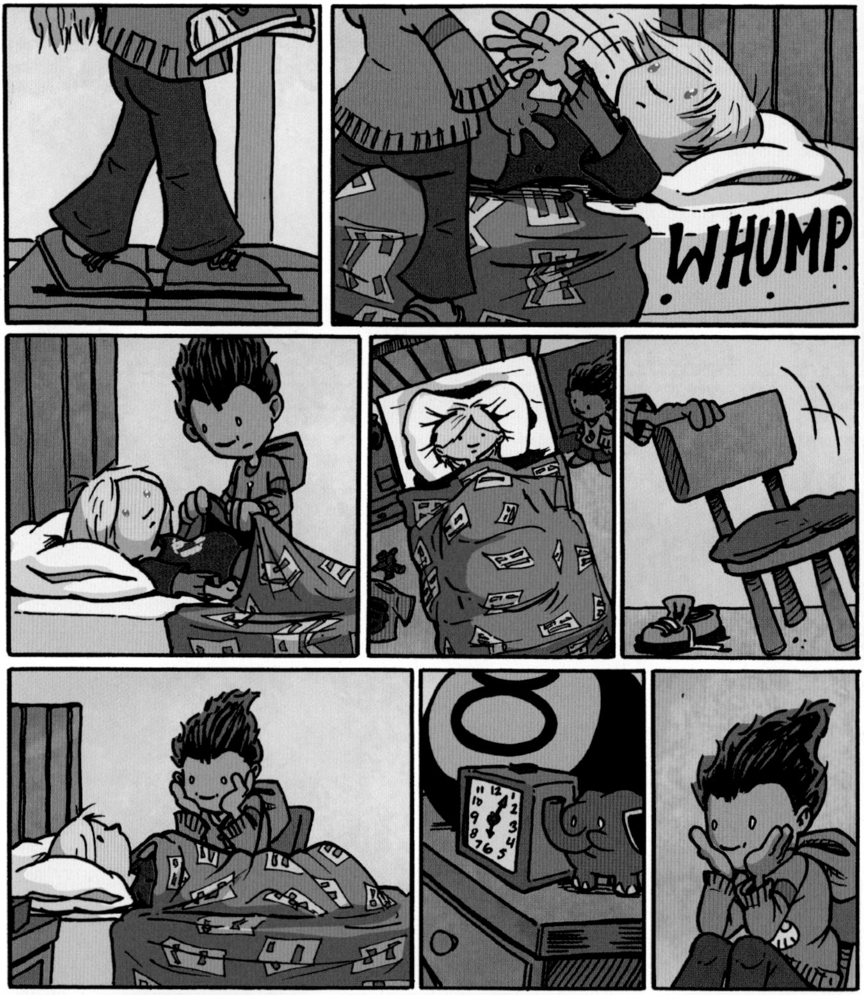
WHUMP
Z Z Z Z
Z Z Z
IS THIS YOUR LABORATORY?

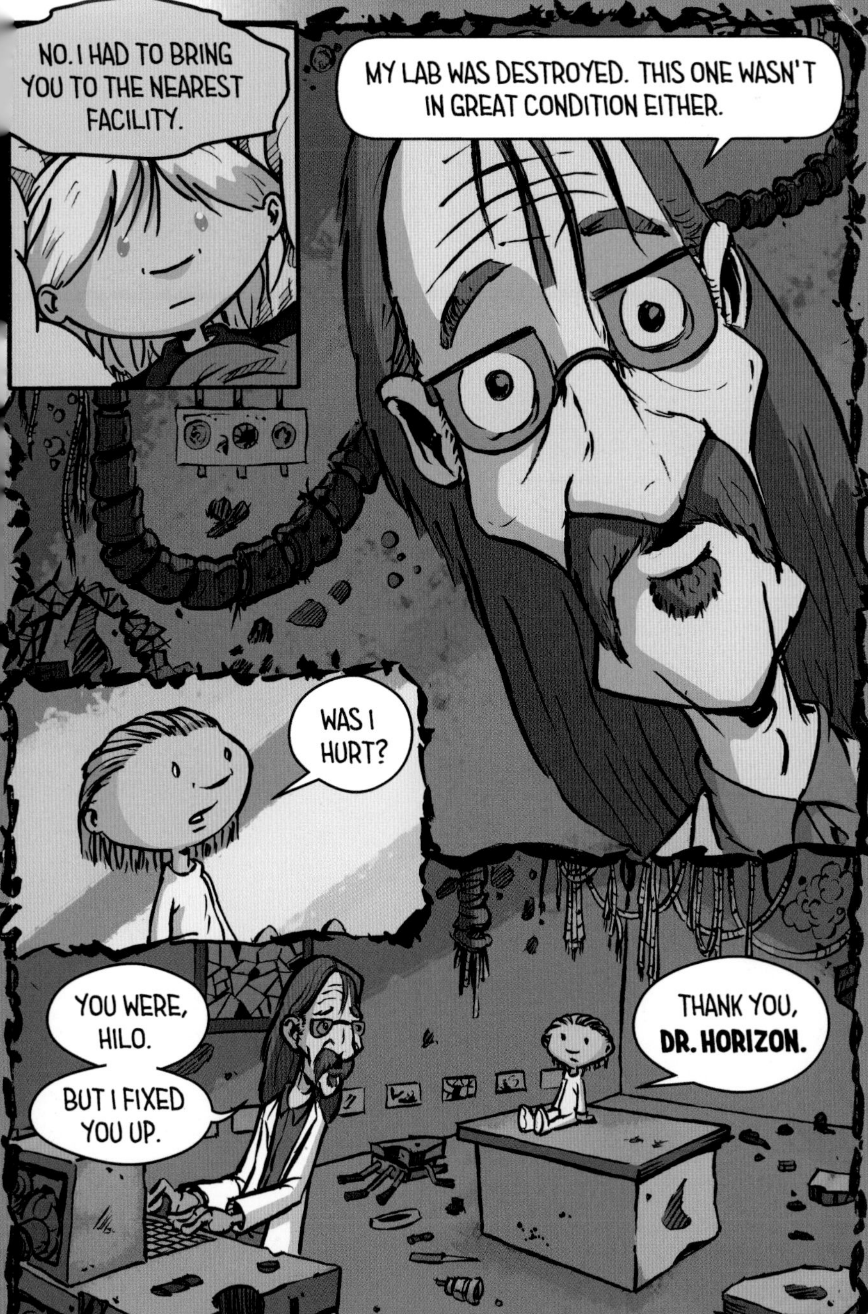
NO. I HAD TO BRING YOU TO THE NEAREST FACILITY.
MY LAB WAS DESTROYED. THIS ONE WASN'T IN GREAT CONDITION EITHER.
WAS I HURT?
YOU WERE, HILO.
BUT I FIXED YOU UP.
THANK YOU, **DR. HORIZON.**

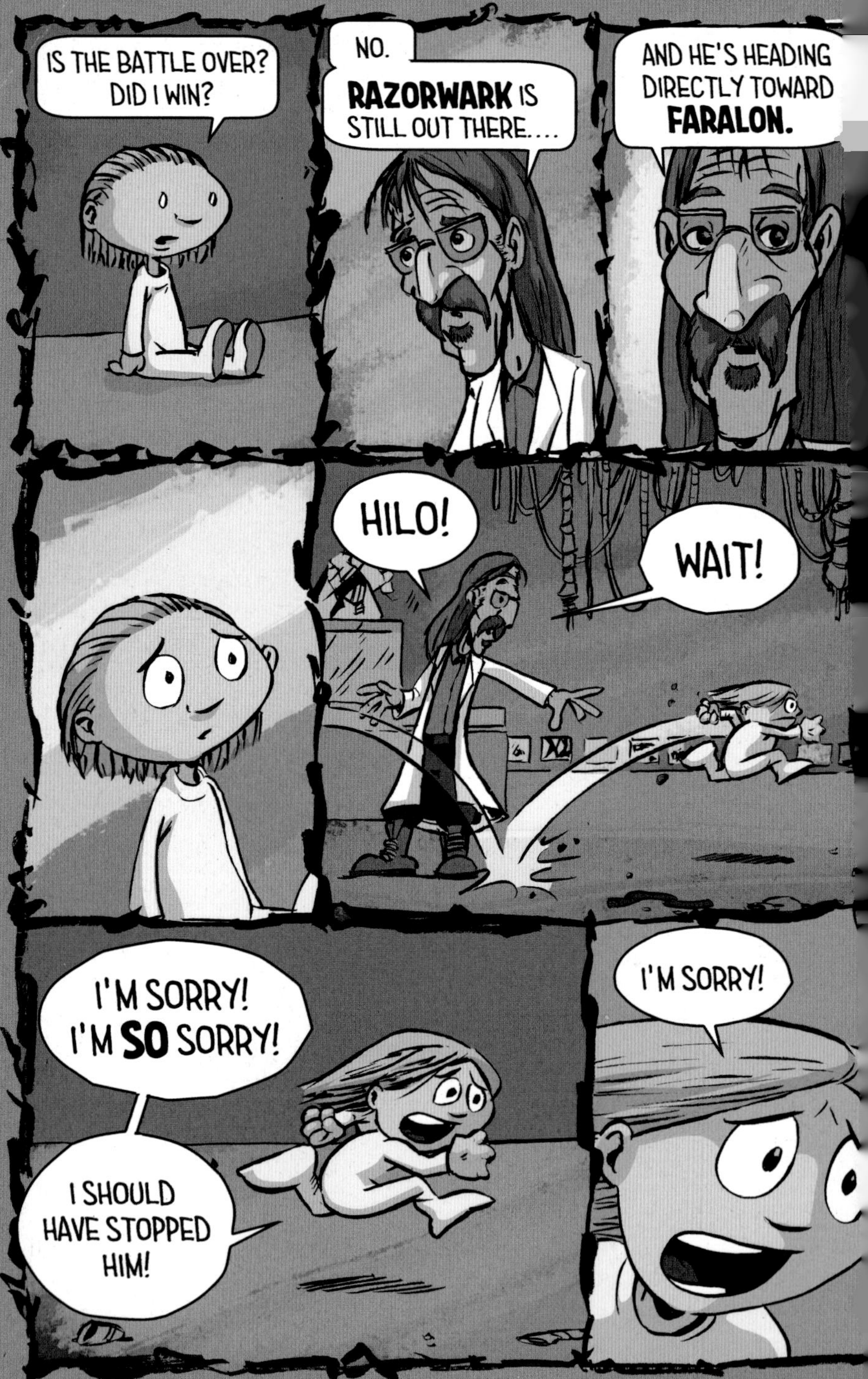
IS THE BATTLE OVER? DID I WIN?
NO.
RAZORWARK IS STILL OUT THERE....
AND HE'S HEADING DIRECTLY TOWARD **FARALON.**
HILO!
WAIT!
I'M SORRY! I'M **SO** SORRY!
I SHOULD HAVE STOPPED HIM!
I'M SORRY!

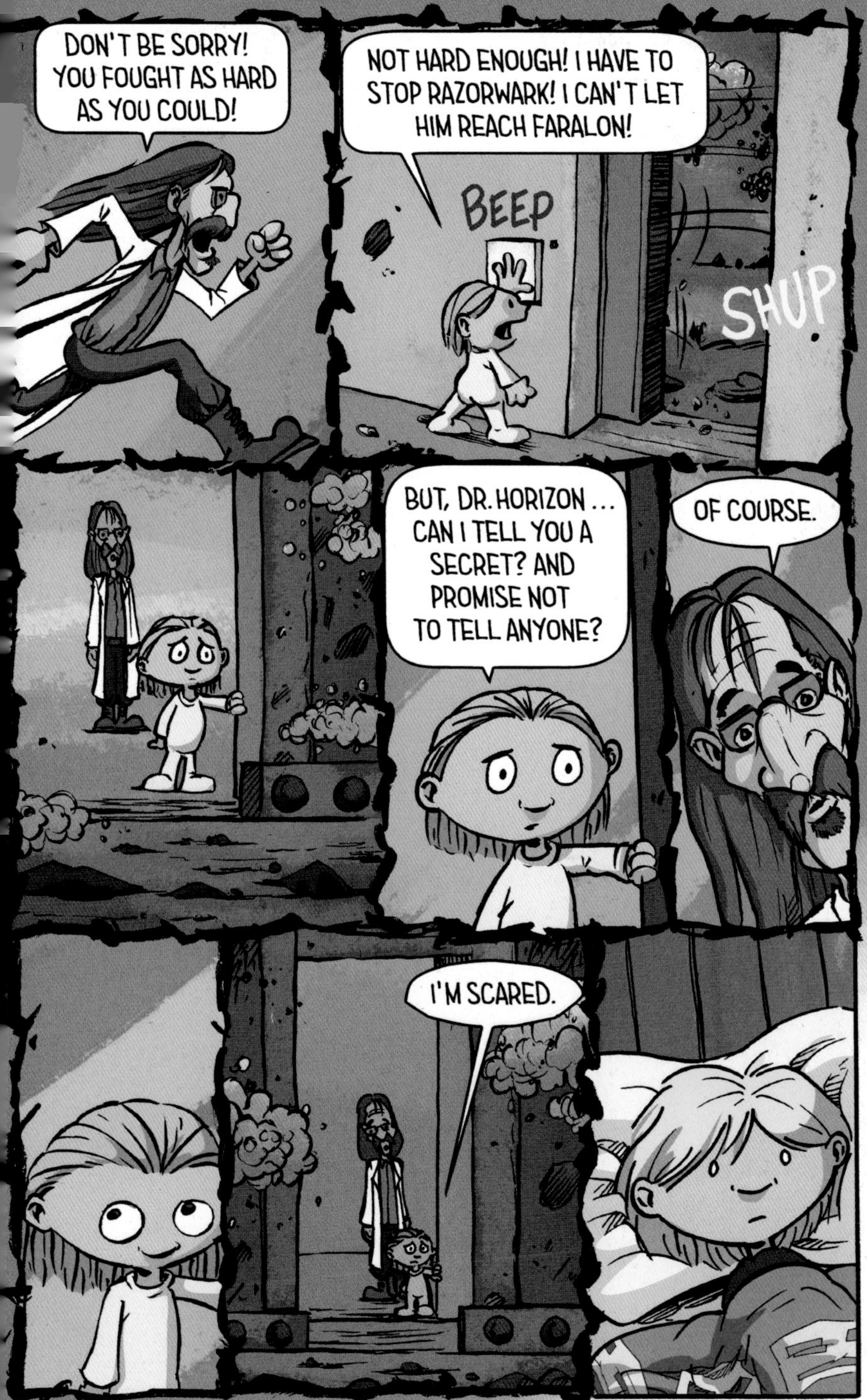
DON'T BE SORRY! YOU FOUGHT AS HARD AS YOU COULD!
NOT HARD ENOUGH! I HAVE TO STOP RAZORWARK! I CAN'T LET HIM REACH FARALON!
BEEP
SHUP
BUT, DR. HORIZON ... CAN I TELL YOU A SECRET? AND PROMISE NOT TO TELL ANYONE?
OF COURSE.
I'M SCARED.

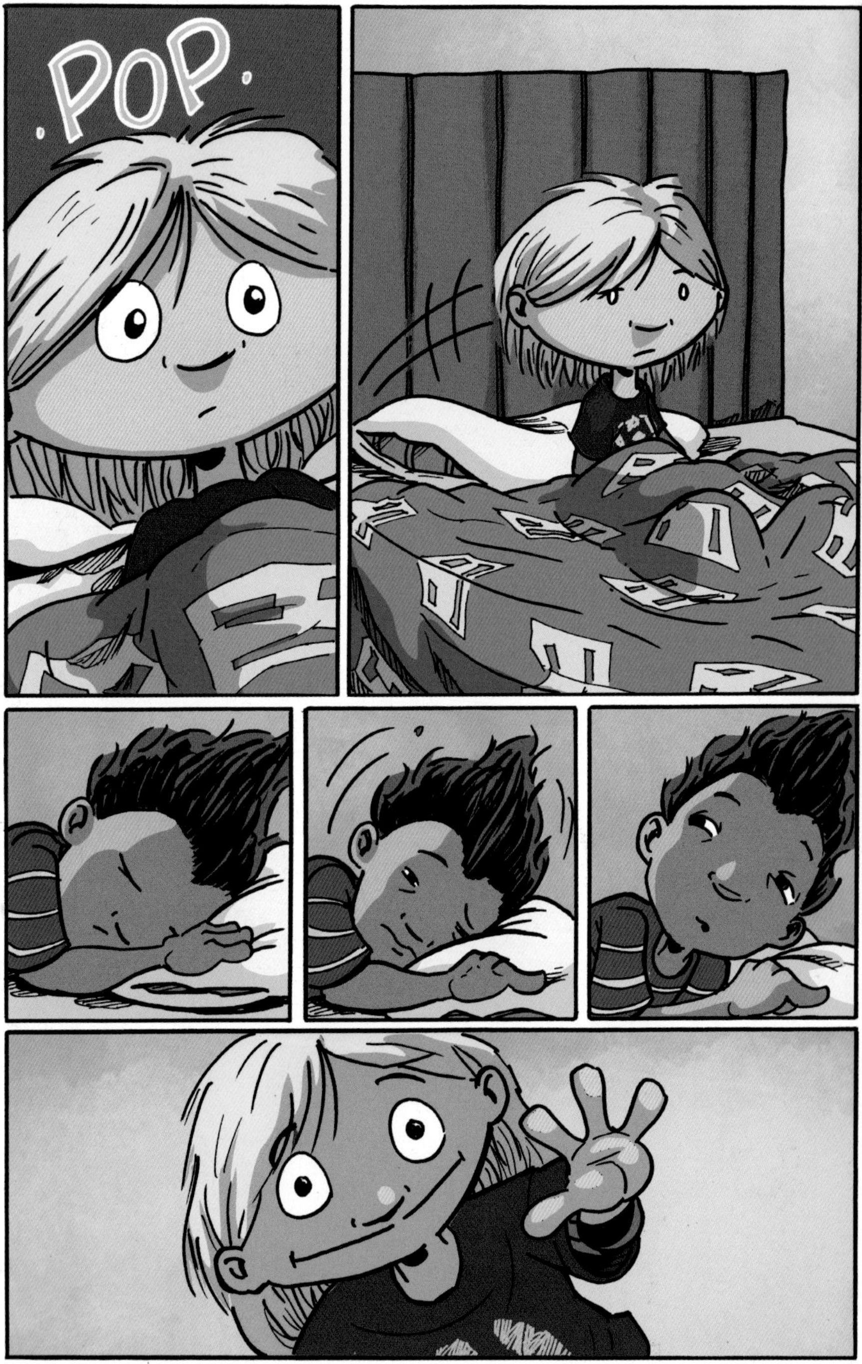
POP

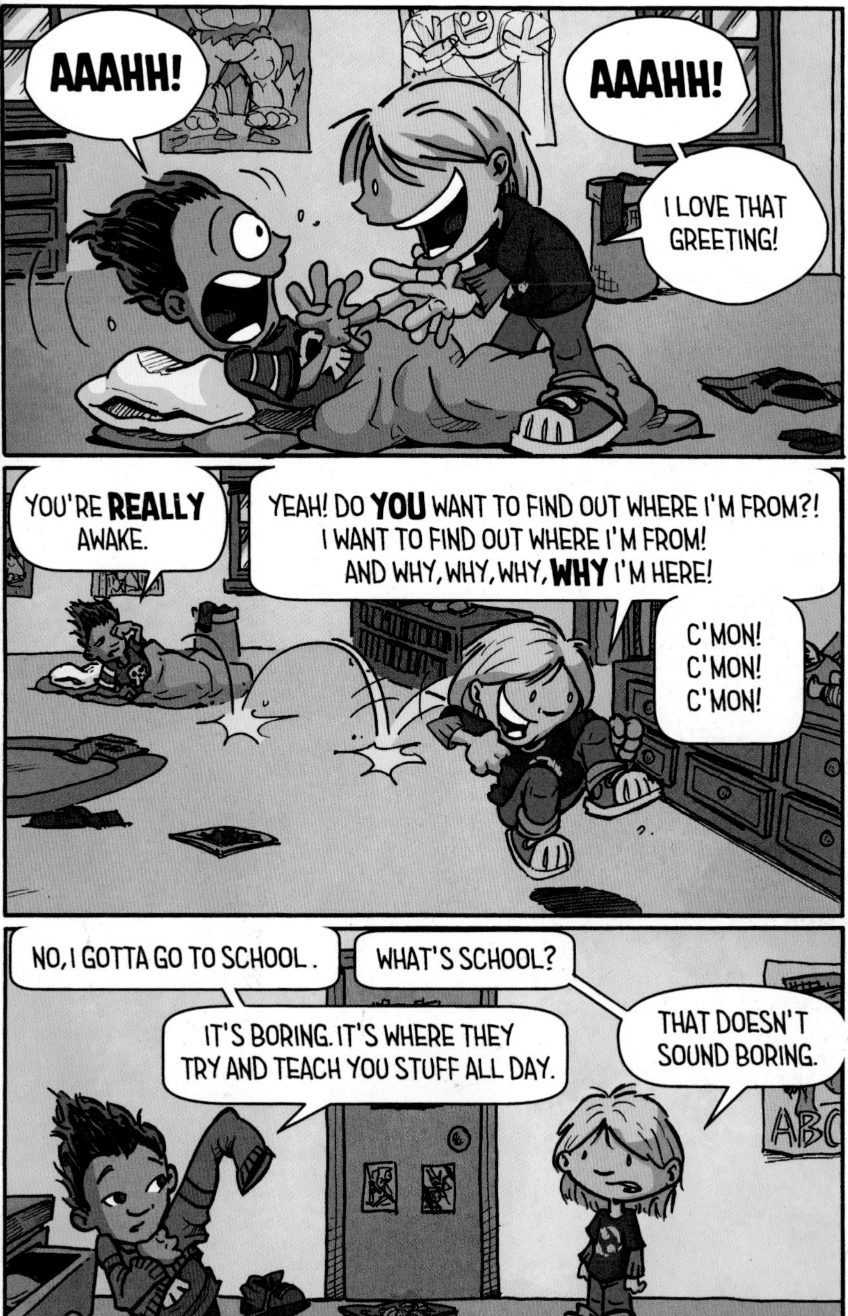
AAAHH!
AAAHH!
I LOVE THAT GREETING!
YOU'RE **REALLY** AWAKE.
YEAH! DO **YOU** WANT TO FIND OUT WHERE I'M FROM?! I WANT TO FIND OUT WHERE I'M FROM! AND WHY, WHY, WHY, **WHY** I'M HERE!
C'MON! C'MON! C'MON!
NO, I GOTTA GO TO SCHOOL.
WHAT'S SCHOOL?
IT'S BORING. IT'S WHERE THEY TRY AND TEACH YOU STUFF ALL DAY.
THAT DOESN'T SOUND BORING.
ABC

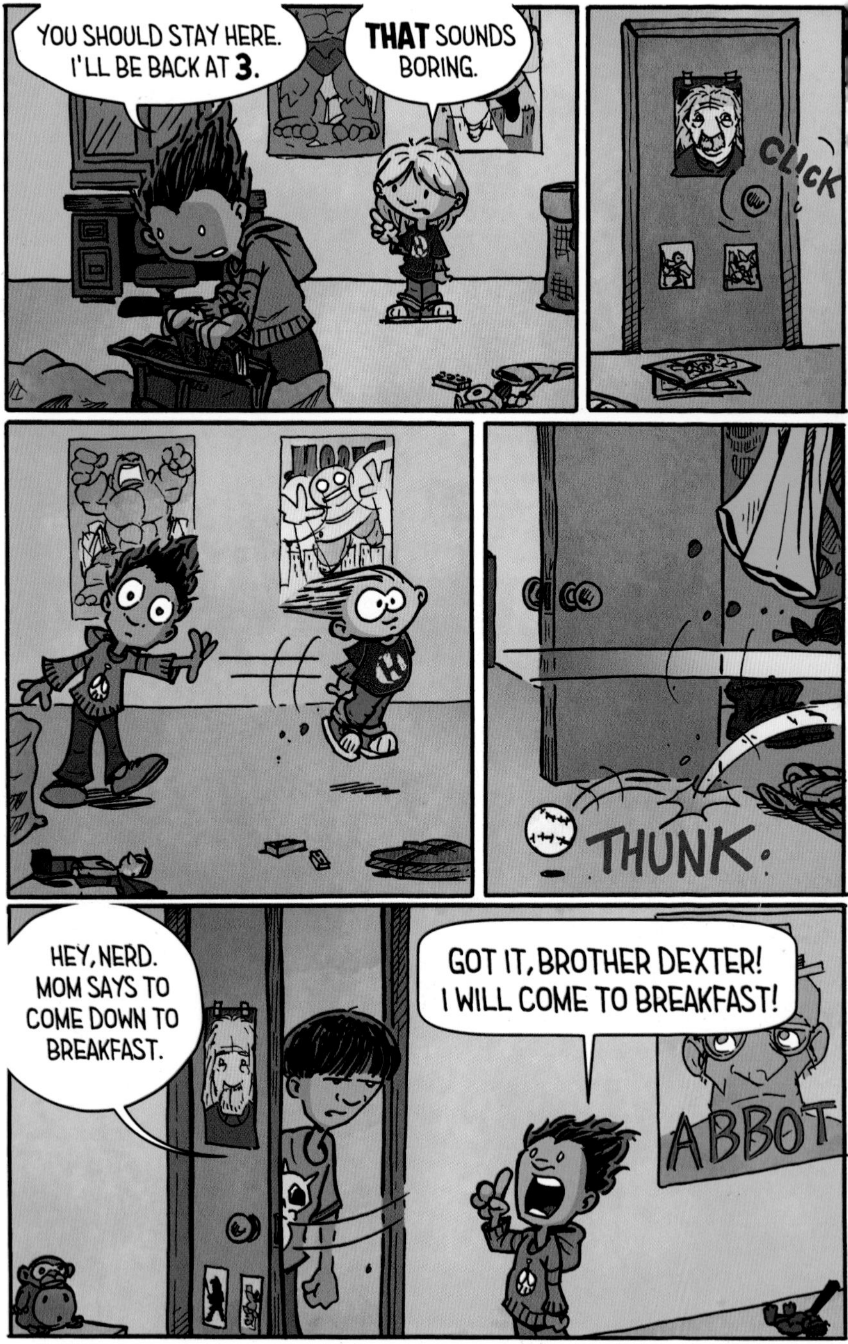
YOU SHOULD STAY HERE. I'LL BE BACK AT 3.
THAT SOUNDS BORING.
CLICK
THUNK.
HEY, NERD. MOM SAYS TO COME DOWN TO BREAKFAST.
GOT IT, BROTHER DEXTER! I WILL COME TO BREAKFAST!
ABBOT

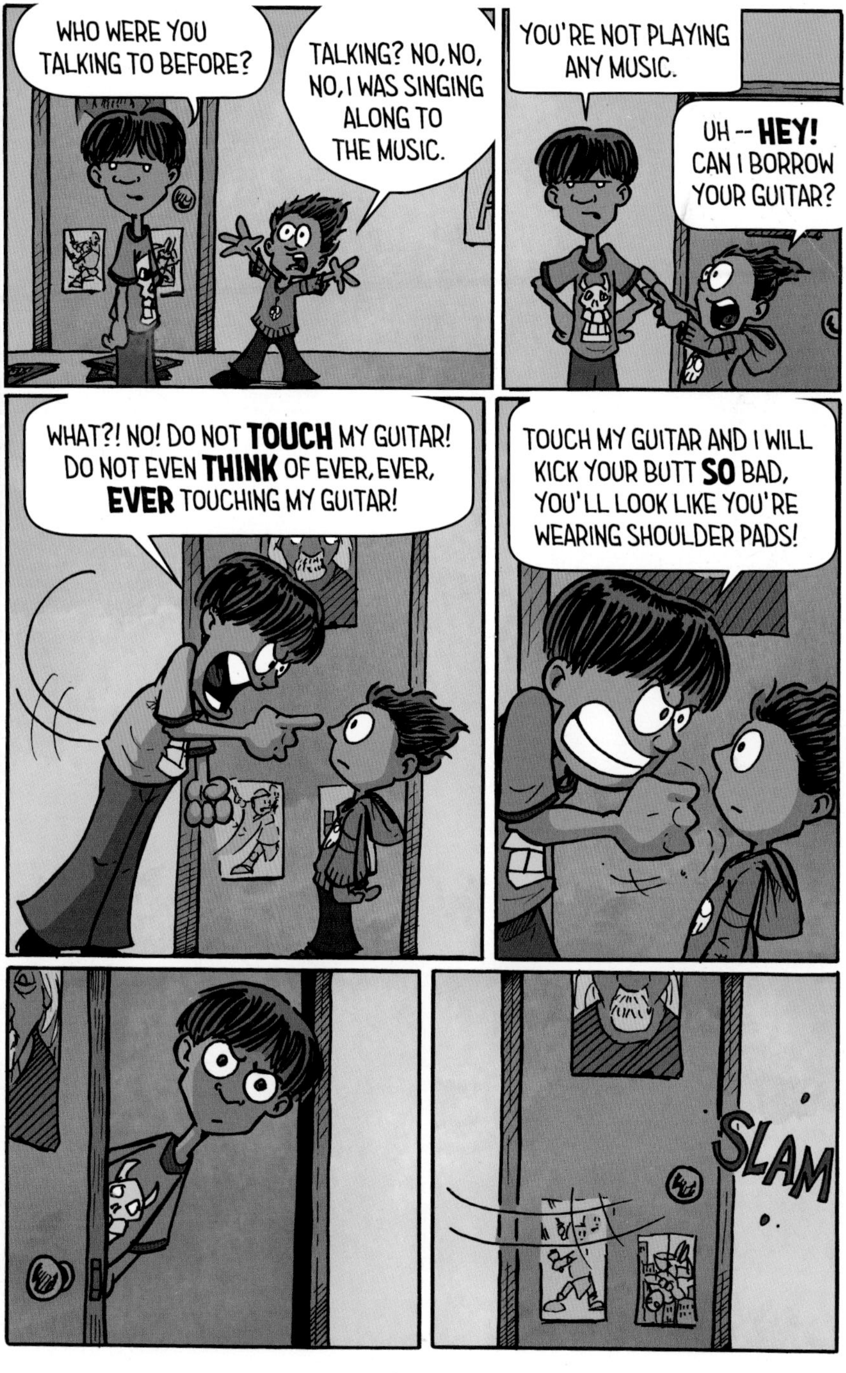
WHO WERE YOU TALKING TO BEFORE?
TALKING? NO, NO, NO, I WAS SINGING ALONG TO THE MUSIC.
YOU'RE NOT PLAYING ANY MUSIC.
UH -- HEY! CAN I BORROW YOUR GUITAR?
WHAT?! NO! DO NOT TOUCH MY GUITAR! DO NOT EVEN THINK OF EVER, EVER, EVER TOUCHING MY GUITAR!
TOUCH MY GUITAR AND I WILL KICK YOUR BUTT SO BAD, YOU'LL LOOK LIKE YOU'RE WEARING SHOULDER PADS!
SLAM

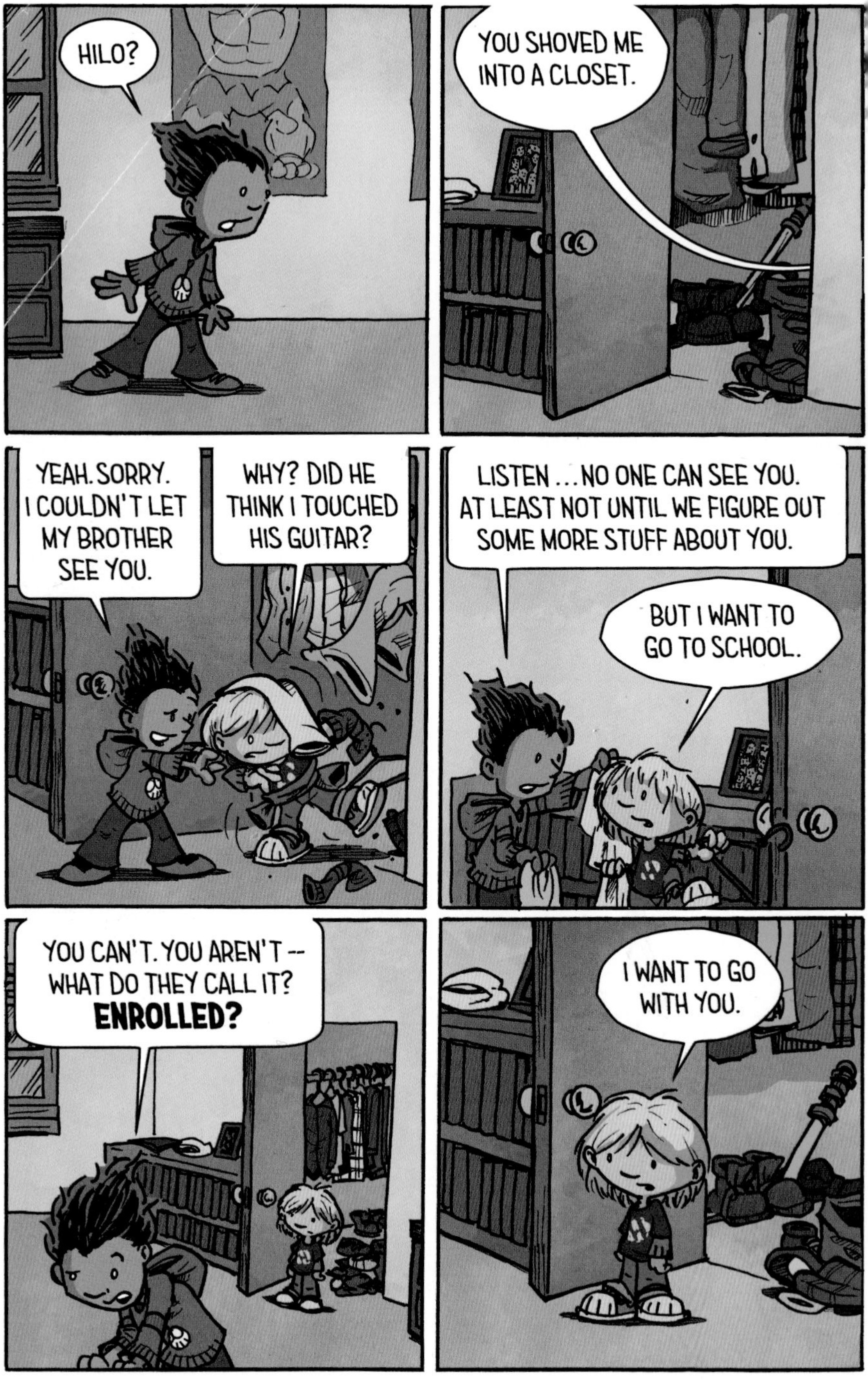
HILO?
YOU SHOVED ME INTO A CLOSET.
YEAH. SORRY. I COULDN'T LET MY BROTHER SEE YOU.
WHY? DID HE THINK I TOUCHED HIS GUITAR?
LISTEN ... NO ONE CAN SEE YOU. AT LEAST NOT UNTIL WE FIGURE OUT SOME MORE STUFF ABOUT YOU.
BUT I WANT TO GO TO SCHOOL.
YOU CAN'T. YOU AREN'T -- WHAT DO THEY CALL IT? **ENROLLED?**
I WANT TO GO WITH YOU.

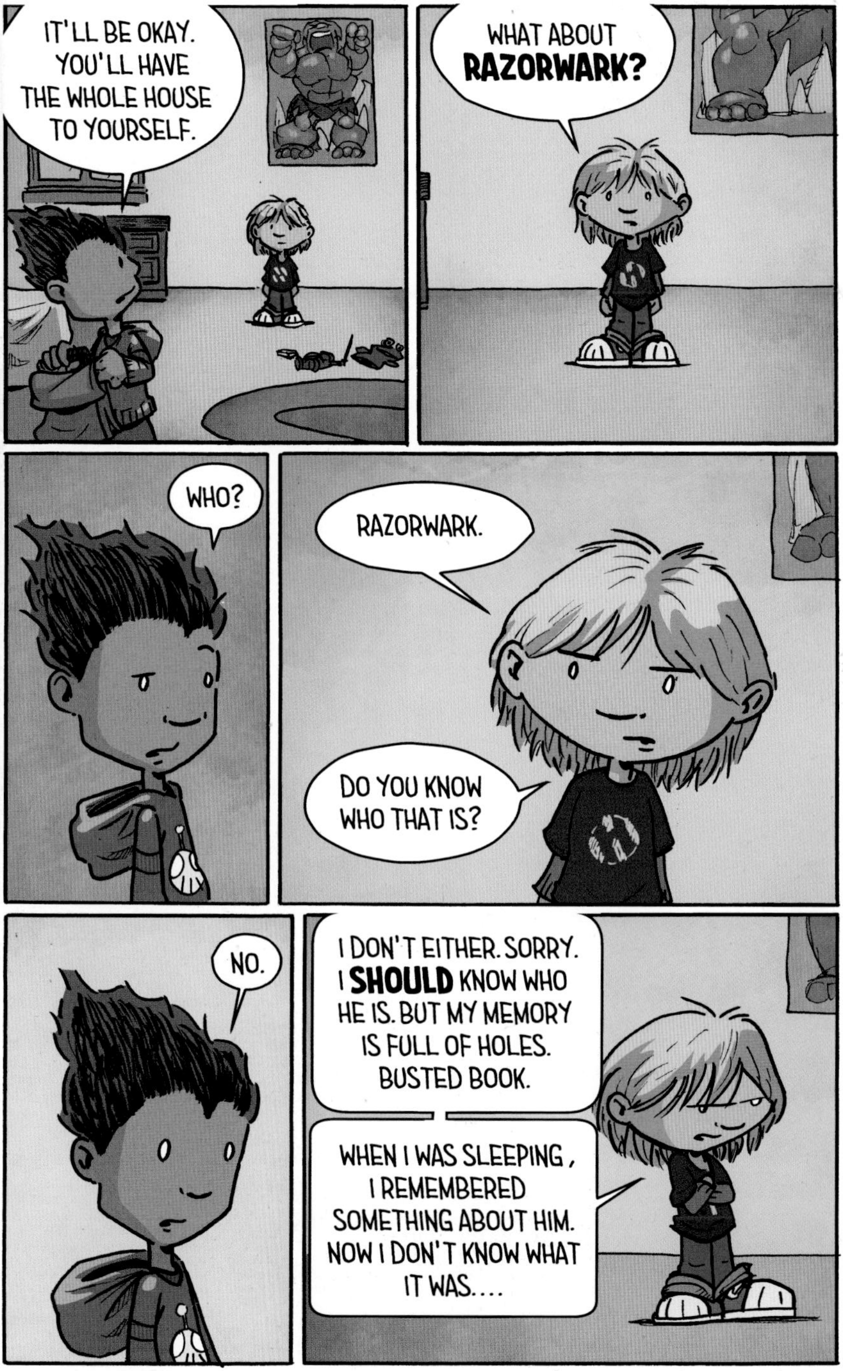
IT'LL BE OKAY. YOU'LL HAVE THE WHOLE HOUSE TO YOURSELF.
WHAT ABOUT **RAZORWARK?**
WHO?
RAZORWARK.
DO YOU KNOW WHO THAT IS?
NO.
I DON'T EITHER. SORRY. I **SHOULD** KNOW WHO HE IS. BUT MY MEMORY IS FULL OF HOLES. BUSTED BOOK.
WHEN I WAS SLEEPING, I REMEMBERED SOMETHING ABOUT HIM. NOW I DON'T KNOW WHAT IT WAS....

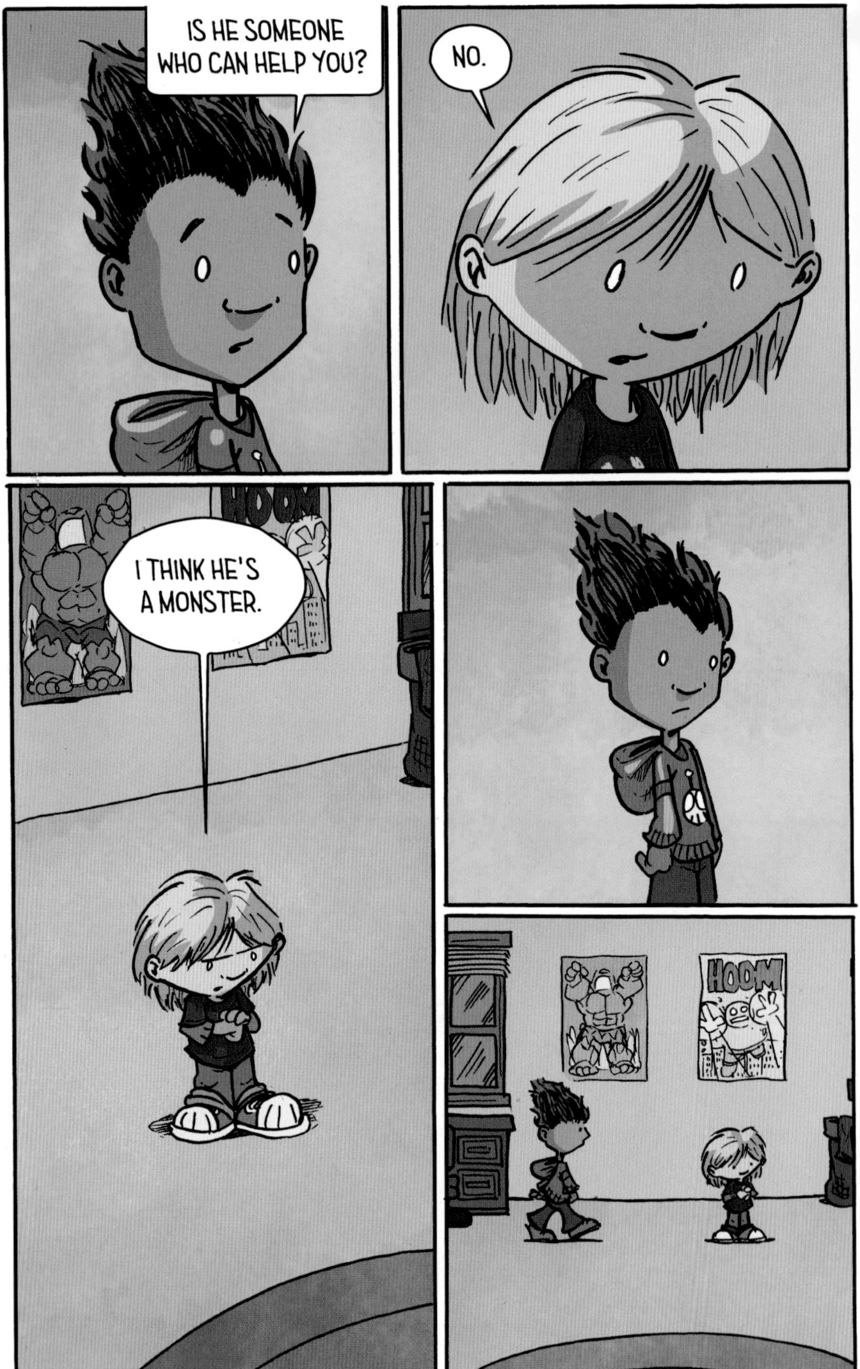
IS HE SOMEONE WHO CAN HELP YOU?
NO.
HOOM
I THINK HE'S A MONSTER.
HOOM

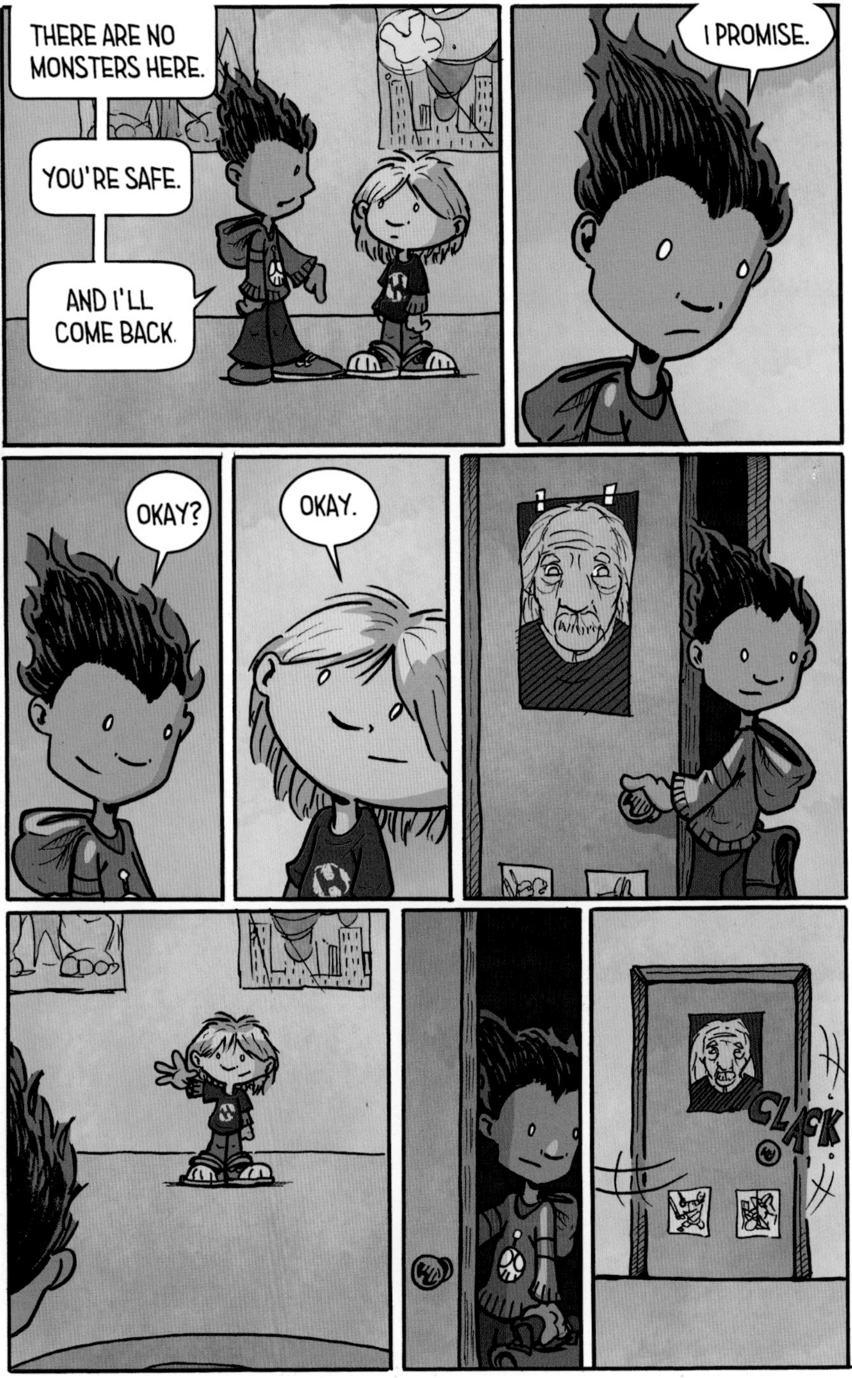
THERE ARE NO MONSTERS HERE.
YOU'RE SAFE.
AND I'LL COME BACK.
I PROMISE.
OKAY?
OKAY.
CLACK

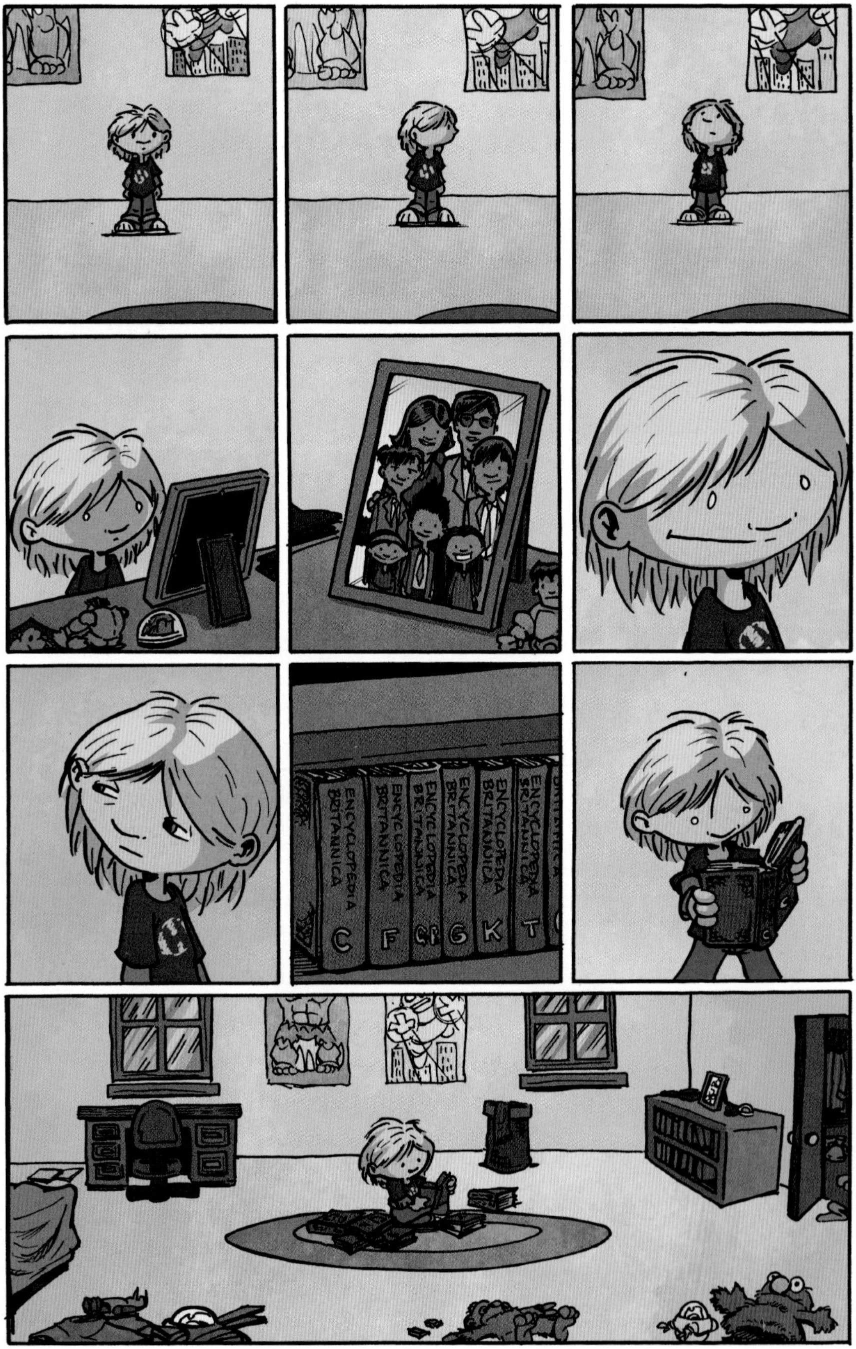
ENCYCLOPEDIA BRITANNICA C
ENCYCLOPEDIA BRITANNICA F
ENCYCLOPEDIA BRITANNICA G
ENCYCLOPEDIA BRITANNICA K
ENCYCLOPEDIA BRITANNICA T

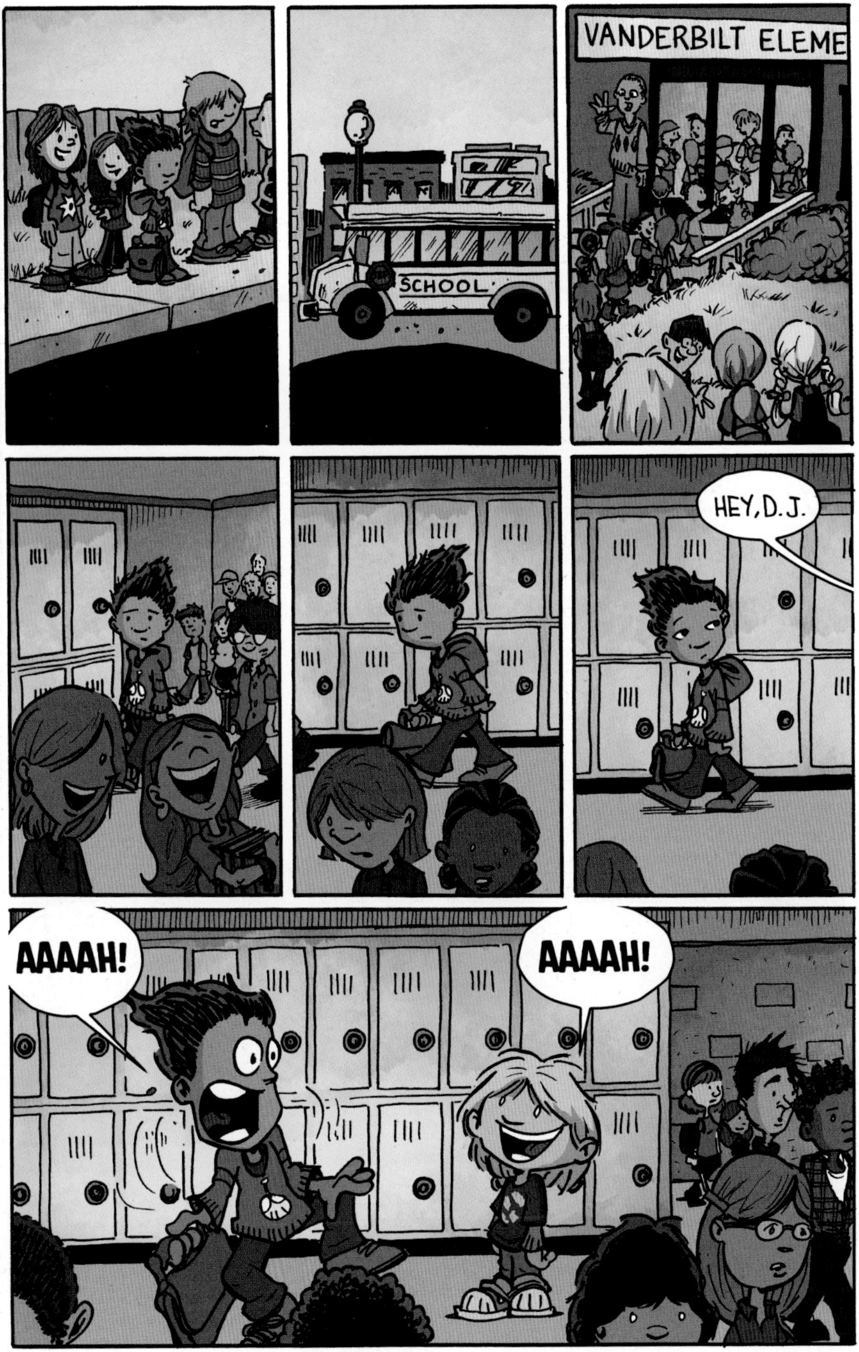
VANDERBILT ELEME
SCHOOL
HEY, D.J.
AAAAH!
AAAAH!

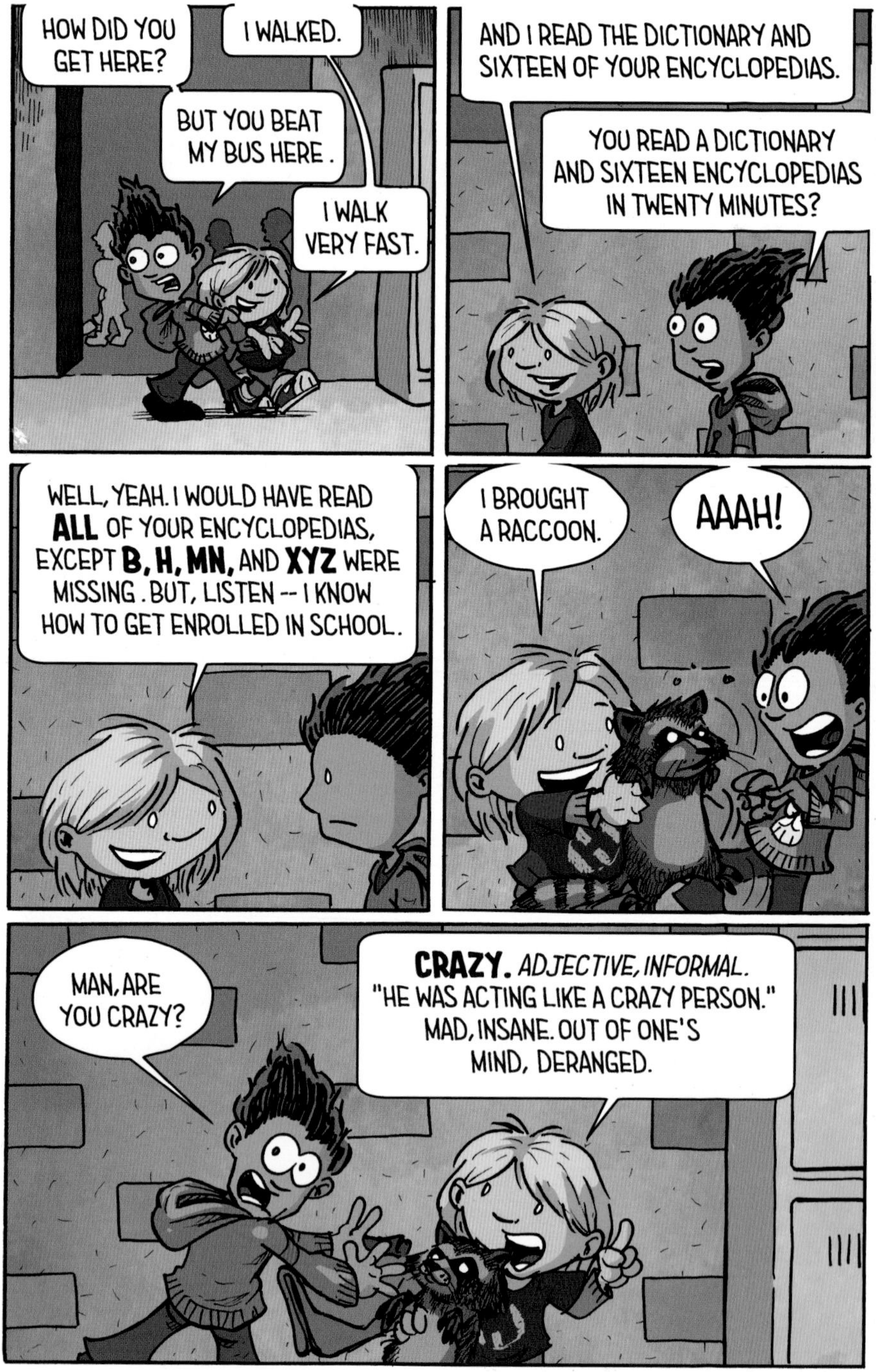
HOW DID YOU GET HERE?
I WALKED.
BUT YOU BEAT MY BUS HERE.
I WALK VERY FAST.
AND I READ THE DICTIONARY AND SIXTEEN OF YOUR ENCYCLOPEDIAS.
YOU READ A DICTIONARY AND SIXTEEN ENCYCLOPEDIAS IN TWENTY MINUTES?
WELL, YEAH. I WOULD HAVE READ ALL OF YOUR ENCYCLOPEDIAS, EXCEPT B, H, MN, AND XYZ WERE MISSING. BUT, LISTEN -- I KNOW HOW TO GET ENROLLED IN SCHOOL.
I BROUGHT A RACCOON.
AAAH!
MAN, ARE YOU CRAZY?
CRAZY. ADJECTIVE, INFORMAL. "HE WAS ACTING LIKE A CRAZY PERSON." MAD, INSANE. OUT OF ONE'S MIND, DERANGED.

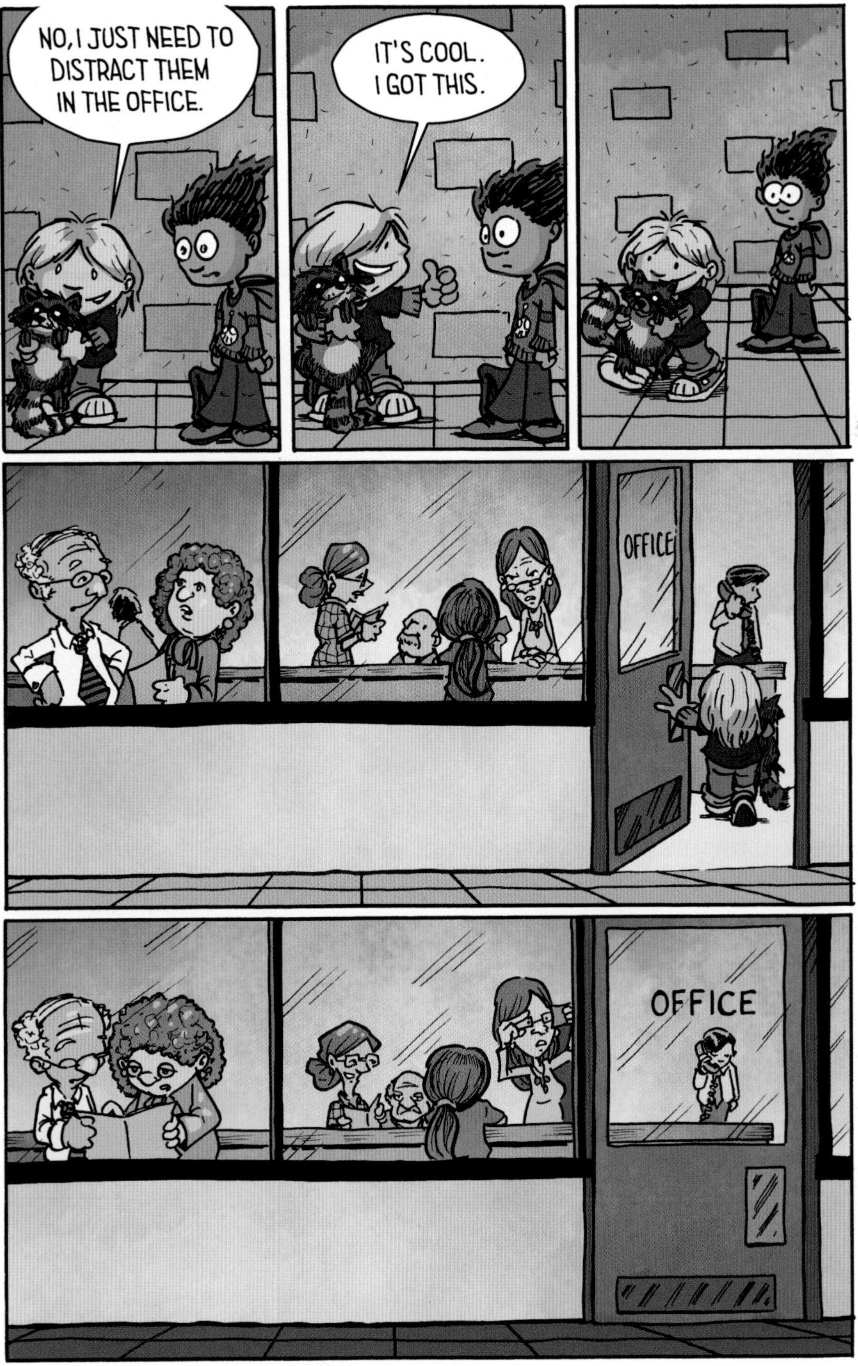
NO, I JUST NEED TO DISTRACT THEM IN THE OFFICE.
IT'S COOL. I GOT THIS.
OFFICE
OFFICE

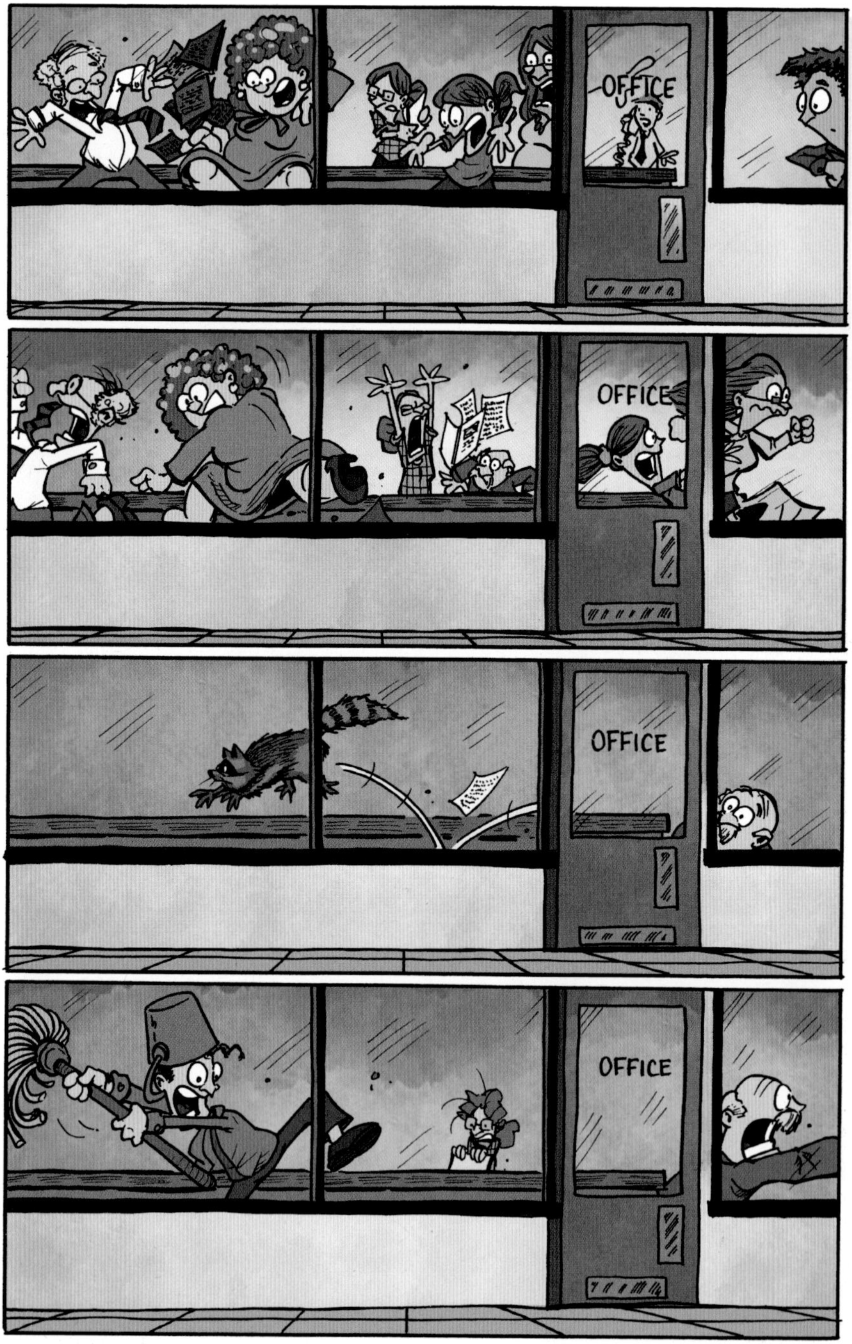
OFFICE
OFFICE
OFFICE
OFFICE

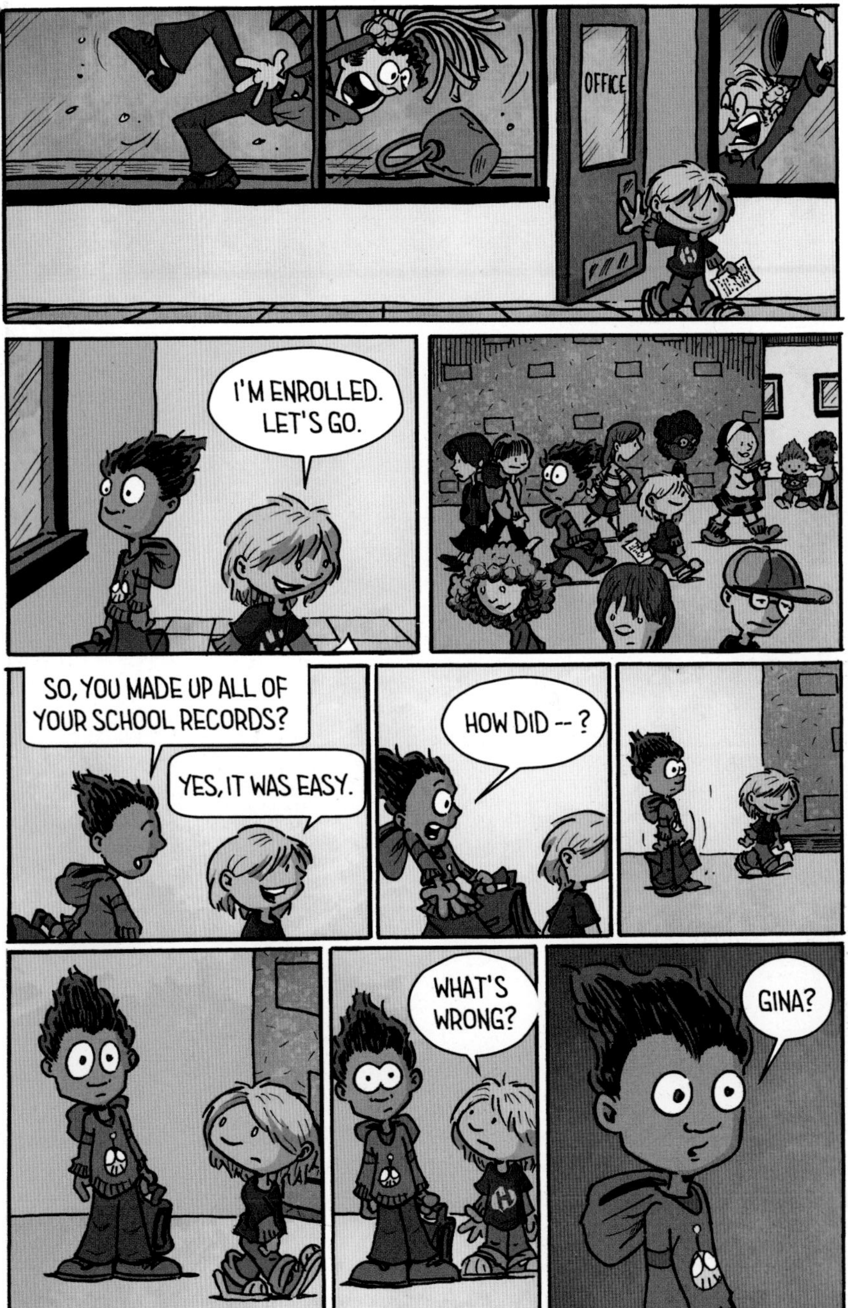
OFFICE
I'M ENROLLED. LET'S GO.
SO, YOU MADE UP ALL OF YOUR SCHOOL RECORDS?
YES, IT WAS EASY.
HOW DID -- ?
WHAT'S WRONG?
GINA?

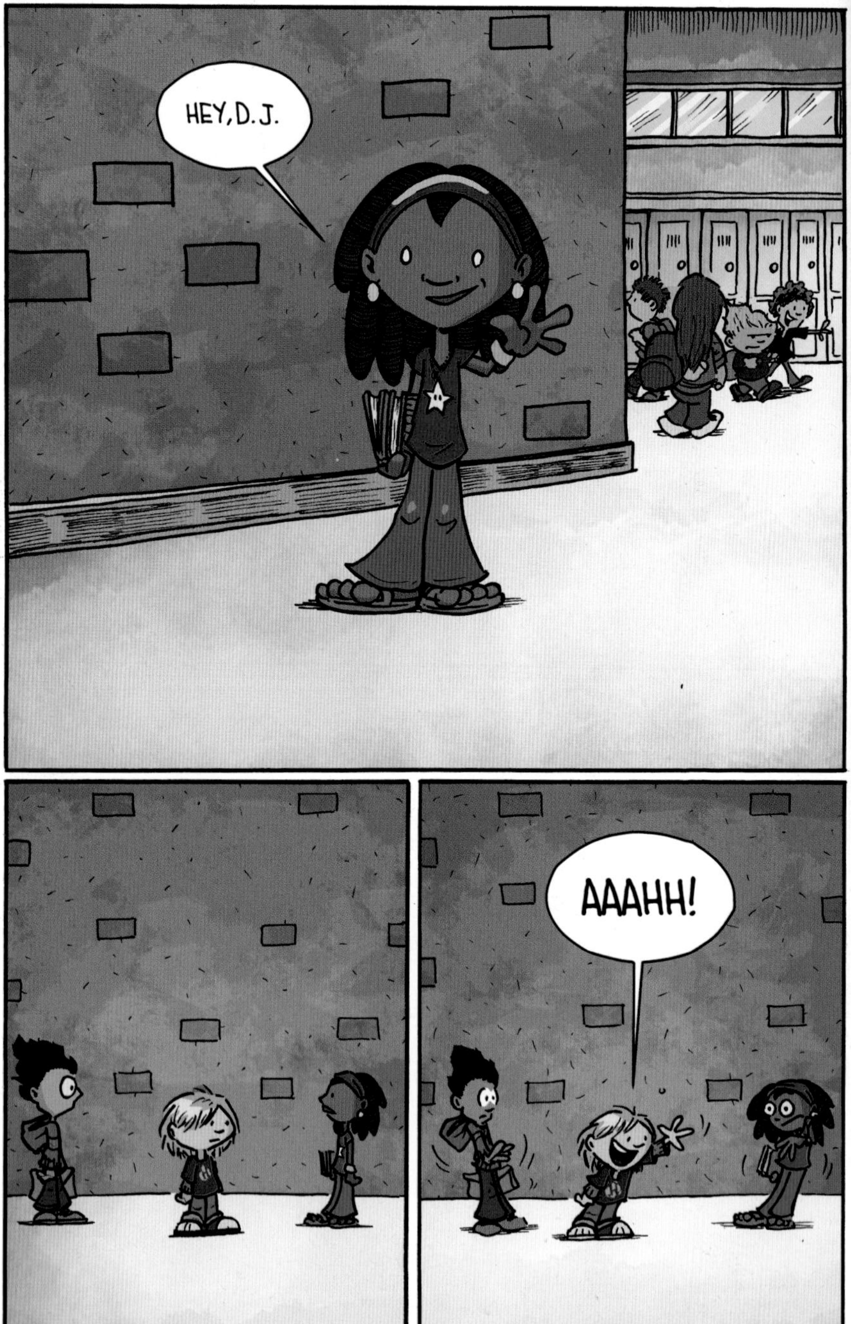
HEY, D.J.
AAAHH!

CHAPTER 4

GINA

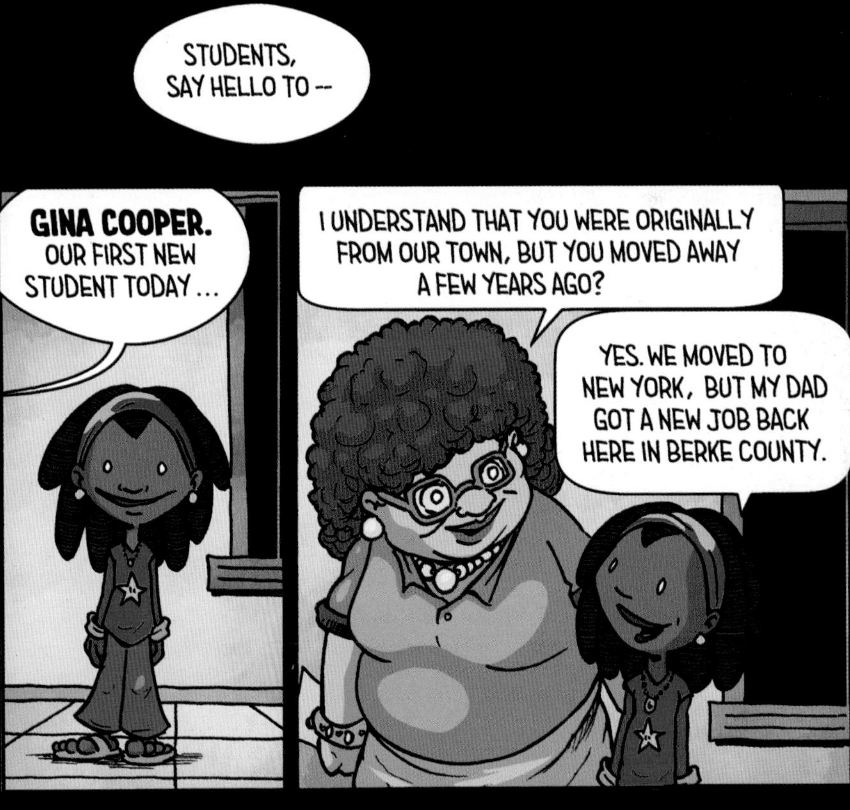
STUDENTS, SAY HELLO TO --
GINA COOPER. OUR FIRST NEW STUDENT TODAY . . .
I UNDERSTAND THAT YOU WERE ORIGINALLY FROM OUR TOWN, BUT YOU MOVED AWAY A FEW YEARS AGO?
YES. WE MOVED TO NEW YORK, BUT MY DAD GOT A NEW JOB BACK HERE IN BERKE COUNTY.

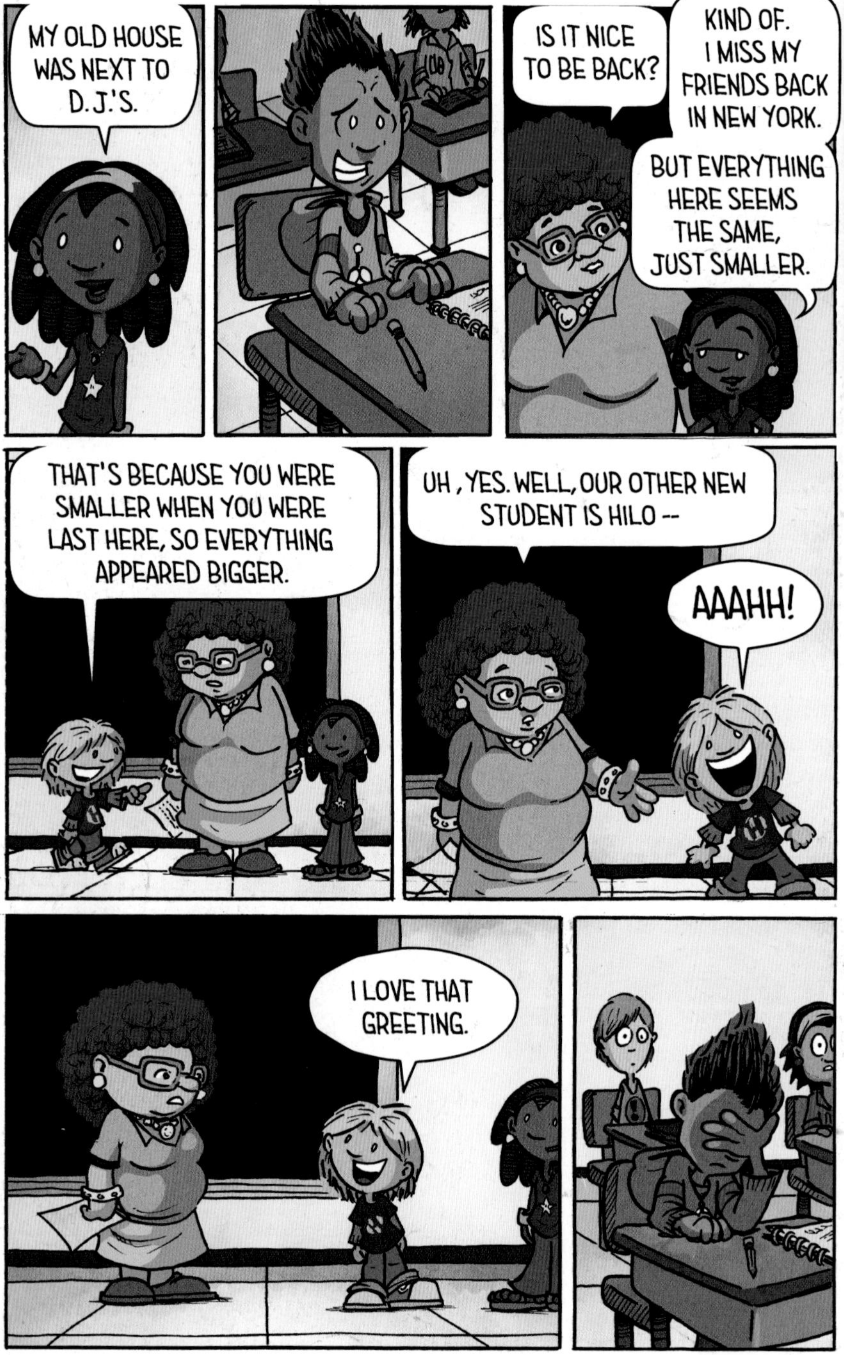
MY OLD HOUSE WAS NEXT TO D.J.'S.
IS IT NICE TO BE BACK?
KIND OF. I MISS MY FRIENDS BACK IN NEW YORK.
BUT EVERYTHING HERE SEEMS THE SAME, JUST SMALLER.
THAT'S BECAUSE YOU WERE SMALLER WHEN YOU WERE LAST HERE, SO EVERYTHING APPEARED BIGGER.
UH, YES. WELL, OUR OTHER NEW STUDENT IS HILO --
AAAHH!
I LOVE THAT GREETING.

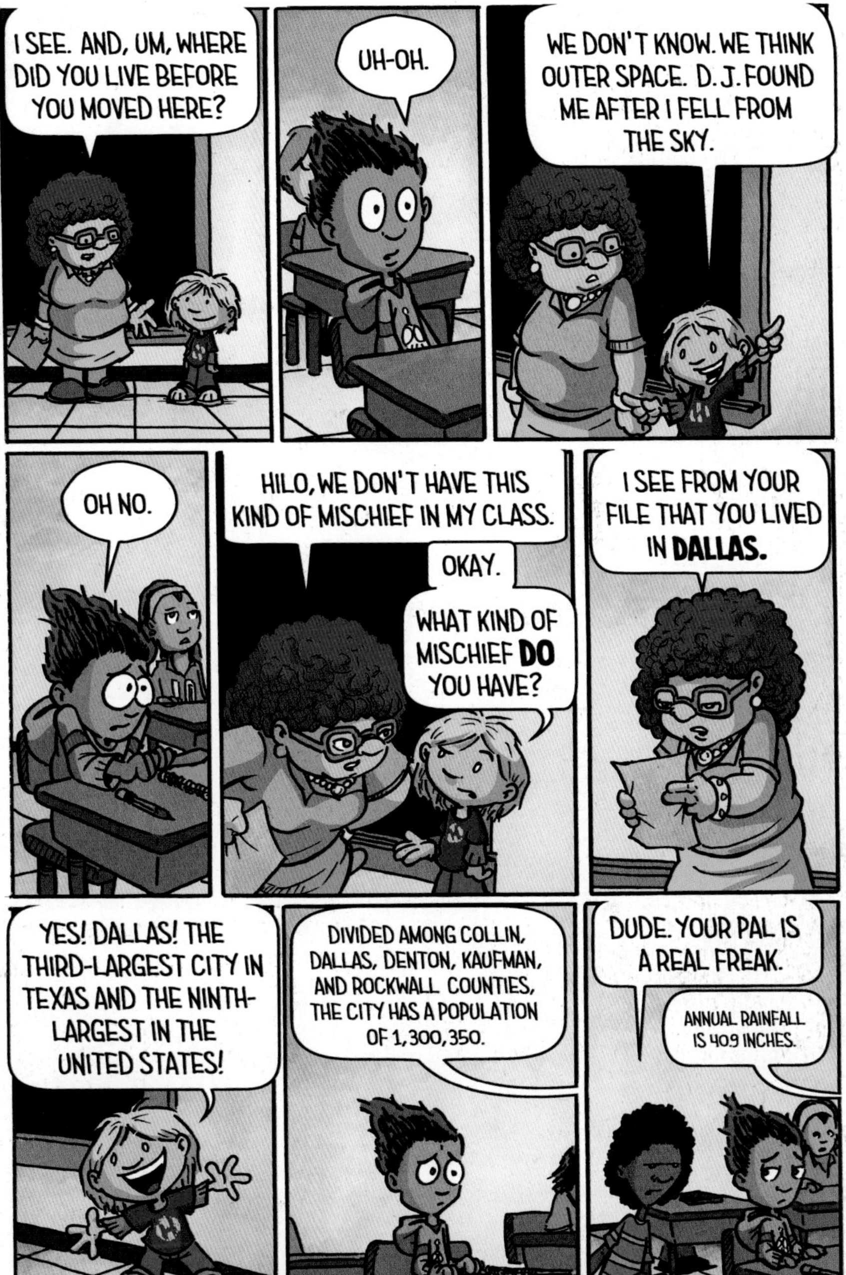
I SEE. AND, UM, WHERE DID YOU LIVE BEFORE YOU MOVED HERE?
UH-OH.
WE DON'T KNOW. WE THINK OUTER SPACE. D.J. FOUND ME AFTER I FELL FROM THE SKY.
OH NO.
HILO, WE DON'T HAVE THIS KIND OF MISCHIEF IN MY CLASS.
OKAY.
WHAT KIND OF MISCHIEF **DO** YOU HAVE?
I SEE FROM YOUR FILE THAT YOU LIVED IN **DALLAS.**
YES! DALLAS! THE THIRD-LARGEST CITY IN TEXAS AND THE NINTH-LARGEST IN THE UNITED STATES!
DIVIDED AMONG COLLIN, DALLAS, DENTON, KAUFMAN, AND ROCKWALL COUNTIES, THE CITY HAS A POPULATION OF 1,300,350.
DUDE. YOUR PAL IS A REAL FREAK.
ANNUAL RAINFALL IS 40.9 INCHES.

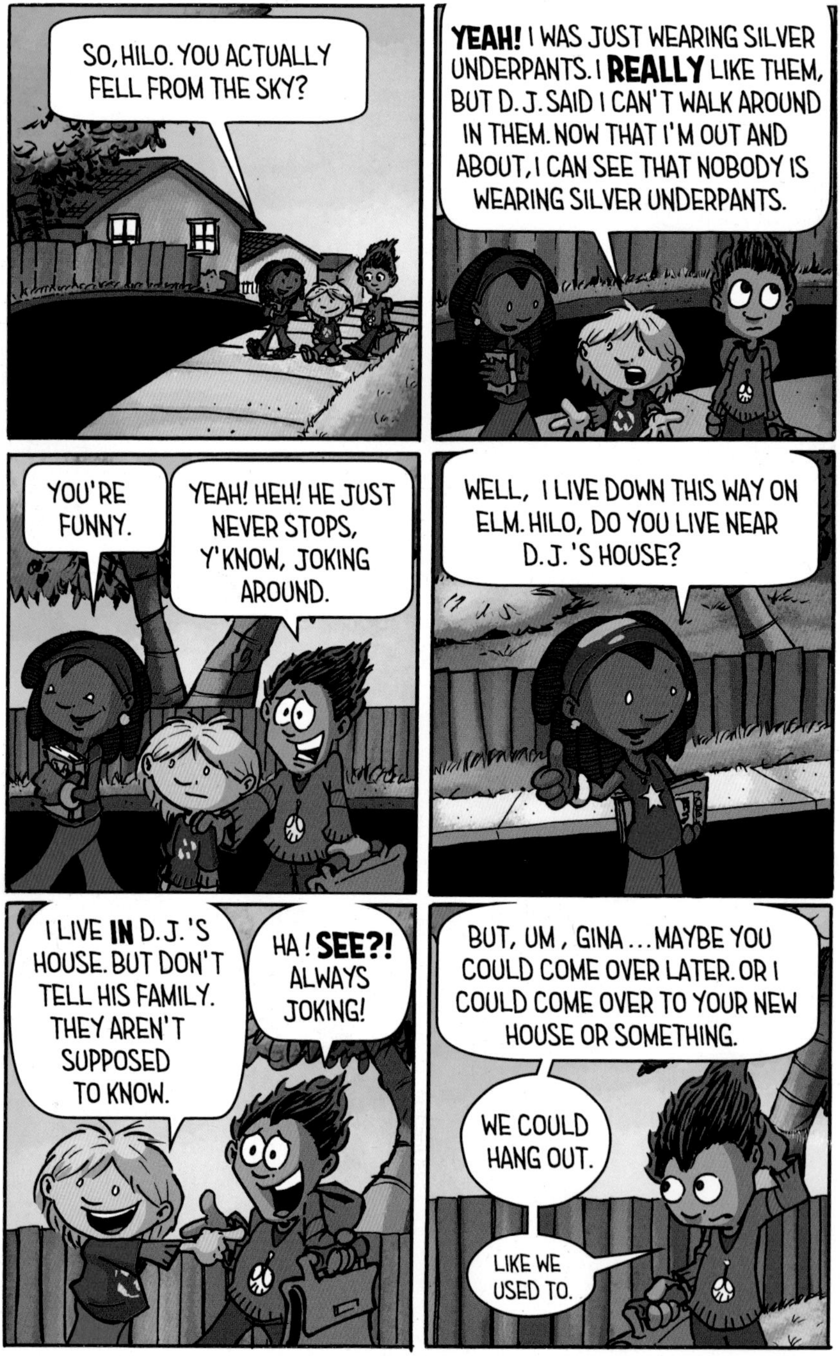
SO, HILO. YOU ACTUALLY FELL FROM THE SKY?
YEAH! I WAS JUST WEARING SILVER UNDERPANTS. I **REALLY** LIKE THEM, BUT D. J. SAID I CAN'T WALK AROUND IN THEM. NOW THAT I'M OUT AND ABOUT, I CAN SEE THAT NOBODY IS WEARING SILVER UNDERPANTS.
YOU'RE FUNNY.
YEAH! HEH! HE JUST NEVER STOPS, Y'KNOW, JOKING AROUND.
WELL, I LIVE DOWN THIS WAY ON ELM. HILO, DO YOU LIVE NEAR D. J.'S HOUSE?
I LIVE **IN** D. J.'S HOUSE. BUT DON'T TELL HIS FAMILY. THEY AREN'T SUPPOSED TO KNOW.
HA! **SEE?!** ALWAYS JOKING!
BUT, UM, GINA... MAYBE YOU COULD COME OVER LATER. OR I COULD COME OVER TO YOUR NEW HOUSE OR SOMETHING.
WE COULD HANG OUT.
LIKE WE USED TO.

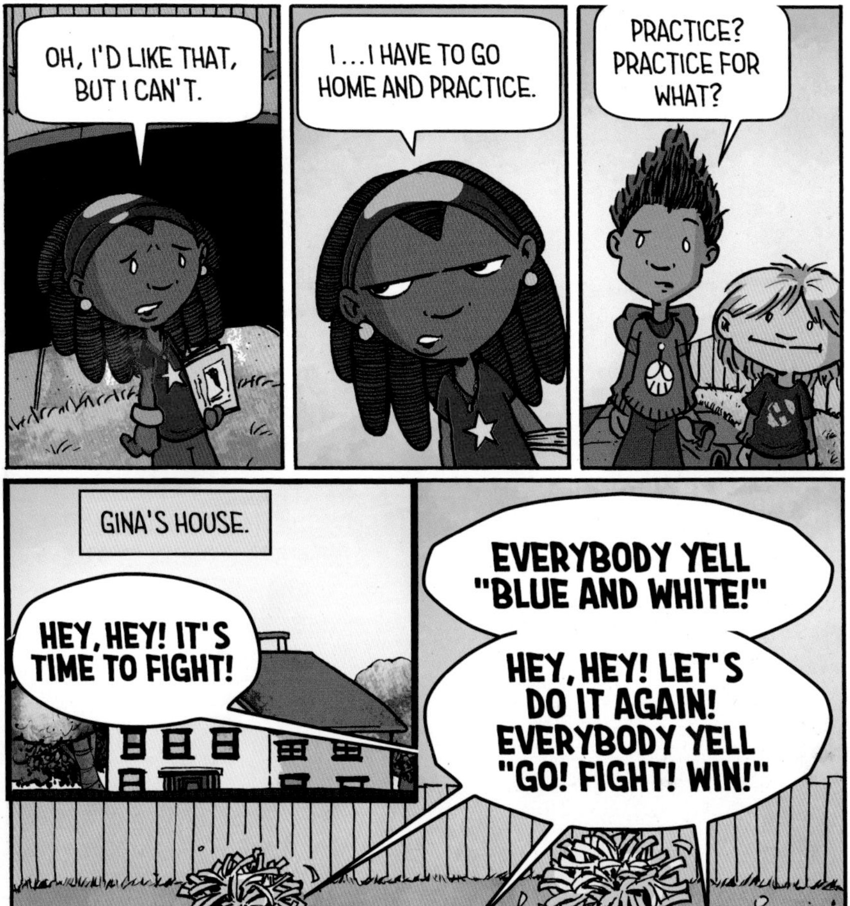
OH, I'D LIKE THAT, BUT I CAN'T.
I...I HAVE TO GO HOME AND PRACTICE.
PRACTICE? PRACTICE FOR WHAT?
GINA'S HOUSE.
HEY, HEY! IT'S TIME TO FIGHT!
EVERYBODY YELL "BLUE AND WHITE!"
HEY, HEY! LET'S DO IT AGAIN! EVERYBODY YELL "GO! FIGHT! WIN!"

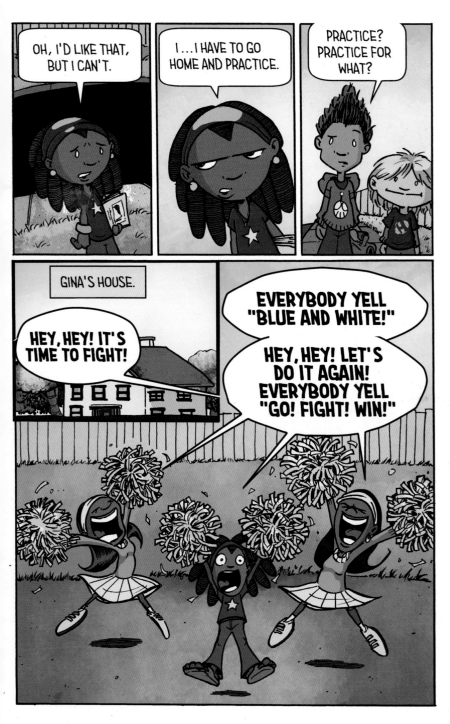

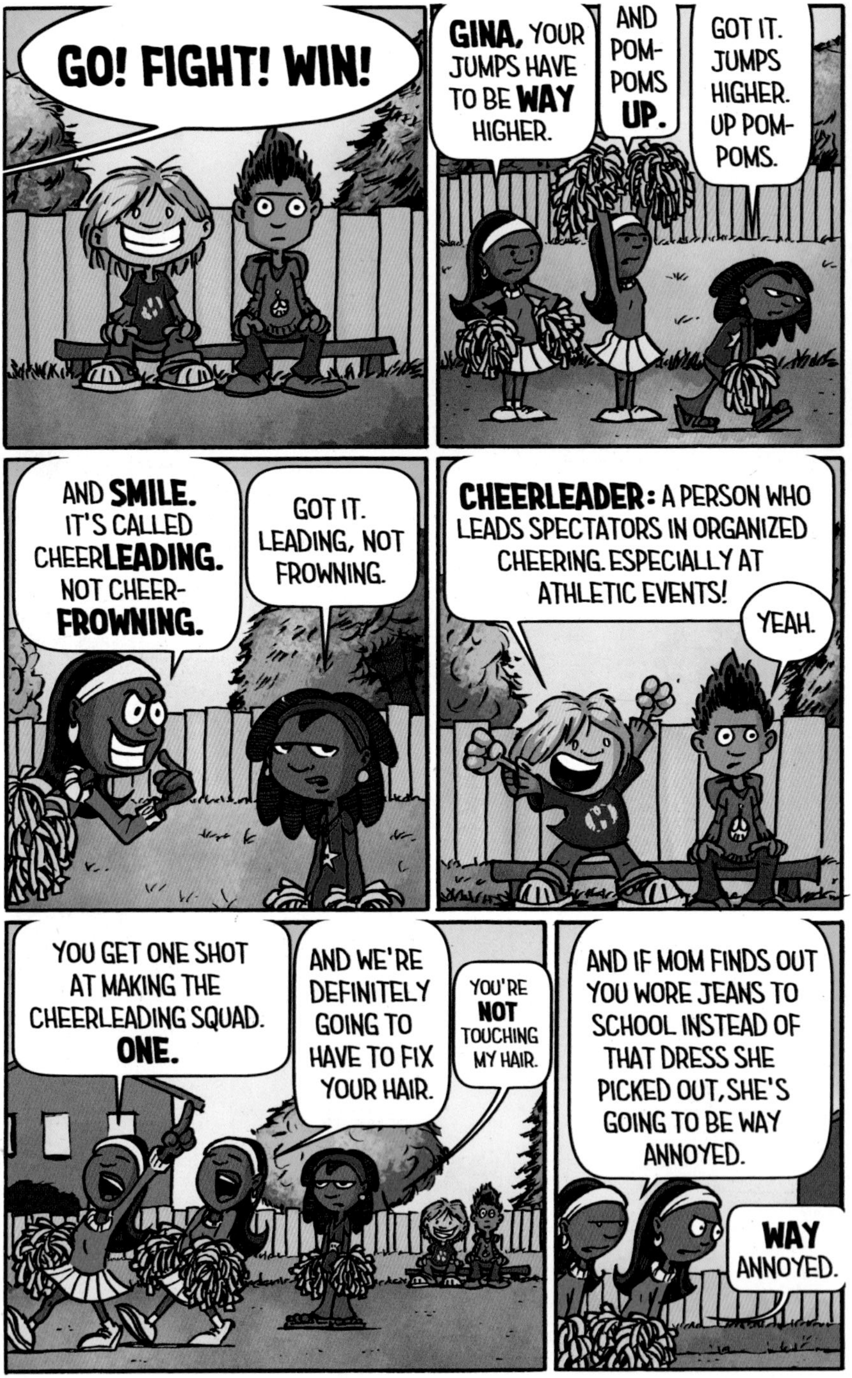
GO! FIGHT! WIN!
GINA, YOUR JUMPS HAVE TO BE WAY HIGHER.
AND POM-POMS UP.
GOT IT. JUMPS HIGHER. UP POM-POMS.
AND SMILE. IT'S CALLED CHEERLEADING. NOT CHEER-FROWNING.
GOT IT. LEADING, NOT FROWNING.
CHEERLEADER: A PERSON WHO LEADS SPECTATORS IN ORGANIZED CHEERING, ESPECIALLY AT ATHLETIC EVENTS!
YEAH.
YOU GET ONE SHOT AT MAKING THE CHEERLEADING SQUAD. ONE.
AND WE'RE DEFINITELY GOING TO HAVE TO FIX YOUR HAIR.
YOU'RE NOT TOUCHING MY HAIR.
AND IF MOM FINDS OUT YOU WORE JEANS TO SCHOOL INSTEAD OF THAT DRESS SHE PICKED OUT, SHE'S GOING TO BE WAY ANNOYED.
WAY ANNOYED.

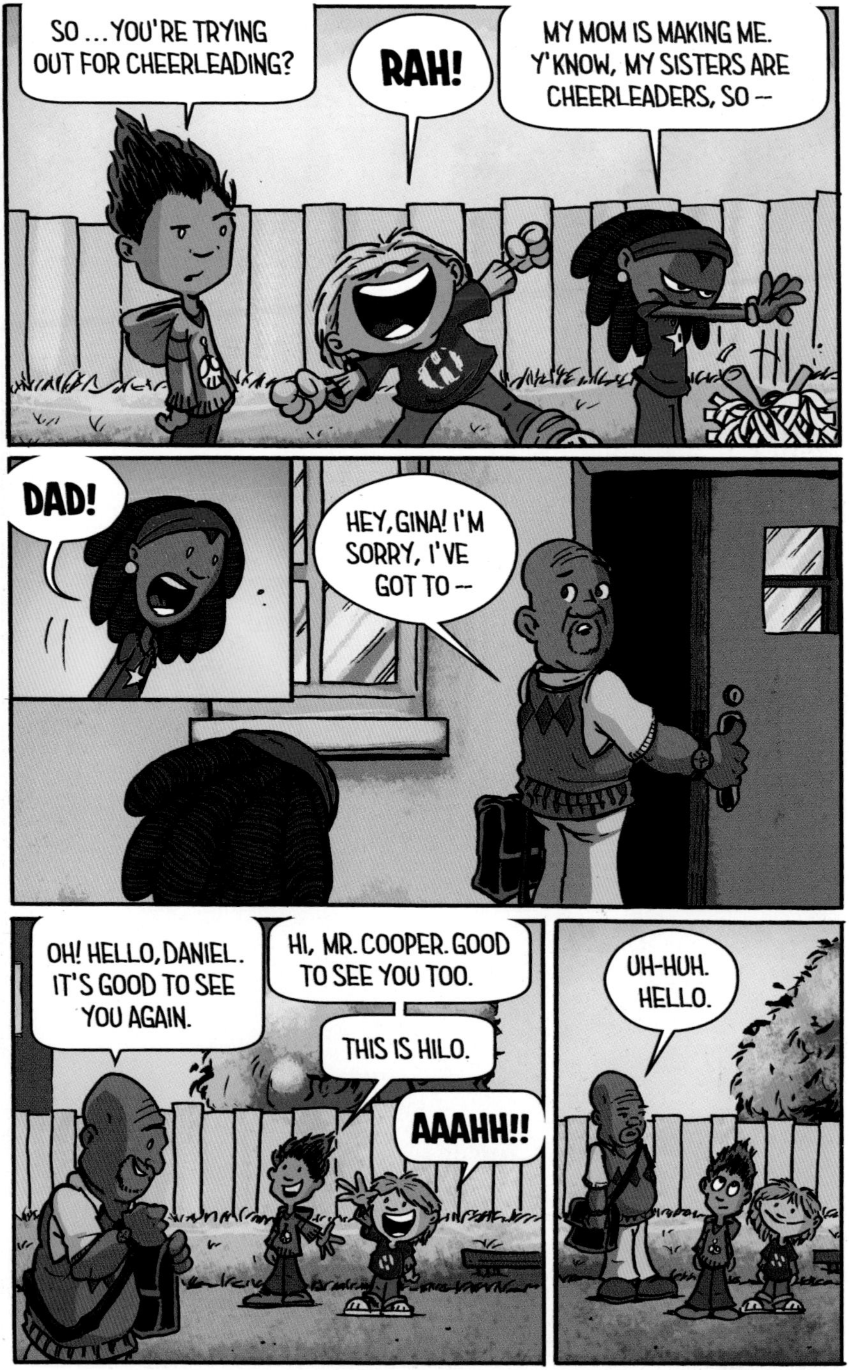
SO ... YOU'RE TRYING OUT FOR CHEERLEADING?
RAH!
MY MOM IS MAKING ME. Y'KNOW, MY SISTERS ARE CHEERLEADERS, SO --
DAD!
HEY, GINA! I'M SORRY, I'VE GOT TO --
OH! HELLO, DANIEL. IT'S GOOD TO SEE YOU AGAIN.
HI, MR. COOPER. GOOD TO SEE YOU TOO.
THIS IS HILO.
AAAHH!!
UH-HUH. HELLO.

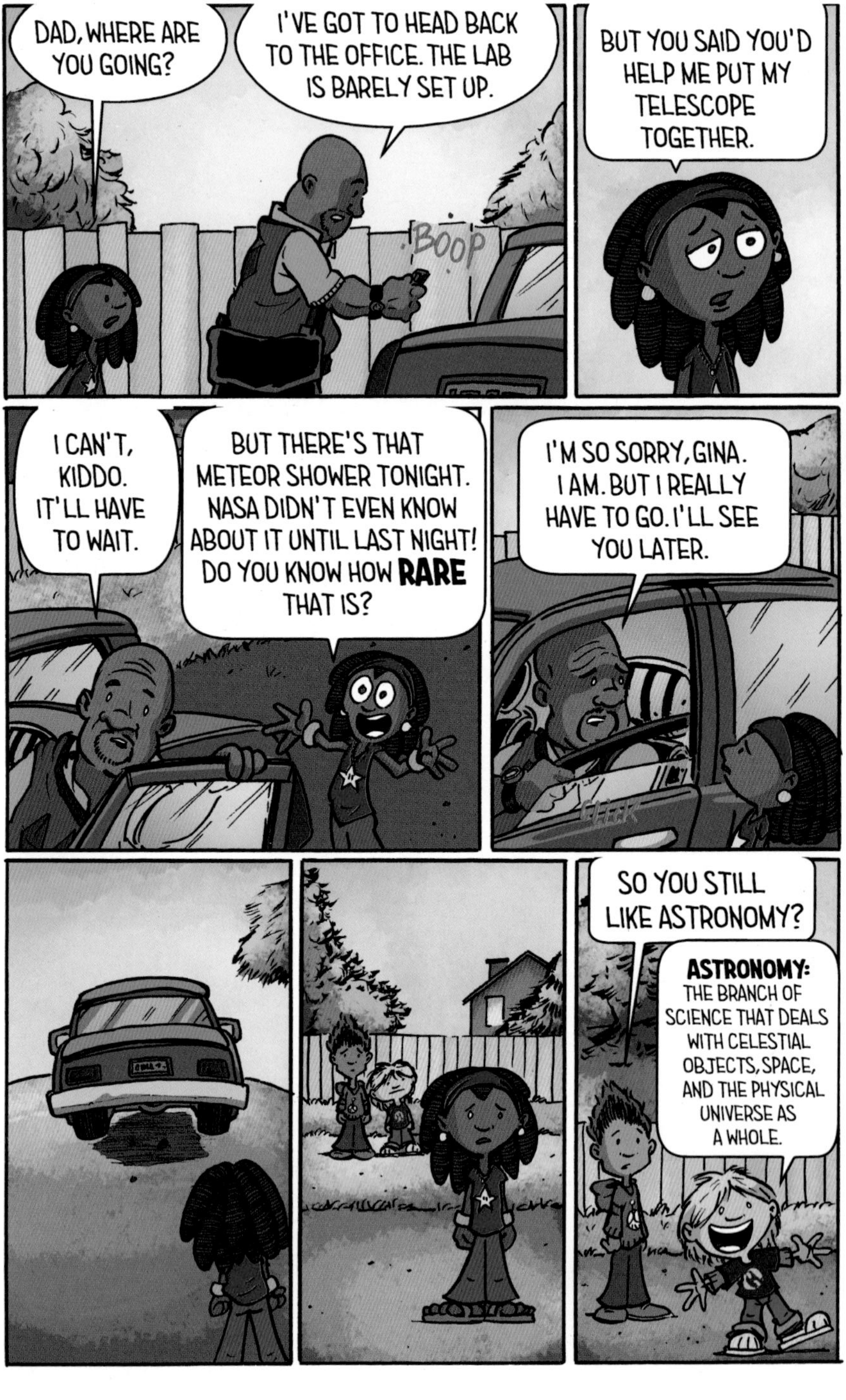
DAD, WHERE ARE YOU GOING?
I'VE GOT TO HEAD BACK TO THE OFFICE. THE LAB IS BARELY SET UP.
BOOP
BUT YOU SAID YOU'D HELP ME PUT MY TELESCOPE TOGETHER.
I CAN'T, KIDDO. IT'LL HAVE TO WAIT.
BUT THERE'S THAT METEOR SHOWER TONIGHT. NASA DIDN'T EVEN KNOW ABOUT IT UNTIL LAST NIGHT! DO YOU KNOW HOW **RARE** THAT IS?
I'M SO SORRY, GINA. I AM. BUT I REALLY HAVE TO GO. I'LL SEE YOU LATER.
CLICK
SO YOU STILL LIKE ASTRONOMY?
ASTRONOMY: THE BRANCH OF SCIENCE THAT DEALS WITH CELESTIAL OBJECTS, SPACE, AND THE PHYSICAL UNIVERSE AS A WHOLE.

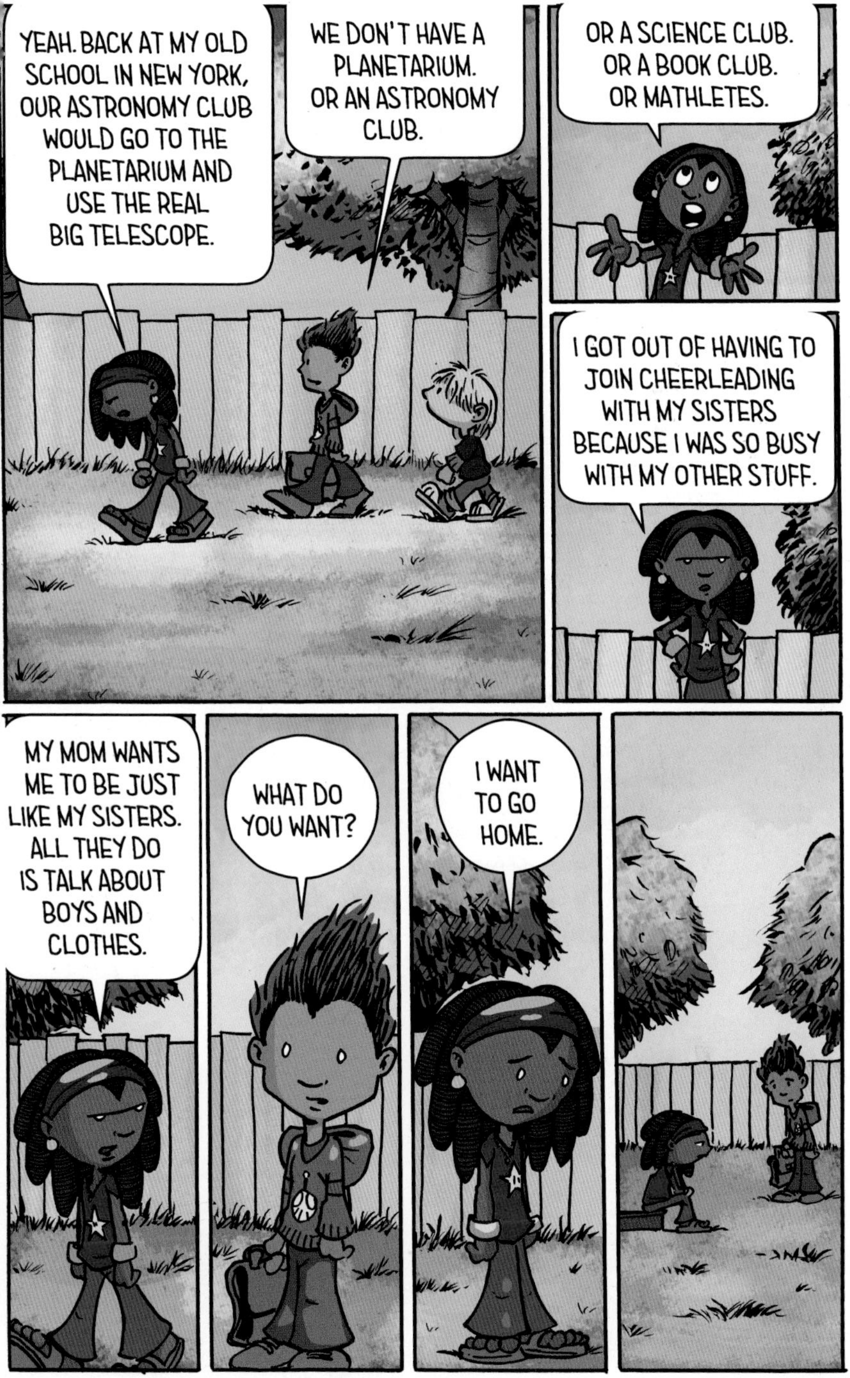
YEAH. BACK AT MY OLD SCHOOL IN NEW YORK, OUR ASTRONOMY CLUB WOULD GO TO THE PLANETARIUM AND USE THE REAL BIG TELESCOPE.
WE DON'T HAVE A PLANETARIUM. OR AN ASTRONOMY CLUB.
OR A SCIENCE CLUB. OR A BOOK CLUB. OR MATHLETES.
I GOT OUT OF HAVING TO JOIN CHEERLEADING WITH MY SISTERS BECAUSE I WAS SO BUSY WITH MY OTHER STUFF.
MY MOM WANTS ME TO BE JUST LIKE MY SISTERS. ALL THEY DO IS TALK ABOUT BOYS AND CLOTHES.
WHAT DO YOU WANT?
I WANT TO GO HOME.

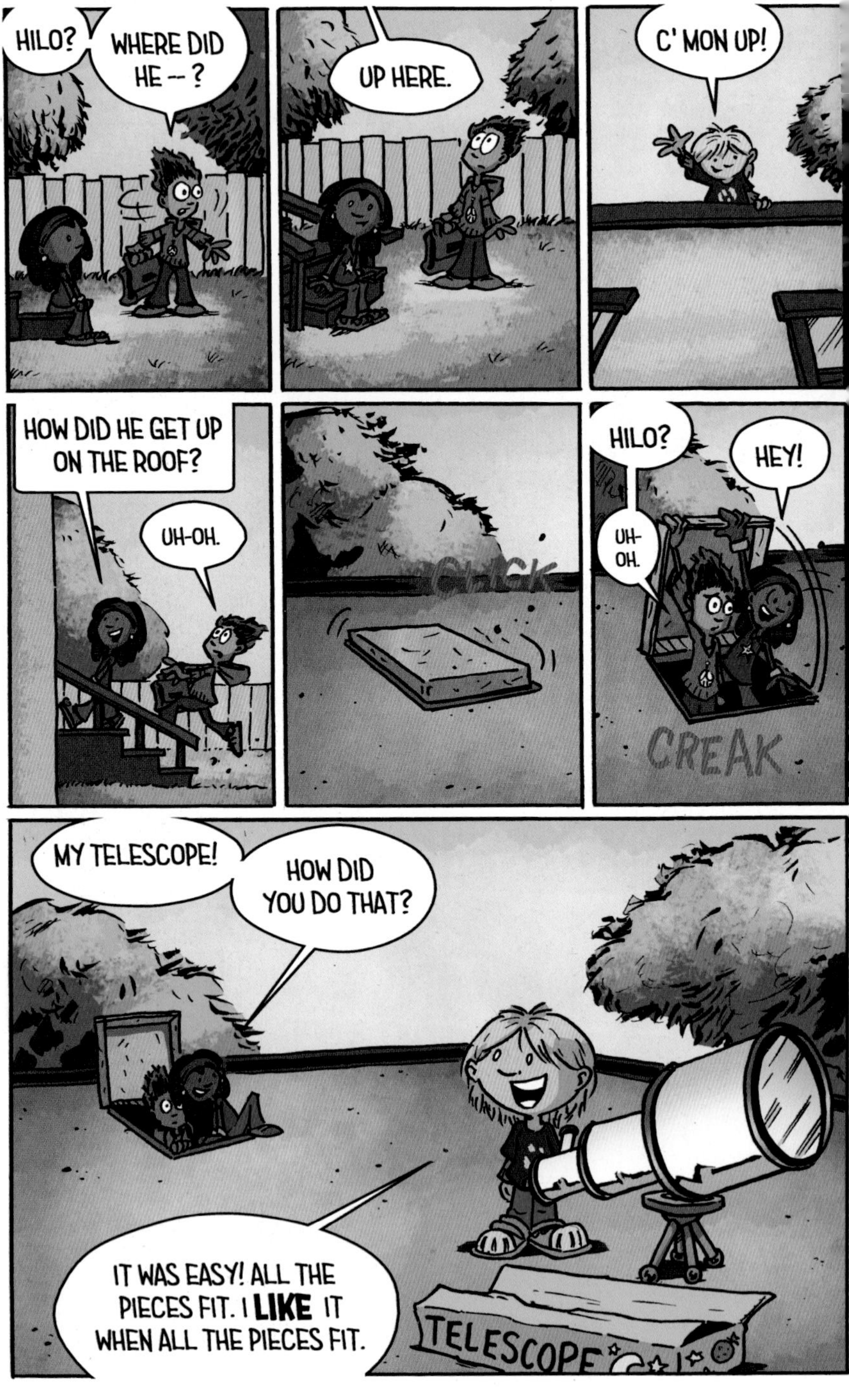
HILO?
WHERE DID HE -- ?
UP HERE.
C' MON UP!
HOW DID HE GET UP ON THE ROOF?
UH-OH.
CLICK
HILO?
UH-OH.
HEY!
CREAK
MY TELESCOPE!
HOW DID YOU DO THAT?
IT WAS EASY! ALL THE PIECES FIT. I **LIKE** IT WHEN ALL THE PIECES FIT.
TELESCOPE

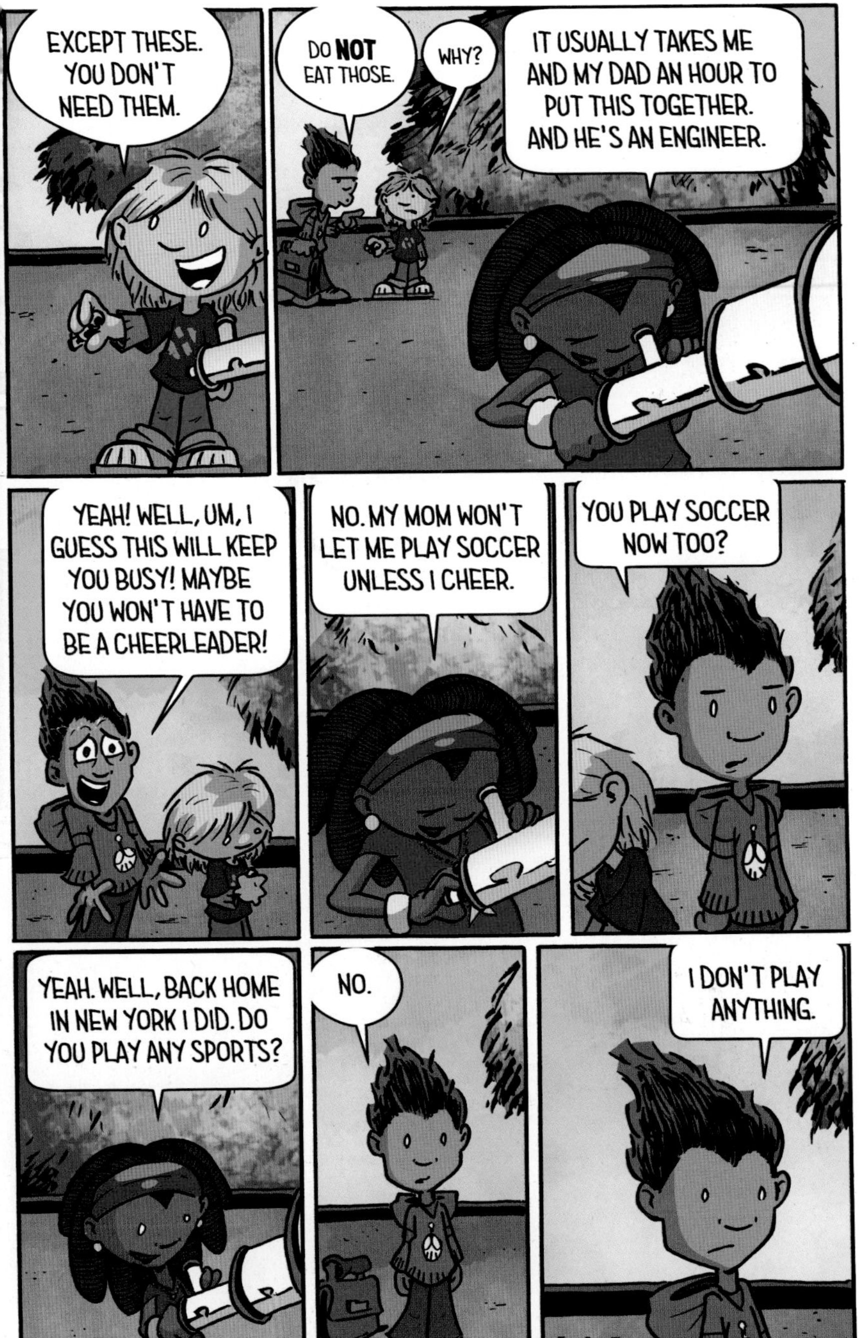
EXCEPT THESE. YOU DON'T NEED THEM.
DO **NOT** EAT THOSE.
WHY?
IT USUALLY TAKES ME AND MY DAD AN HOUR TO PUT THIS TOGETHER. AND HE'S AN ENGINEER.
YEAH! WELL, UM, I GUESS THIS WILL KEEP YOU BUSY! MAYBE YOU WON'T HAVE TO BE A CHEERLEADER!
NO. MY MOM WON'T LET ME PLAY SOCCER UNLESS I CHEER.
YOU PLAY SOCCER NOW TOO?
YEAH. WELL, BACK HOME IN NEW YORK I DID. DO YOU PLAY ANY SPORTS?
NO.
I DON'T PLAY ANYTHING.

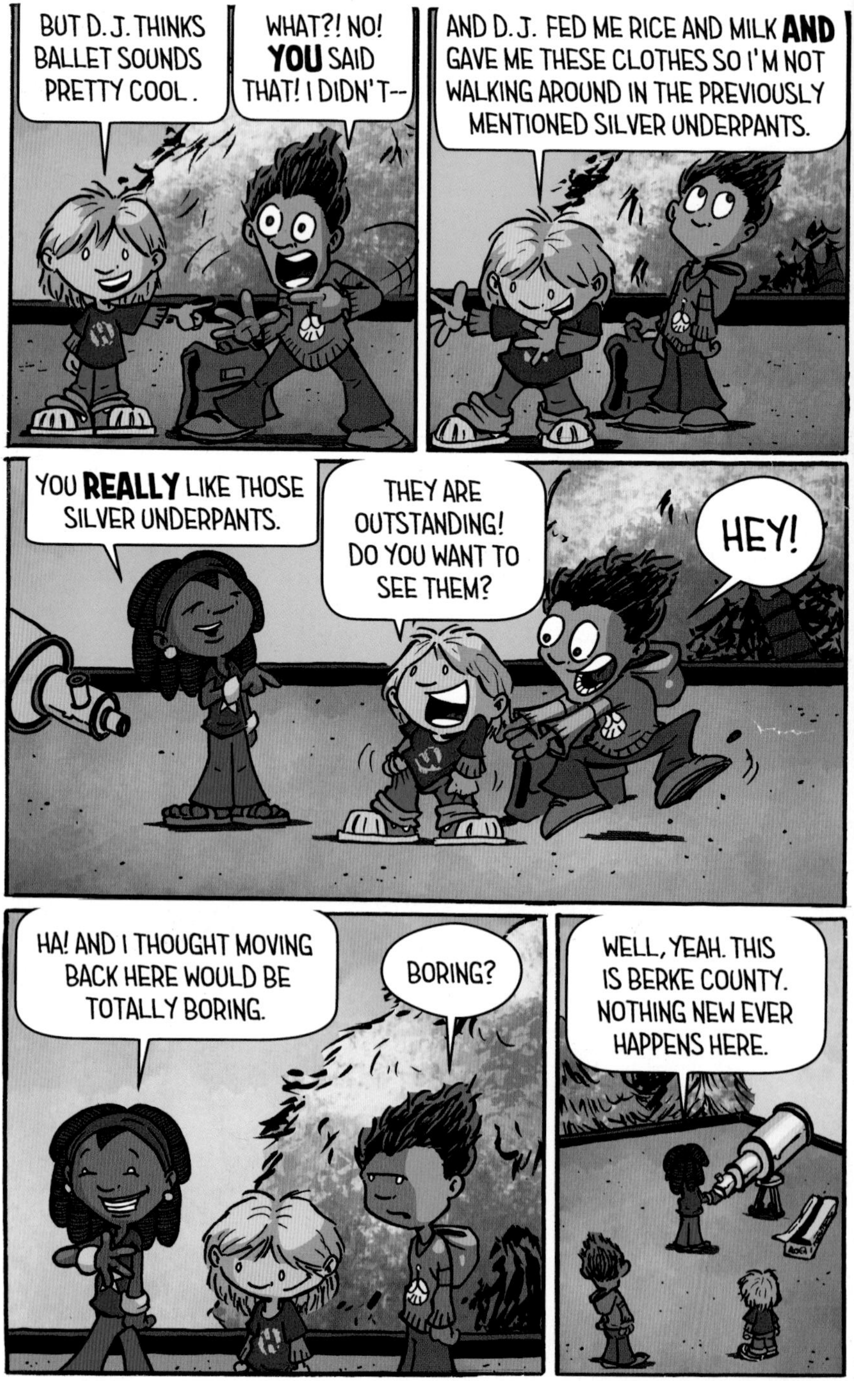
BUT D. J. THINKS BALLET SOUNDS PRETTY COOL.
WHAT?! NO! **YOU** SAID THAT! I DIDN'T--
AND D. J. FED ME RICE AND MILK **AND** GAVE ME THESE CLOTHES SO I'M NOT WALKING AROUND IN THE PREVIOUSLY MENTIONED SILVER UNDERPANTS.
YOU **REALLY** LIKE THOSE SILVER UNDERPANTS.
THEY ARE OUTSTANDING! DO YOU WANT TO SEE THEM?
HEY!
HA! AND I THOUGHT MOVING BACK HERE WOULD BE TOTALLY BORING.
BORING?
WELL, YEAH. THIS IS BERKE COUNTY. NOTHING NEW EVER HAPPENS HERE.

CHAPTER

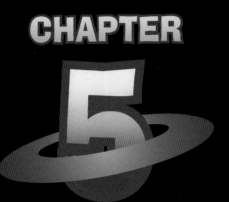

NOTHING NEW
EVER HAPPENS HERE

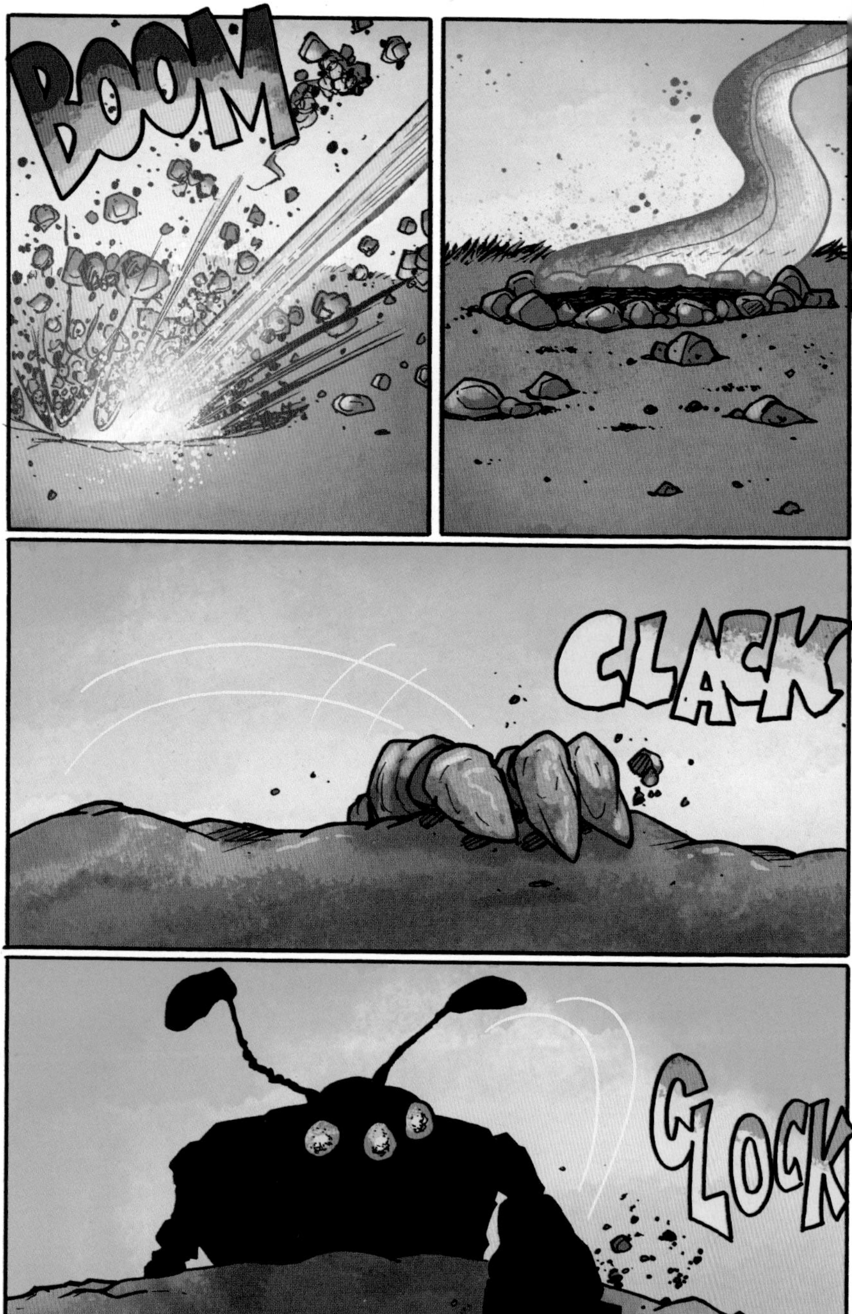
BOOM
CLACK
CLOCK

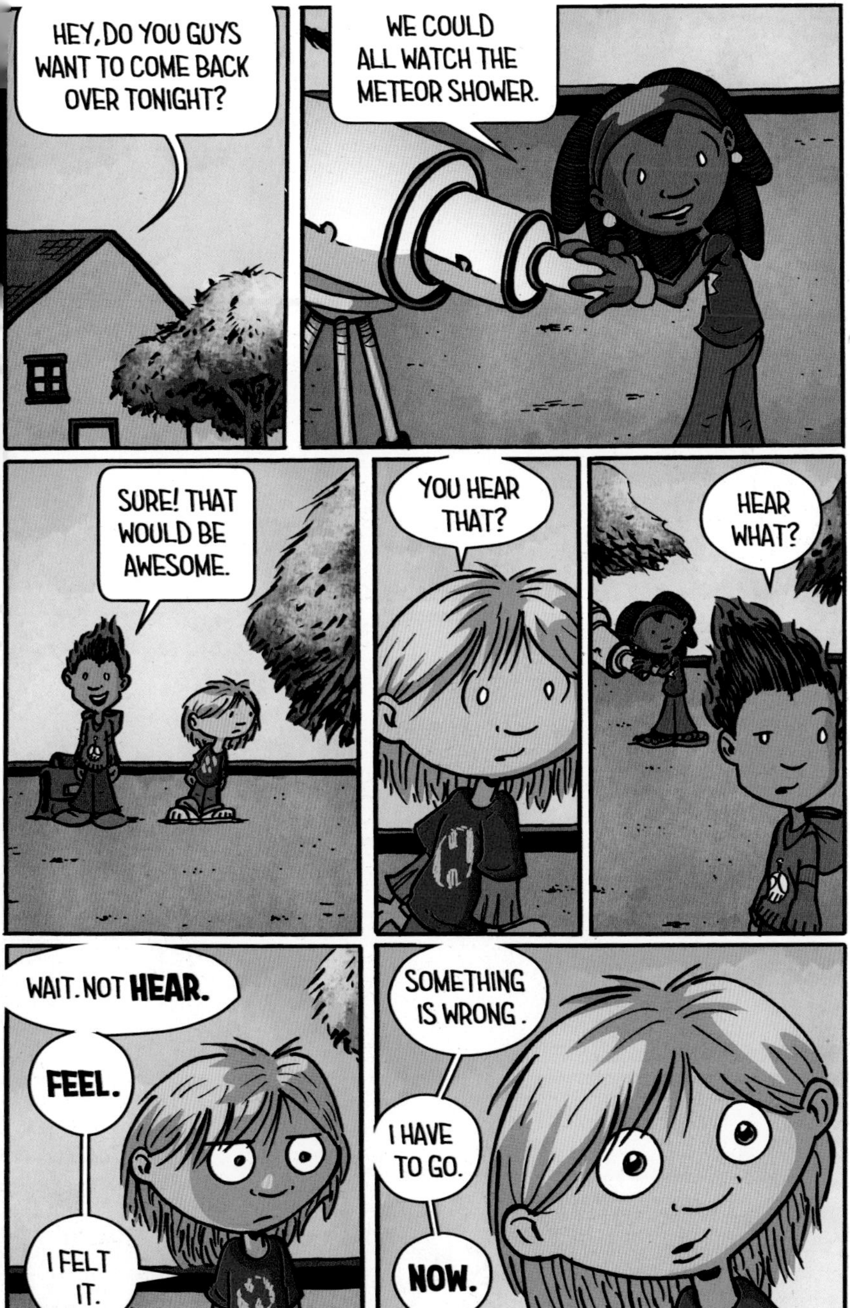
HEY, DO YOU GUYS WANT TO COME BACK OVER TONIGHT?
WE COULD ALL WATCH THE METEOR SHOWER.
SURE! THAT WOULD BE AWESOME.
YOU HEAR THAT?
HEAR WHAT?
WAIT. NOT HEAR.
FEEL.
I FELT IT.
SOMETHING IS WRONG.
I HAVE TO GO.
NOW.

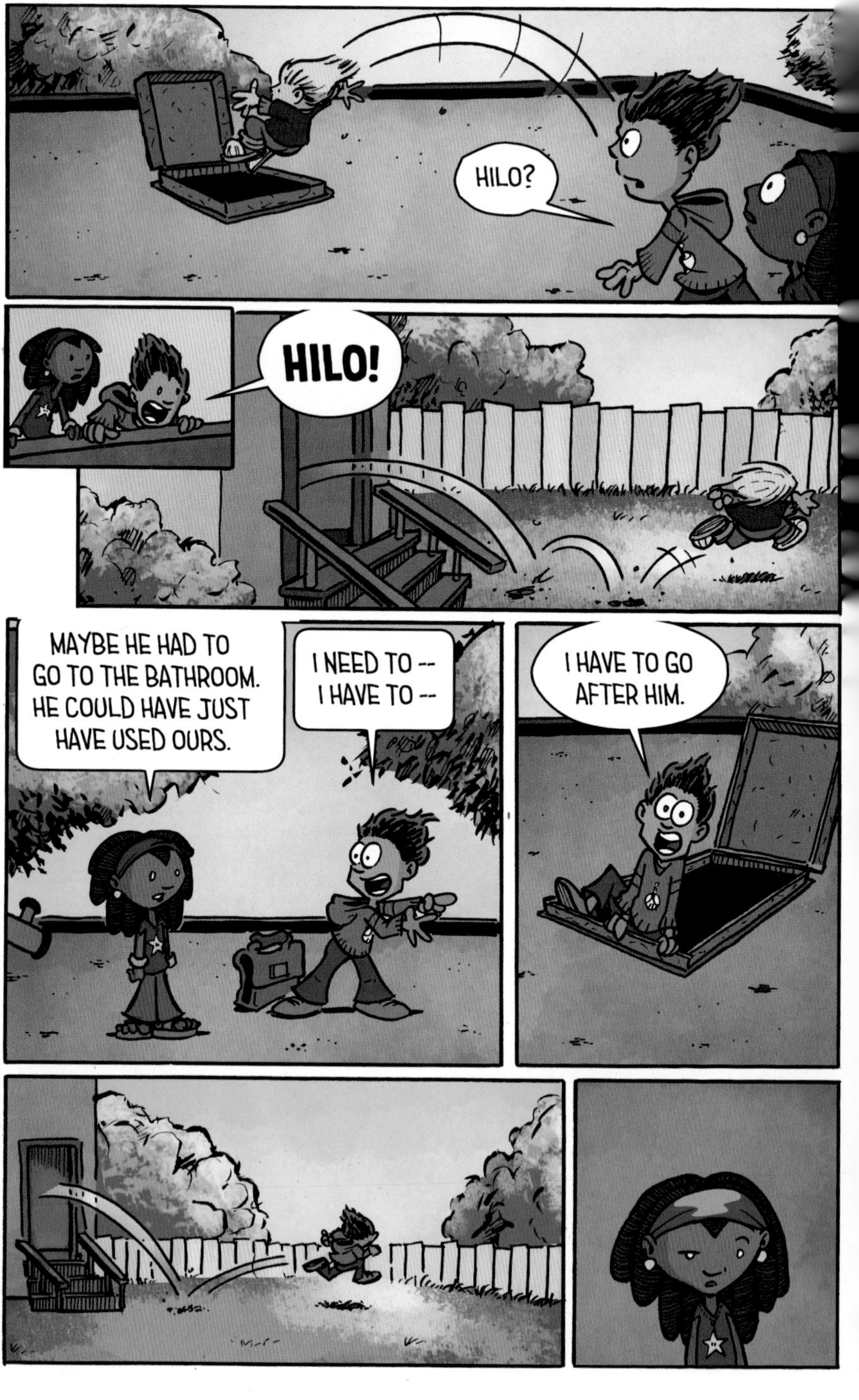

HILO?
HILO!
MAYBE HE HAD TO GO TO THE BATHROOM. HE COULD HAVE JUST HAVE USED OURS.
I NEED TO -- I HAVE TO --
I HAVE TO GO AFTER HIM.

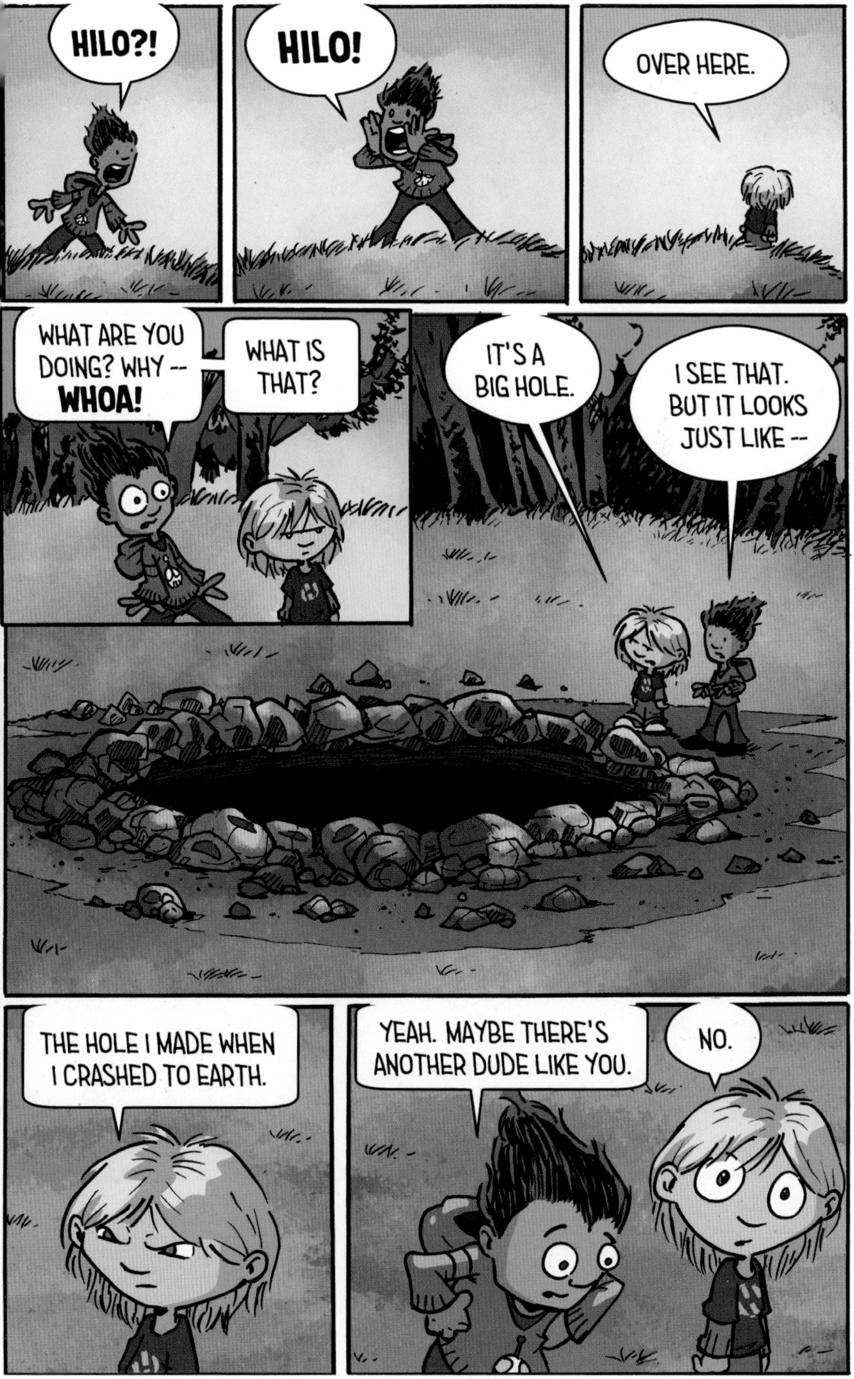
HILO?!
HILO!
OVER HERE.
WHAT ARE YOU DOING? WHY -- WHOA!
WHAT IS THAT?
IT'S A BIG HOLE.
I SEE THAT. BUT IT LOOKS JUST LIKE --
THE HOLE I MADE WHEN I CRASHED TO EARTH.
YEAH. MAYBE THERE'S ANOTHER DUDE LIKE YOU.
NO.

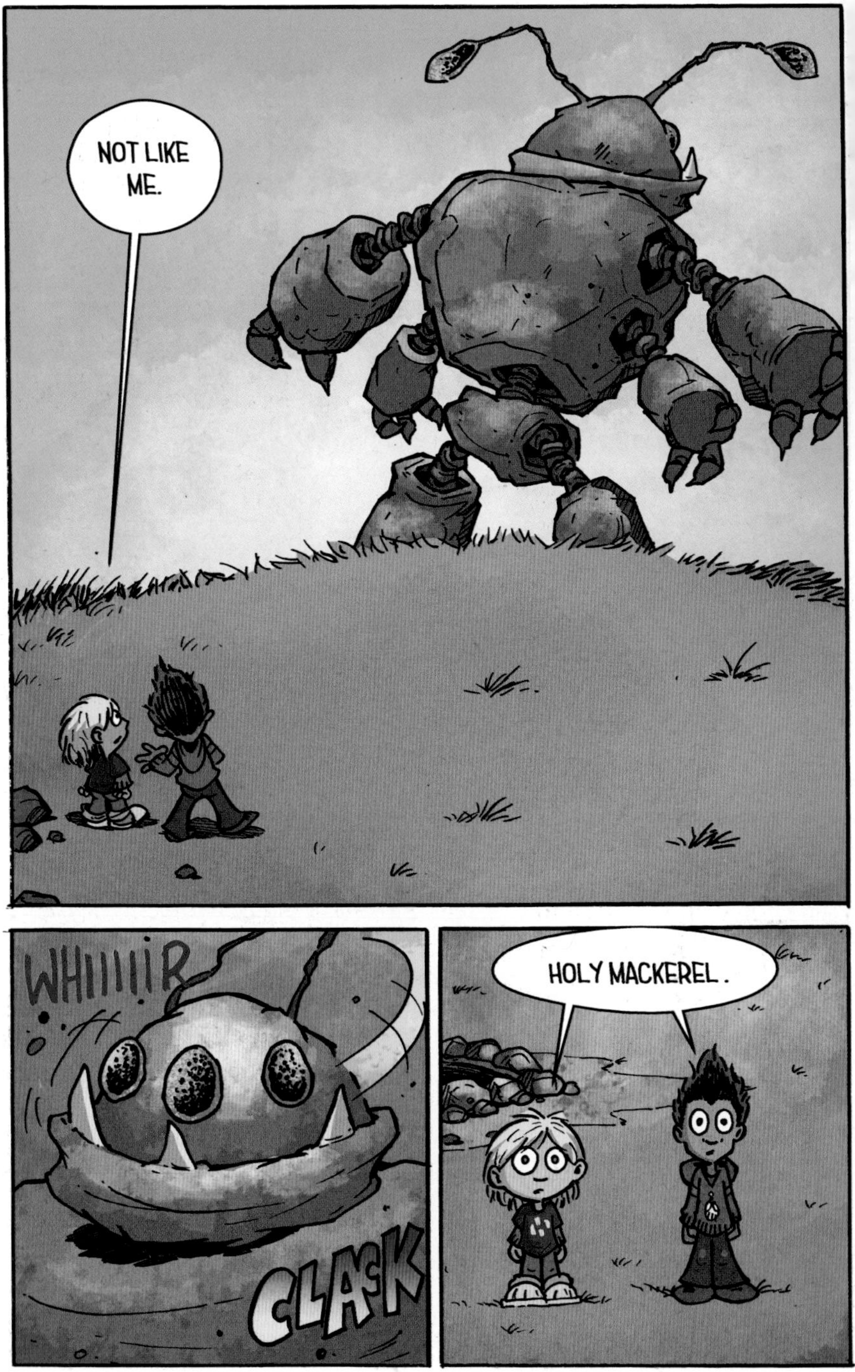
NOT LIKE ME.
WHIIIIR
CLACK
HOLY MACKEREL.

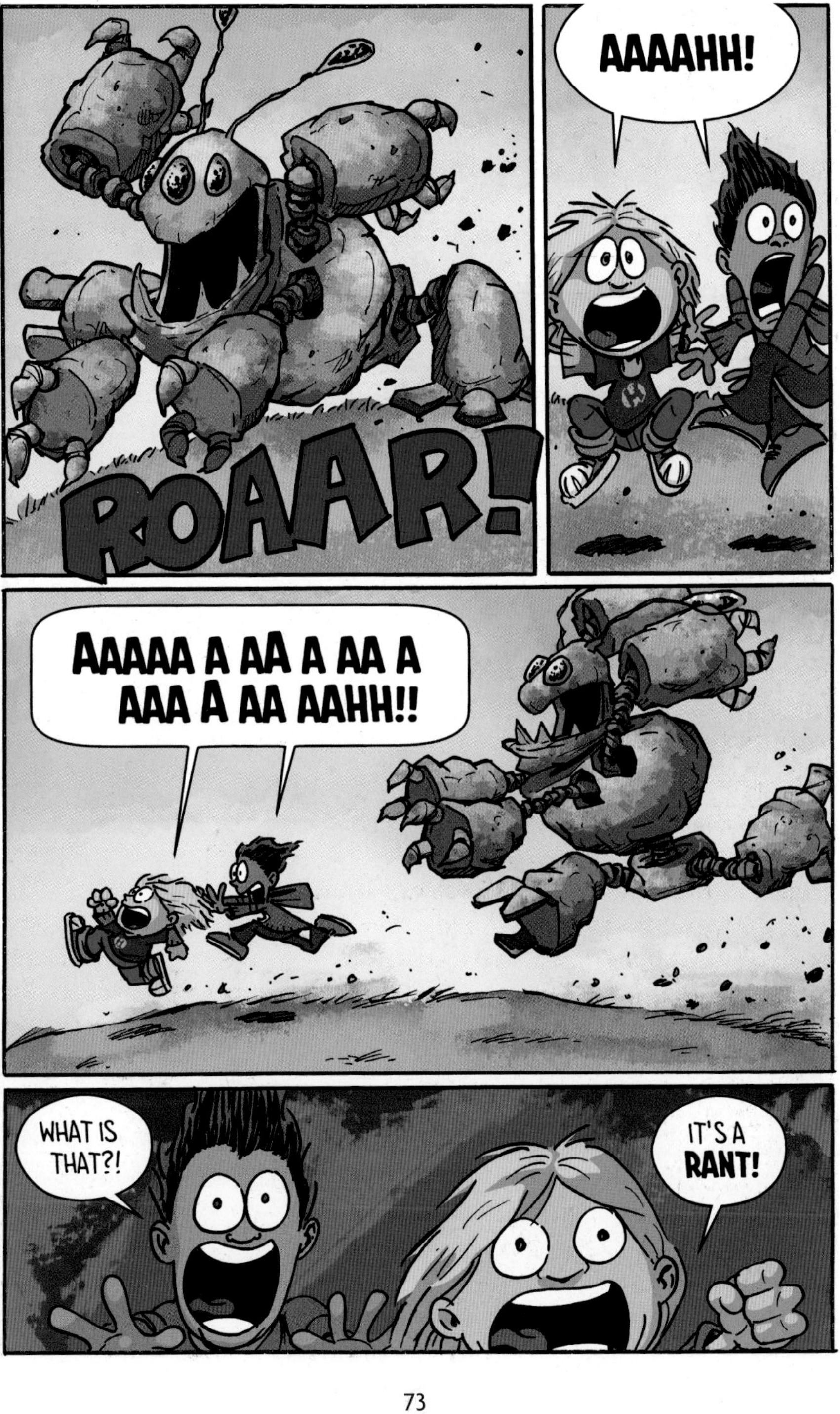
ROAAR!
AAAAHH!
AAAAA A AA A AA A
AAA A AA AAHH!!
WHAT IS
THAT?!
IT'S A
RANT!

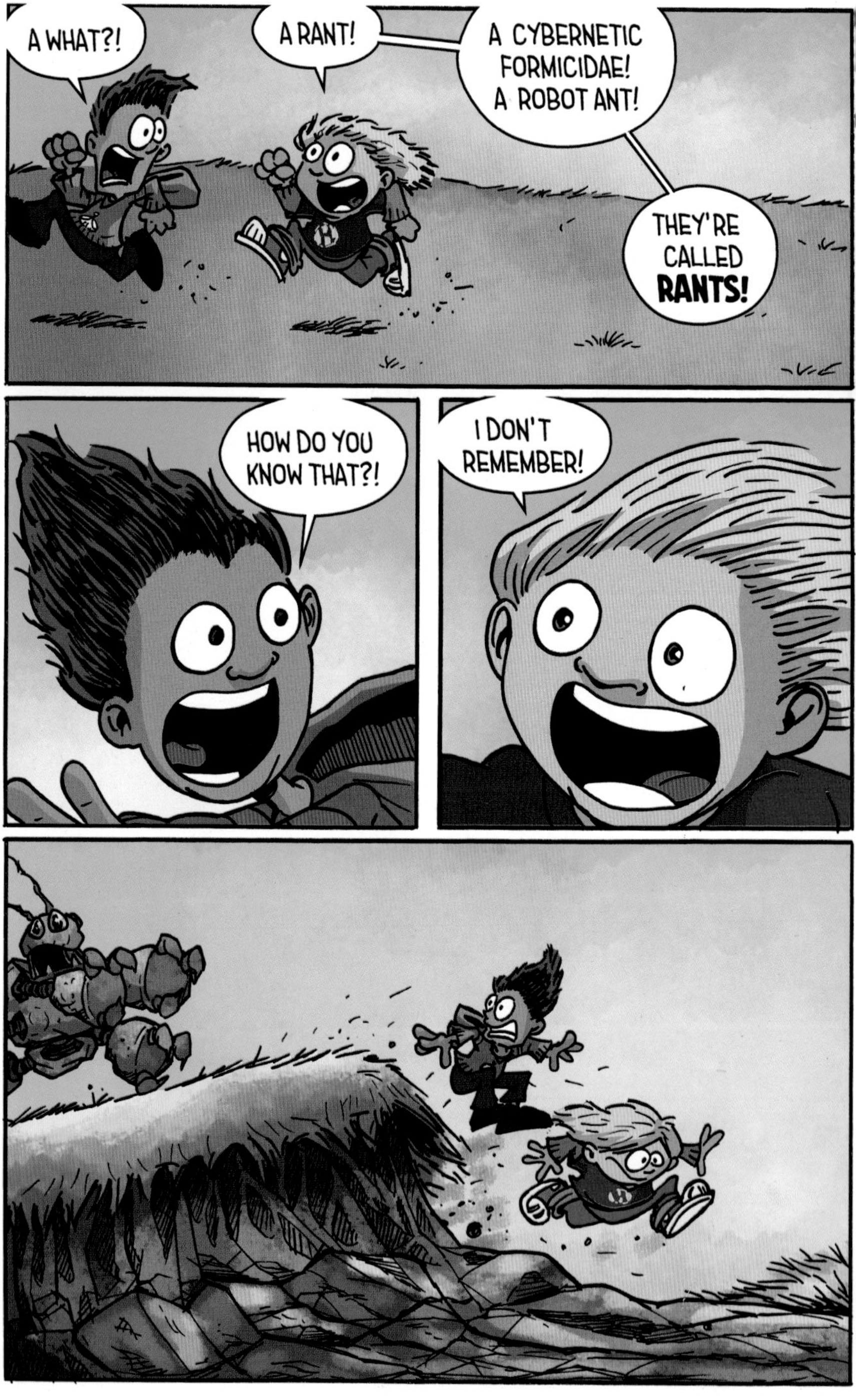
A WHAT?!
A RANT!
A CYBERNETIC FORMICIDAE! A ROBOT ANT!
THEY'RE CALLED **RANTS!**
HOW DO YOU KNOW THAT?!
I DON'T REMEMBER!

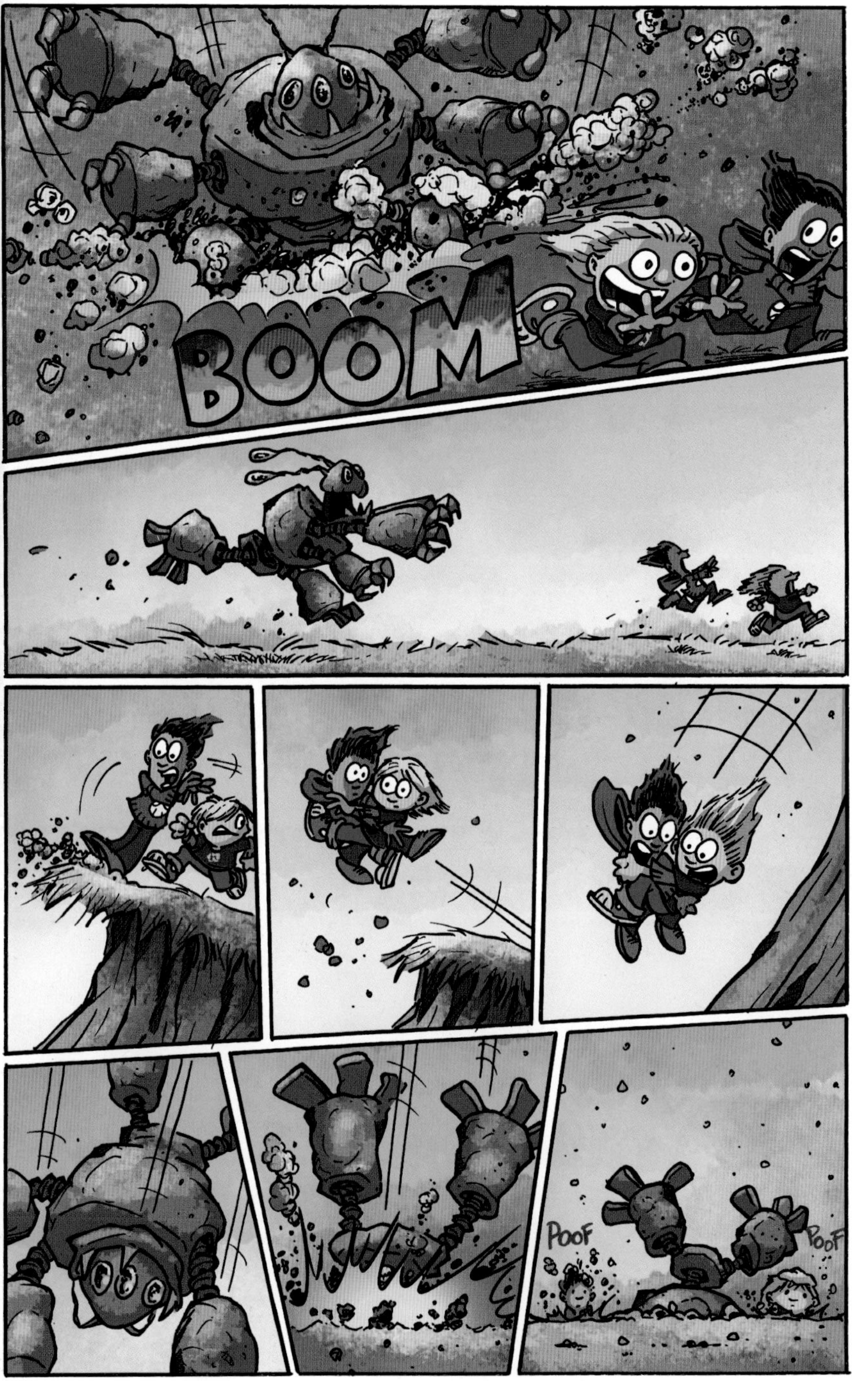
BOOM
POOF
POOF

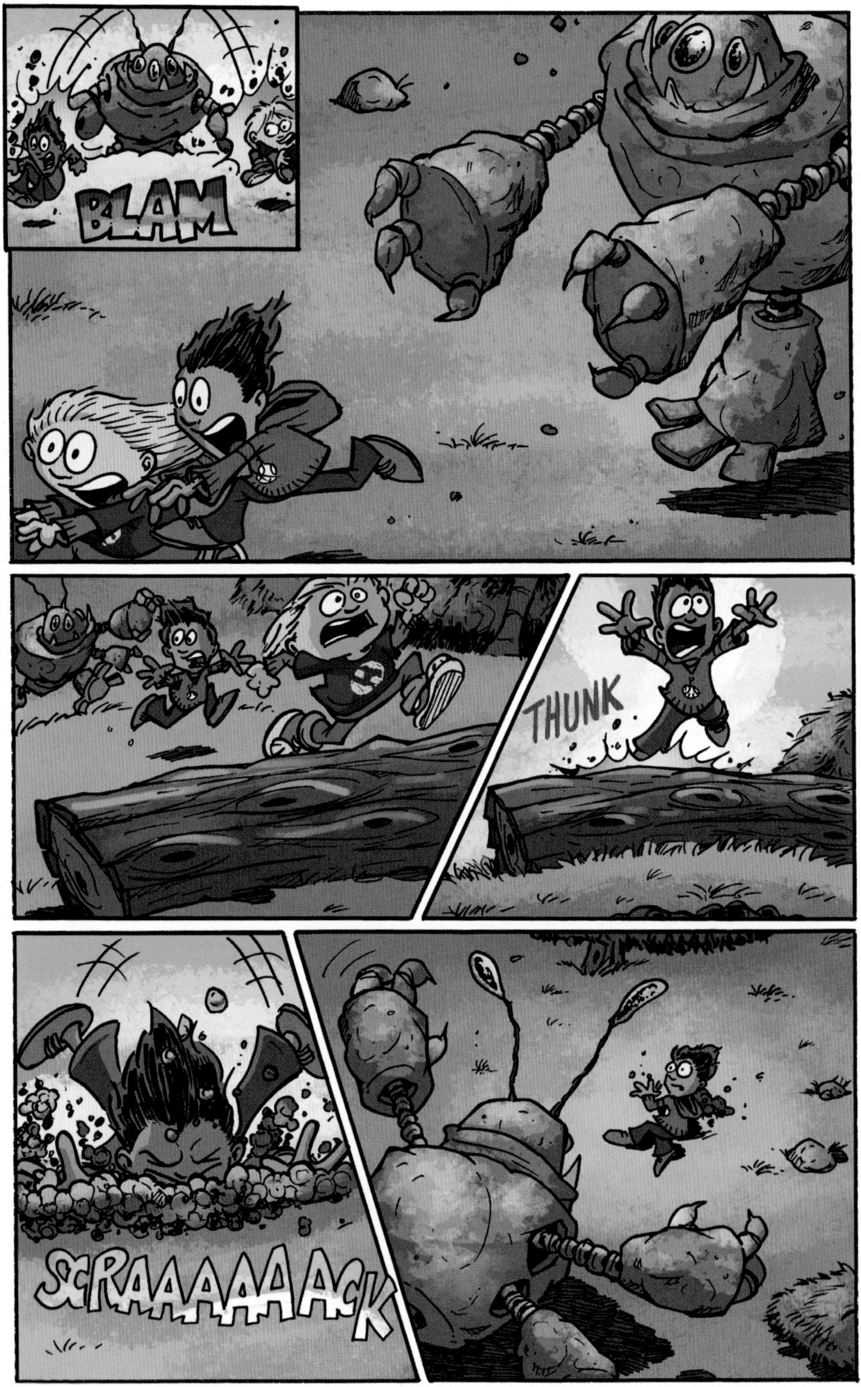
BLAM
THUNK
SCRAAAAAACK

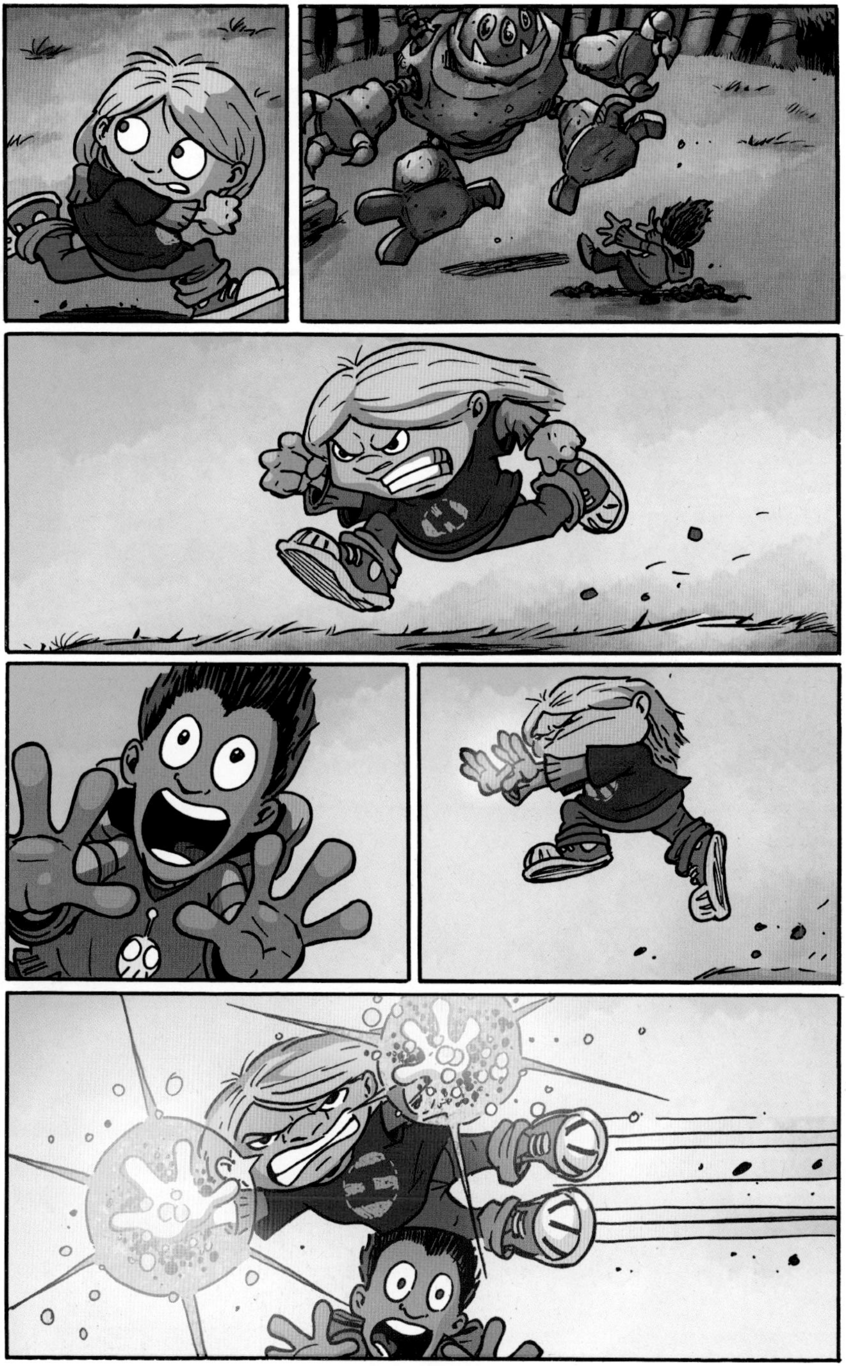

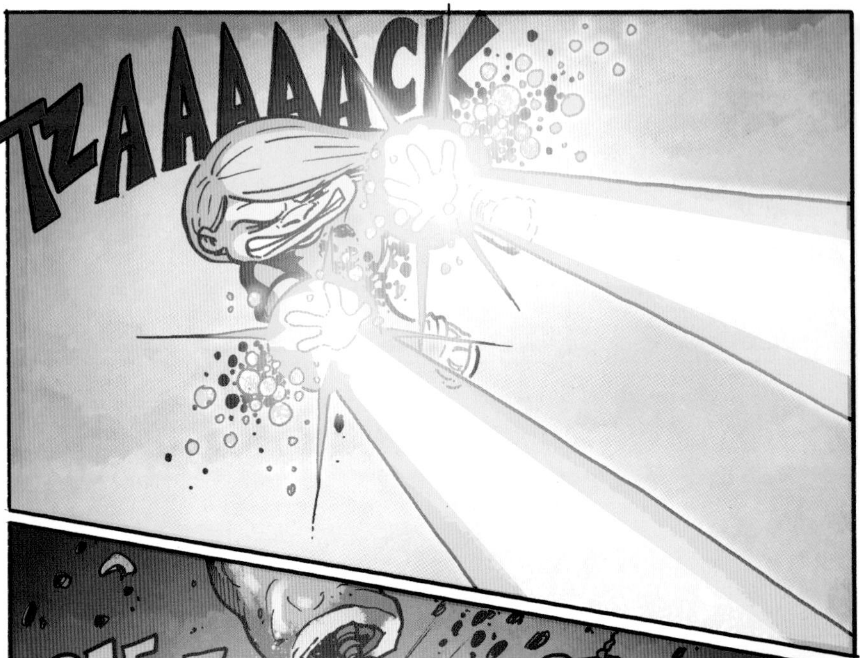
TZAAAACK

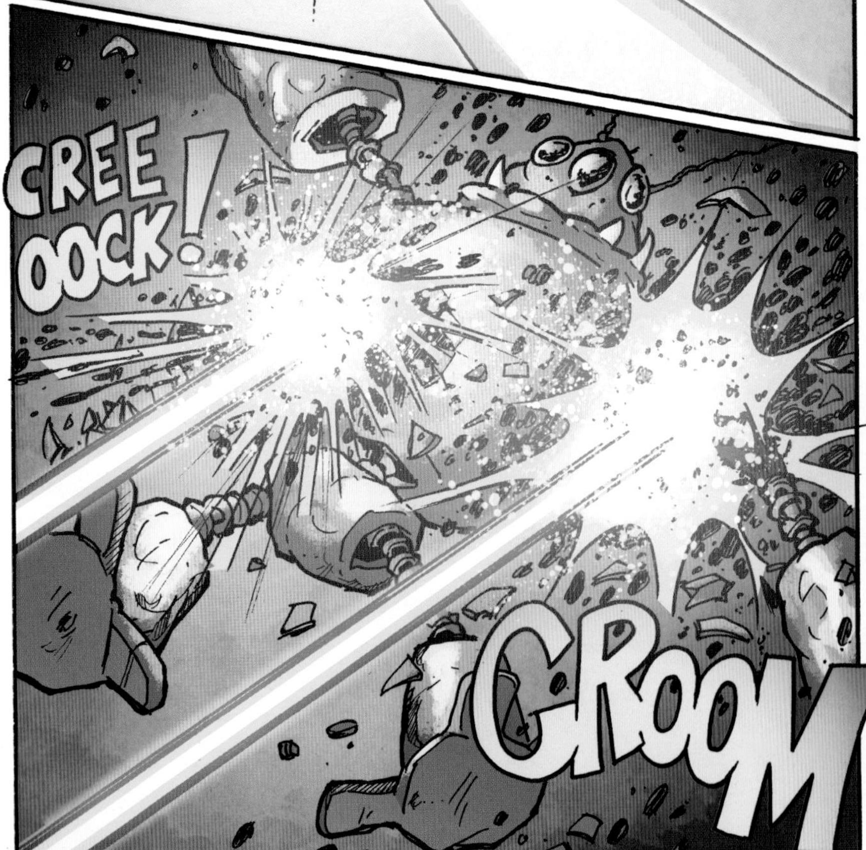
CREE
OOCK!
GROOM

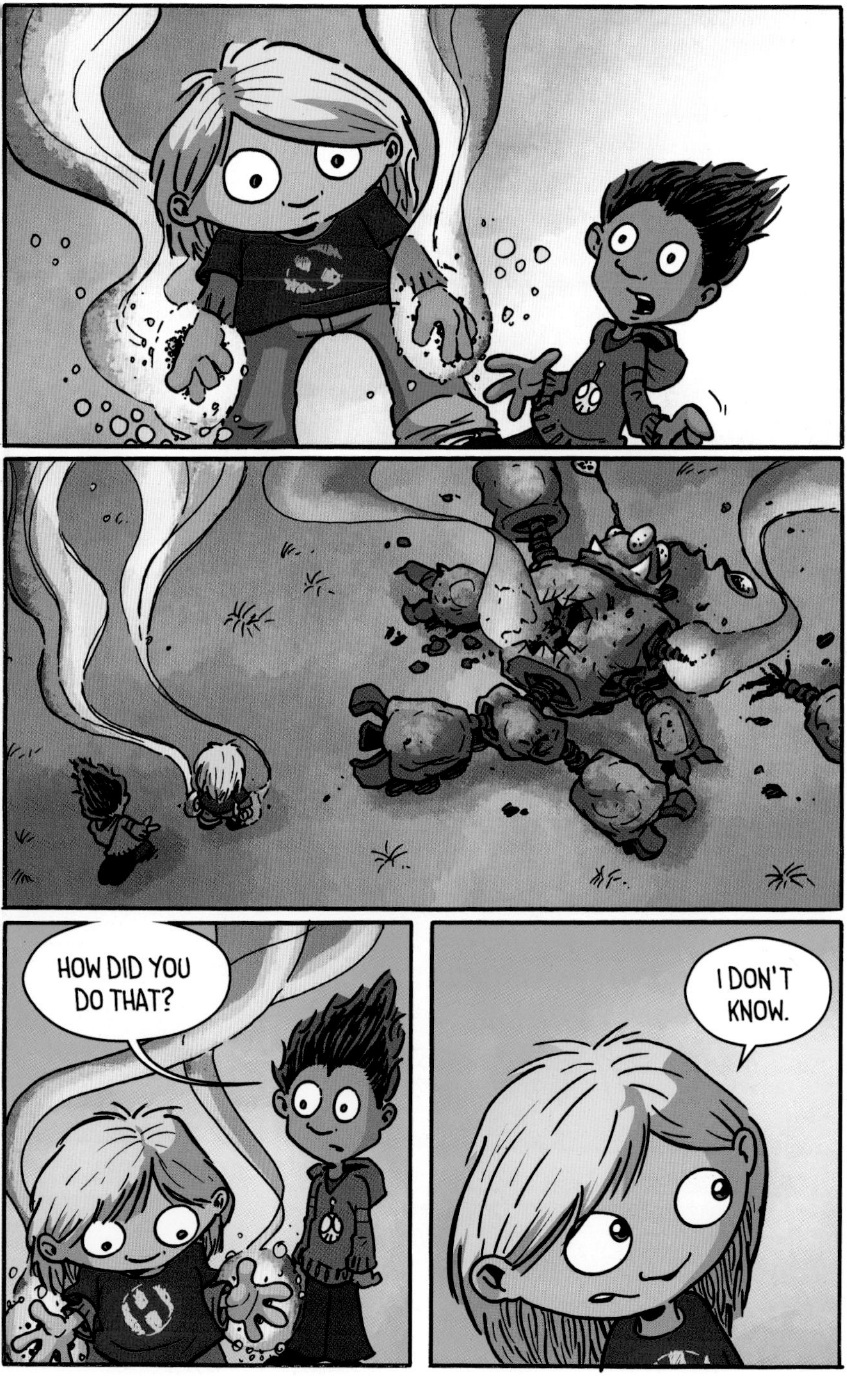
HOW DID YOU DO THAT?
I DON'T KNOW.

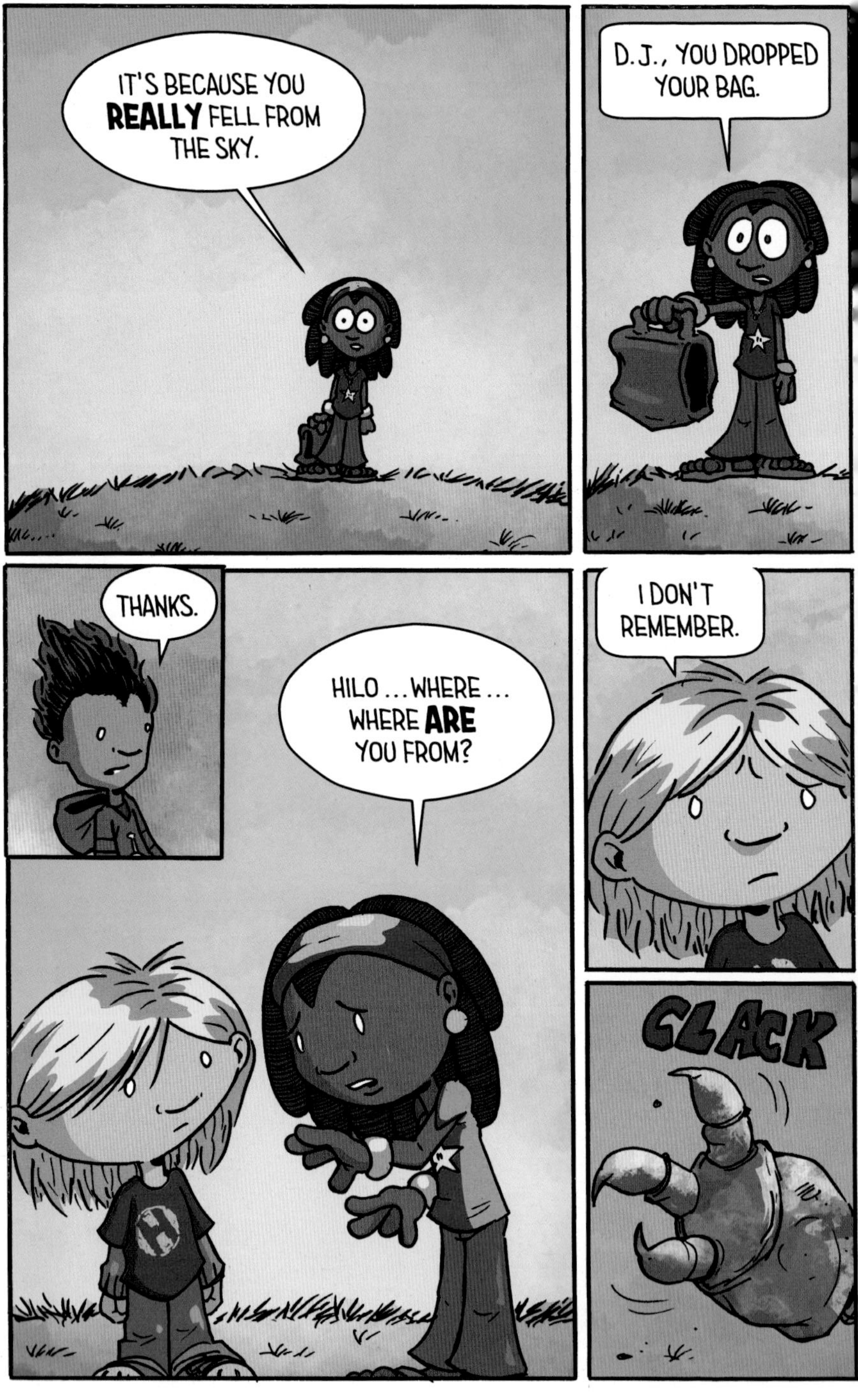
IT'S BECAUSE YOU REALLY FELL FROM THE SKY.
D.J., YOU DROPPED YOUR BAG.
THANKS.
HILO ... WHERE ... WHERE ARE YOU FROM?
I DON'T REMEMBER.
CLACK

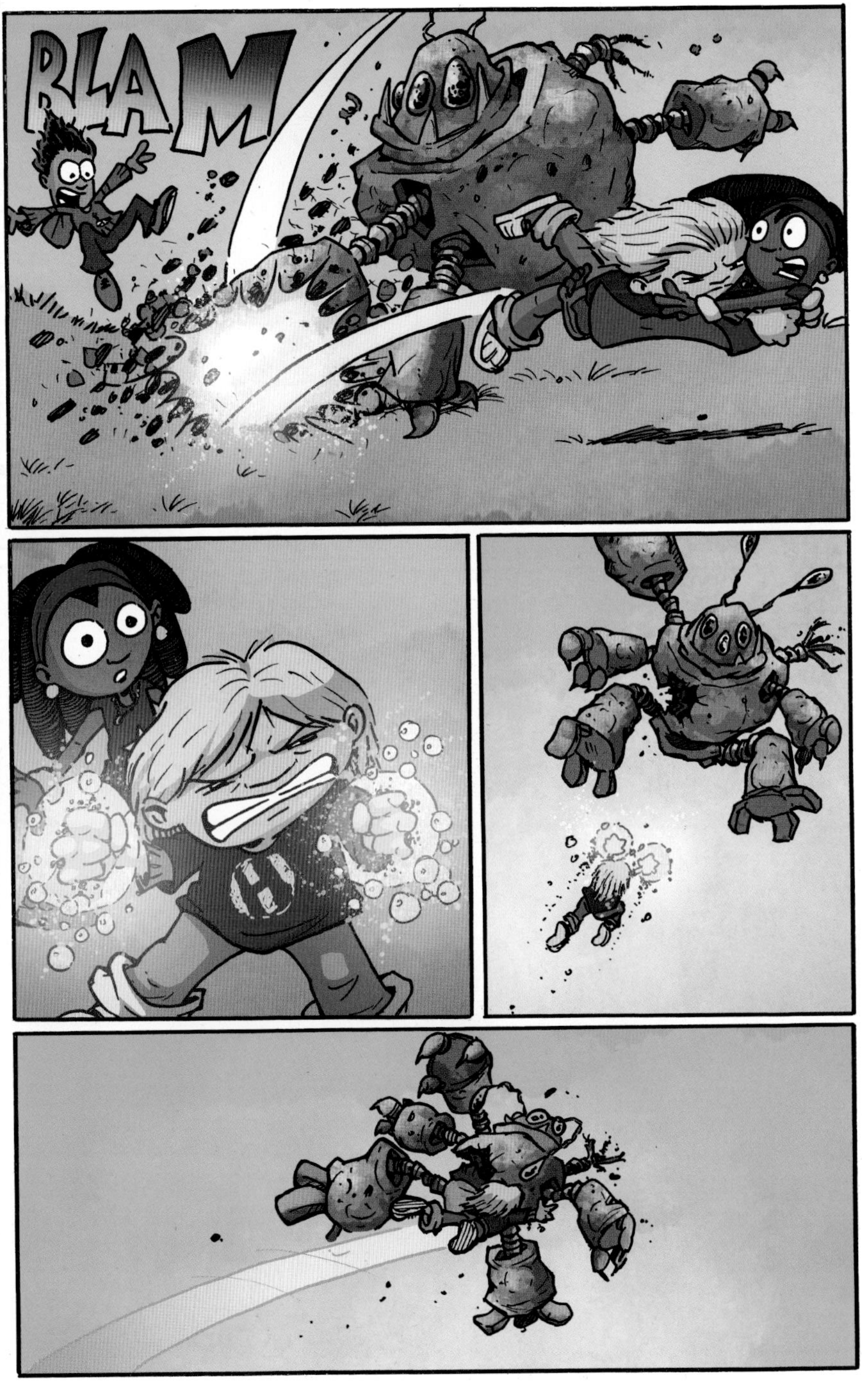
BLAM

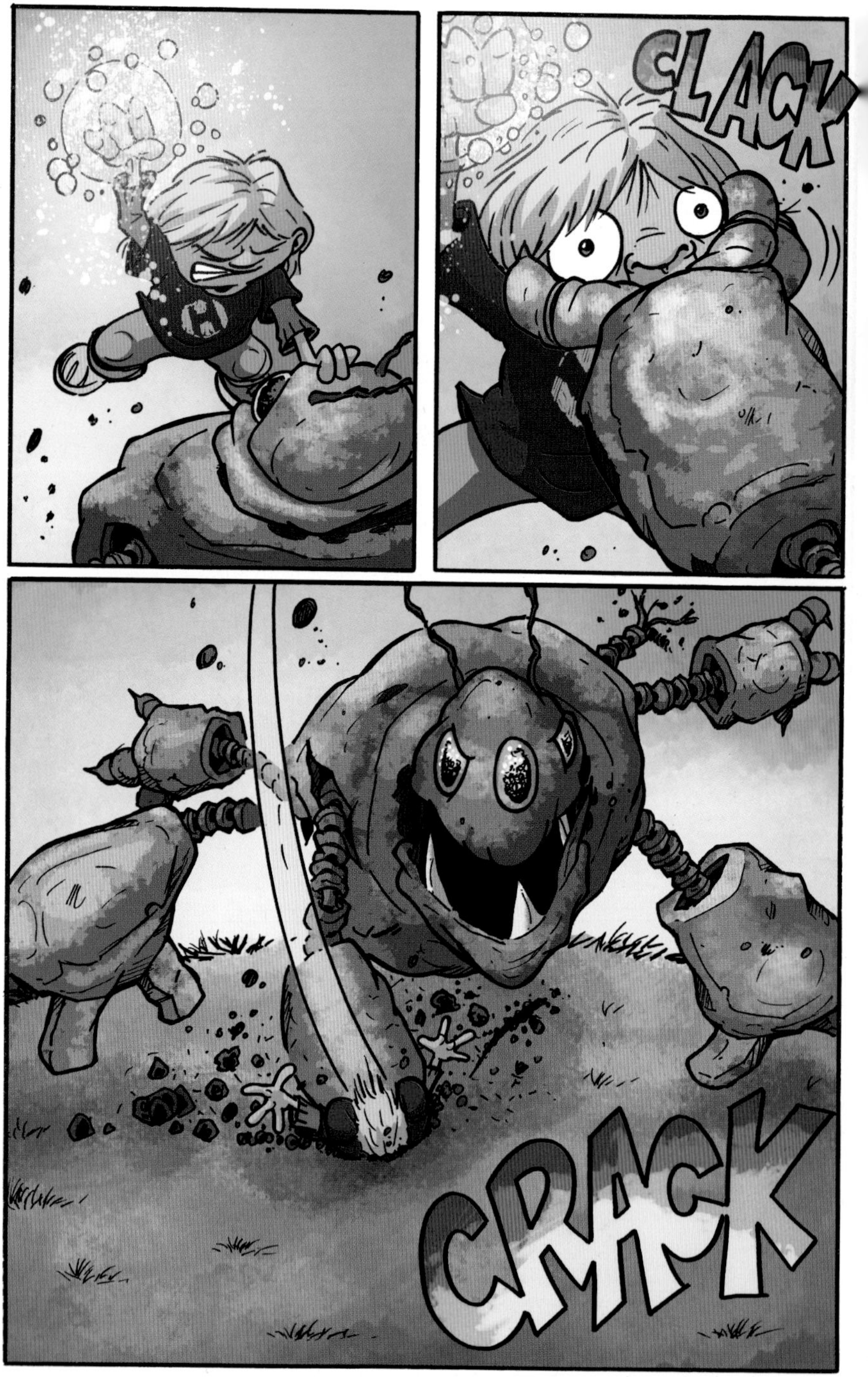
CLACK
CRACK

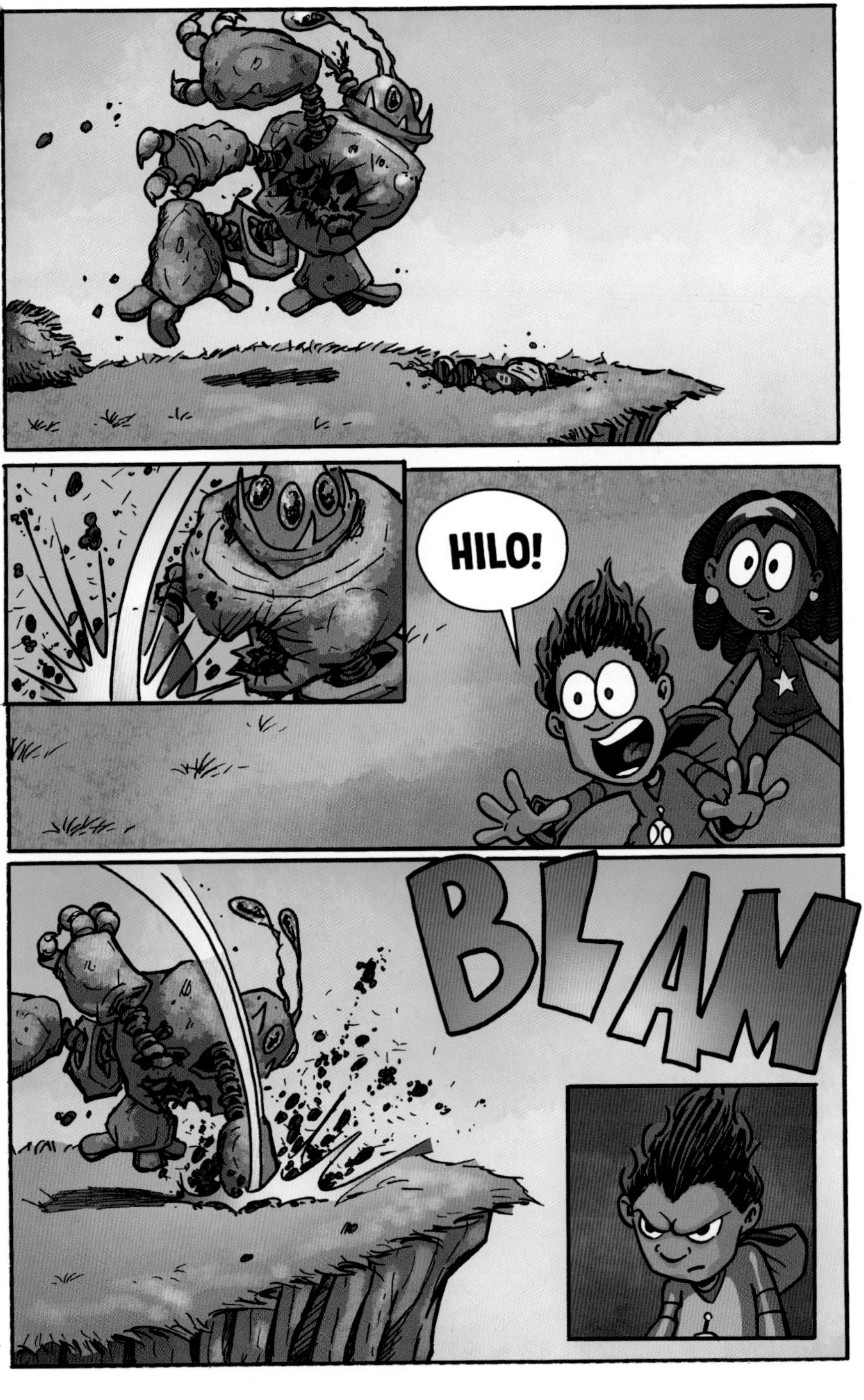

HILO!
BLAM

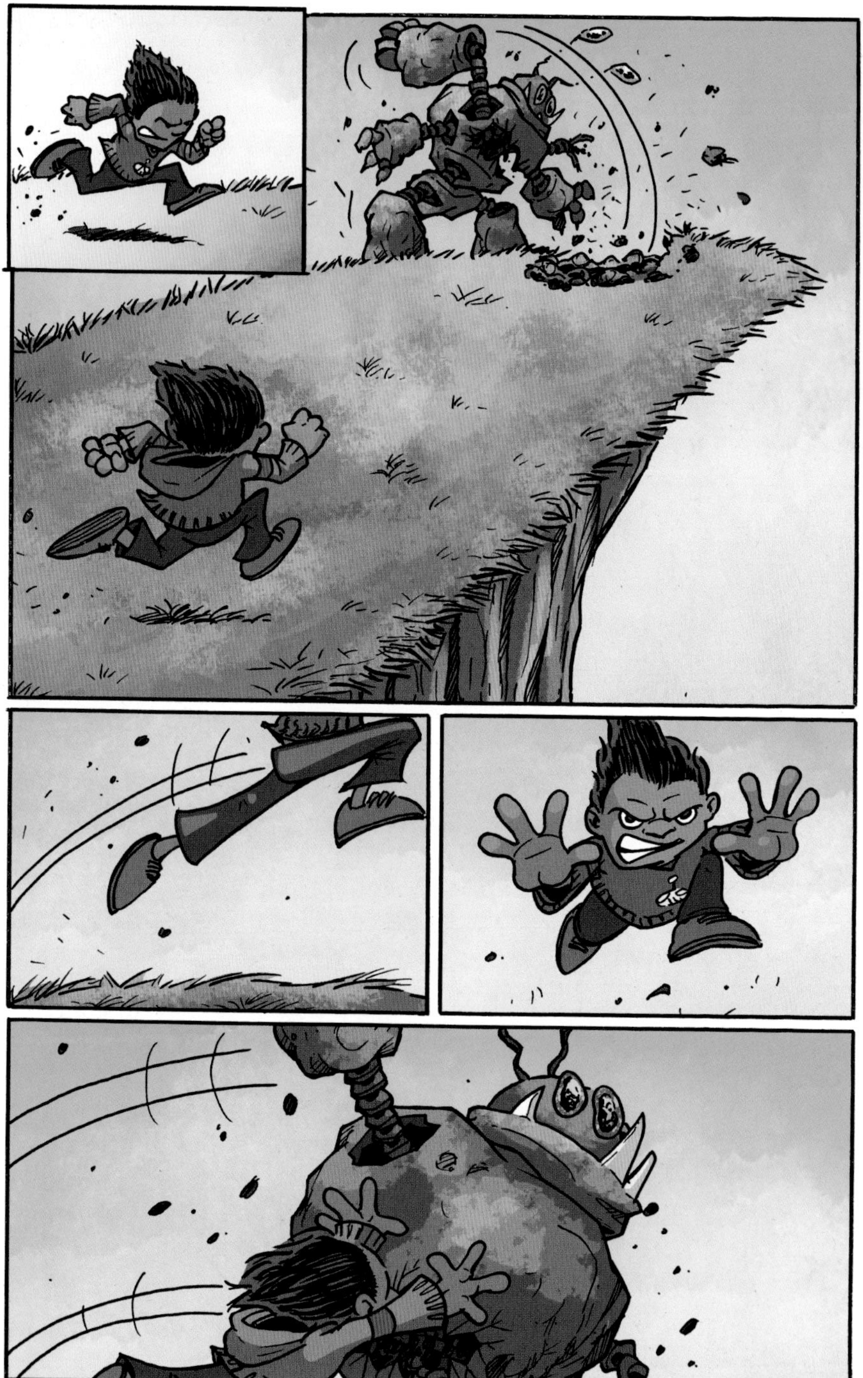

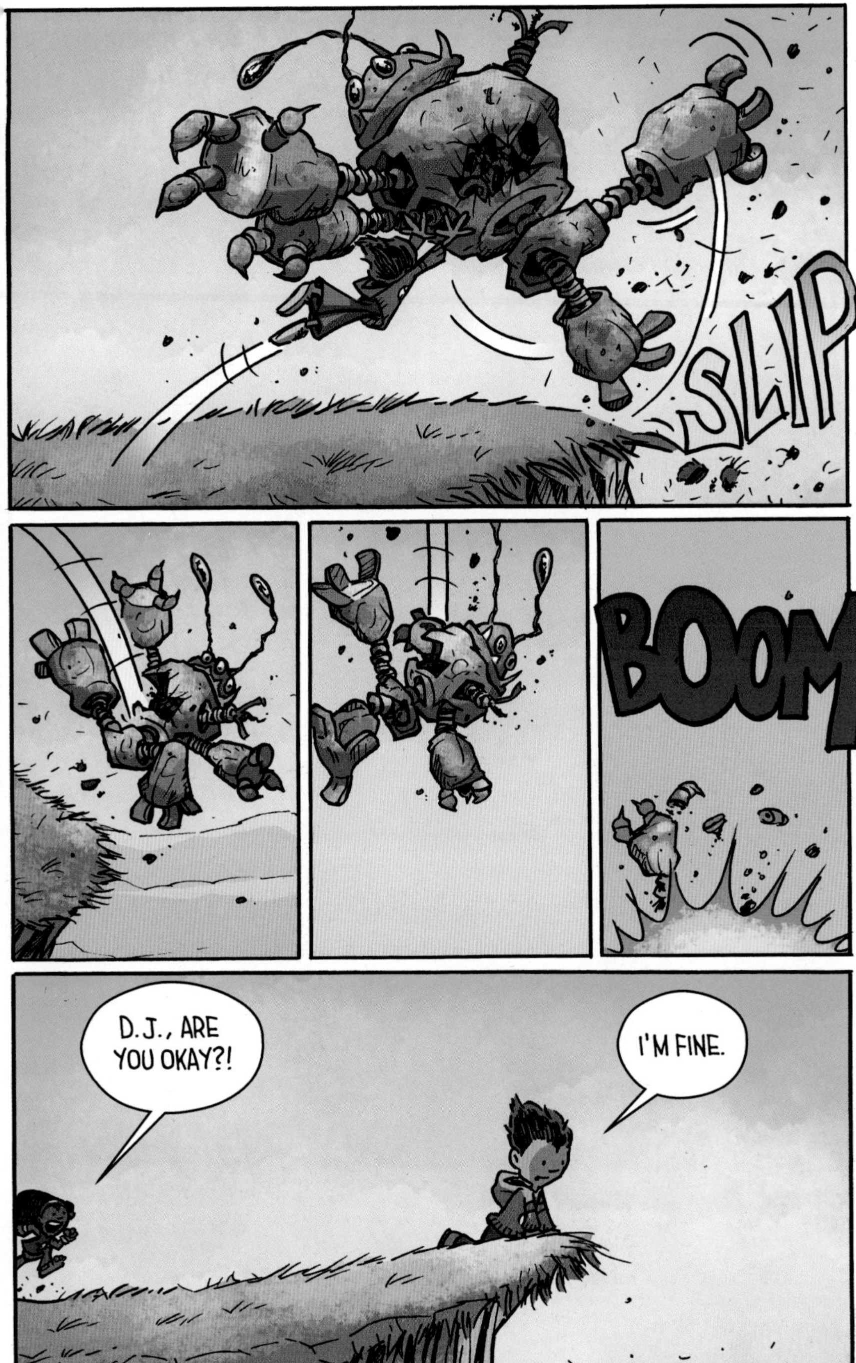
SLIP
BOOM
D.J., ARE YOU OKAY?!
I'M FINE.

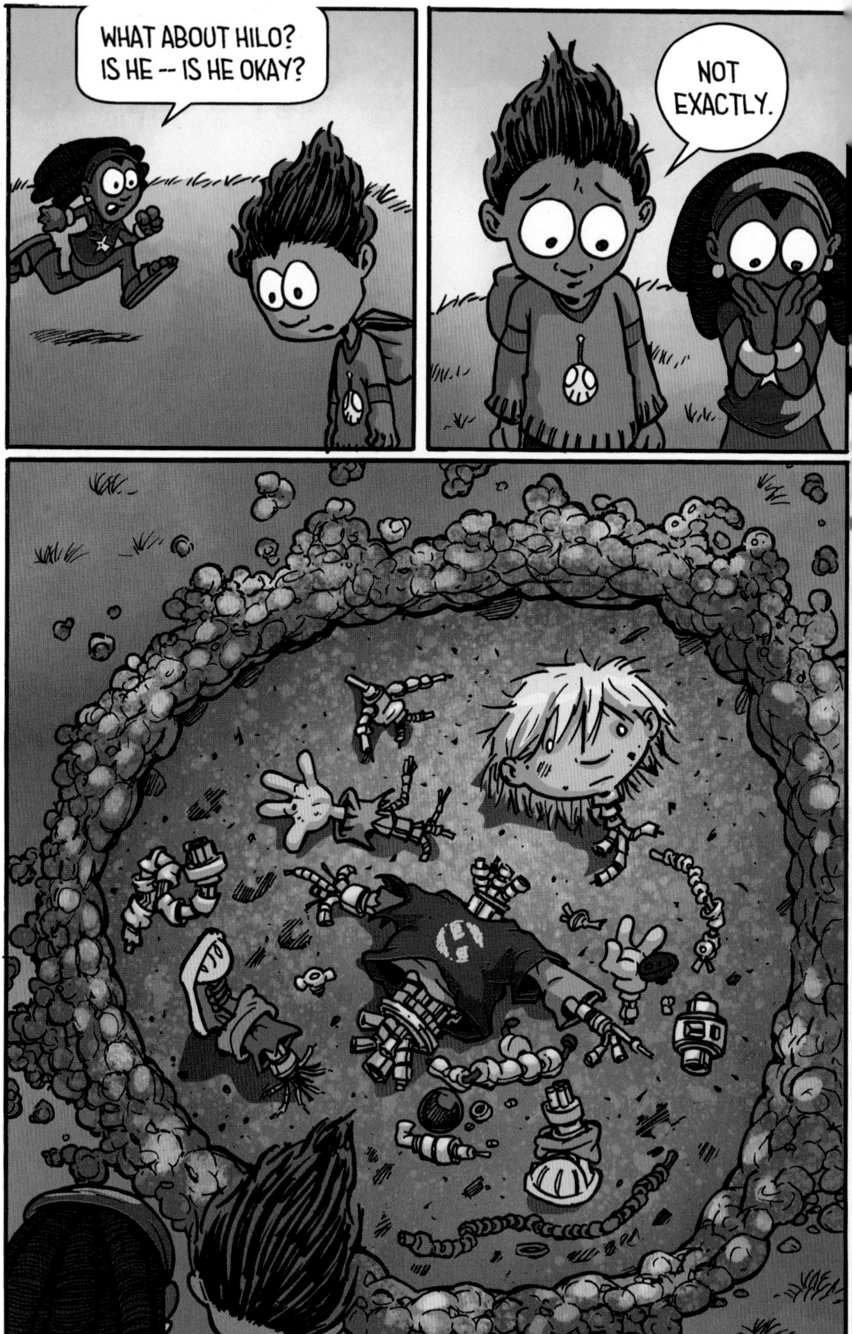
WHAT ABOUT HILO?
IS HE -- IS HE OKAY?
NOT
EXACTLY.

CHAPTER 6

DIG

NO MORE!! NO MORE DESTRUCTION! NO MORE DEATH!
NO MORE RAZORWARK!

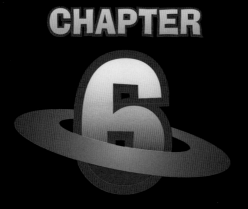

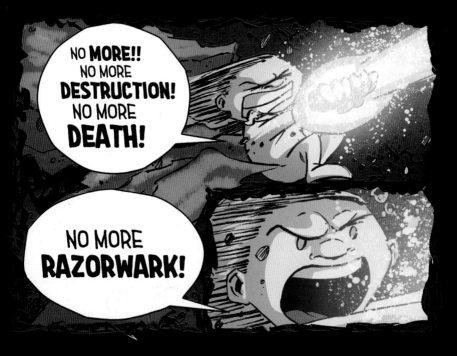

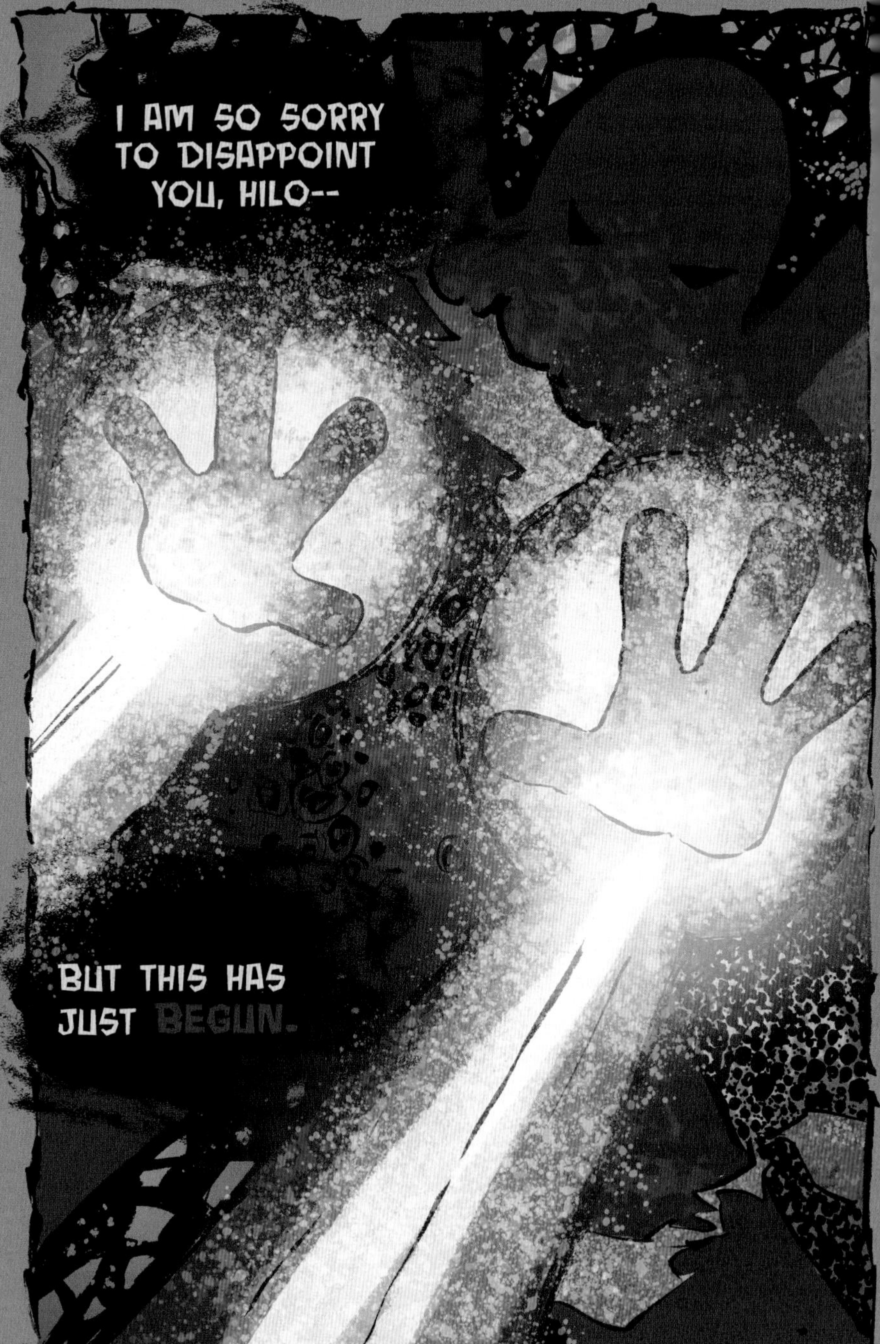
I AM SO SORRY TO DISAPPOINT YOU, HILO--
BUT THIS HAS JUST BEGUN.

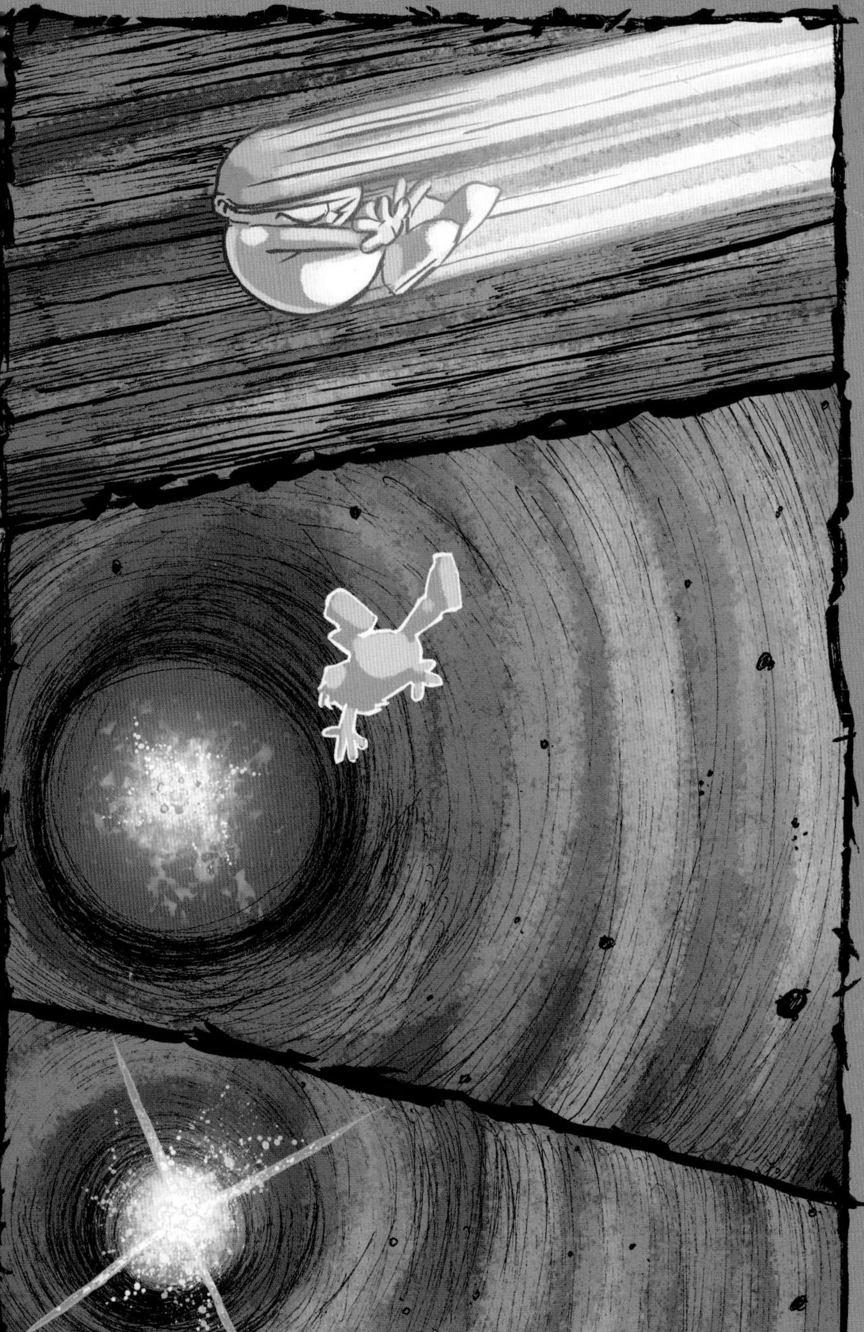

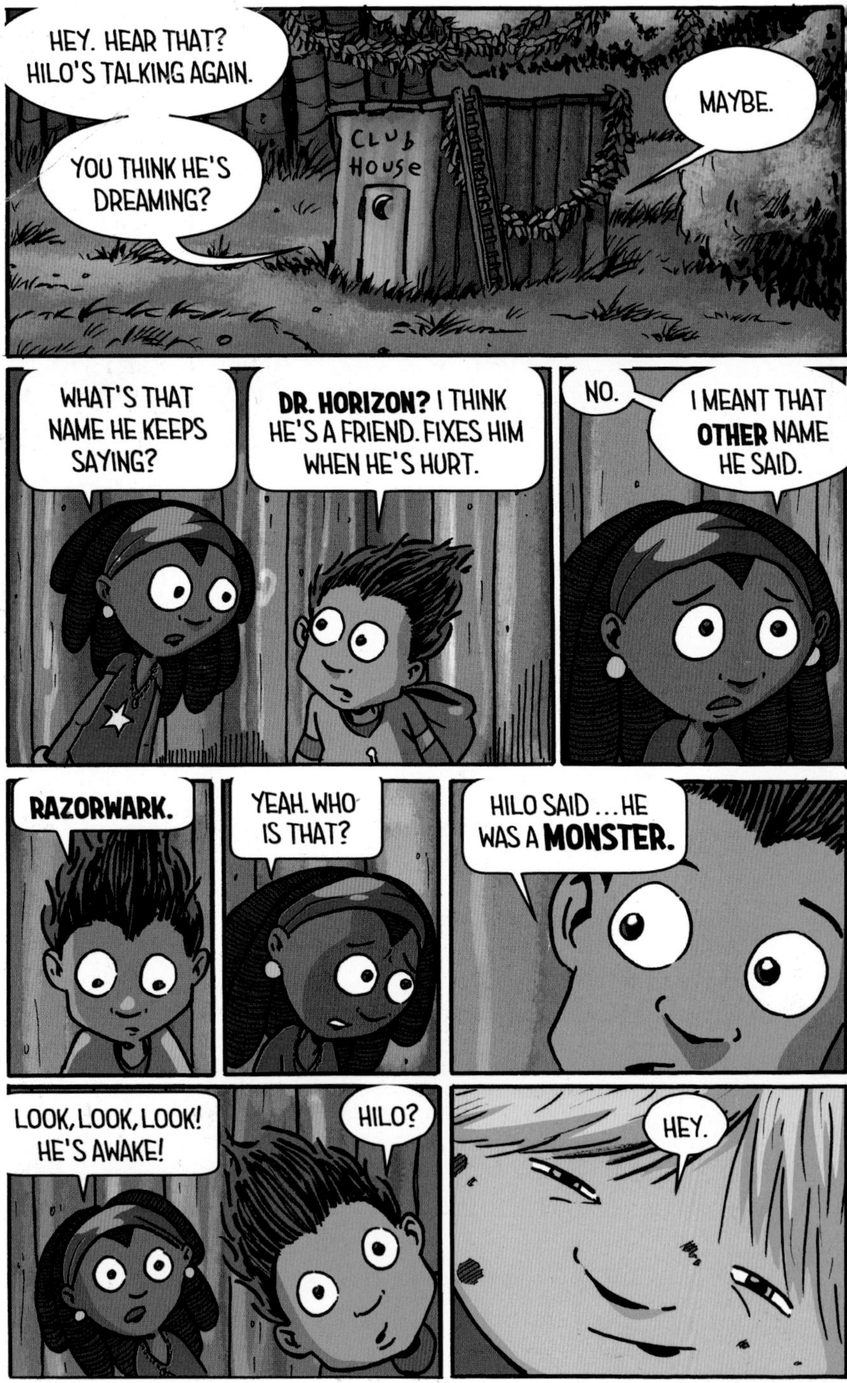
HEY. HEAR THAT? HILO'S TALKING AGAIN.
YOU THINK HE'S DREAMING?
CLUB HOUSE
MAYBE.
WHAT'S THAT NAME HE KEEPS SAYING?
DR. HORIZON? I THINK HE'S A FRIEND. FIXES HIM WHEN HE'S HURT.
NO.
I MEANT THAT **OTHER** NAME HE SAID.
RAZORWARK.
YEAH. WHO IS THAT?
HILO SAID . . . HE WAS A **MONSTER.**
LOOK, LOOK, LOOK! HE'S AWAKE!
HILO?
HEY.

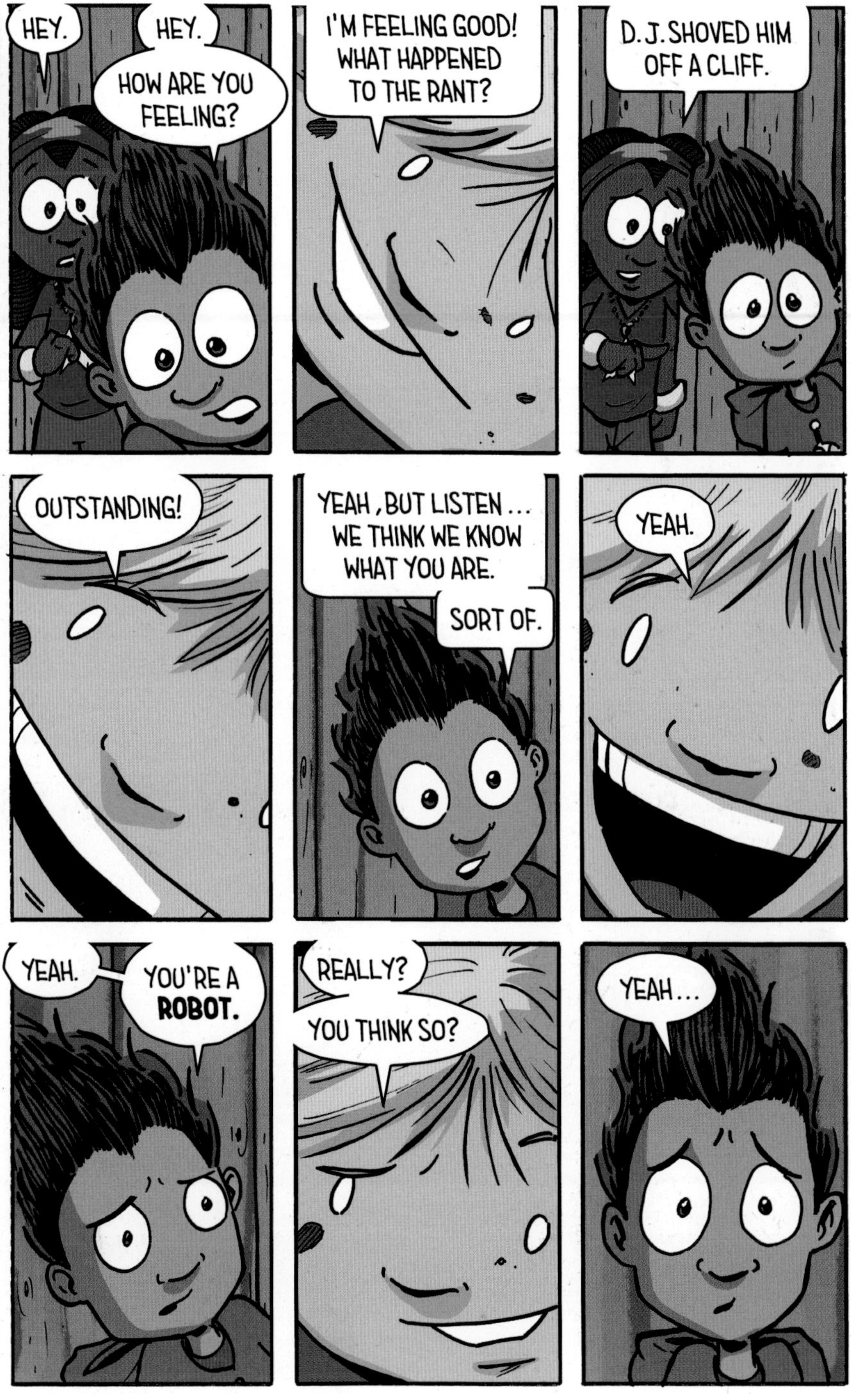
HEY.
HEY.
HOW ARE YOU FEELING?
I'M FEELING GOOD! WHAT HAPPENED TO THE RANT?
D. J. SHOVED HIM OFF A CLIFF.
OUTSTANDING!
YEAH, BUT LISTEN ... WE THINK WE KNOW WHAT YOU ARE.
SORT OF.
YEAH.
YEAH.
YOU'RE A **ROBOT.**
REALLY?
YOU THINK SO?
YEAH ...

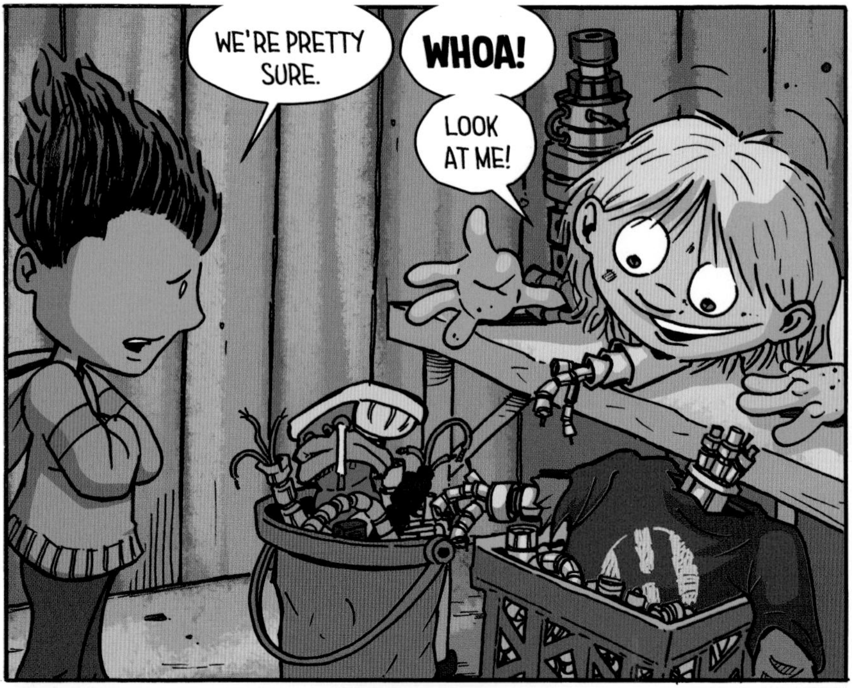
WE'RE PRETTY SURE.
WHOA!
LOOK AT ME!

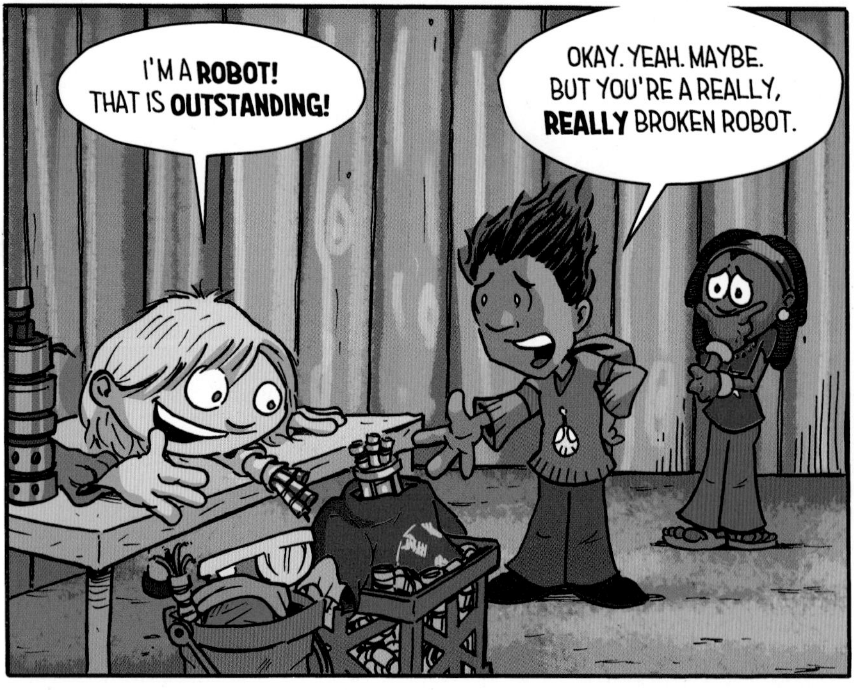
I'M A **ROBOT!** THAT IS **OUTSTANDING!**
OKAY. YEAH. MAYBE. BUT YOU'RE A REALLY, **REALLY** BROKEN ROBOT.

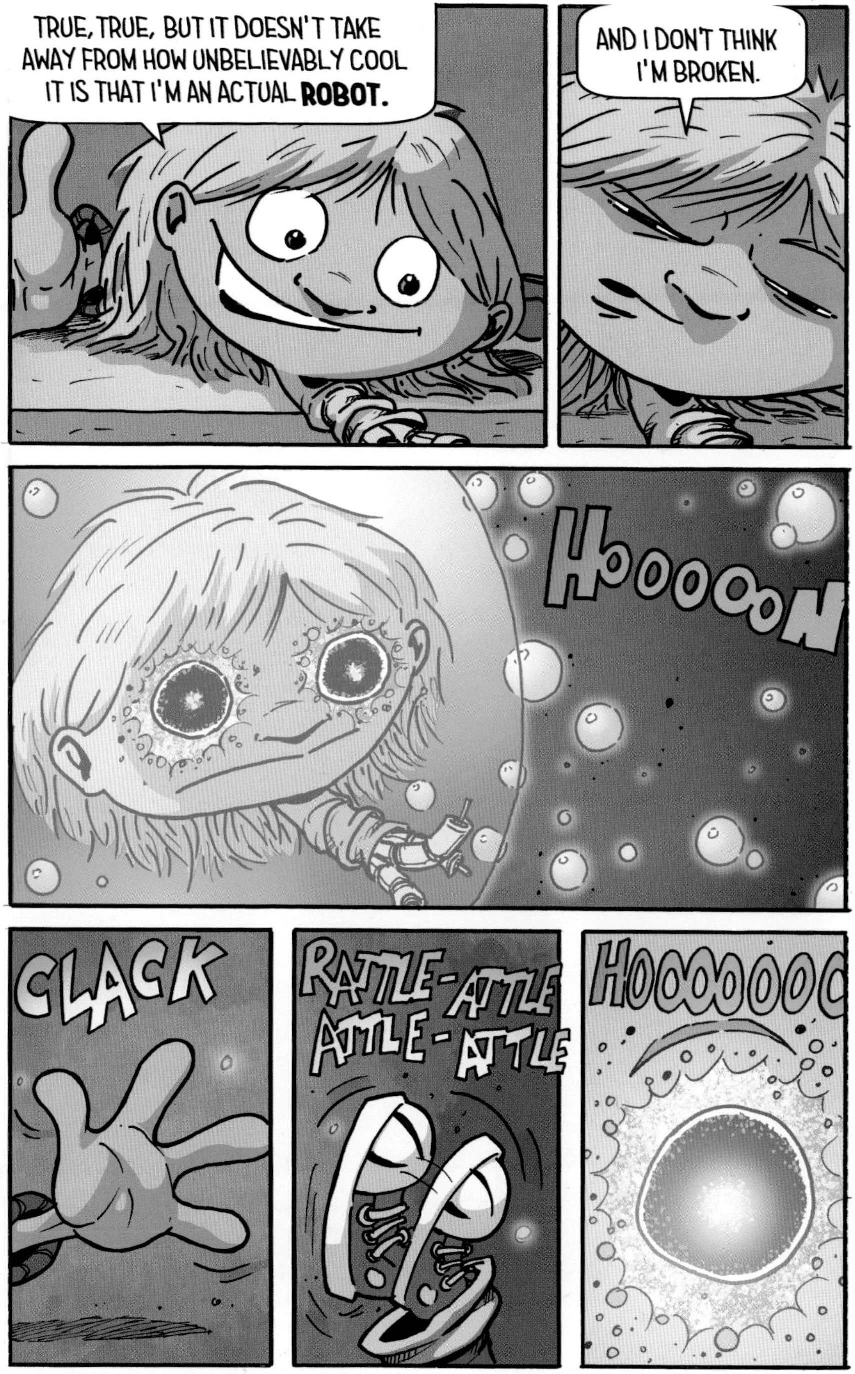
TRUE, TRUE, BUT IT DOESN'T TAKE AWAY FROM HOW UNBELIEVABLY COOL IT IS THAT I'M AN ACTUAL **ROBOT.**
AND I DON'T THINK I'M BROKEN.
HOOOOON
CLACK
RATTLE-ATTLE ATTLE-ATTLE
HOOOOOOO

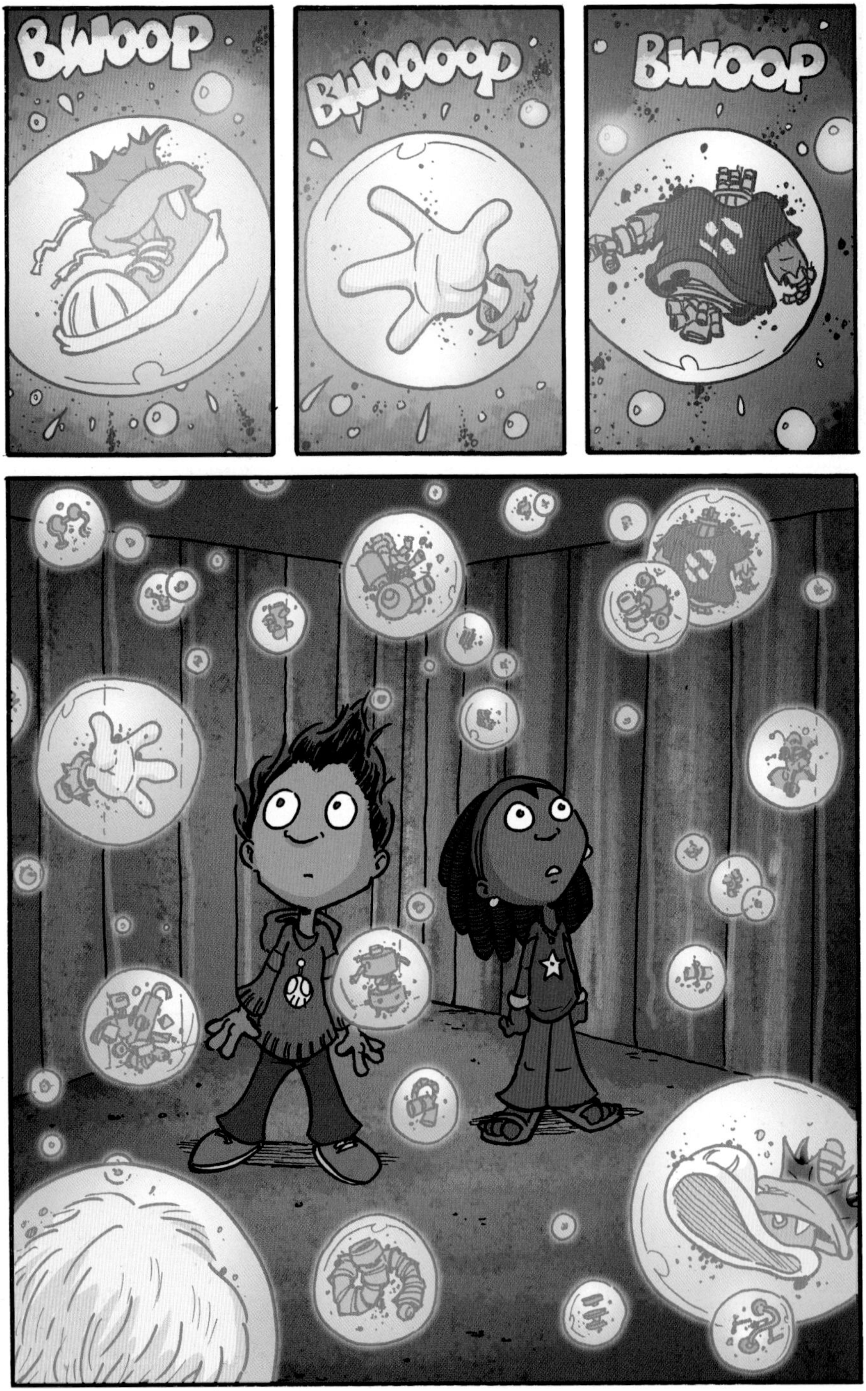
BWOOP
BWOOOOP
BWOOP

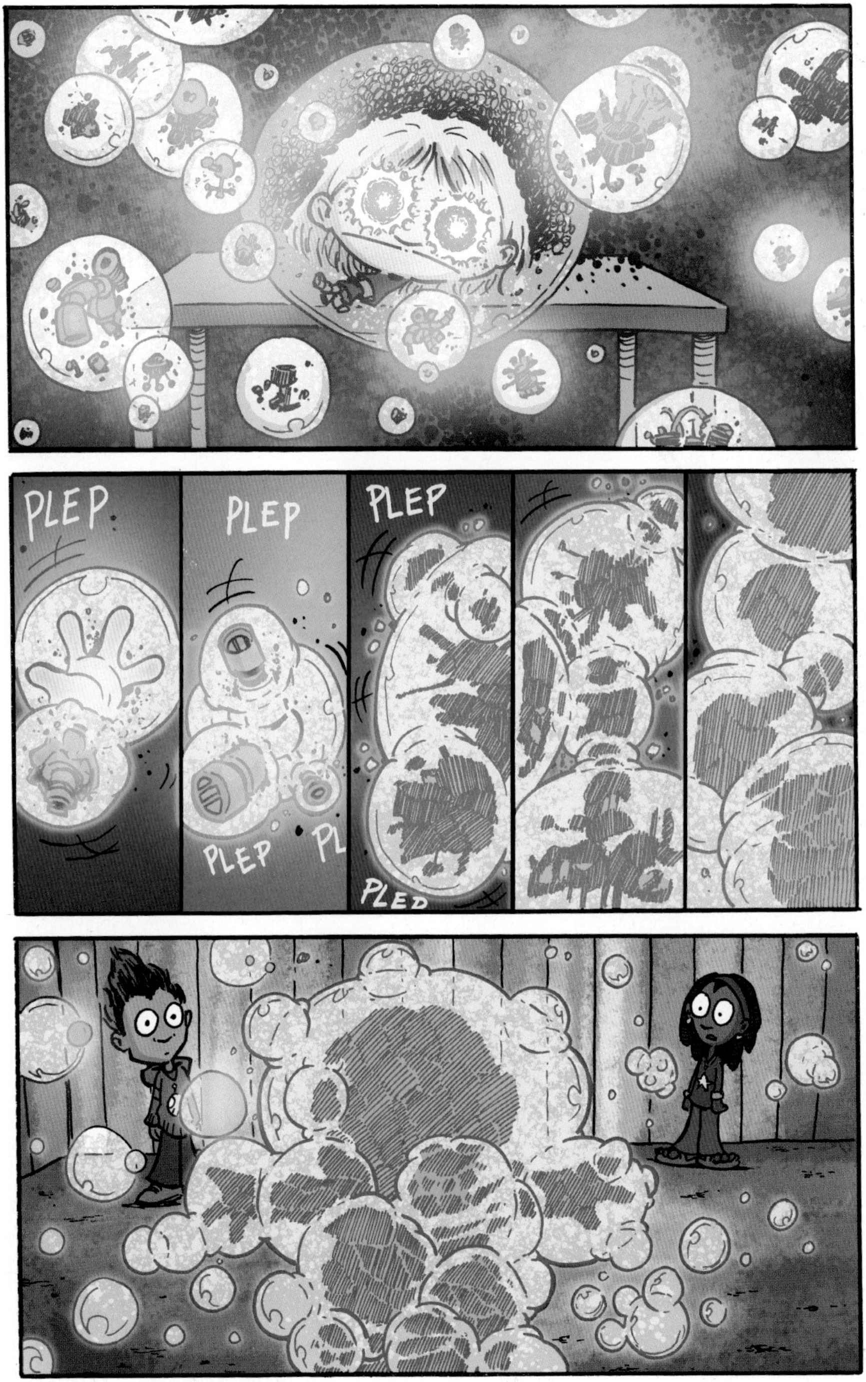

PLEP
PLEP
PLEP
PLEP
PLEP

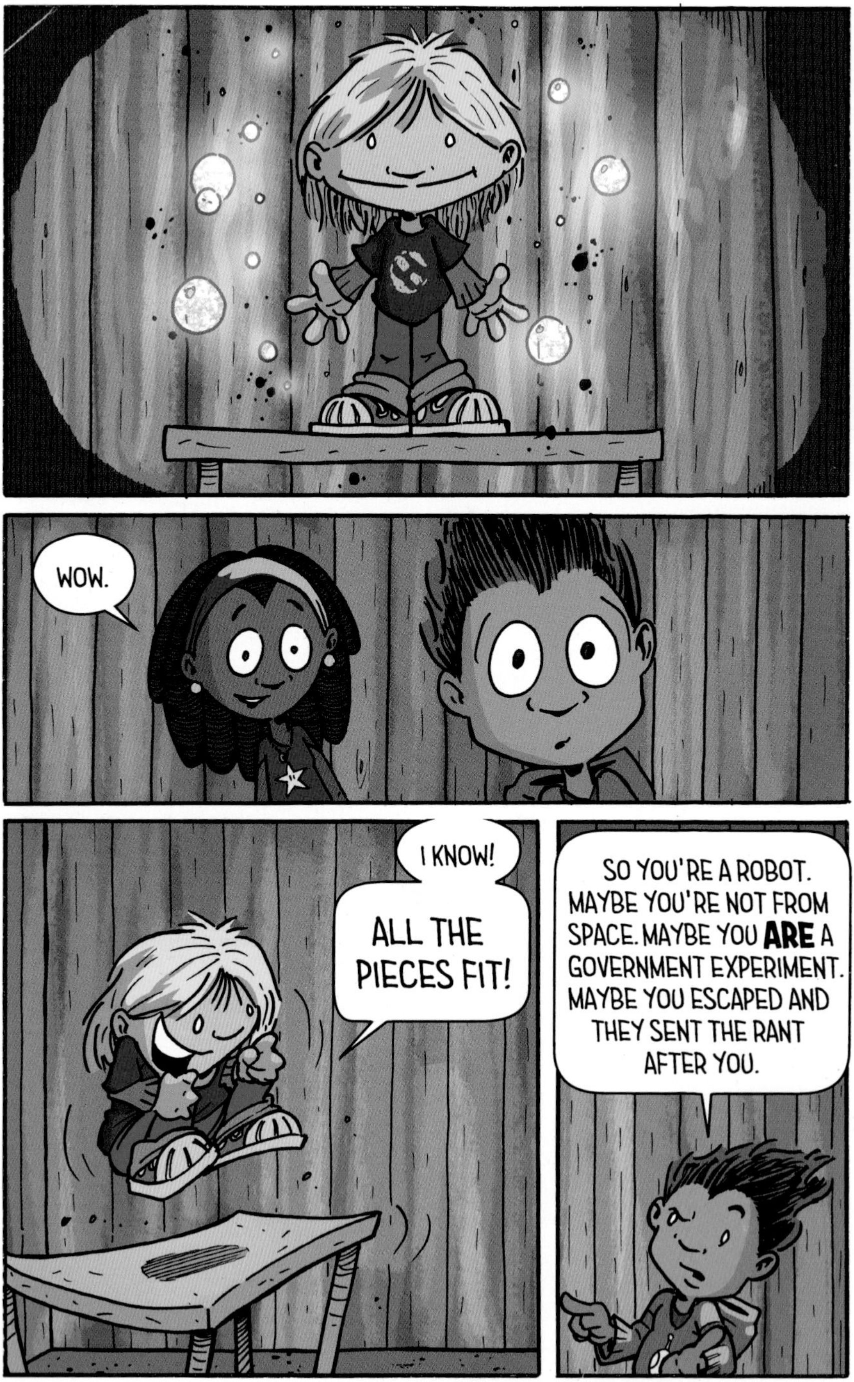
WOW.
I KNOW!
ALL THE PIECES FIT!
SO YOU'RE A ROBOT. MAYBE YOU'RE NOT FROM SPACE. MAYBE YOU **ARE** A GOVERNMENT EXPERIMENT. MAYBE YOU ESCAPED AND THEY SENT THE RANT AFTER YOU.

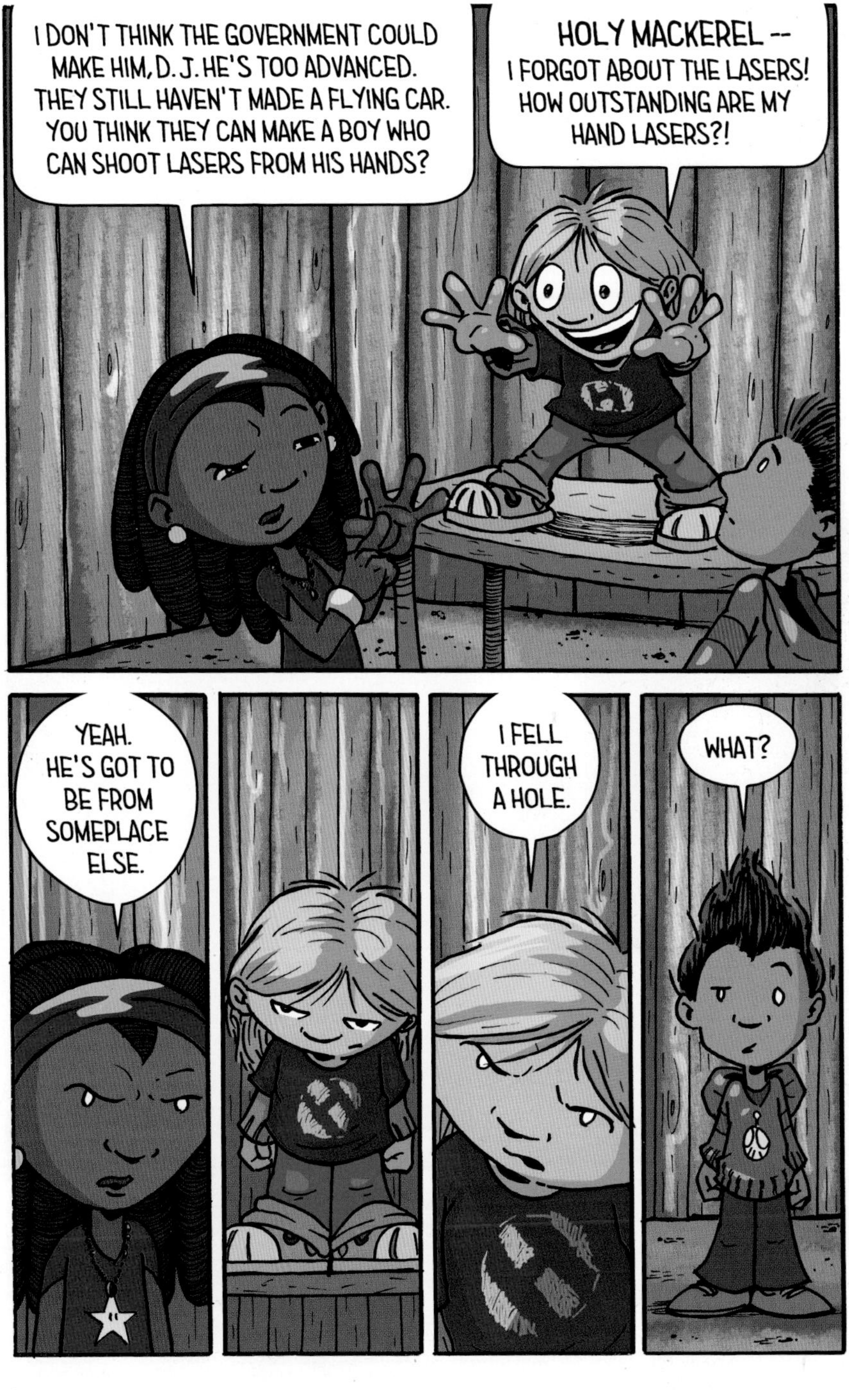
I DON'T THINK THE GOVERNMENT COULD MAKE HIM, D. J. HE'S TOO ADVANCED. THEY STILL HAVEN'T MADE A FLYING CAR. YOU THINK THEY CAN MAKE A BOY WHO CAN SHOOT LASERS FROM HIS HANDS?
HOLY MACKEREL -- I FORGOT ABOUT THE LASERS! HOW OUTSTANDING ARE MY HAND LASERS?!
YEAH. HE'S GOT TO BE FROM SOMEPLACE ELSE.
I FELL THROUGH A HOLE.
WHAT?

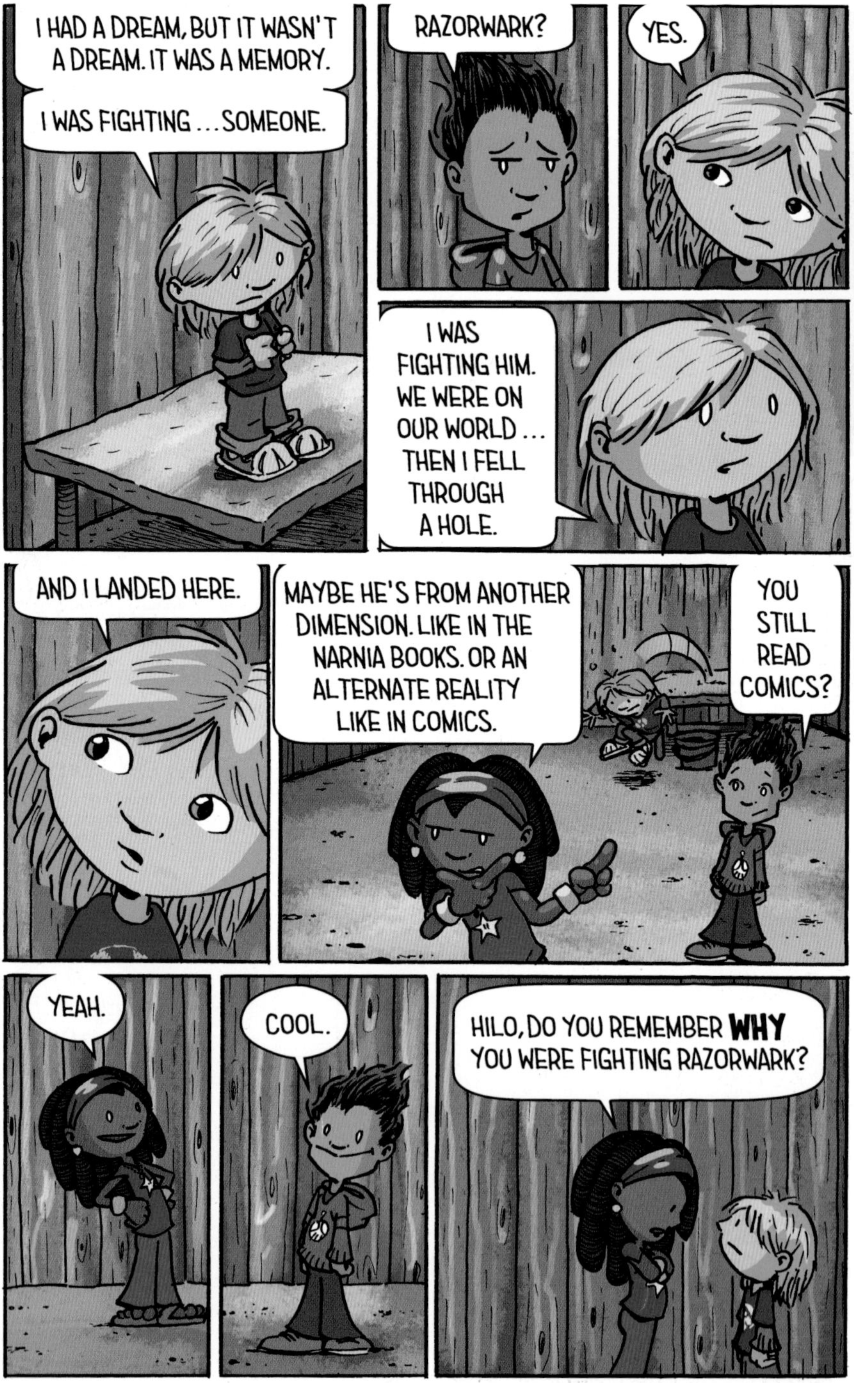
I HAD A DREAM, BUT IT WASN'T A DREAM. IT WAS A MEMORY.
I WAS FIGHTING . . . SOMEONE.
RAZORWARK?
YES.
I WAS FIGHTING HIM. WE WERE ON OUR WORLD . . . THEN I FELL THROUGH A HOLE.
AND I LANDED HERE.
MAYBE HE'S FROM ANOTHER DIMENSION. LIKE IN THE NARNIA BOOKS. OR AN ALTERNATE REALITY LIKE IN COMICS.
YOU STILL READ COMICS?
YEAH.
COOL.
HILO, DO YOU REMEMBER **WHY** YOU WERE FIGHTING RAZORWARK?

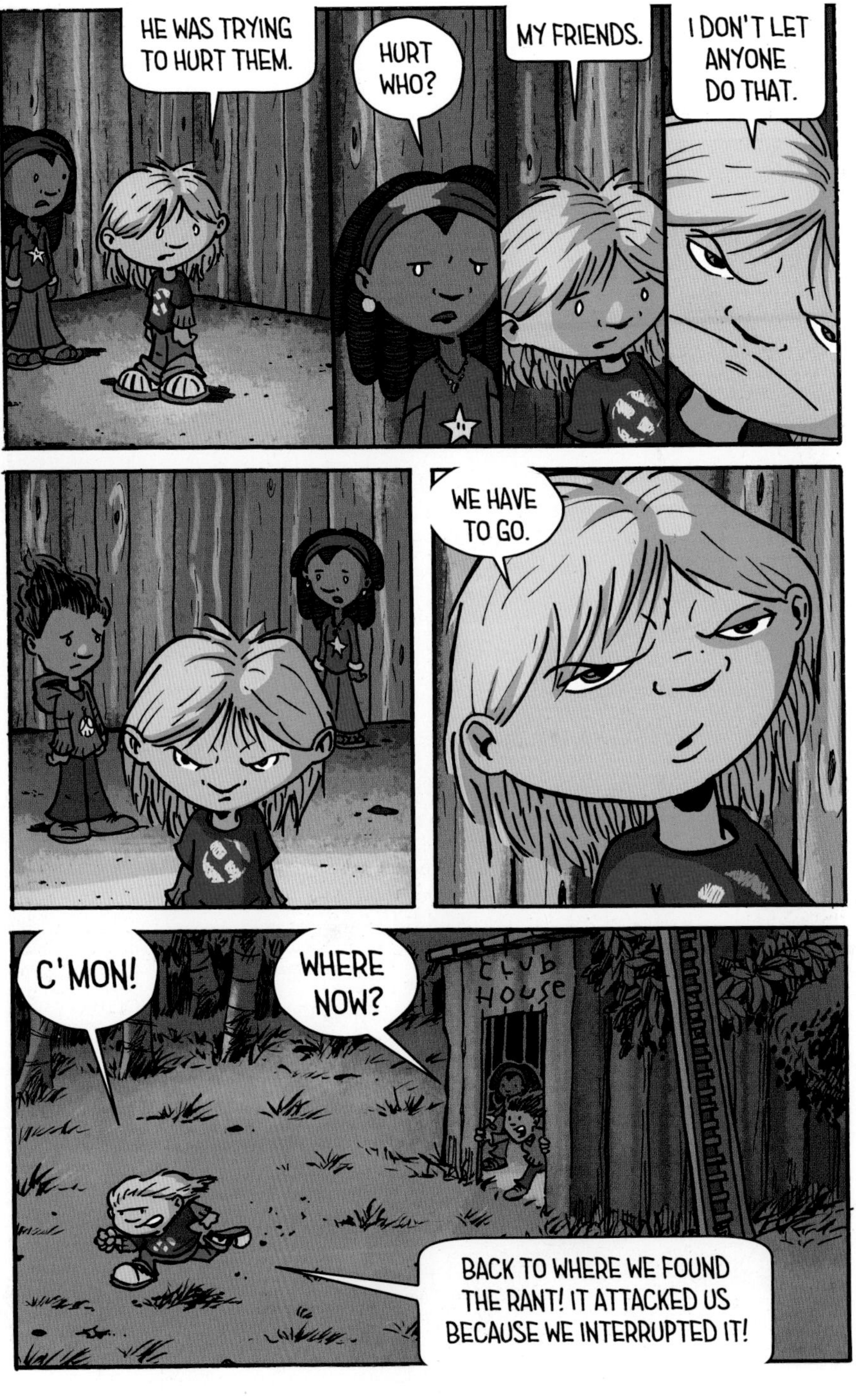
HE WAS TRYING TO HURT THEM.
HURT WHO?
MY FRIENDS.
I DON'T LET ANYONE DO THAT.
WE HAVE TO GO.
C'MON!
WHERE NOW?
CLUB HOUSE
BACK TO WHERE WE FOUND THE RANT! IT ATTACKED US BECAUSE WE INTERRUPTED IT!

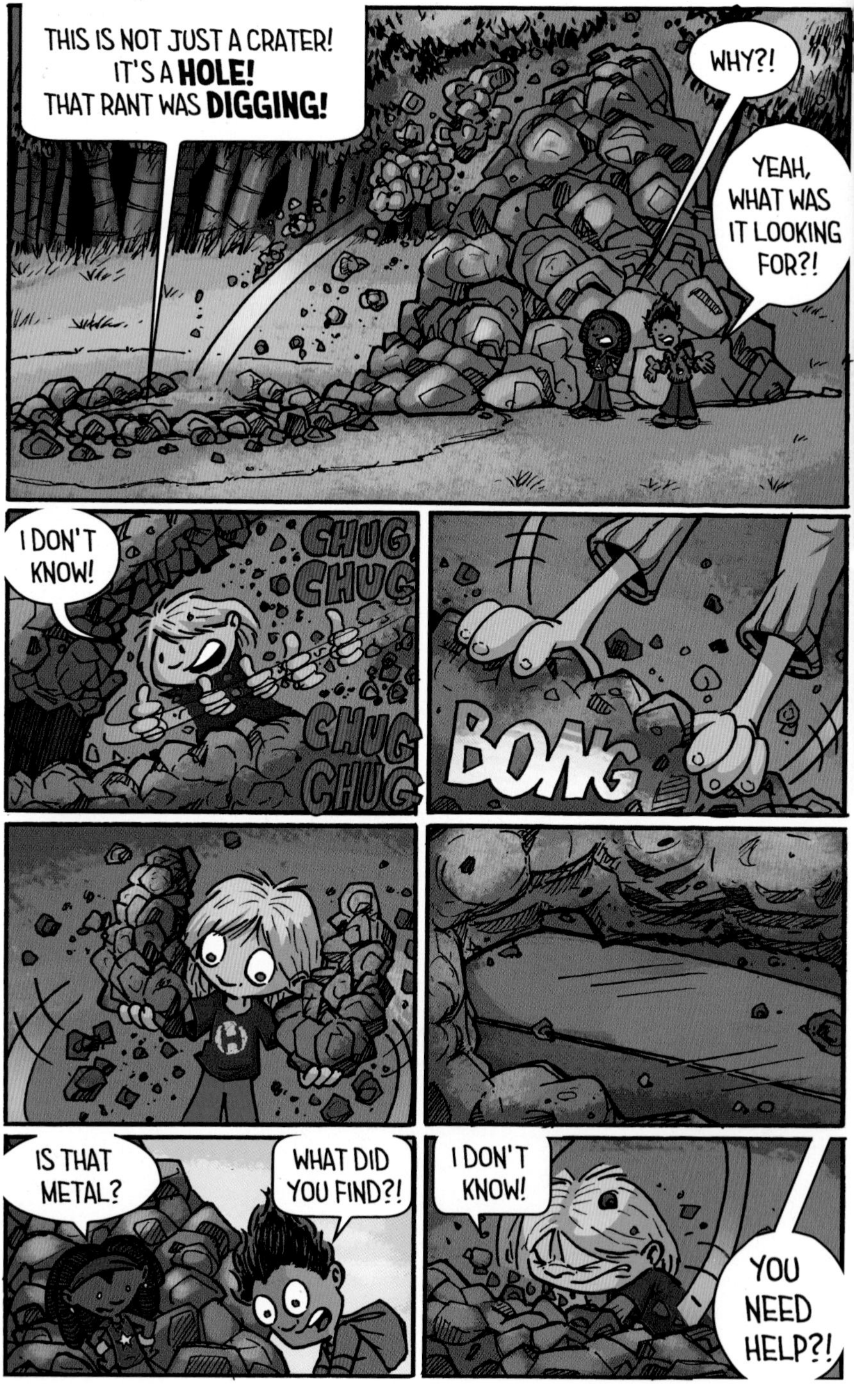
THIS IS NOT JUST A CRATER! IT'S A **HOLE!** THAT RANT WAS **DIGGING!**
WHY?!
YEAH, WHAT WAS IT LOOKING FOR?!
I DON'T KNOW!
CHUG CHUG
CHUG CHUG
BONG
IS THAT METAL?
WHAT DID YOU FIND?!
I DON'T KNOW!
YOU NEED HELP?!

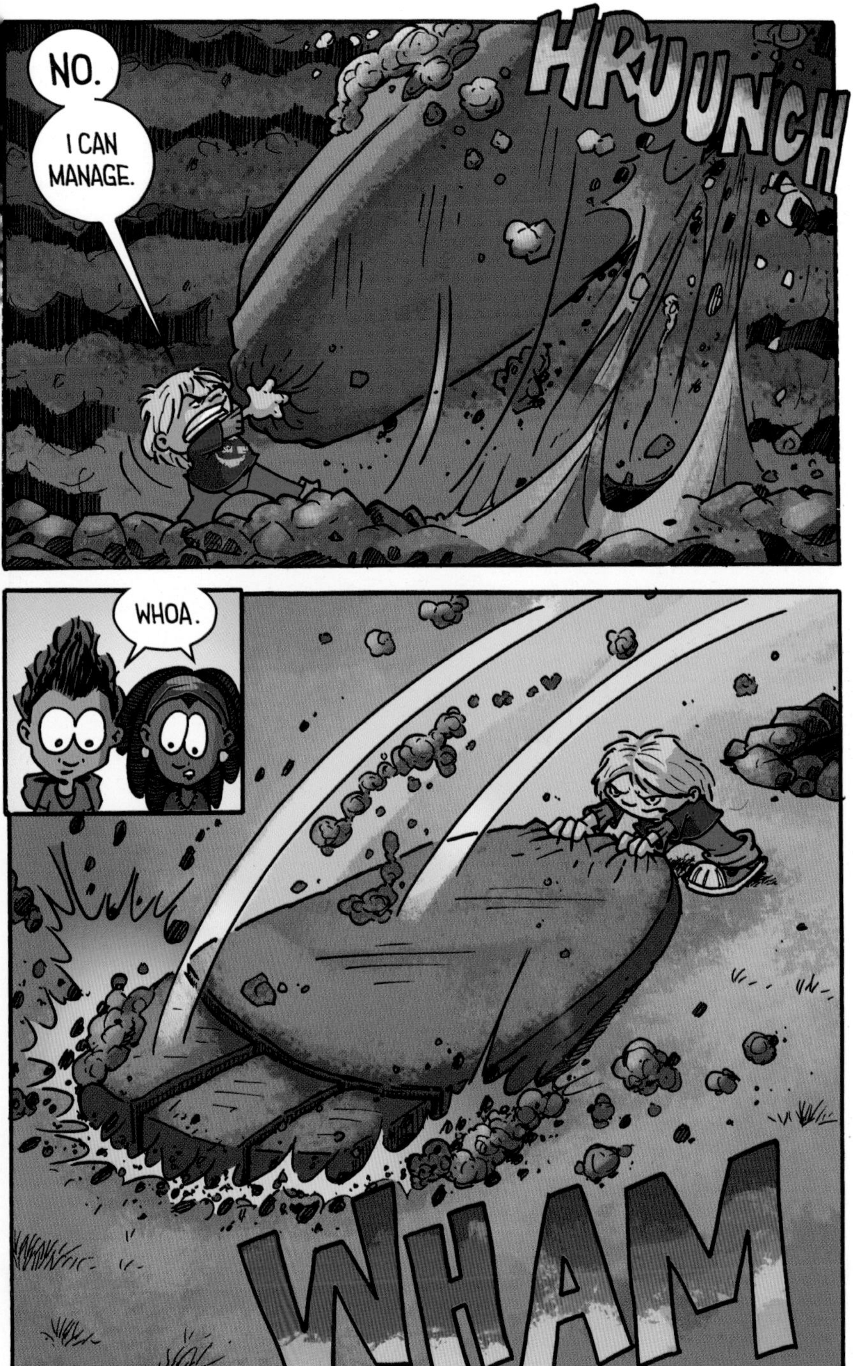
NO.
I CAN MANAGE.
HRUUNCH
WHOA.
WHAM

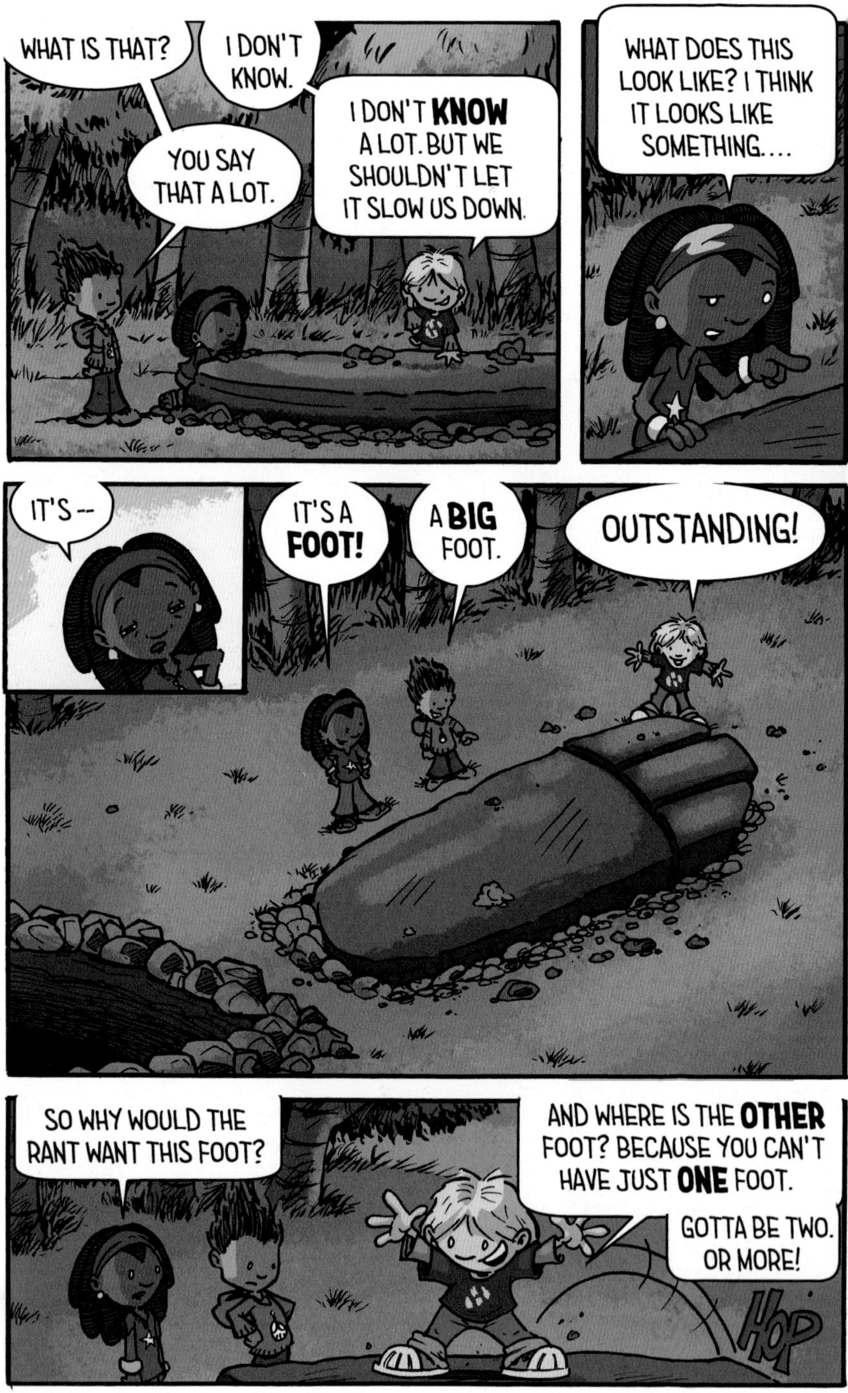

WHAT IS THAT?
I DON'T KNOW.
YOU SAY THAT A LOT.
I DON'T **KNOW** A LOT. BUT WE SHOULDN'T LET IT SLOW US DOWN.
WHAT DOES THIS LOOK LIKE? I THINK IT LOOKS LIKE SOMETHING....
IT'S --
IT'S A **FOOT!**
A **BIG** FOOT.
OUTSTANDING!
SO WHY WOULD THE RANT WANT THIS FOOT?
AND WHERE IS THE **OTHER** FOOT? BECAUSE YOU CAN'T HAVE JUST **ONE** FOOT.
GOTTA BE TWO. OR MORE!
HOP

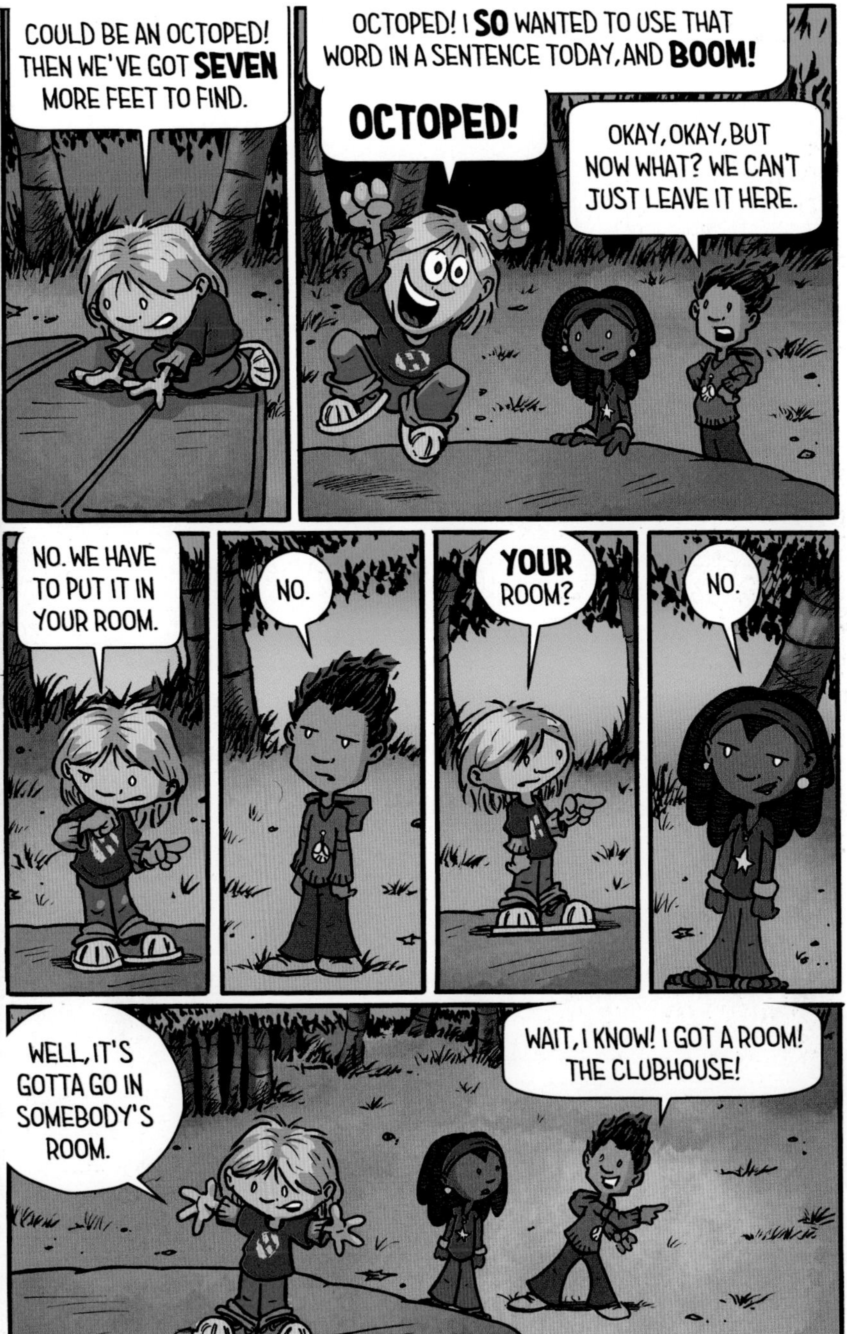

COULD BE AN OCTOPED! THEN WE'VE GOT **SEVEN** MORE FEET TO FIND.
OCTOPED! I **SO** WANTED TO USE THAT WORD IN A SENTENCE TODAY, AND **BOOM!**
OCTOPED!
OKAY, OKAY, BUT NOW WHAT? WE CAN'T JUST LEAVE IT HERE.
NO. WE HAVE TO PUT IT IN YOUR ROOM.
NO.
YOUR ROOM?
NO.
WELL, IT'S GOTTA GO IN SOMEBODY'S ROOM.
WAIT, I KNOW! I GOT A ROOM! THE CLUBHOUSE!

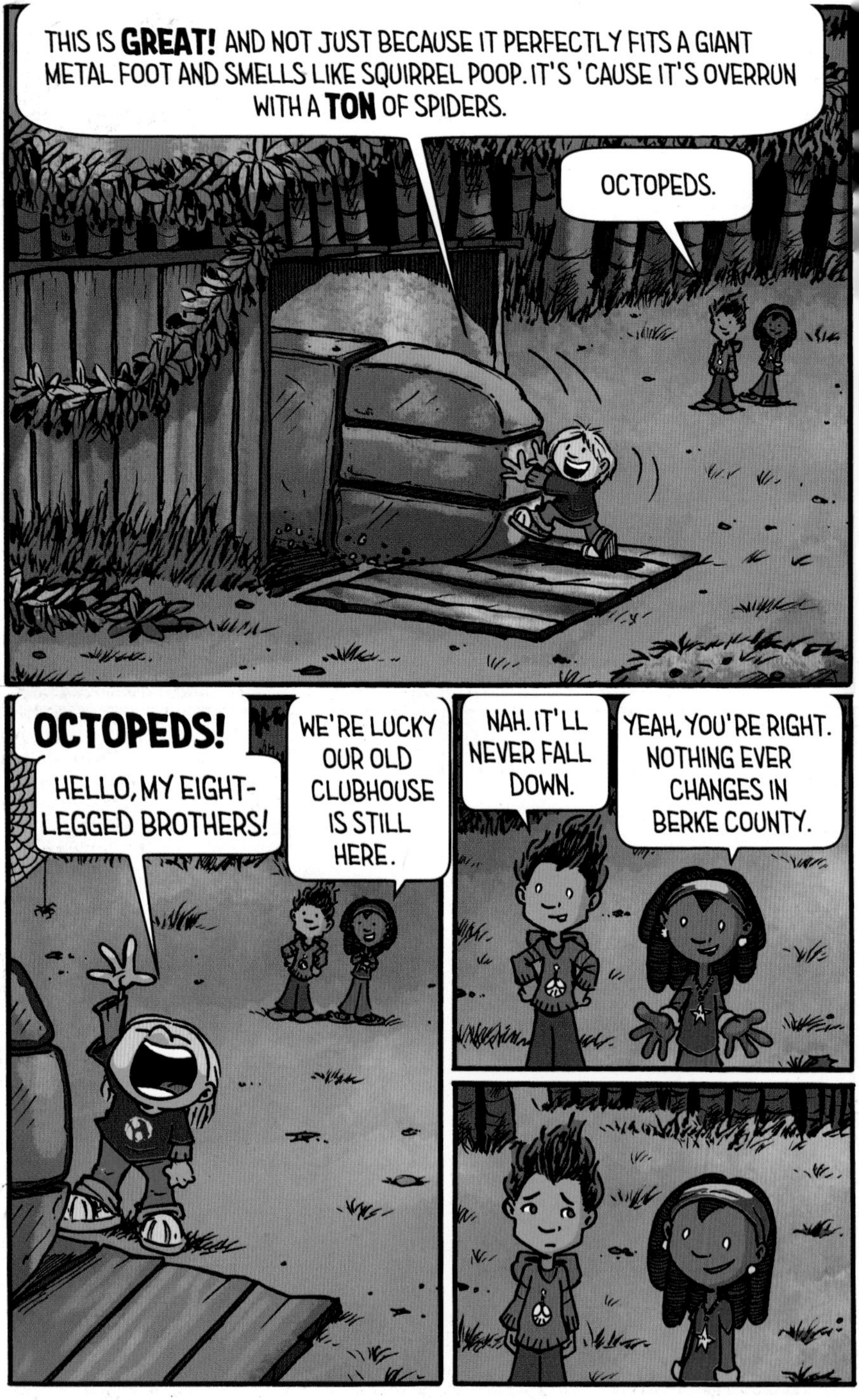
THIS IS GREAT! AND NOT JUST BECAUSE IT PERFECTLY FITS A GIANT METAL FOOT AND SMELLS LIKE SQUIRREL POOP. IT'S 'CAUSE IT'S OVERRUN WITH A TON OF SPIDERS.
OCTOPEDS.
OCTOPEDS!
HELLO, MY EIGHT-LEGGED BROTHERS!
WE'RE LUCKY OUR OLD CLUBHOUSE IS STILL HERE.
NAH. IT'LL NEVER FALL DOWN.
YEAH, YOU'RE RIGHT. NOTHING EVER CHANGES IN BERKE COUNTY.

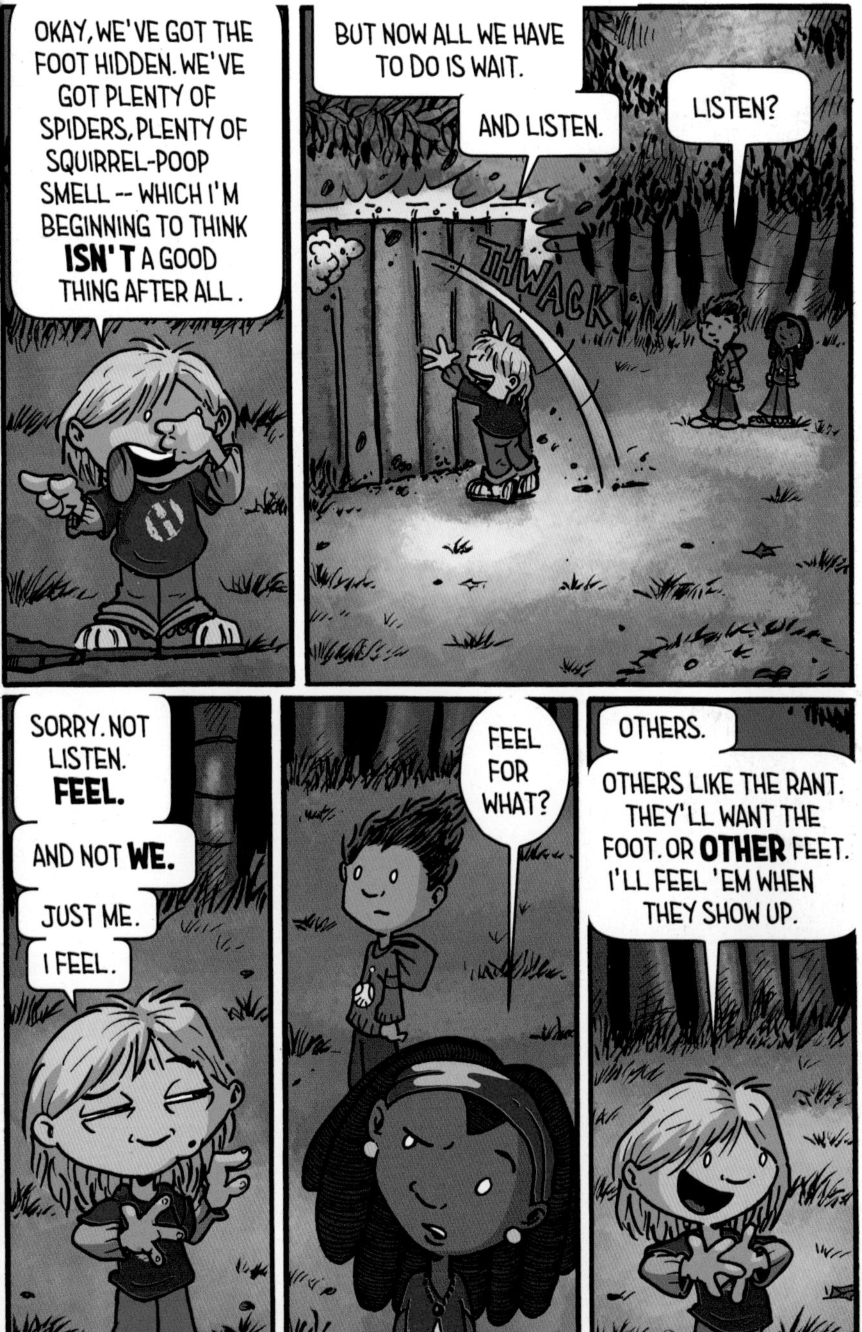
OKAY, WE'VE GOT THE FOOT HIDDEN. WE'VE GOT PLENTY OF SPIDERS, PLENTY OF SQUIRREL-POOP SMELL -- WHICH I'M BEGINNING TO THINK **ISN'T** A GOOD THING AFTER ALL.
BUT NOW ALL WE HAVE TO DO IS WAIT.
AND LISTEN.
THWACK
LISTEN?
SORRY. NOT LISTEN. **FEEL.**
AND NOT **WE.**
JUST ME.
I FEEL.
FEEL FOR WHAT?
OTHERS.
OTHERS LIKE THE RANT. THEY'LL WANT THE FOOT. OR **OTHER** FEET. I'LL FEEL 'EM WHEN THEY SHOW UP.

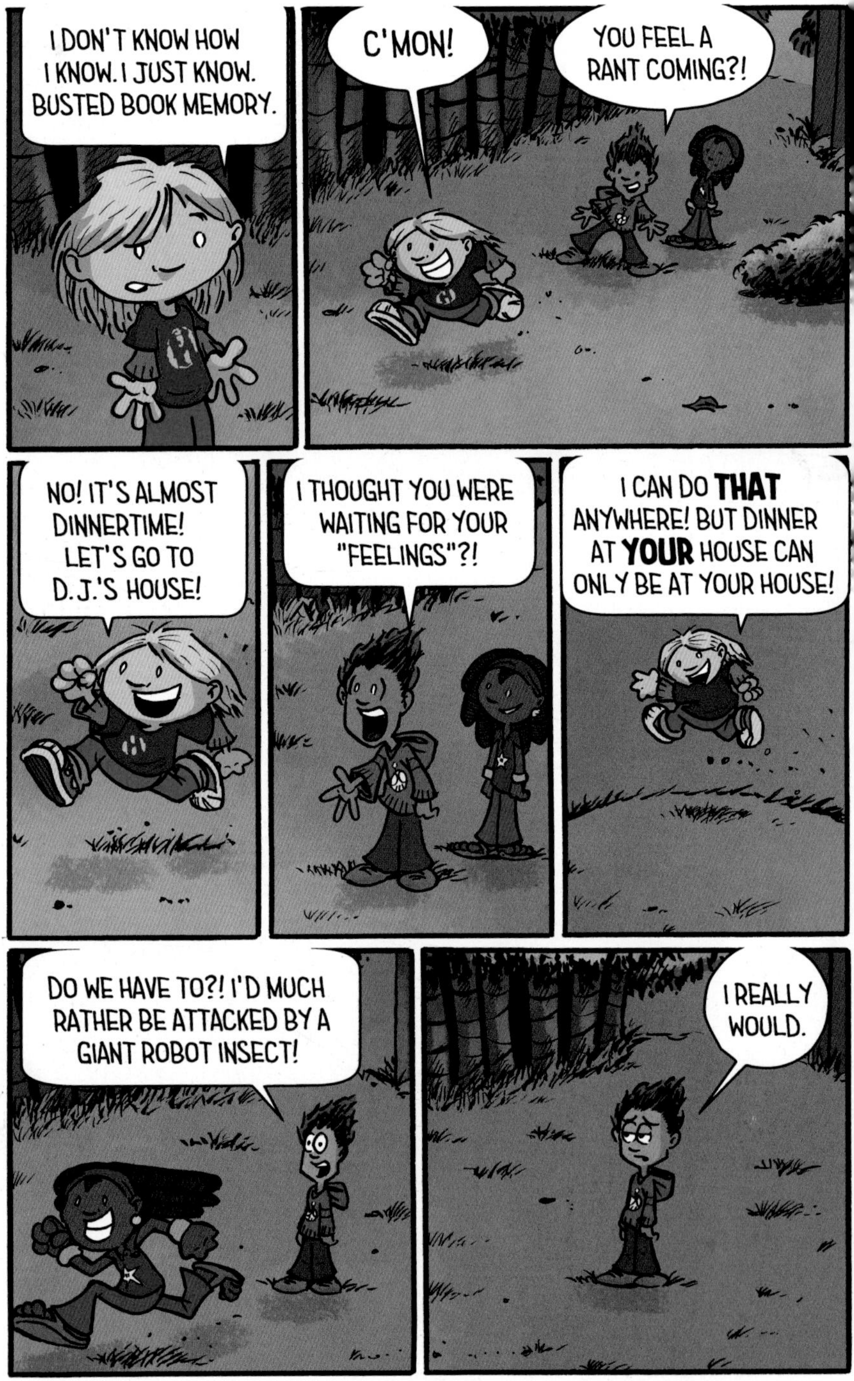
I DON'T KNOW HOW I KNOW. I JUST KNOW. BUSTED BOOK MEMORY.
C'MON!
YOU FEEL A RANT COMING?!
NO! IT'S ALMOST DINNERTIME! LET'S GO TO D.J.'S HOUSE!
I THOUGHT YOU WERE WAITING FOR YOUR "FEELINGS"?!
I CAN DO THAT ANYWHERE! BUT DINNER AT YOUR HOUSE CAN ONLY BE AT YOUR HOUSE!
DO WE HAVE TO?! I'D MUCH RATHER BE ATTACKED BY A GIANT ROBOT INSECT!
I REALLY WOULD.

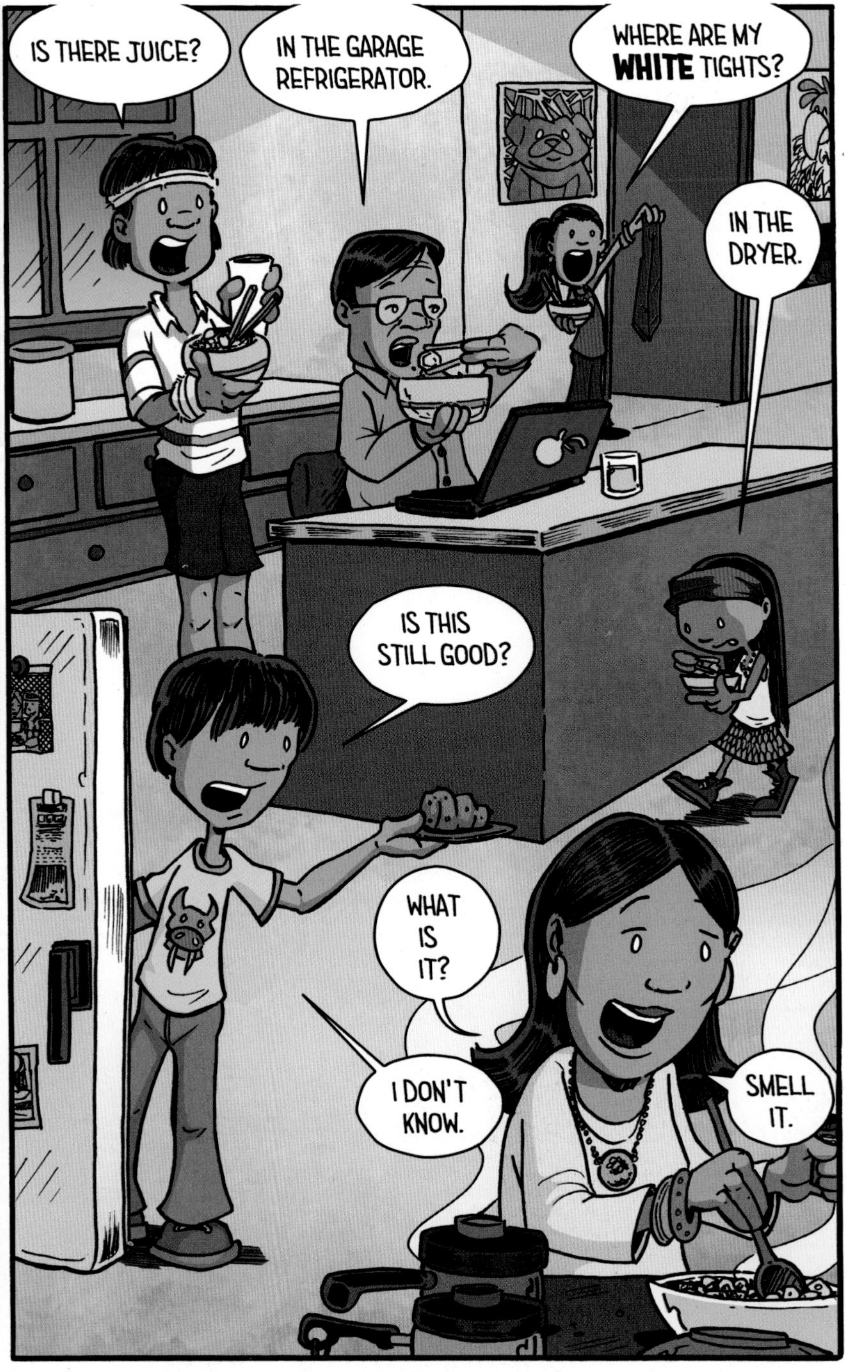
IS THERE JUICE?
IN THE GARAGE REFRIGERATOR.
WHERE ARE MY **WHITE** TIGHTS?
IN THE DRYER.
IS THIS STILL GOOD?
WHAT IS IT?
I DON'T KNOW.
SMELL IT.

CHAPTER

RUN

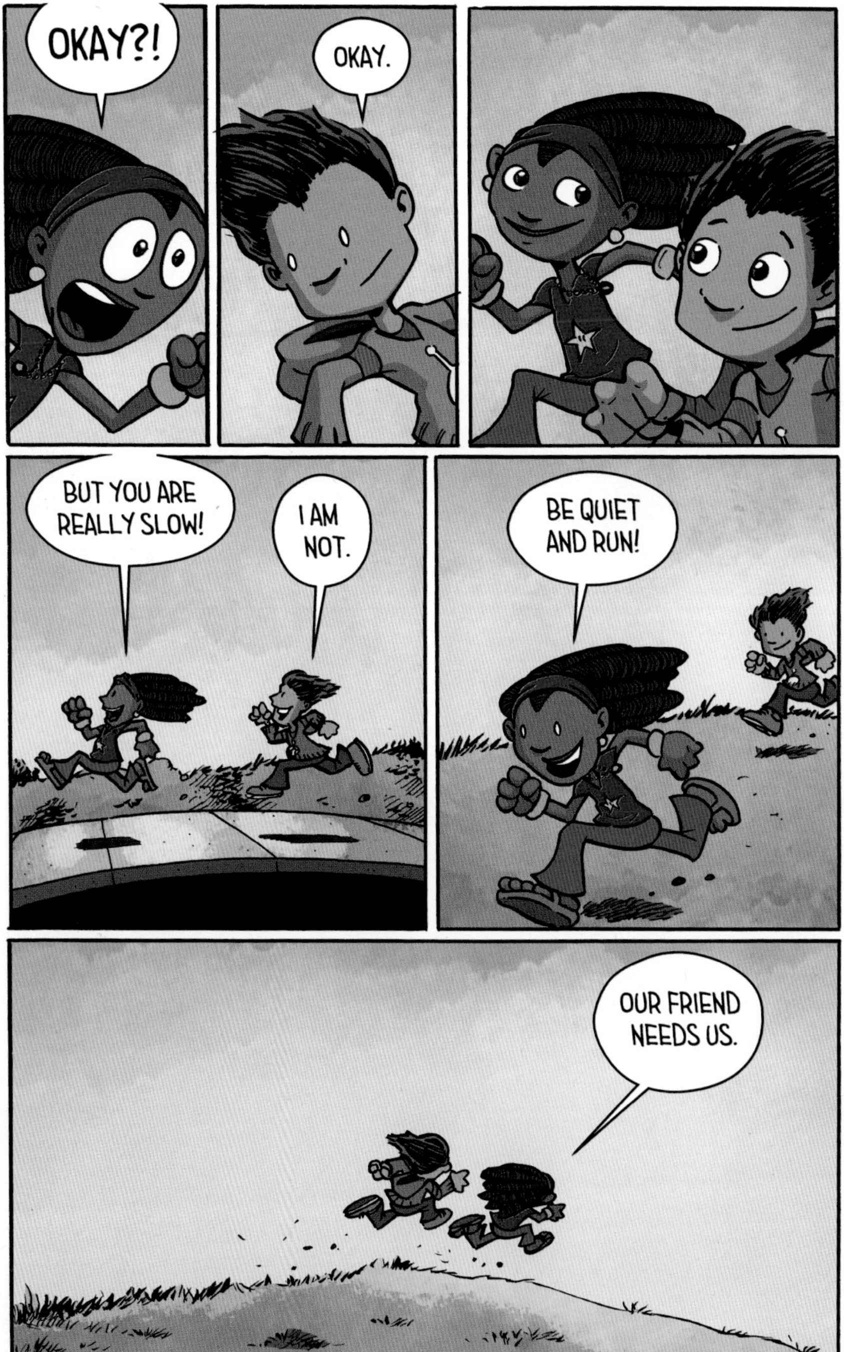
OKAY?!
OKAY.
BUT YOU ARE REALLY SLOW!
I AM NOT.
BE QUIET AND RUN!
OUR FRIEND NEEDS US.

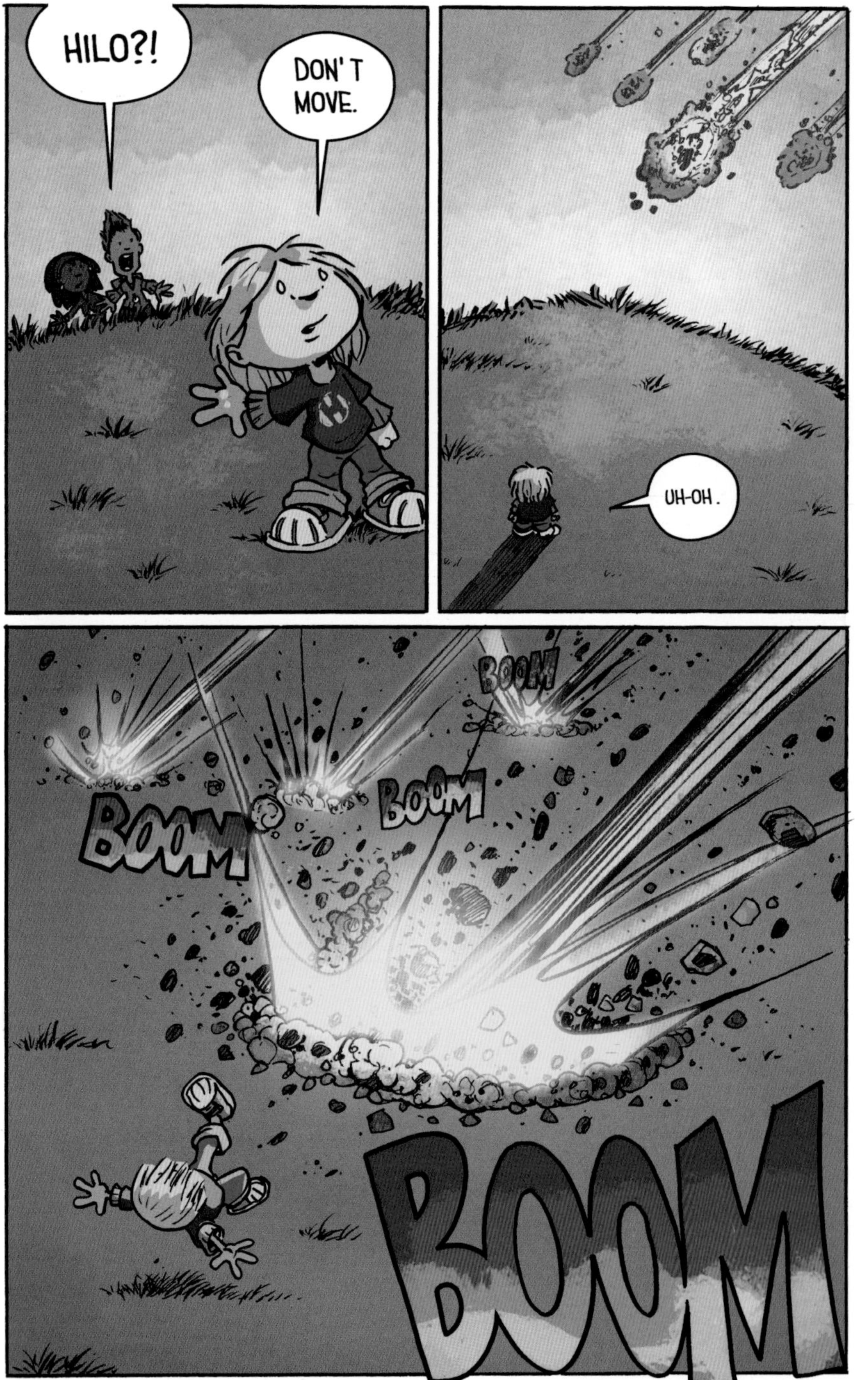
HILO?!
DON'T MOVE.
UH-OH.
BOOM
BOOM
BOOM
BOOM

128

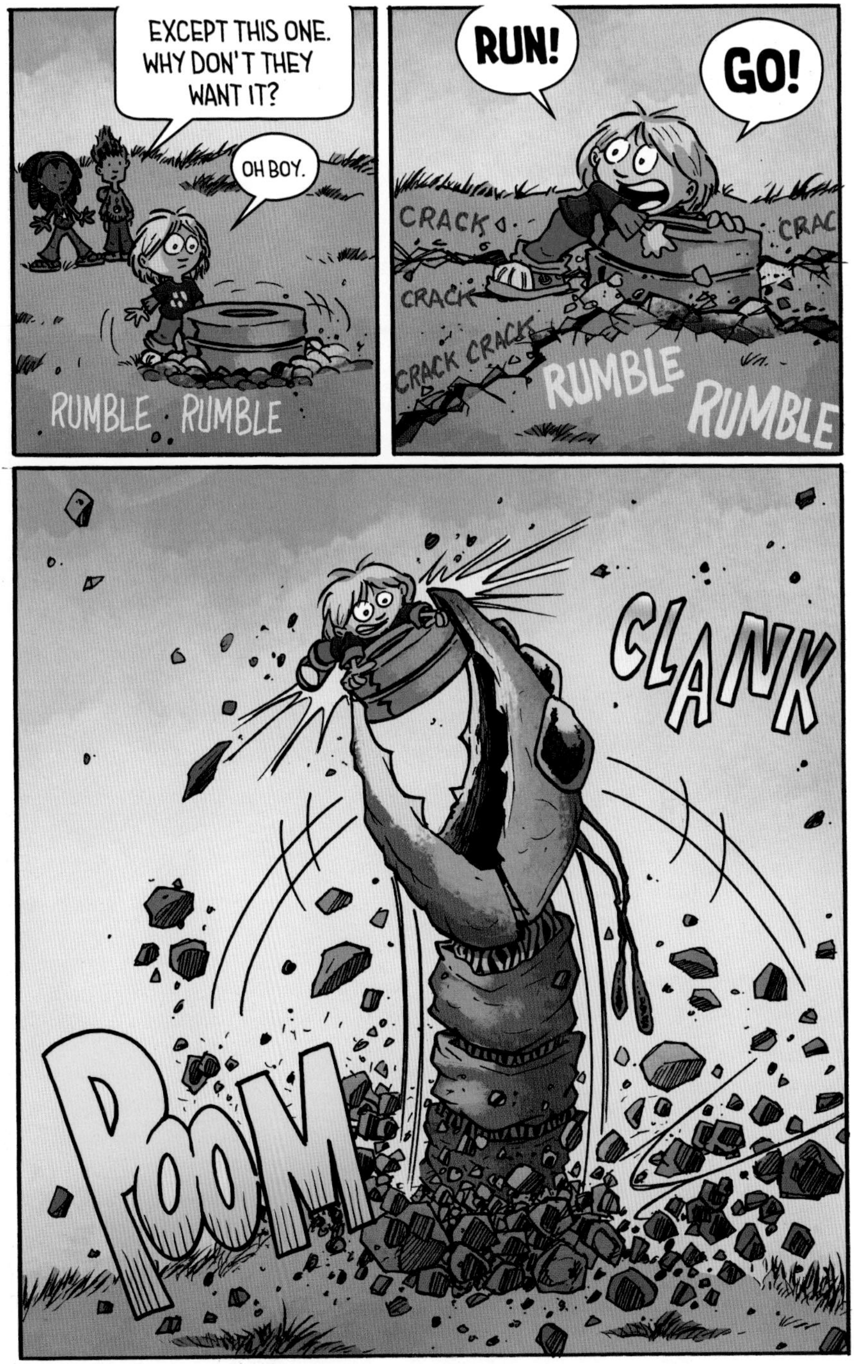
EXCEPT THIS ONE. WHY DON'T THEY WANT IT?
OH BOY.
RUMBLE RUMBLE
RUN!
GO!
CRACK
CRACK
CRACK CRACK
CRAC
RUMBLE
RUMBLE
CLANK
POOM

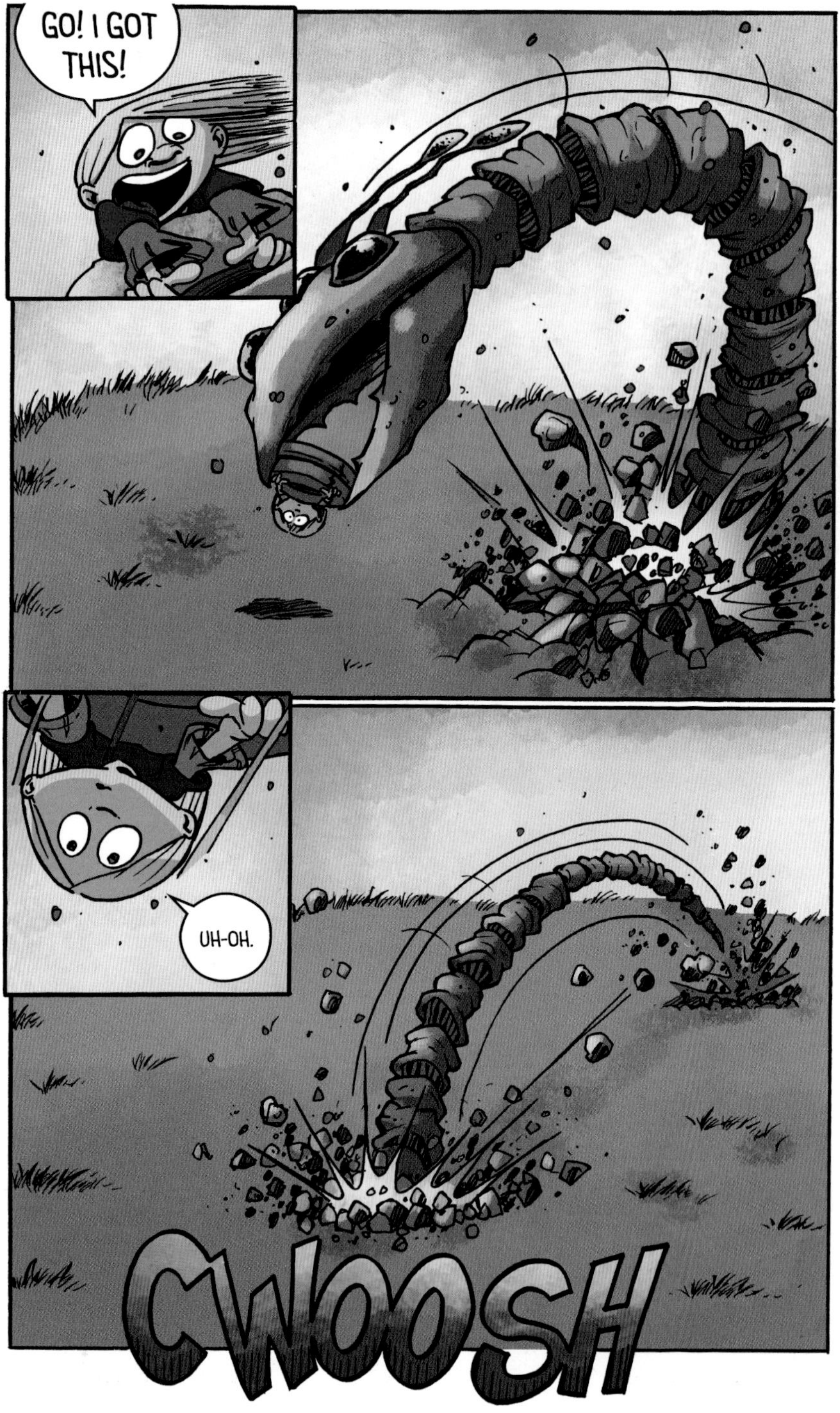
GO! I GOT THIS!
UH-OH.
CWOOSH

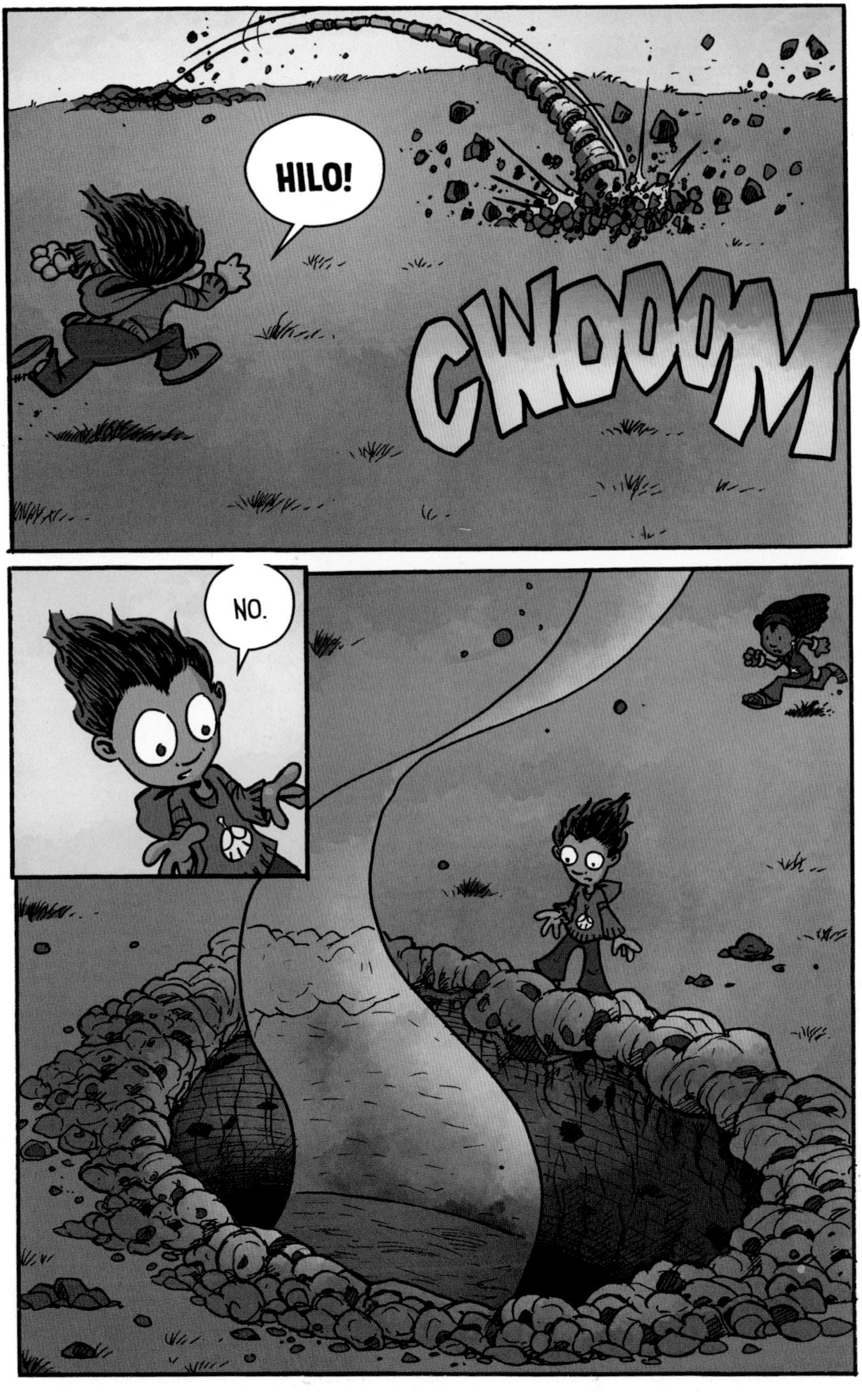
HILO!
CHOOOM
NO.

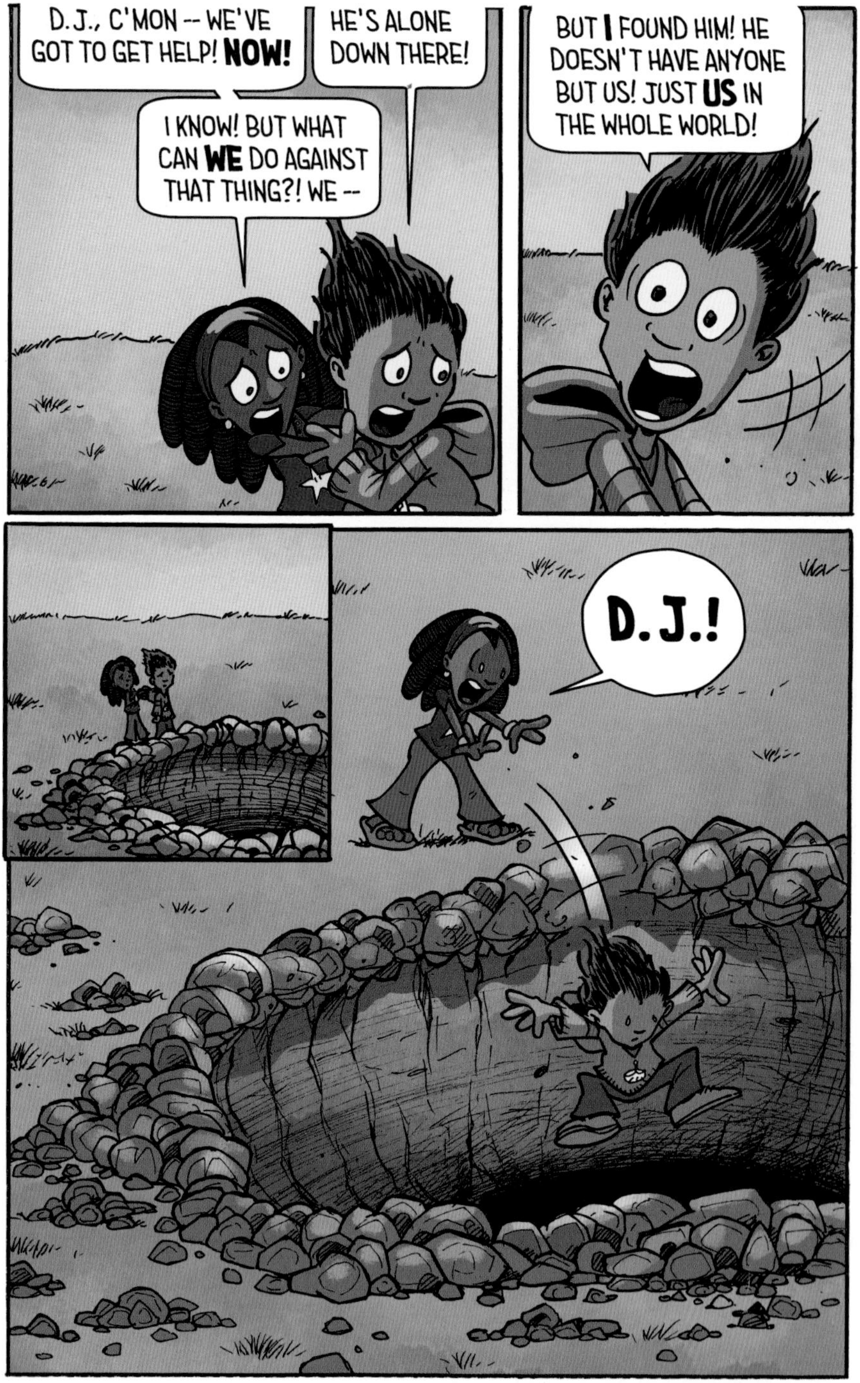
D.J., C'MON -- WE'VE GOT TO GET HELP! **NOW!**
I KNOW! BUT WHAT CAN **WE** DO AGAINST THAT THING?! WE --
HE'S ALONE DOWN THERE!
BUT **I** FOUND HIM! HE DOESN'T HAVE ANYONE BUT US! JUST **US** IN THE WHOLE WORLD!
D.J.!

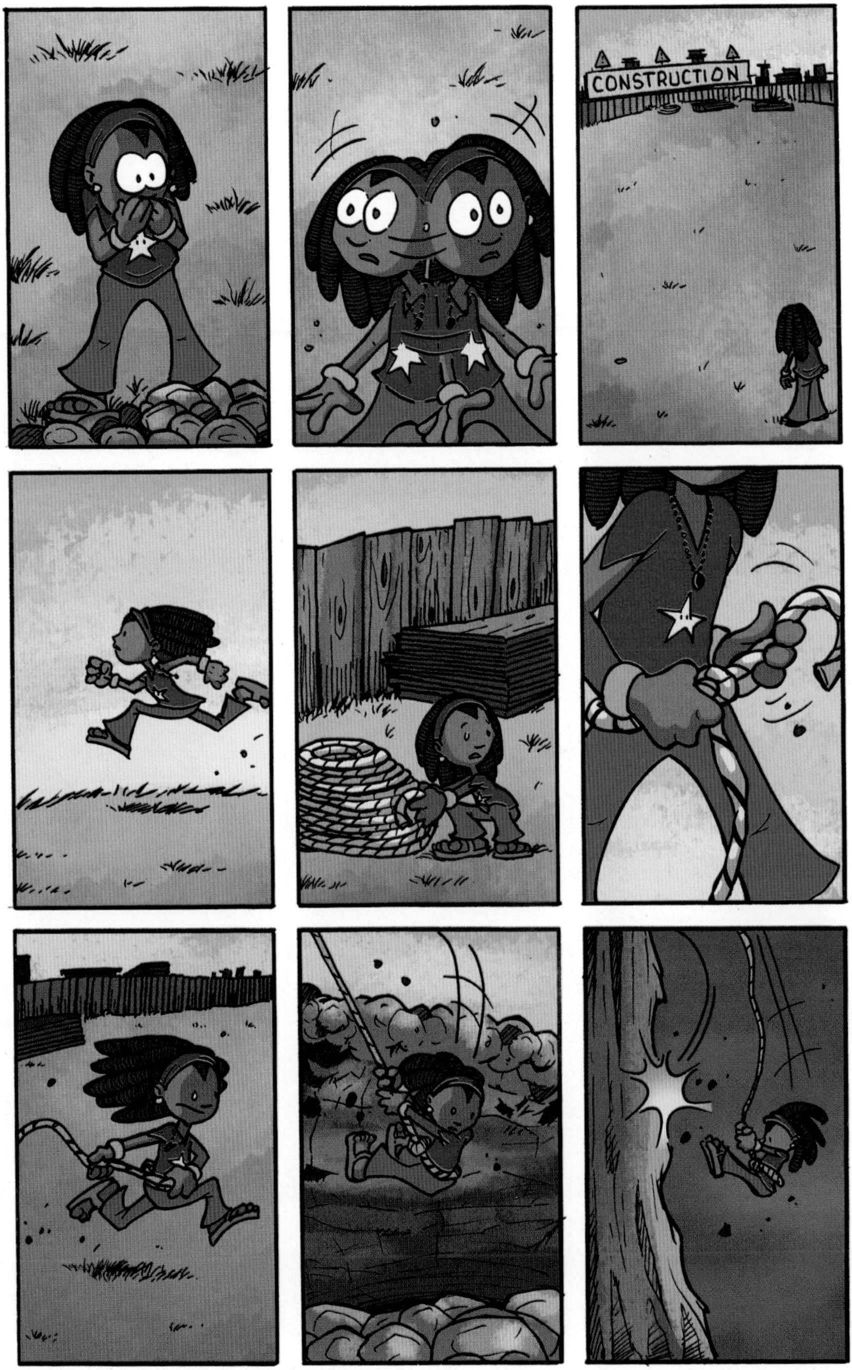
CONSTRUCTION

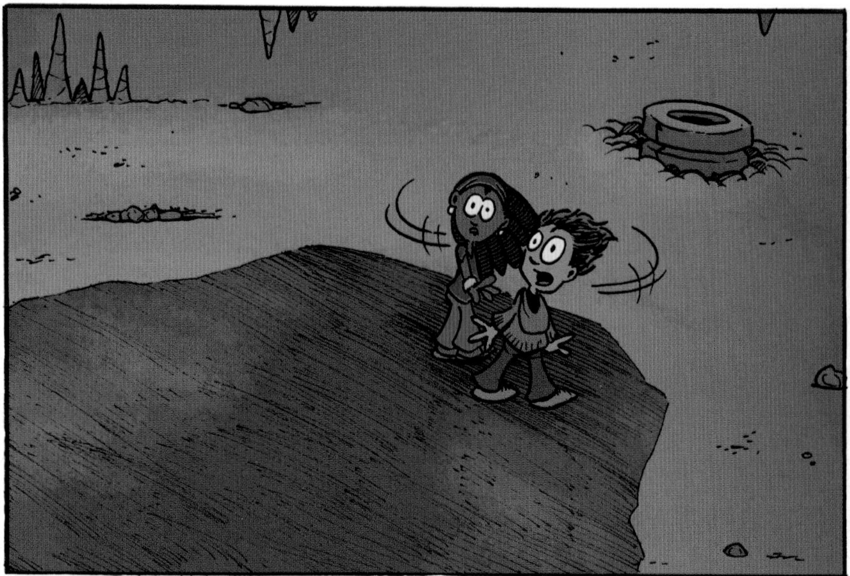

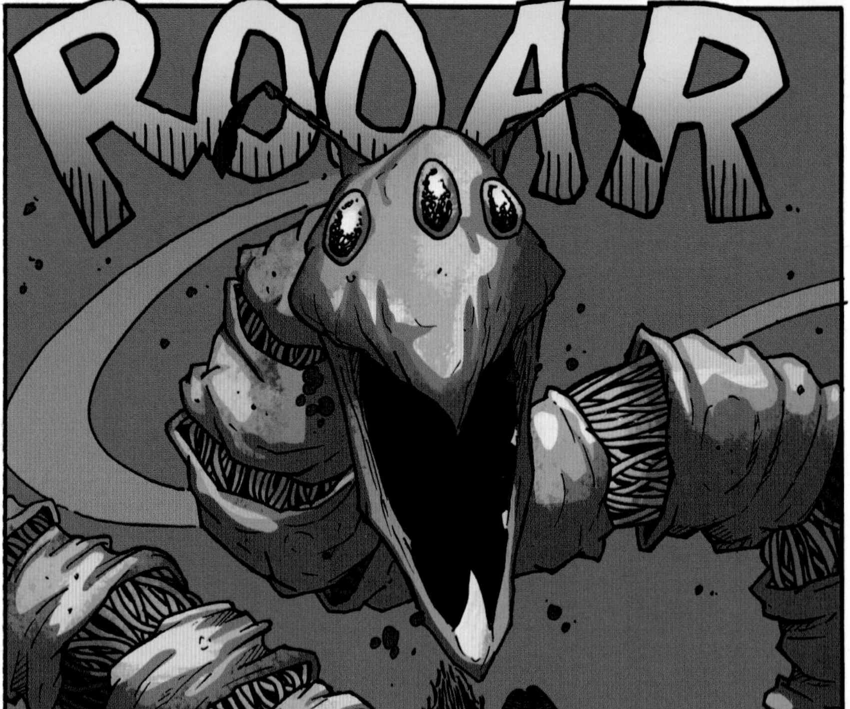
ROOAR

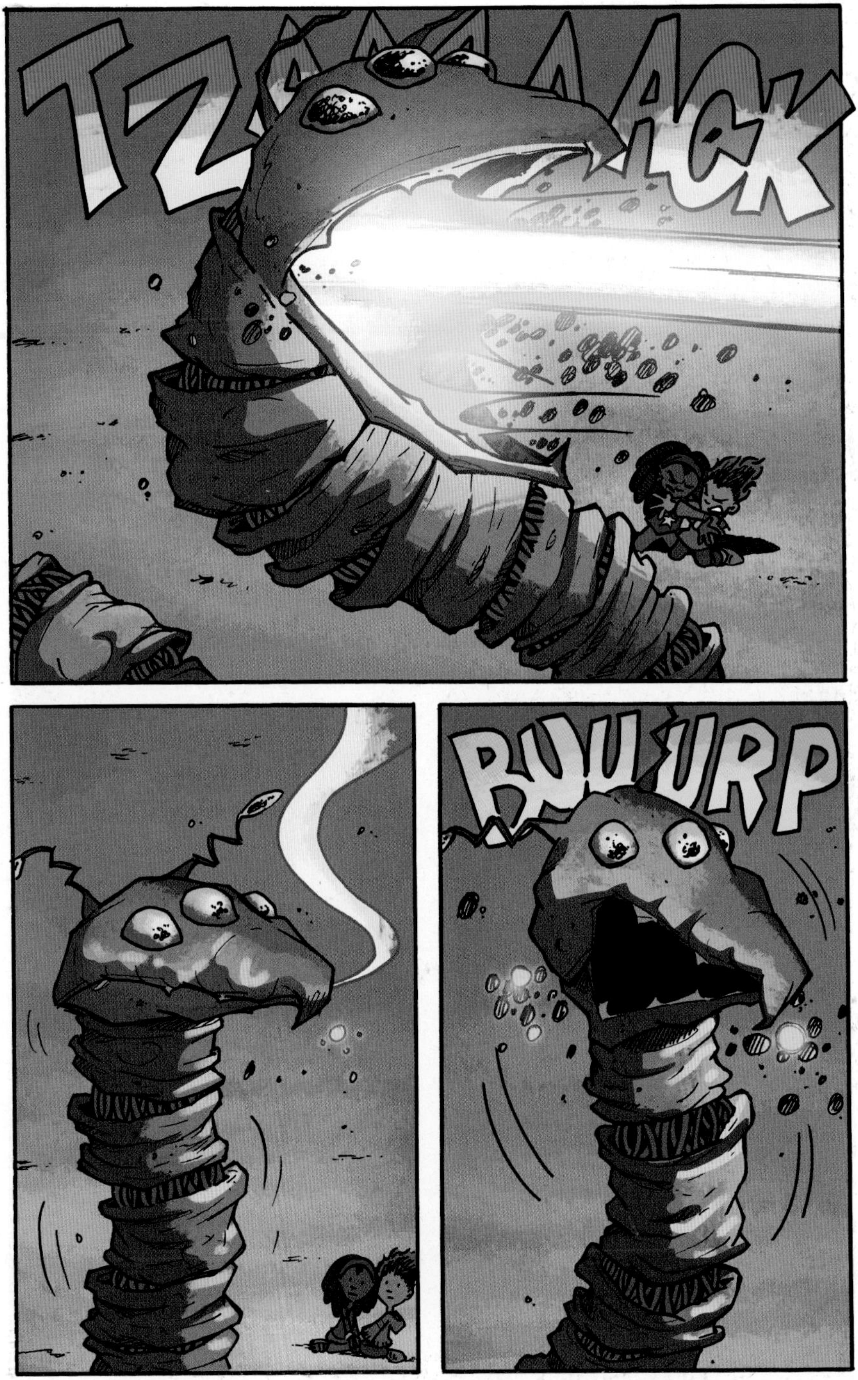
TZAAAAACK
BUUURP

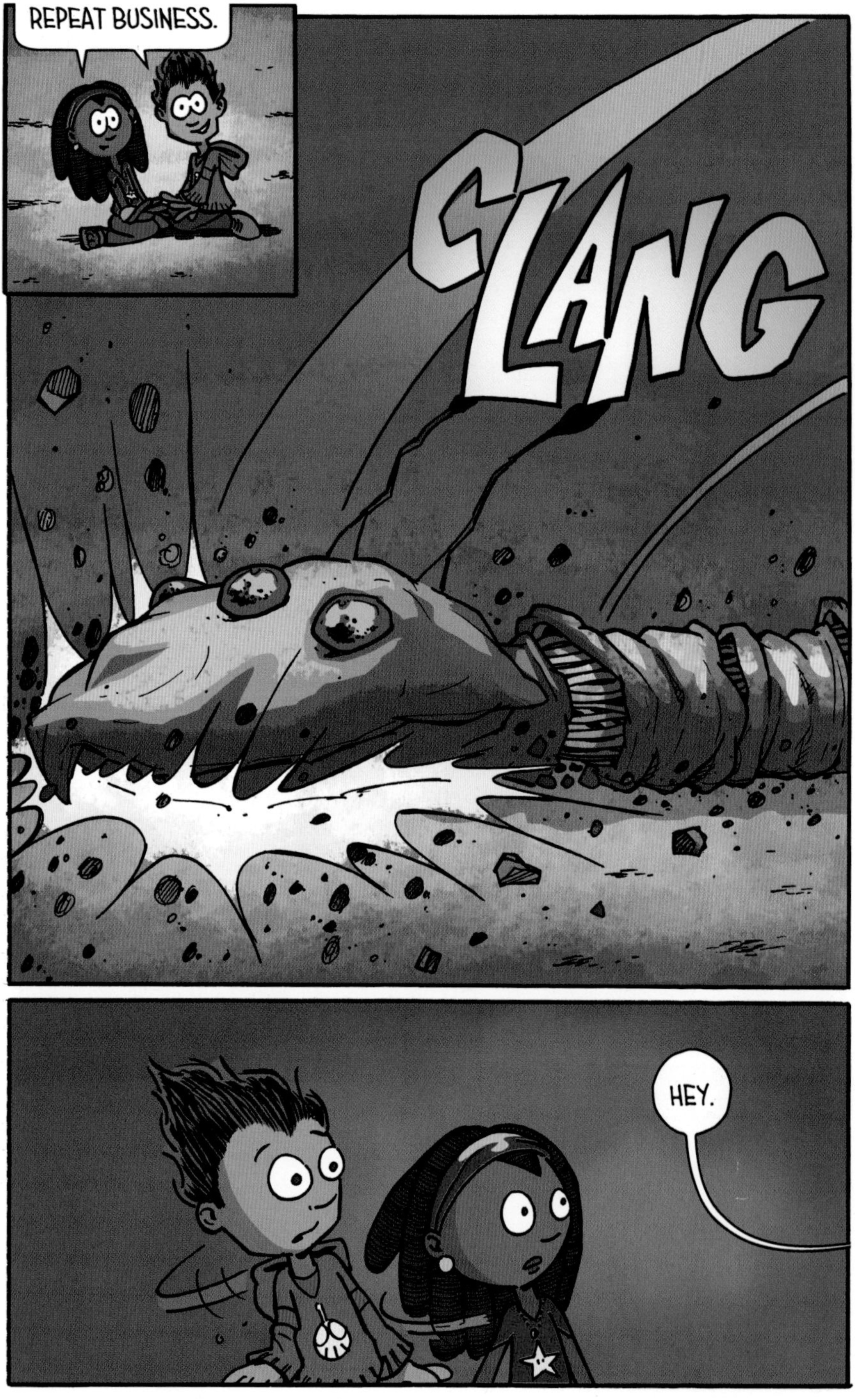
REPEAT BUSINESS.
CLANG
HEY.

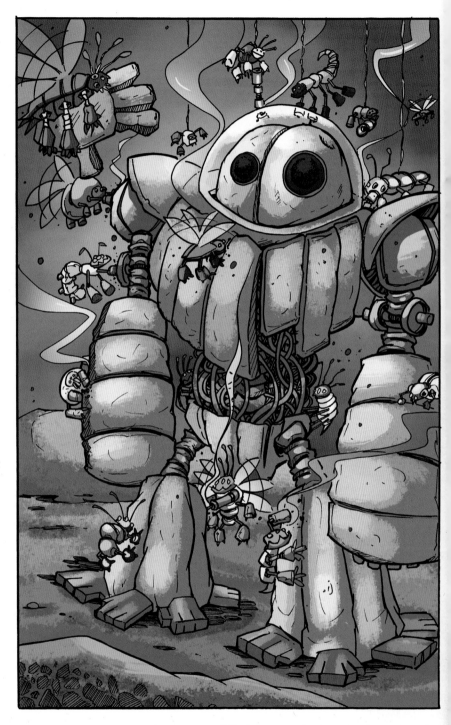

CHAPTER

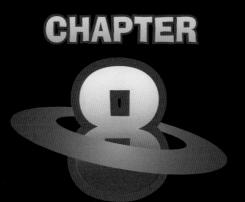

I STOP THEM WHEN THEY GO WRONG

144

145

147

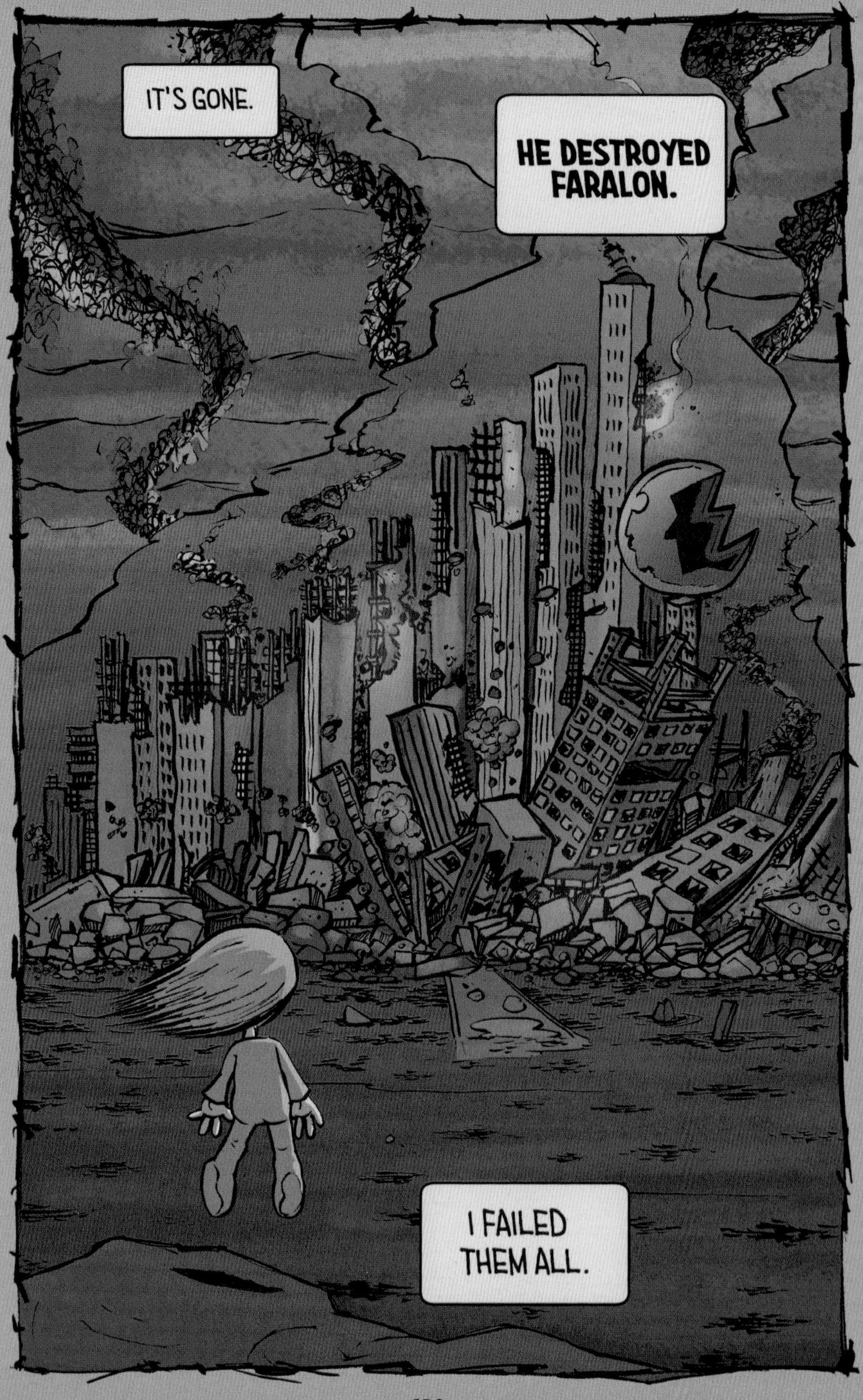
IT'S GONE.
HE DESTROYED FARALON.
I FAILED THEM ALL.

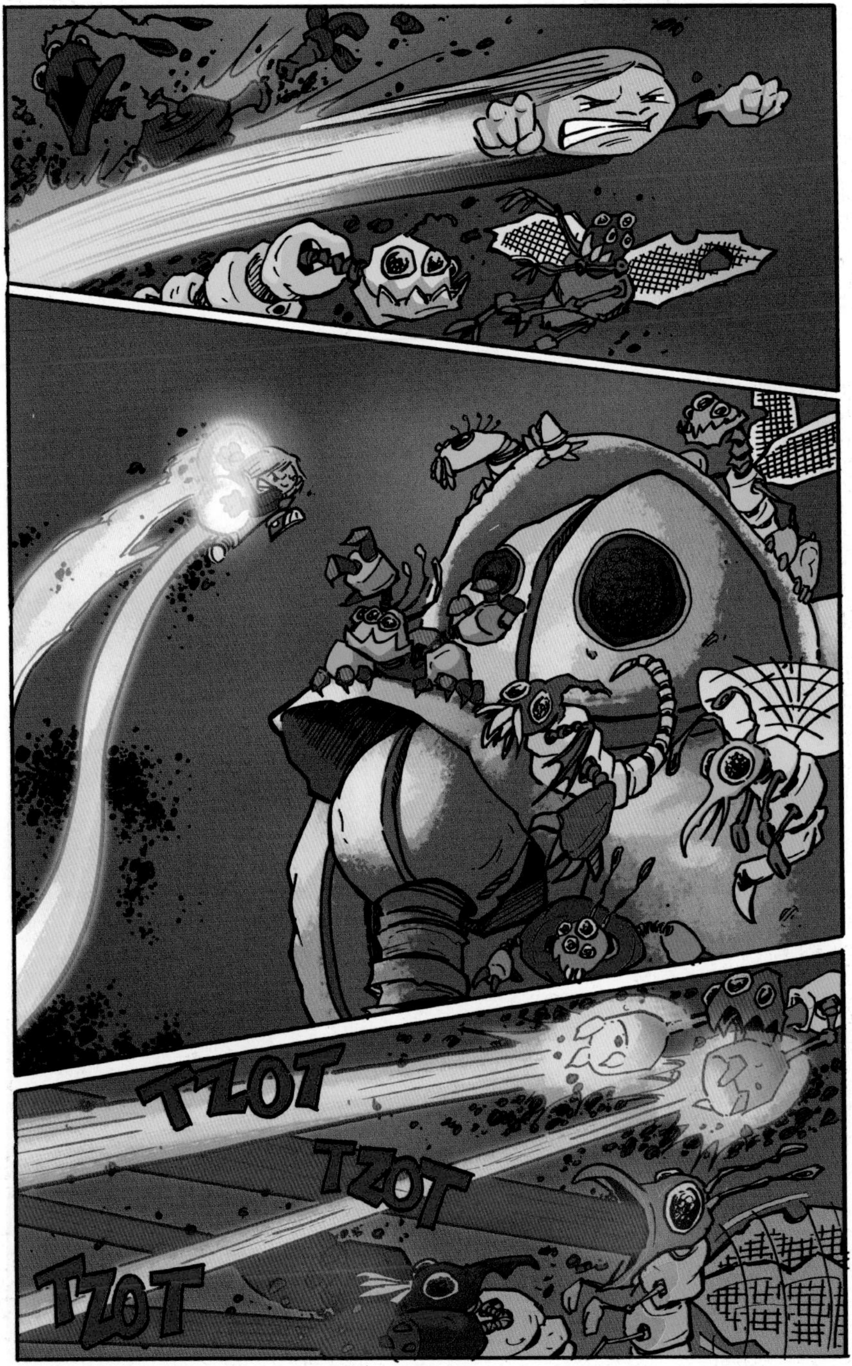
TZOT
TZOT
TZOT

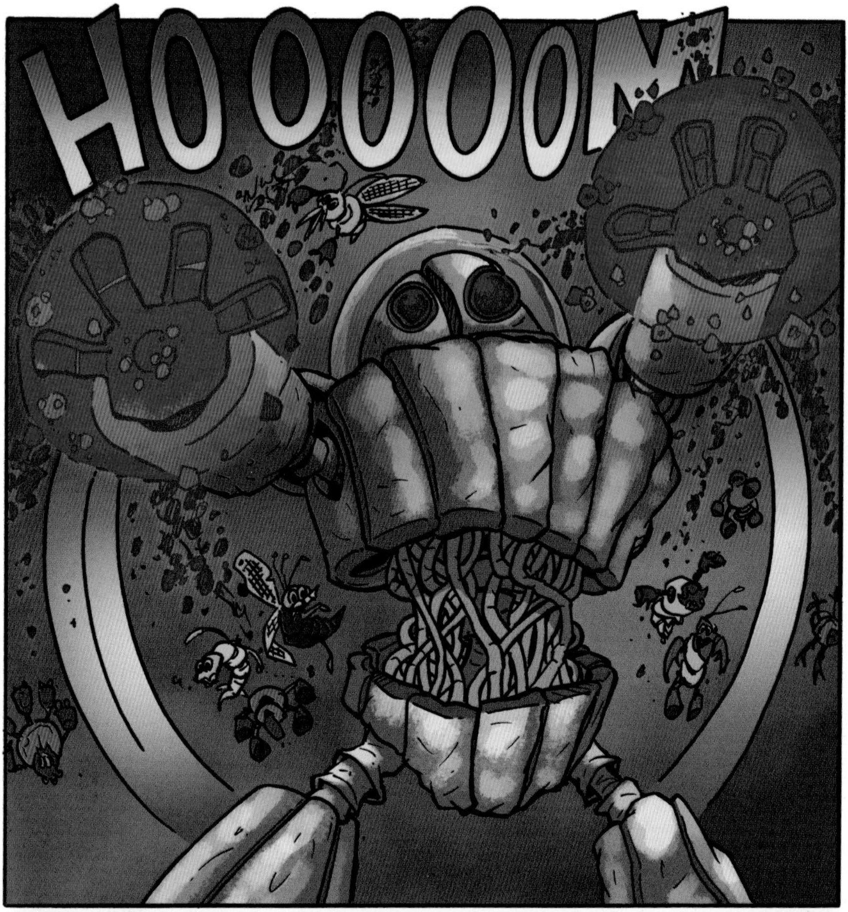
HOOOOOM

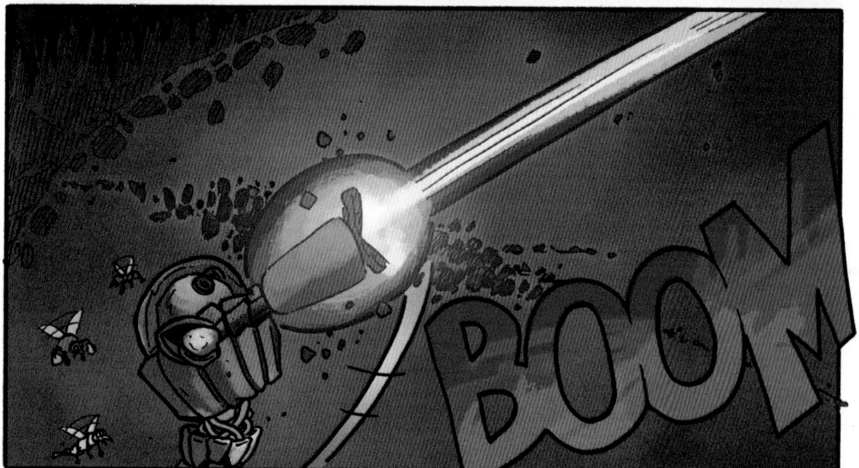
BOOM

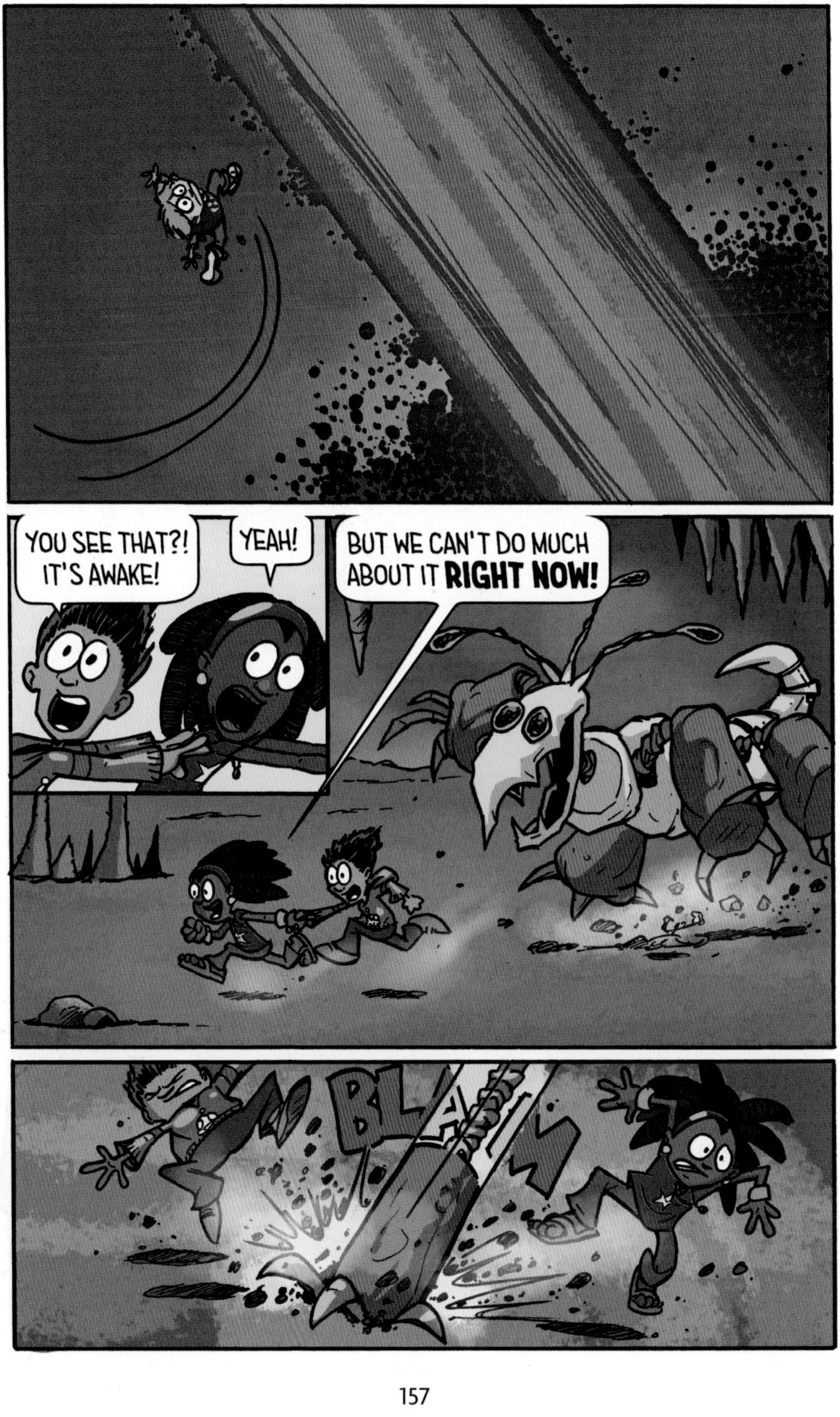
YOU SEE THAT?! IT'S AWAKE!
YEAH!
BUT WE CAN'T DO MUCH ABOUT IT **RIGHT NOW!**

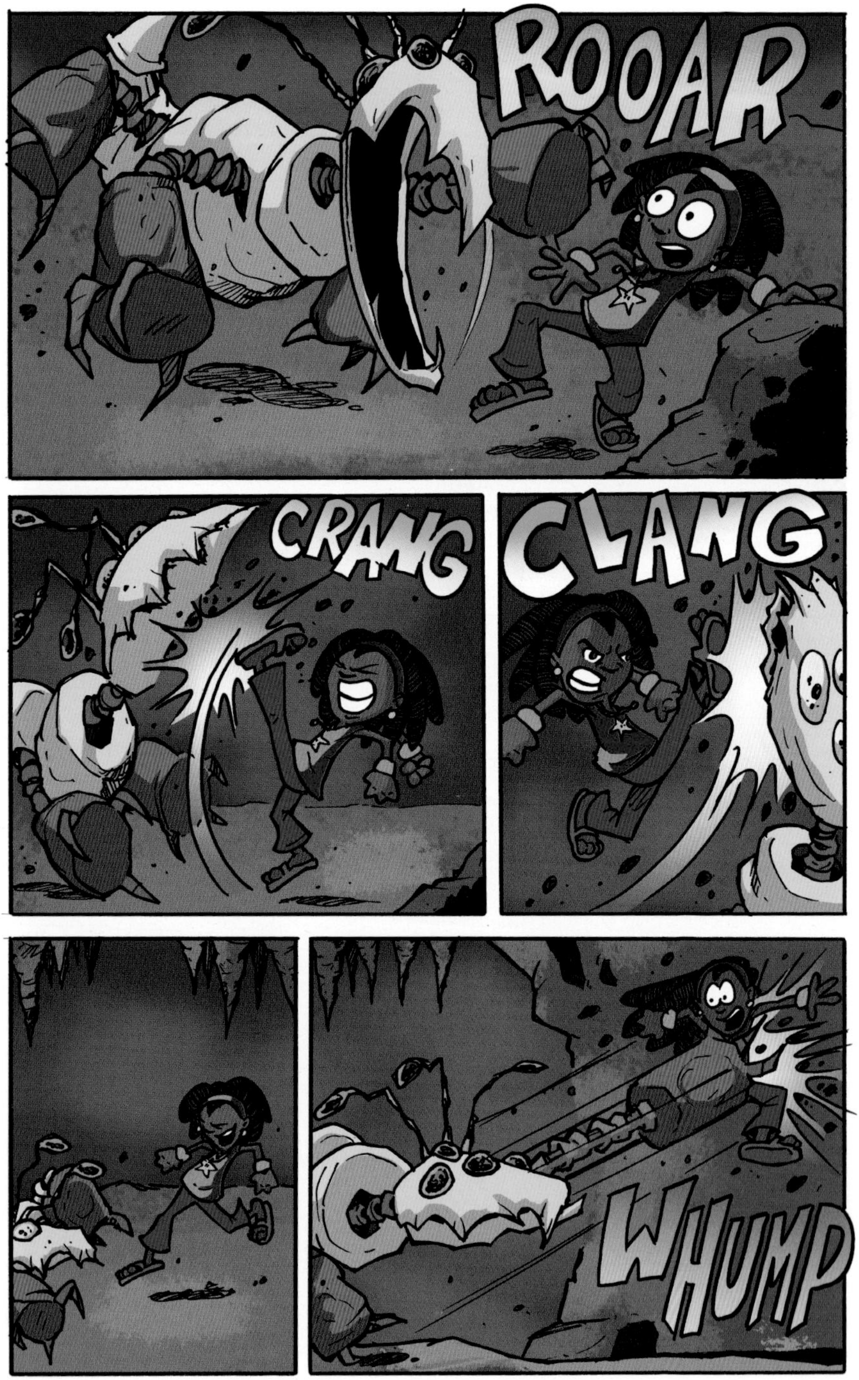
ROOAR
CRANG
CLANG
WHUMP

159

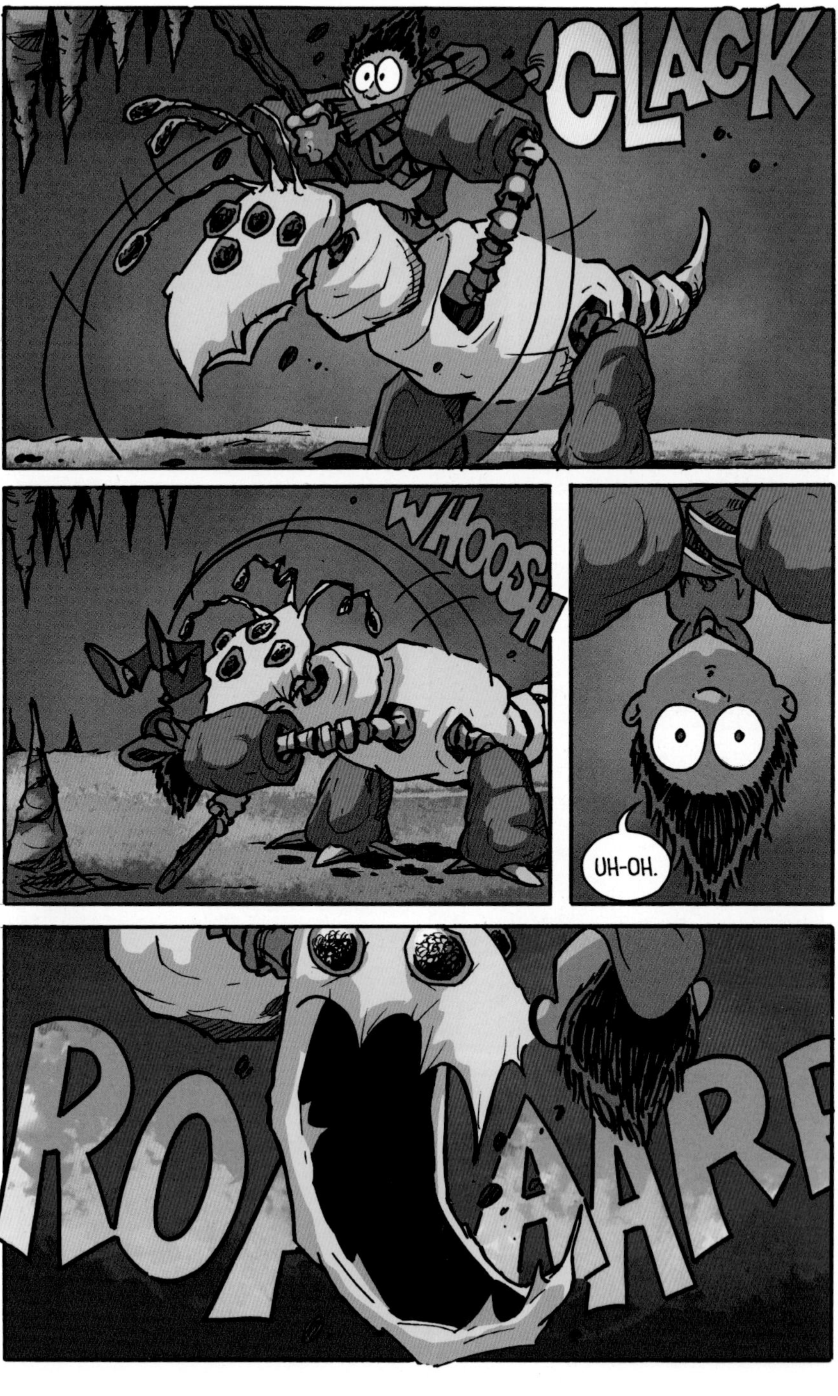
CLACK
WHOOSH
UH-OH.
ROAARR

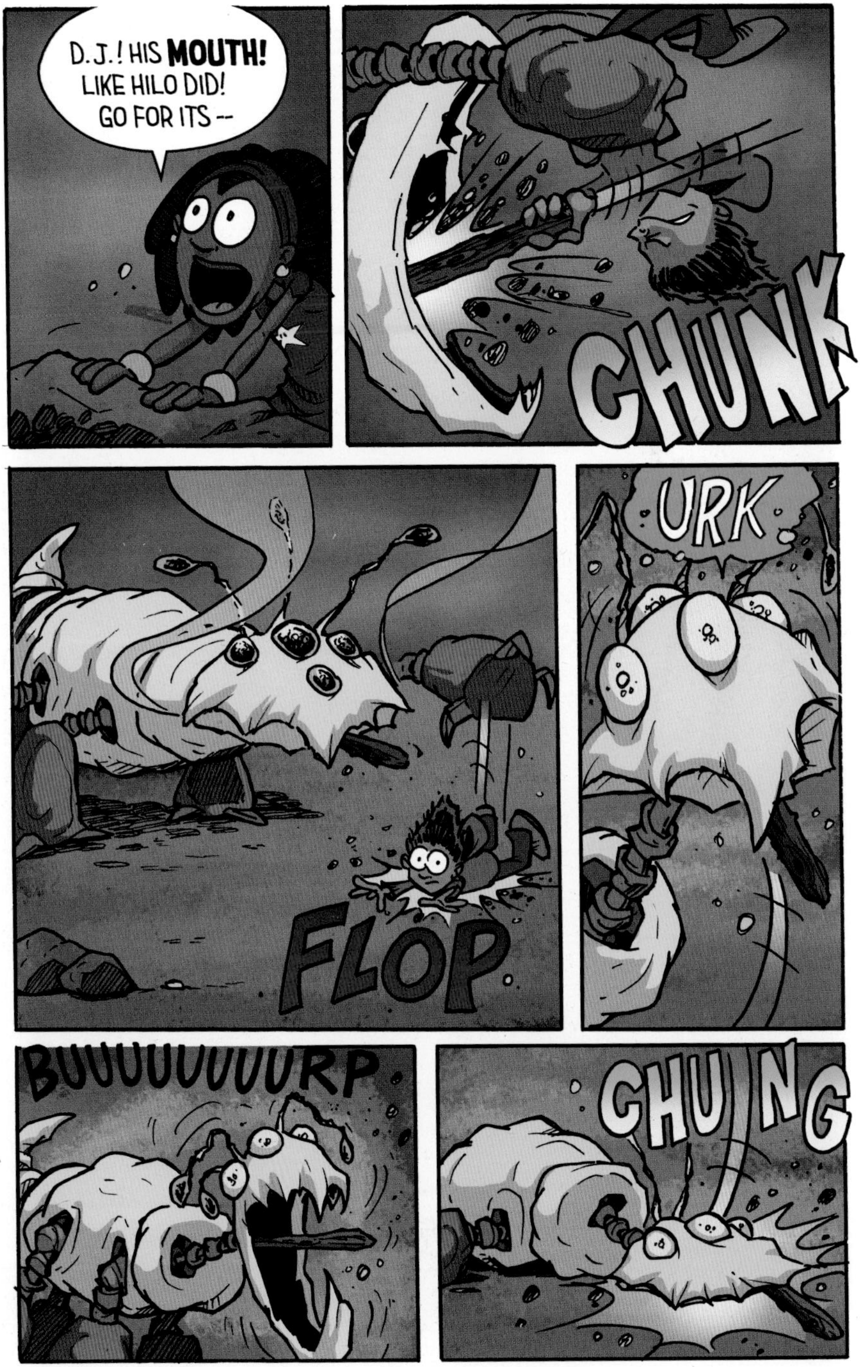
D.J.! HIS **MOUTH!** LIKE HILO DID! GO FOR ITS --
CHUNK
URK
FLOP
BUUUUUUUURP
CHUNG

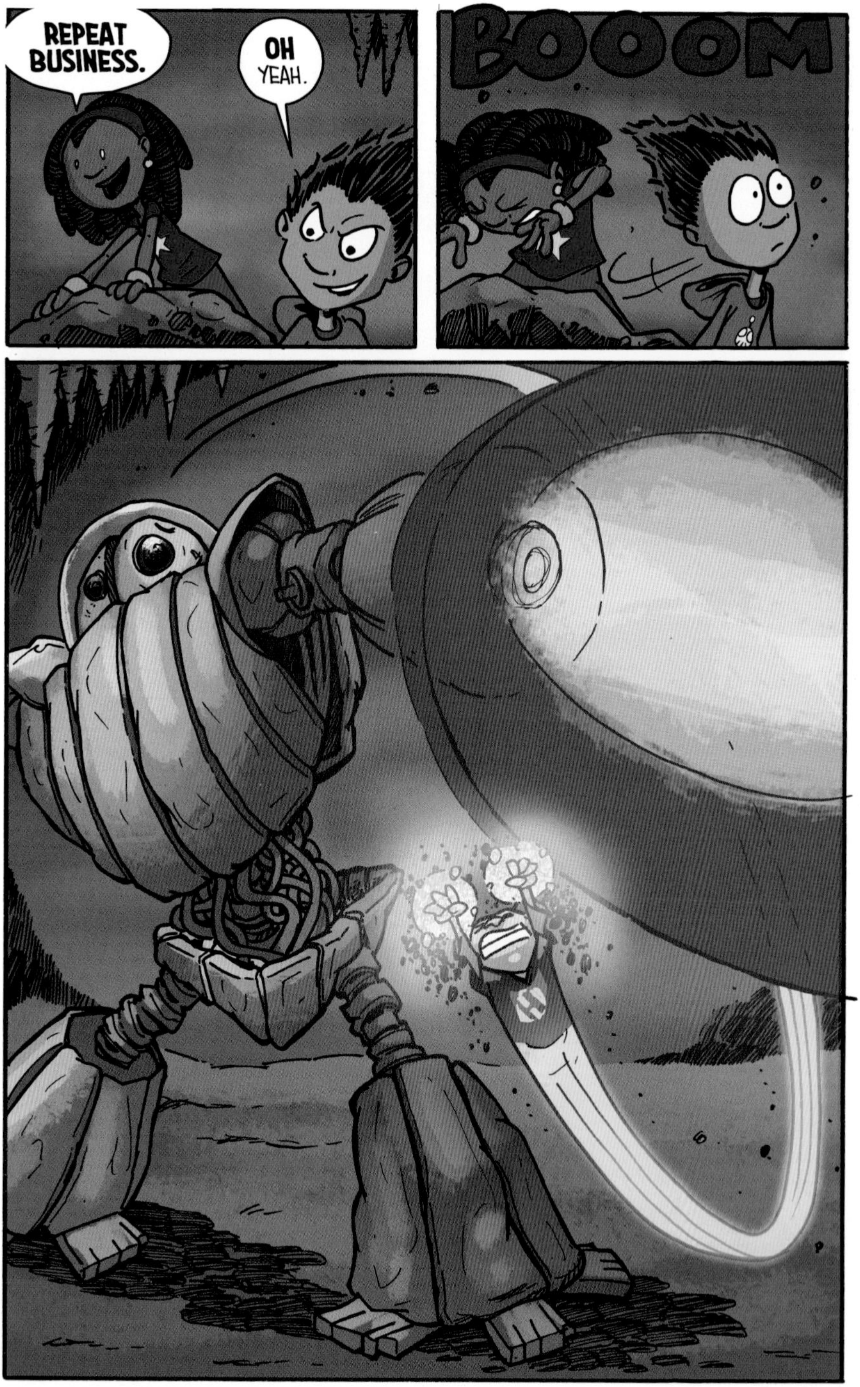
REPEAT BUSINESS.
OH YEAH.
BOOOM

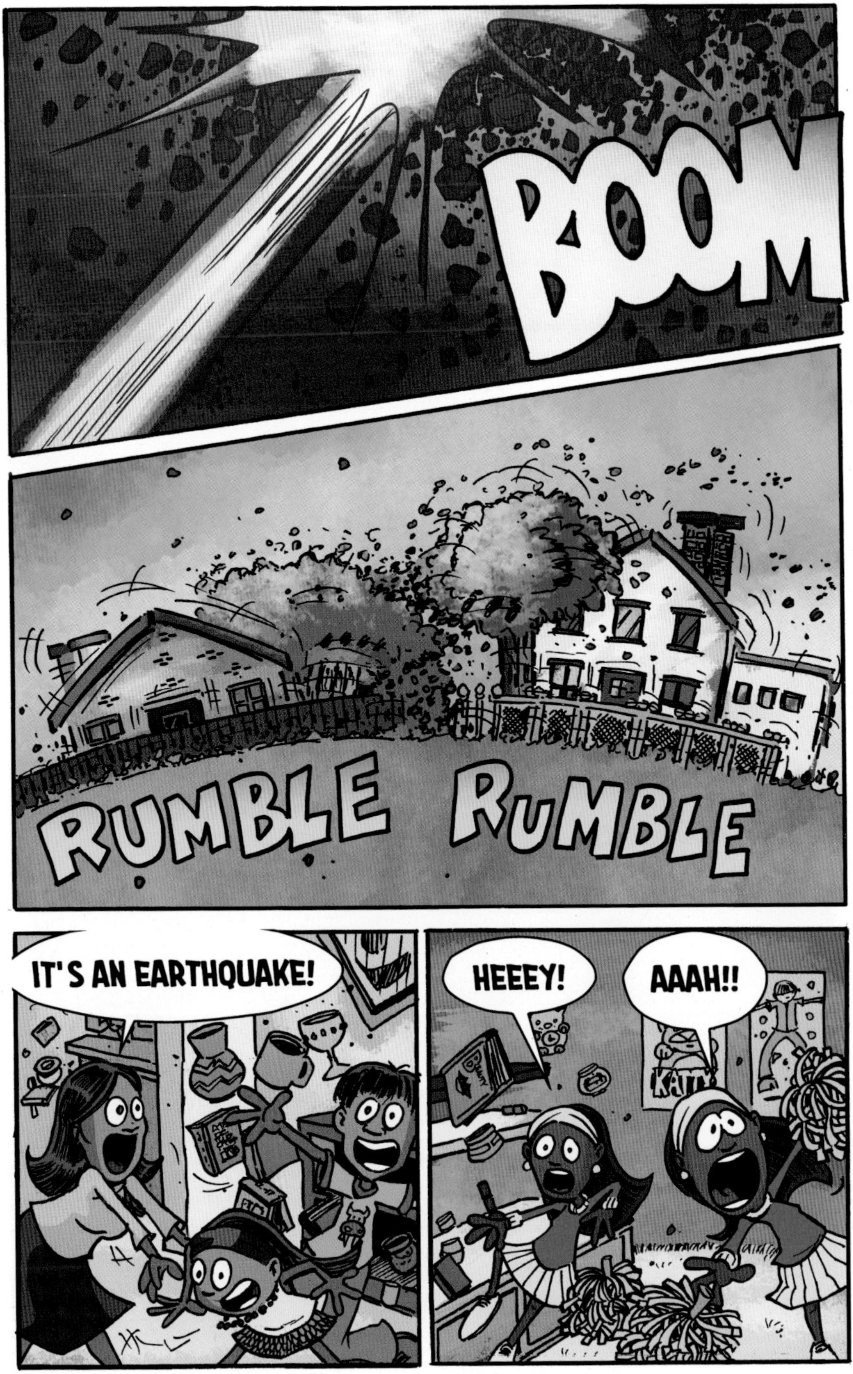
BOOM
RUMBLE RUMBLE
IT'S AN EARTHQUAKE!
HEEEY!
AAAH!!

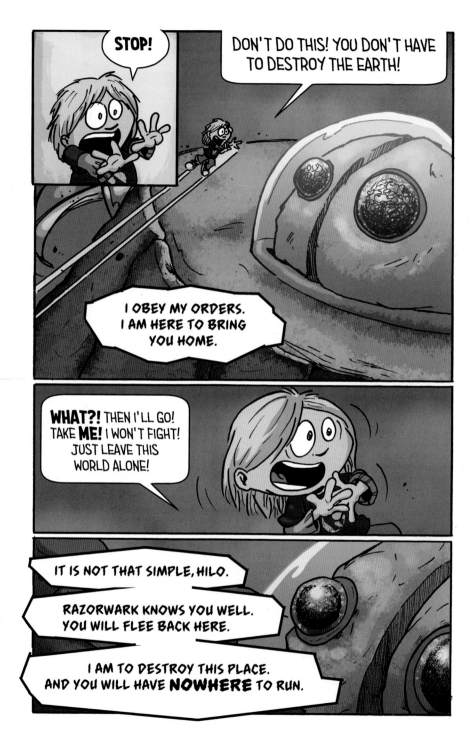

164

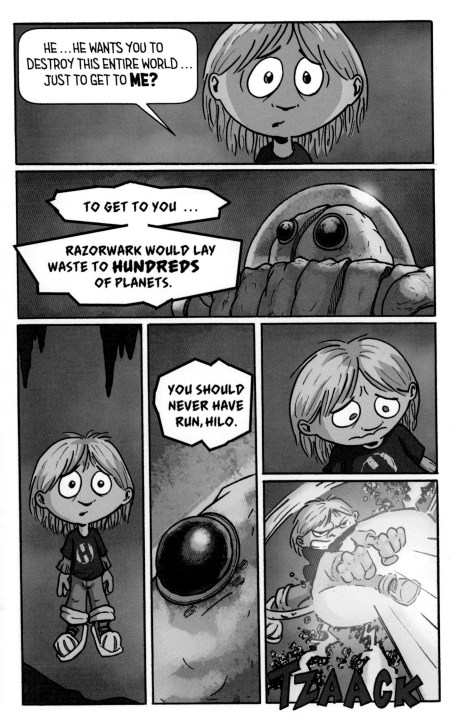

166

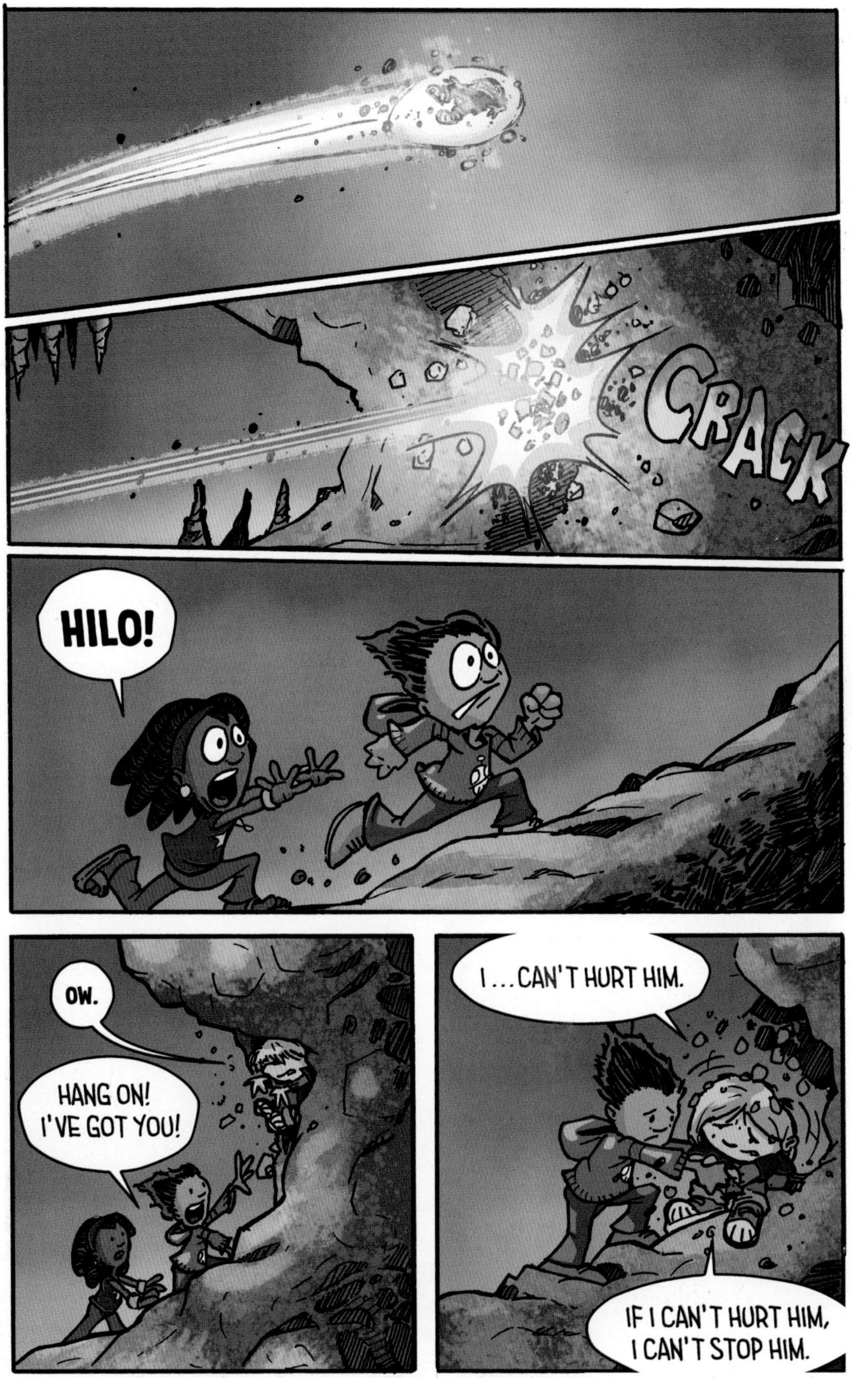
CRACK
HILO!
OW.
HANG ON! I'VE GOT YOU!
I...CAN'T HURT HIM.
IF I CAN'T HURT HIM, I CAN'T STOP HIM.

168

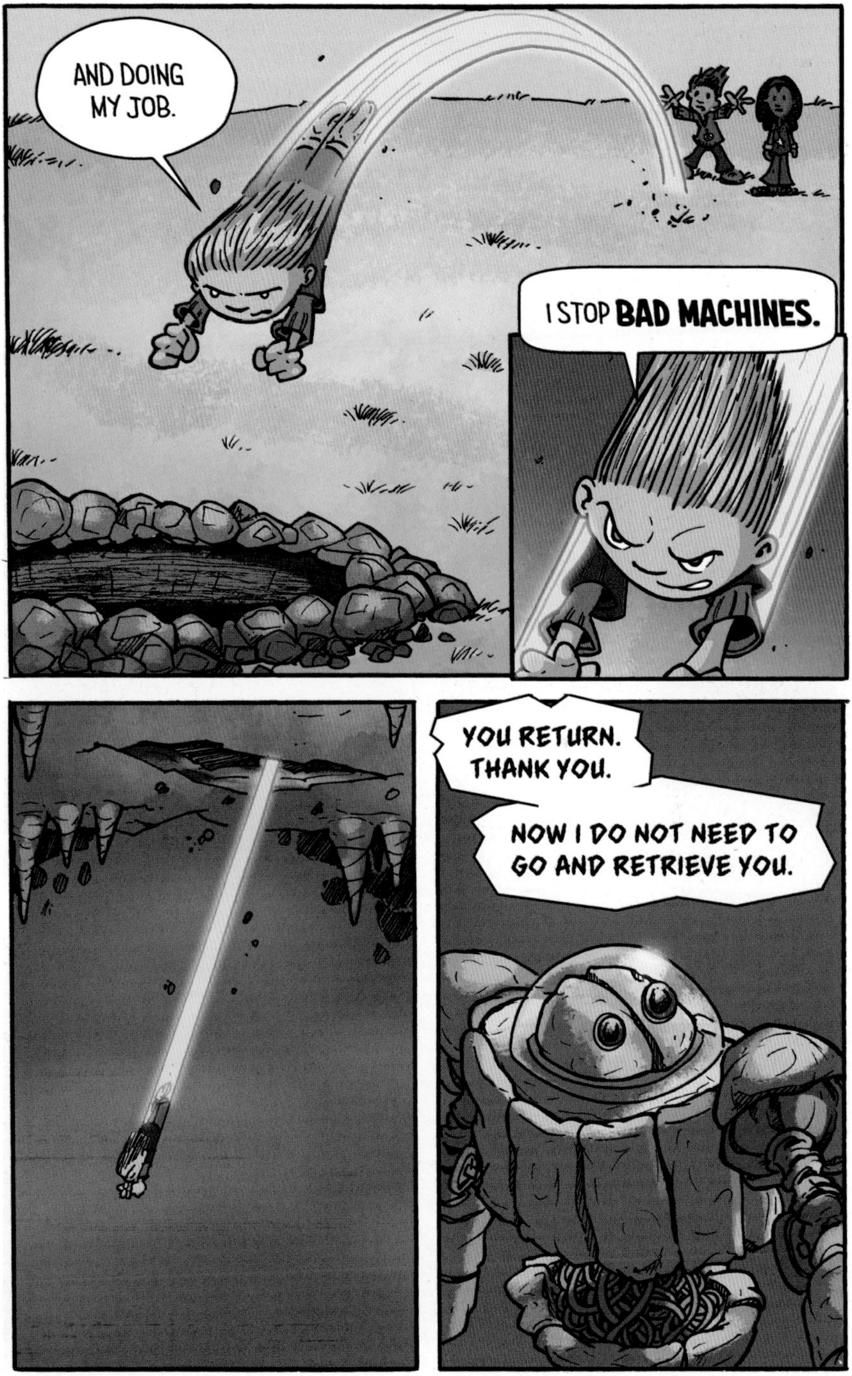
AND DOING MY JOB.
I STOP BAD MACHINES.
YOU RETURN. THANK YOU.
NOW I DO NOT NEED TO GO AND RETRIEVE YOU.

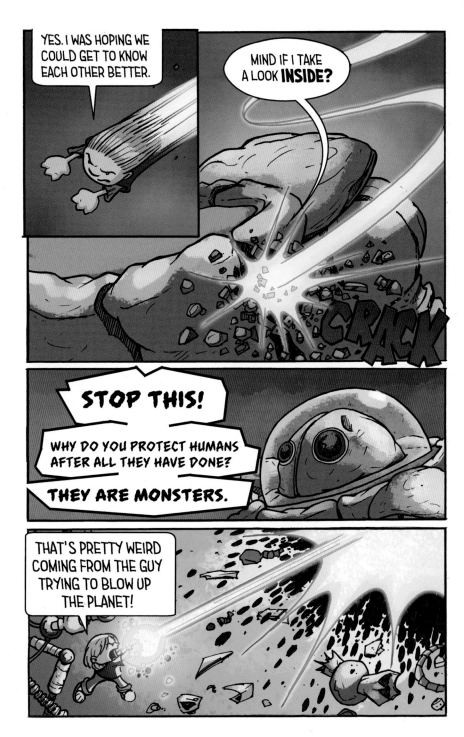

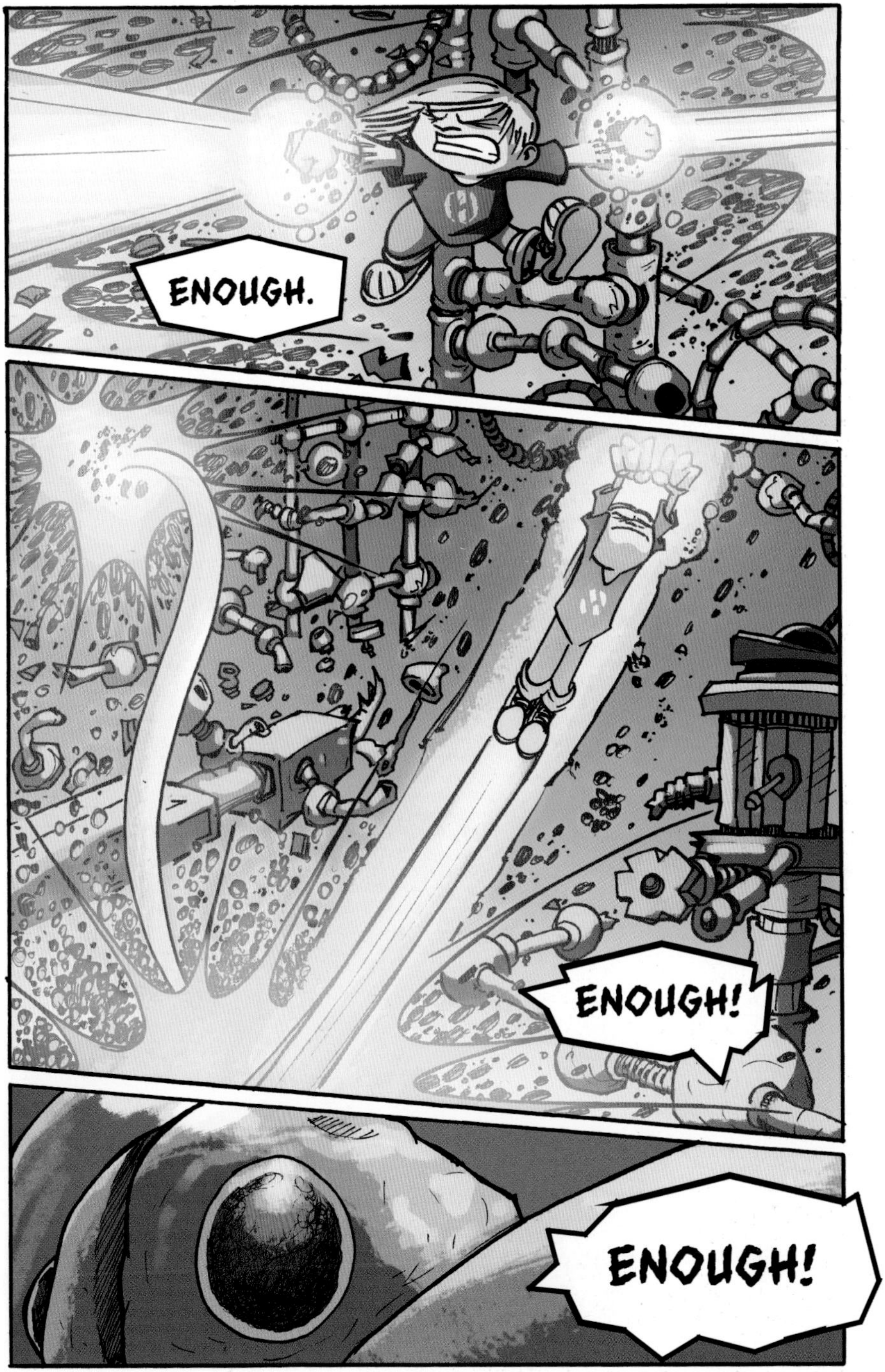
ENOUGH.
ENOUGH!
ENOUGH!

173

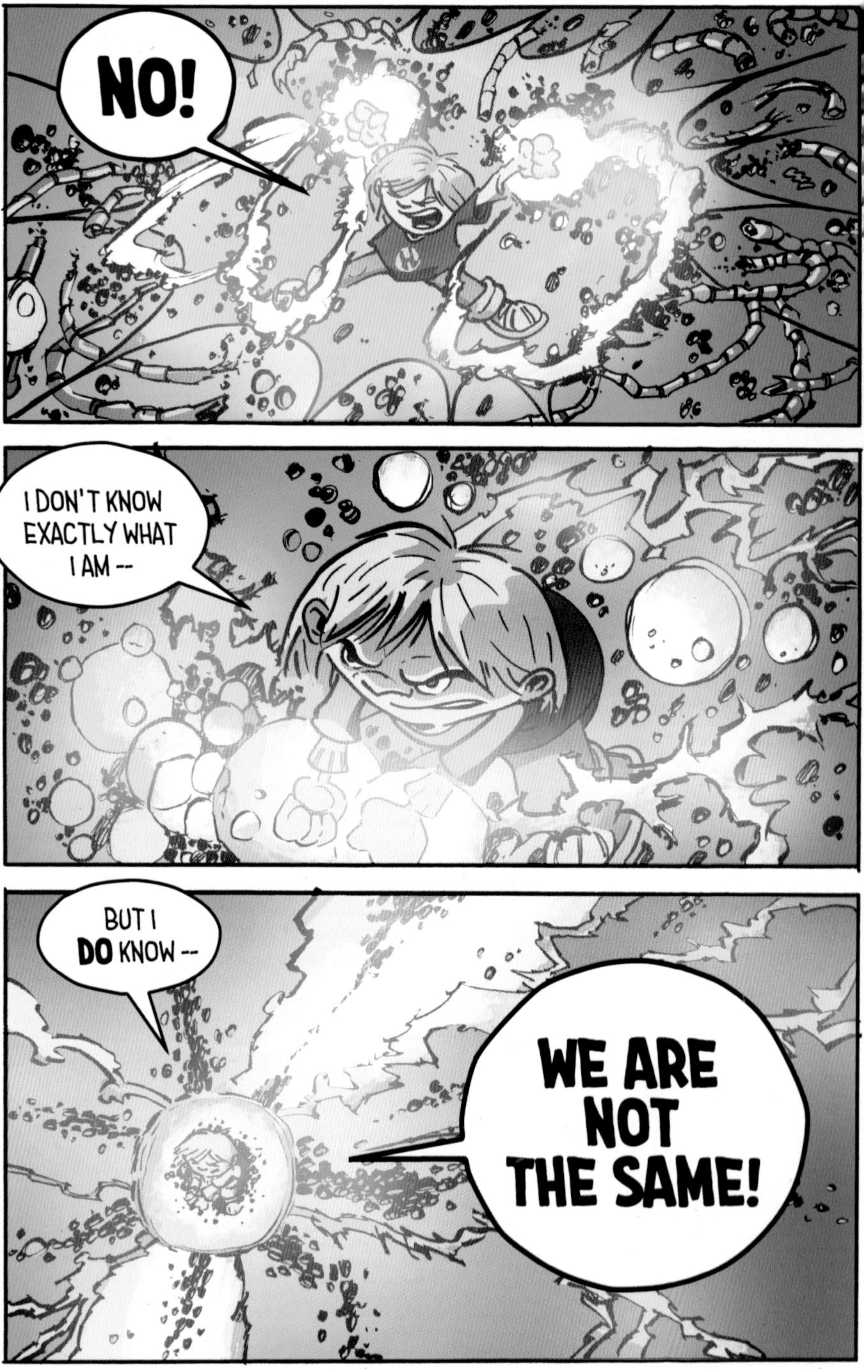
NO!
I DON'T KNOW EXACTLY WHAT I AM --
BUT I **DO** KNOW --
WE ARE NOT THE SAME!

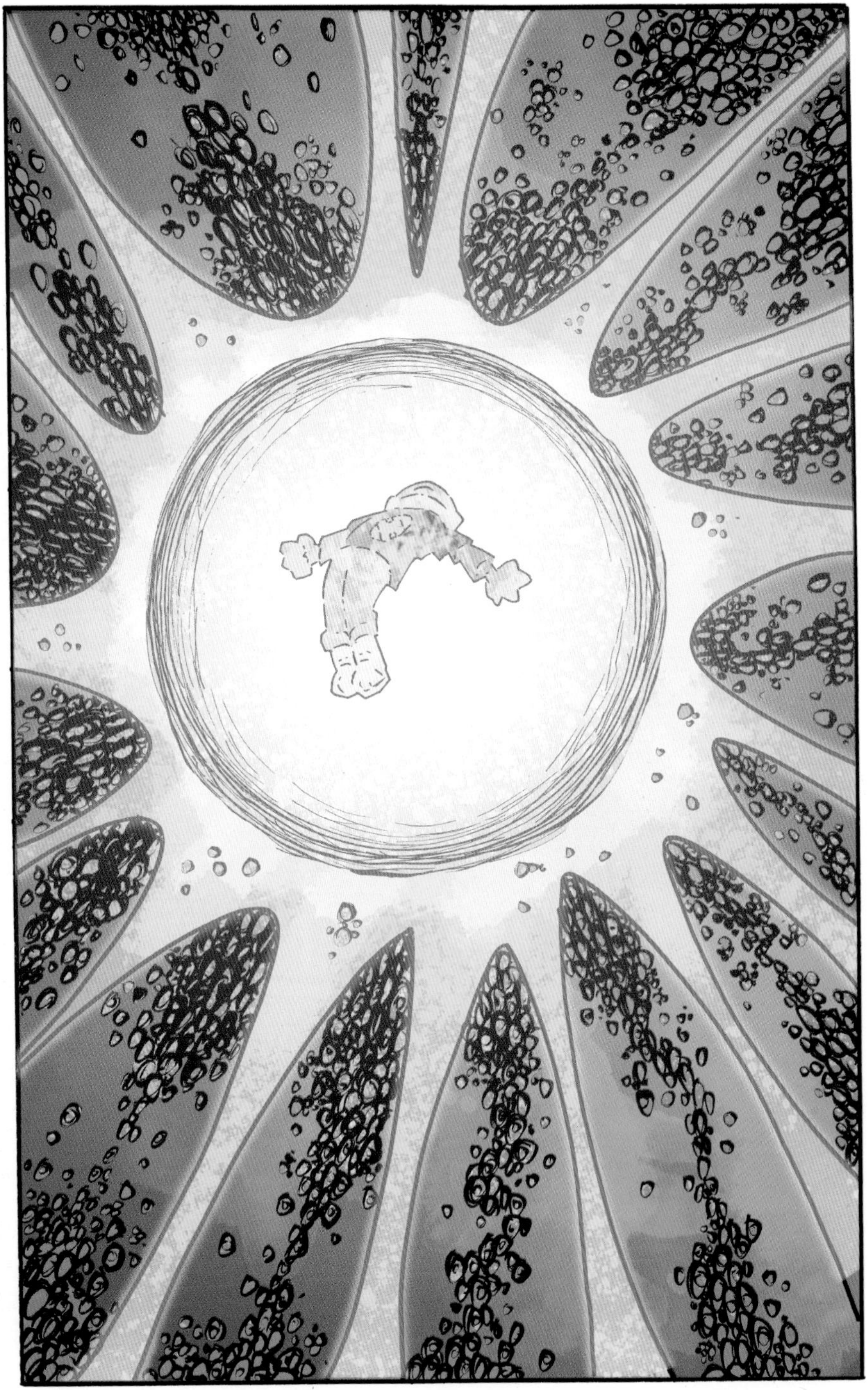

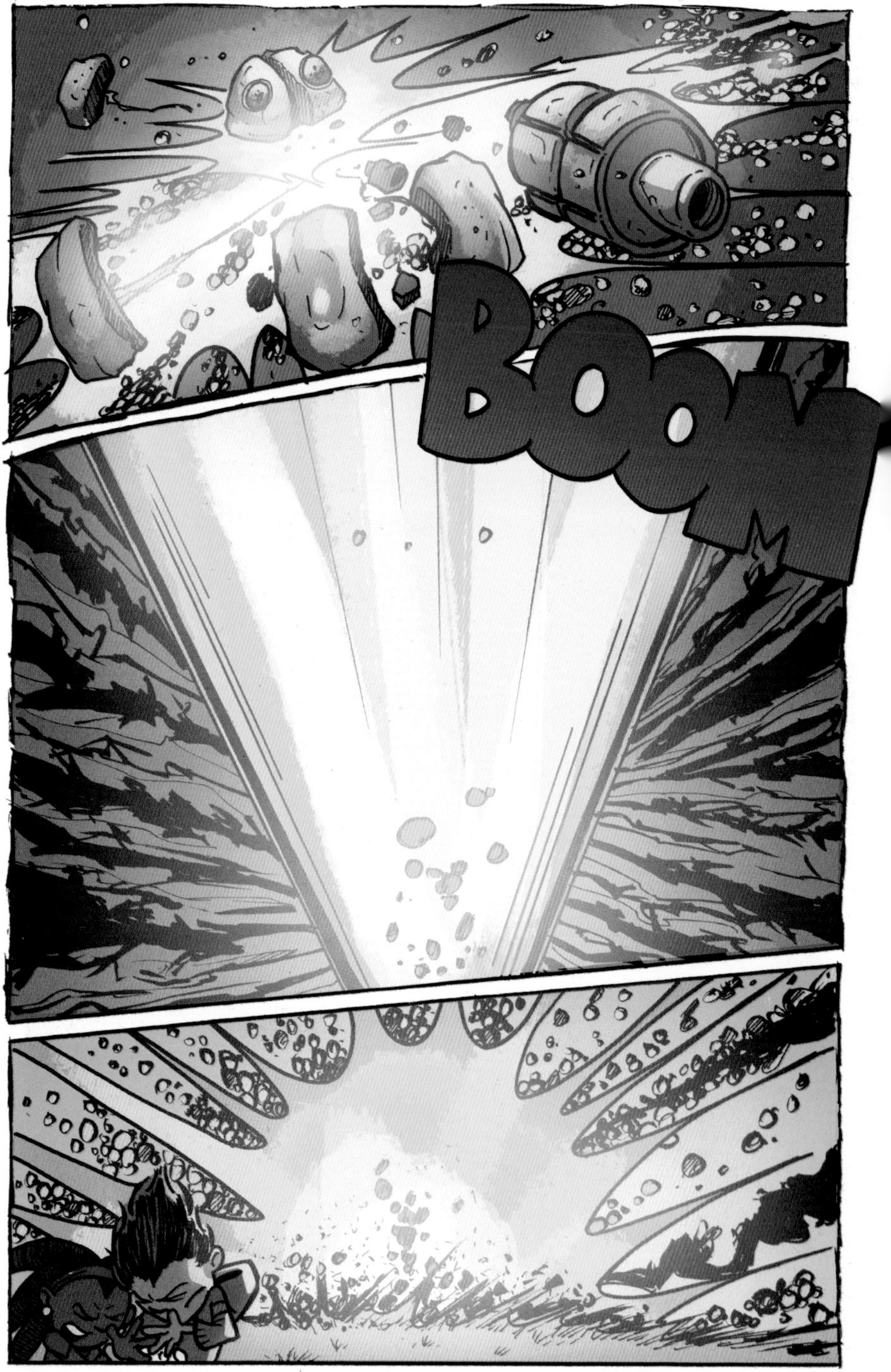
BOOM

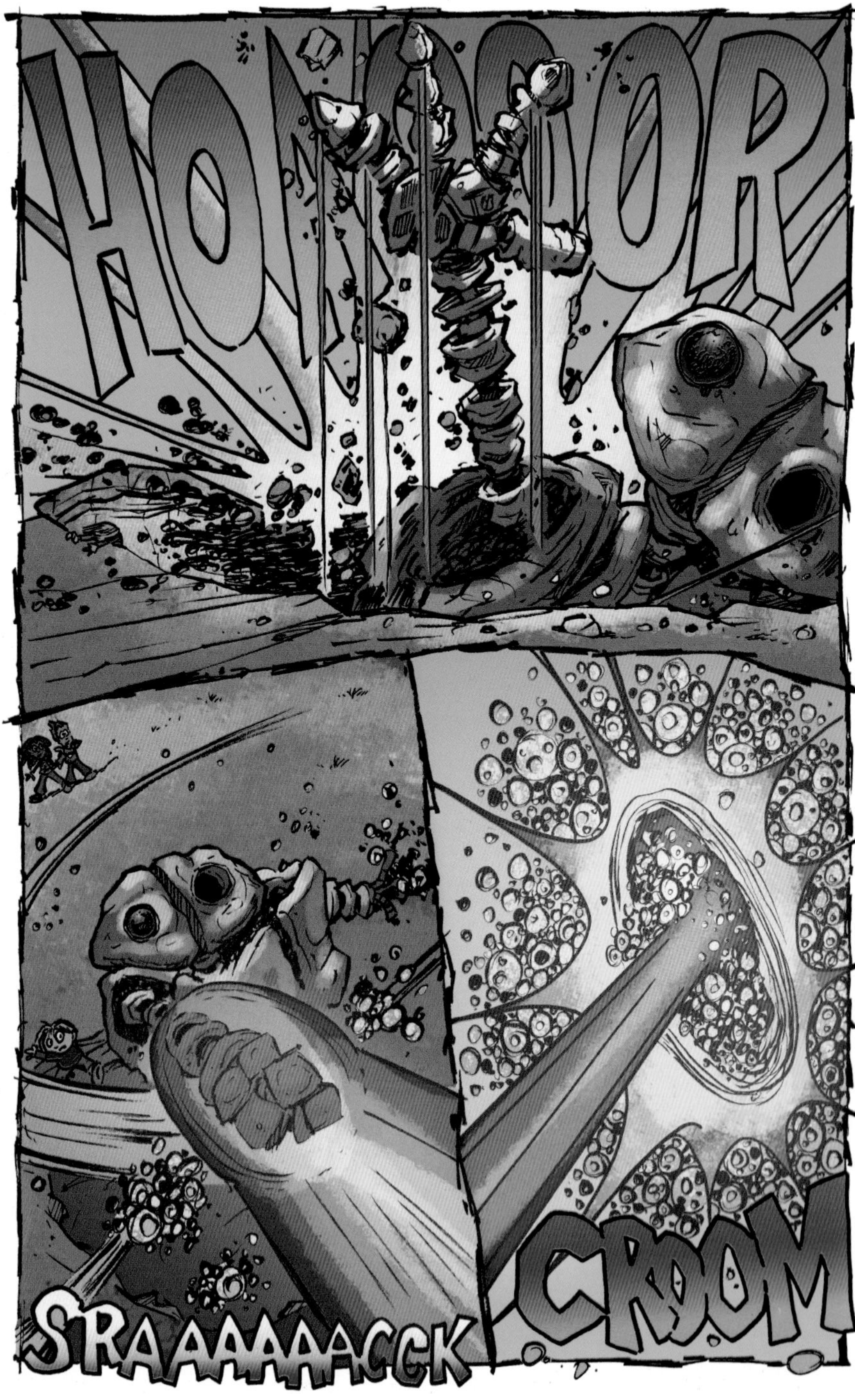
SRAAAAAACCK
CROOM

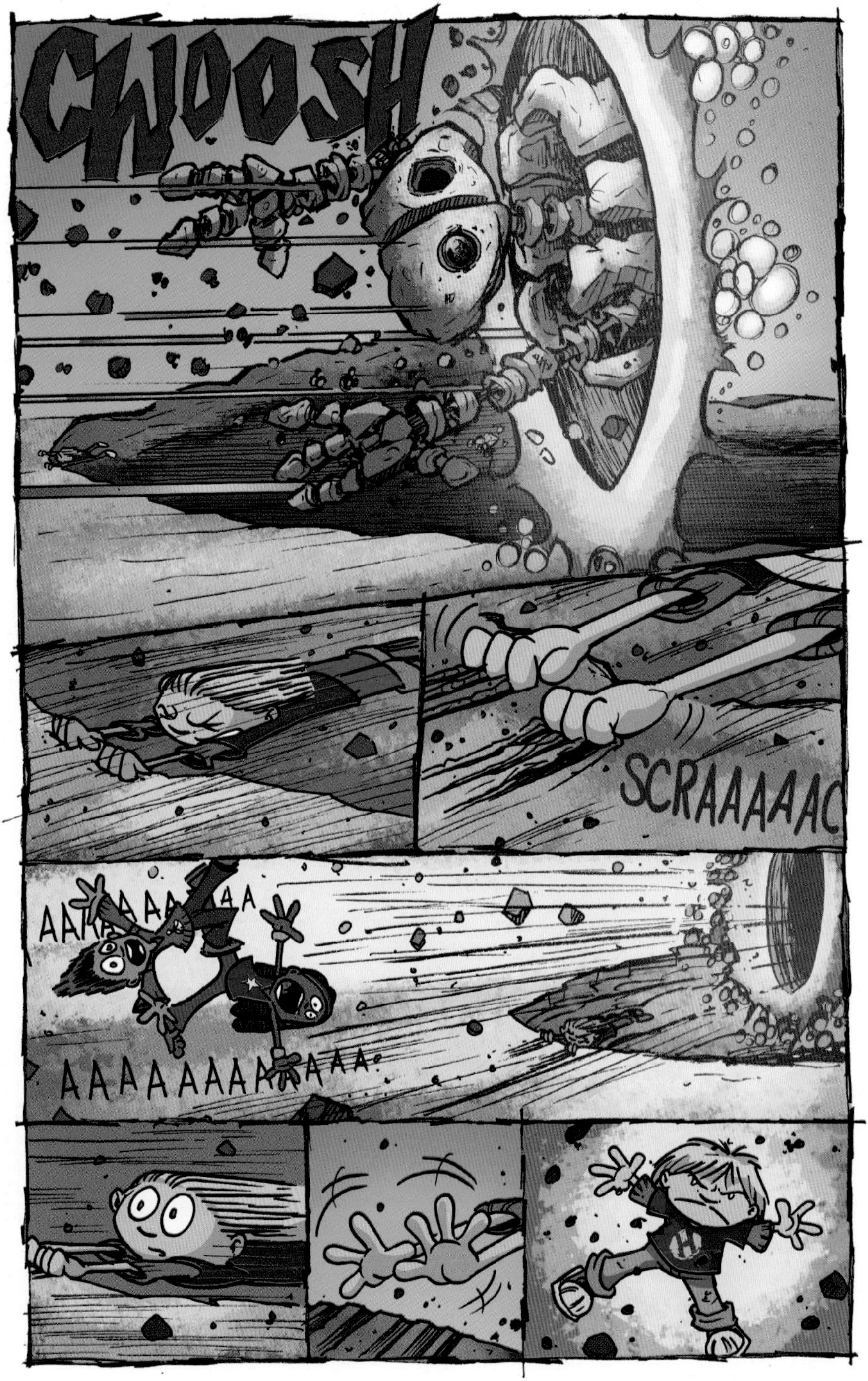
CHOOSH
SCRAAAAAC
AAAAAAAAA
AAAAAAAAAAAA

180

181

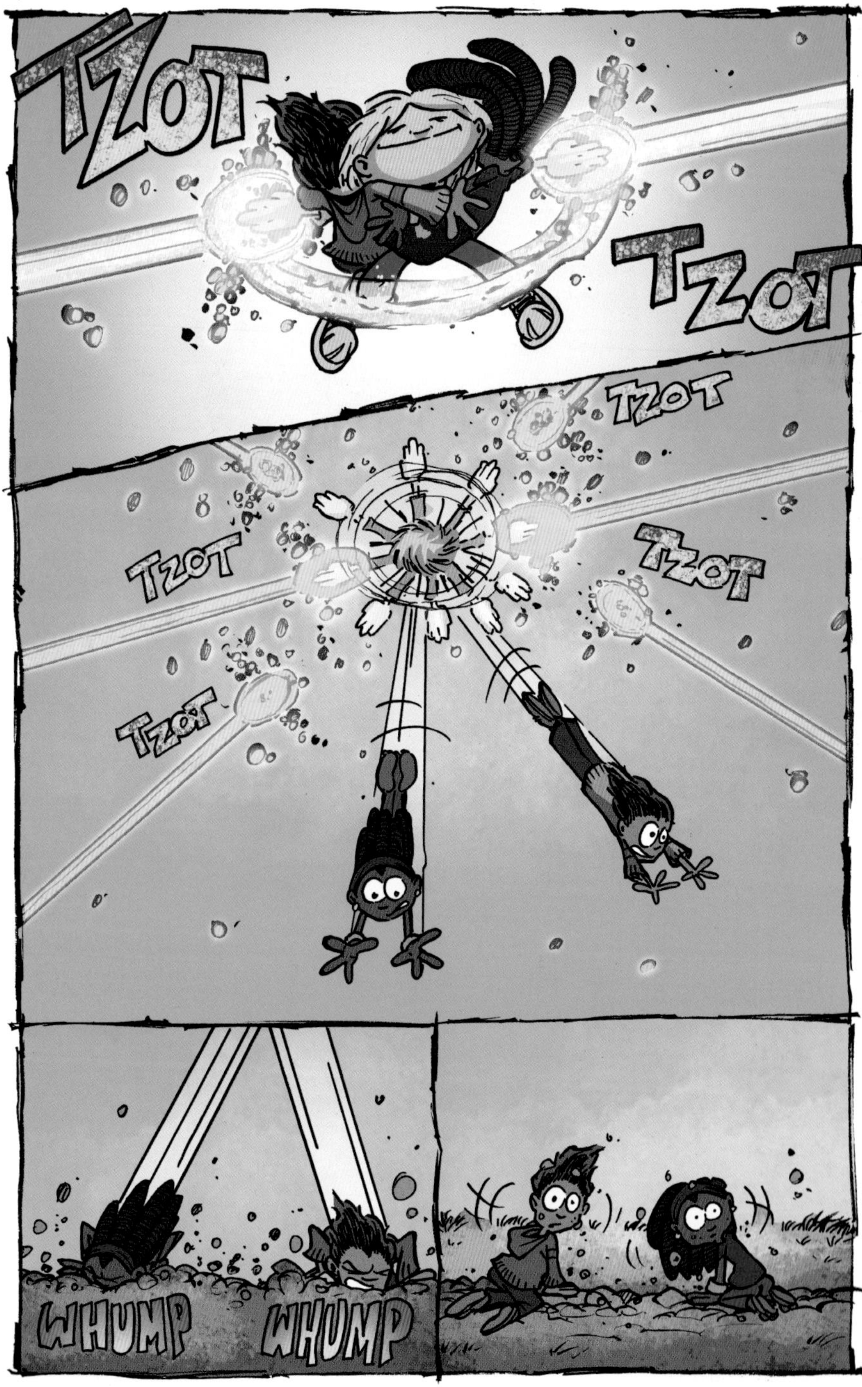
TZOT
TZOT
TZOT
TZOT
TZOT
TZOT
WHUMP
WHUMP

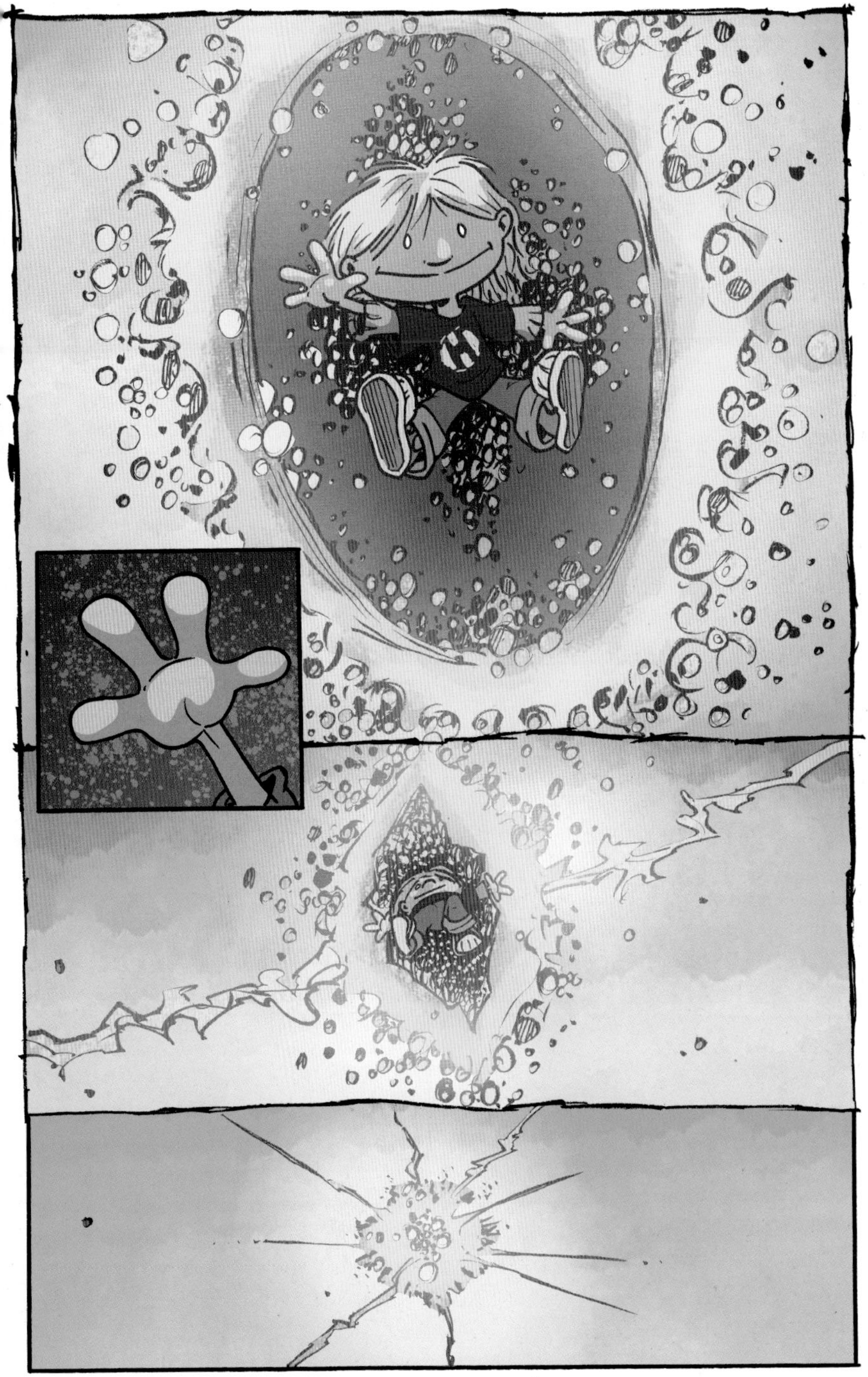

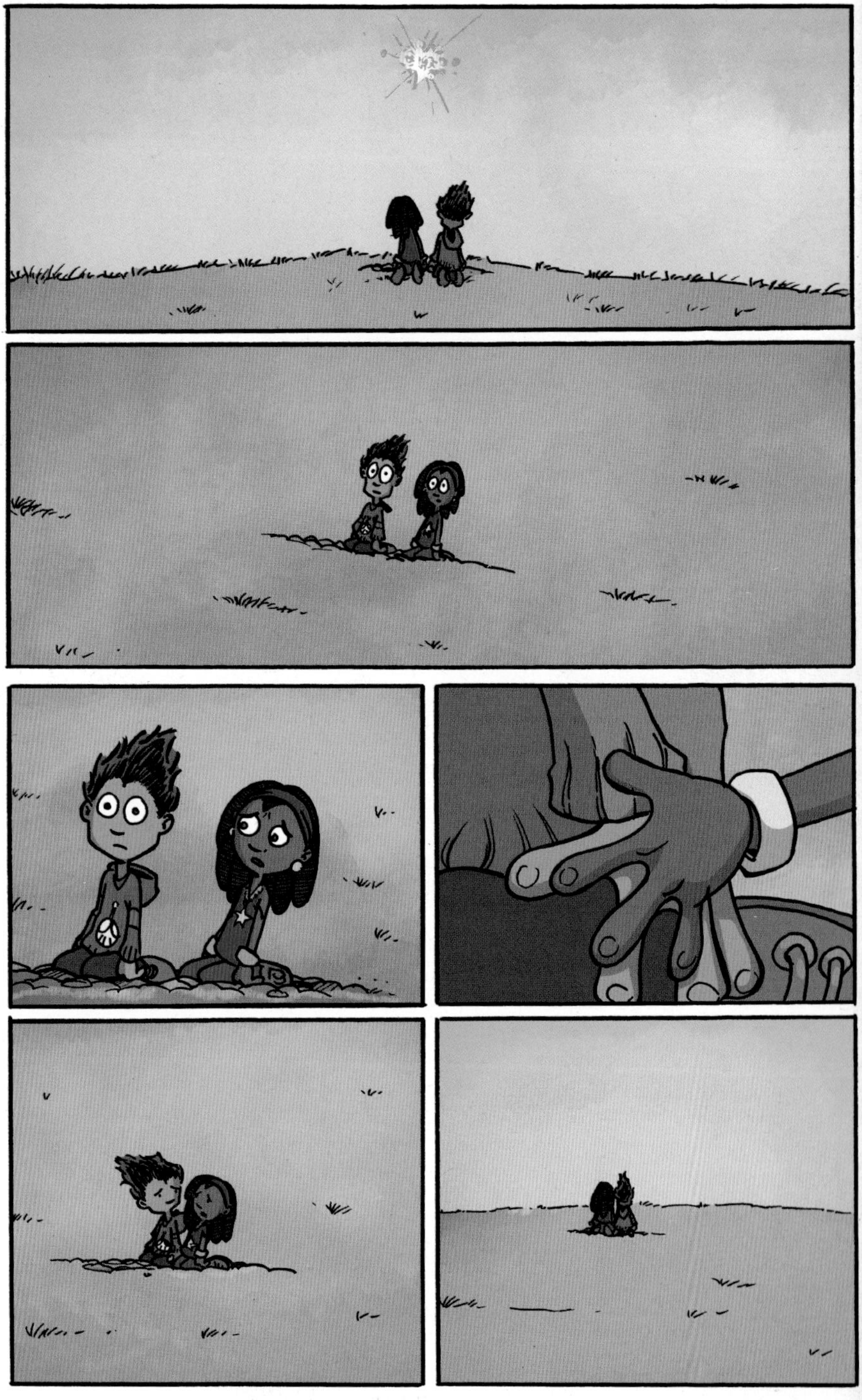

CHAPTER

GONE

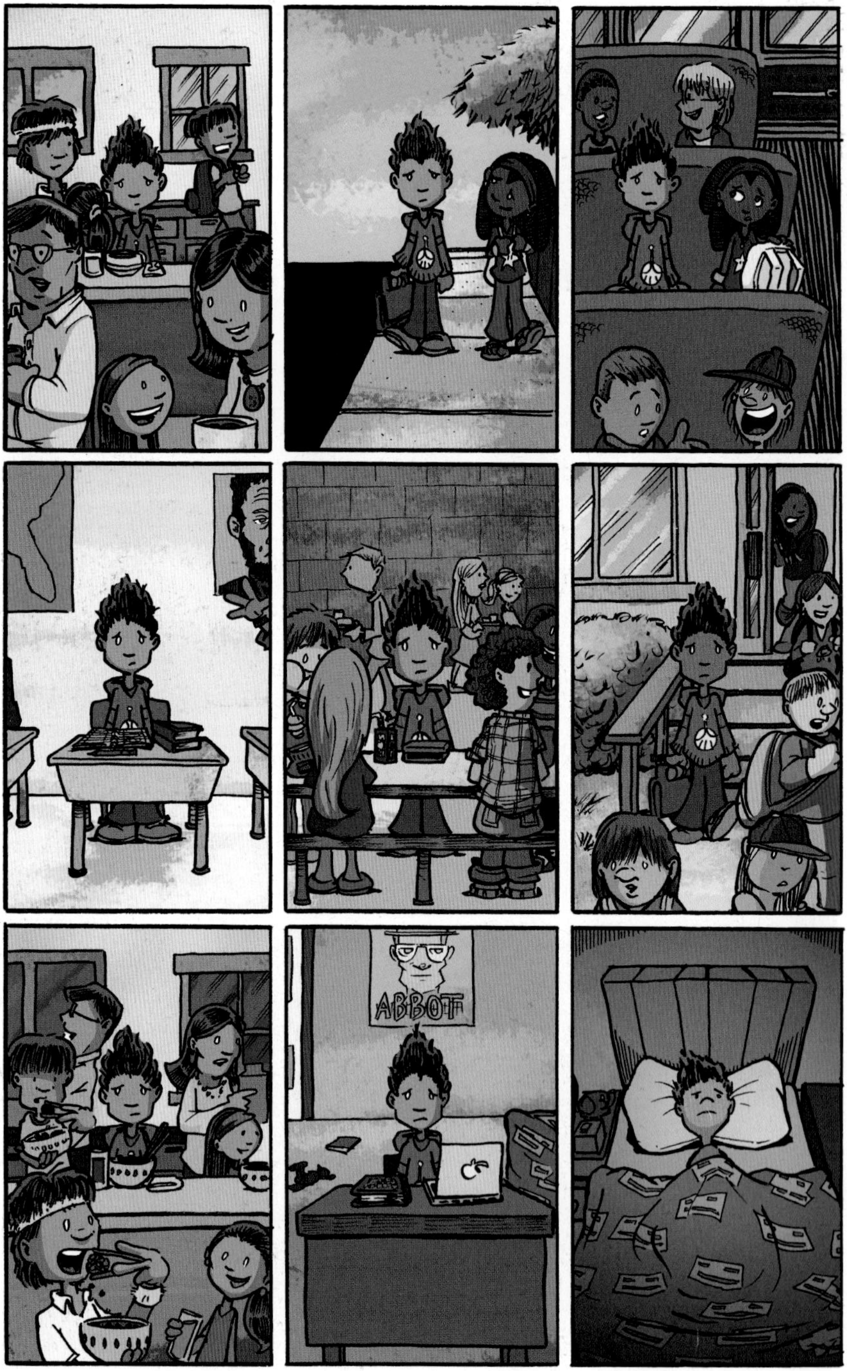
ABBOT

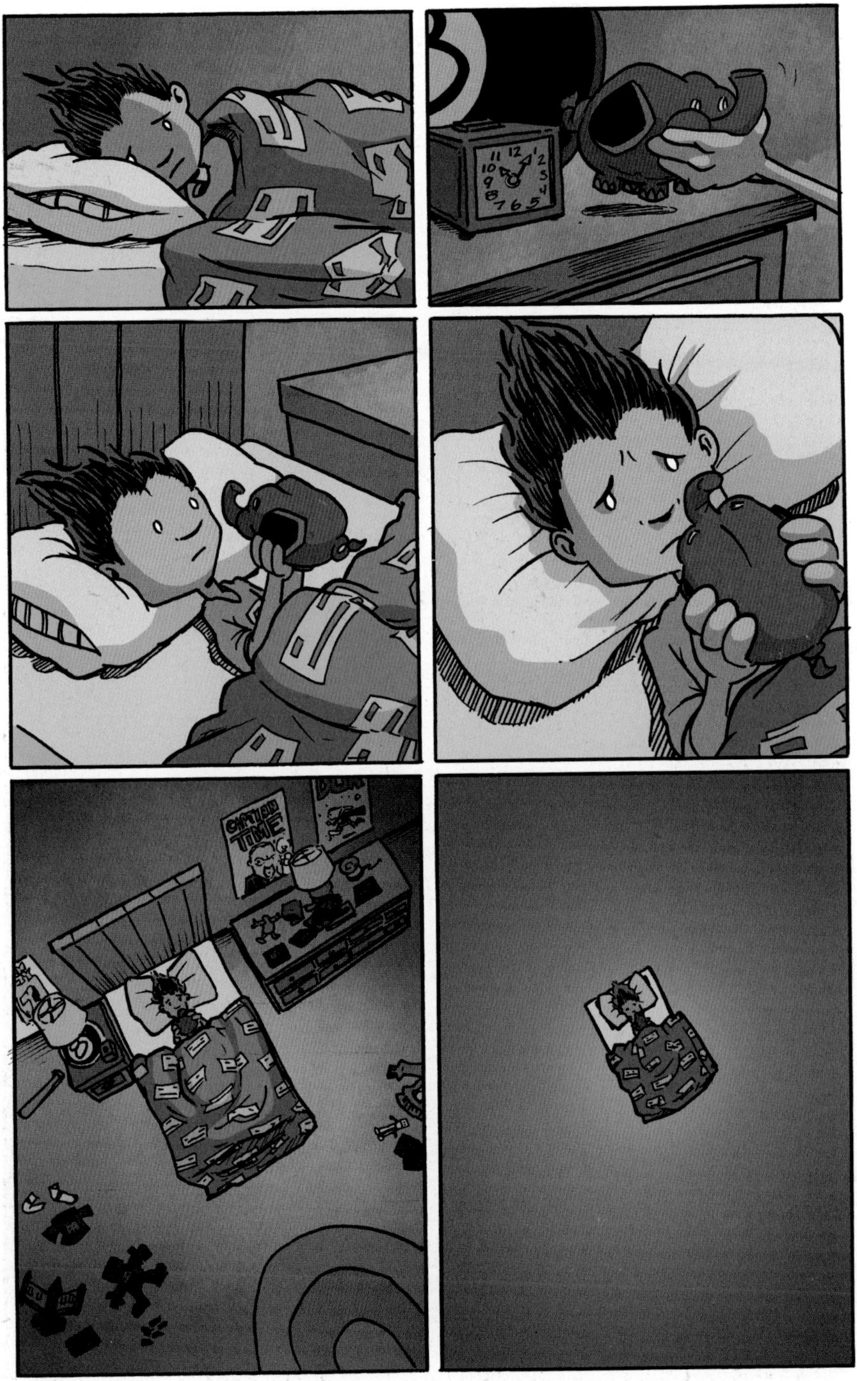
CARTOON TIME

189

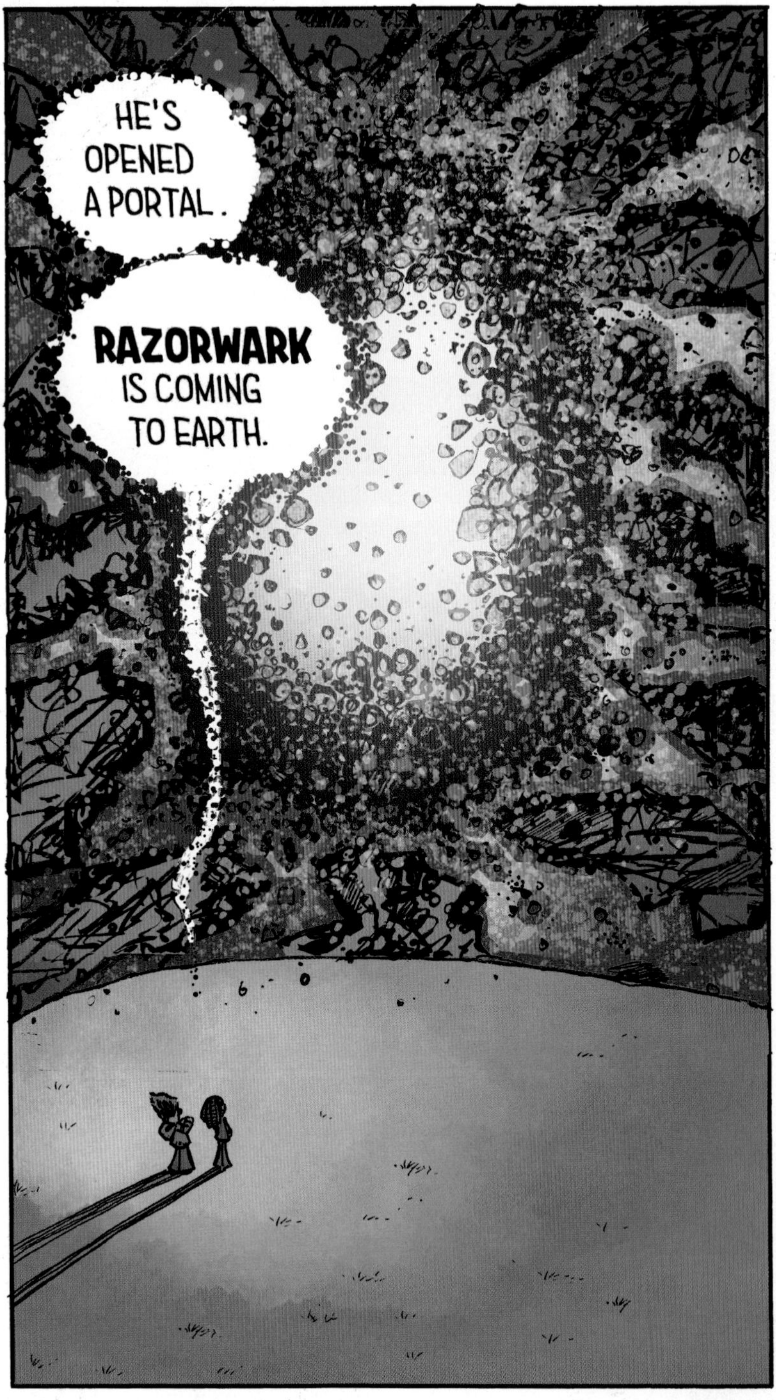
HE'S OPENED A PORTAL.
RAZORWARK IS COMING TO EARTH.

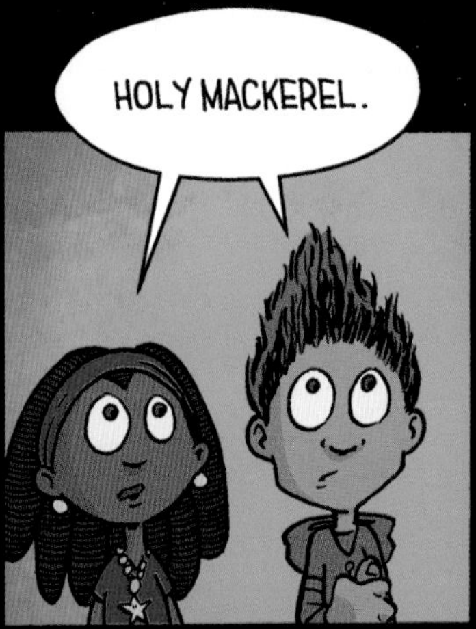
HOLY MACKEREL.

END OF BOOK ONE

DON'T MISS THE NEXT ADVENTURE

AVAILABLE NOW!
KEEP READING FOR A PREVIEW!

Excerpt copyright © 2016 by Judd Winick.
Published by Random House Children's Books, a division of Penguin Random House LLC, New York.

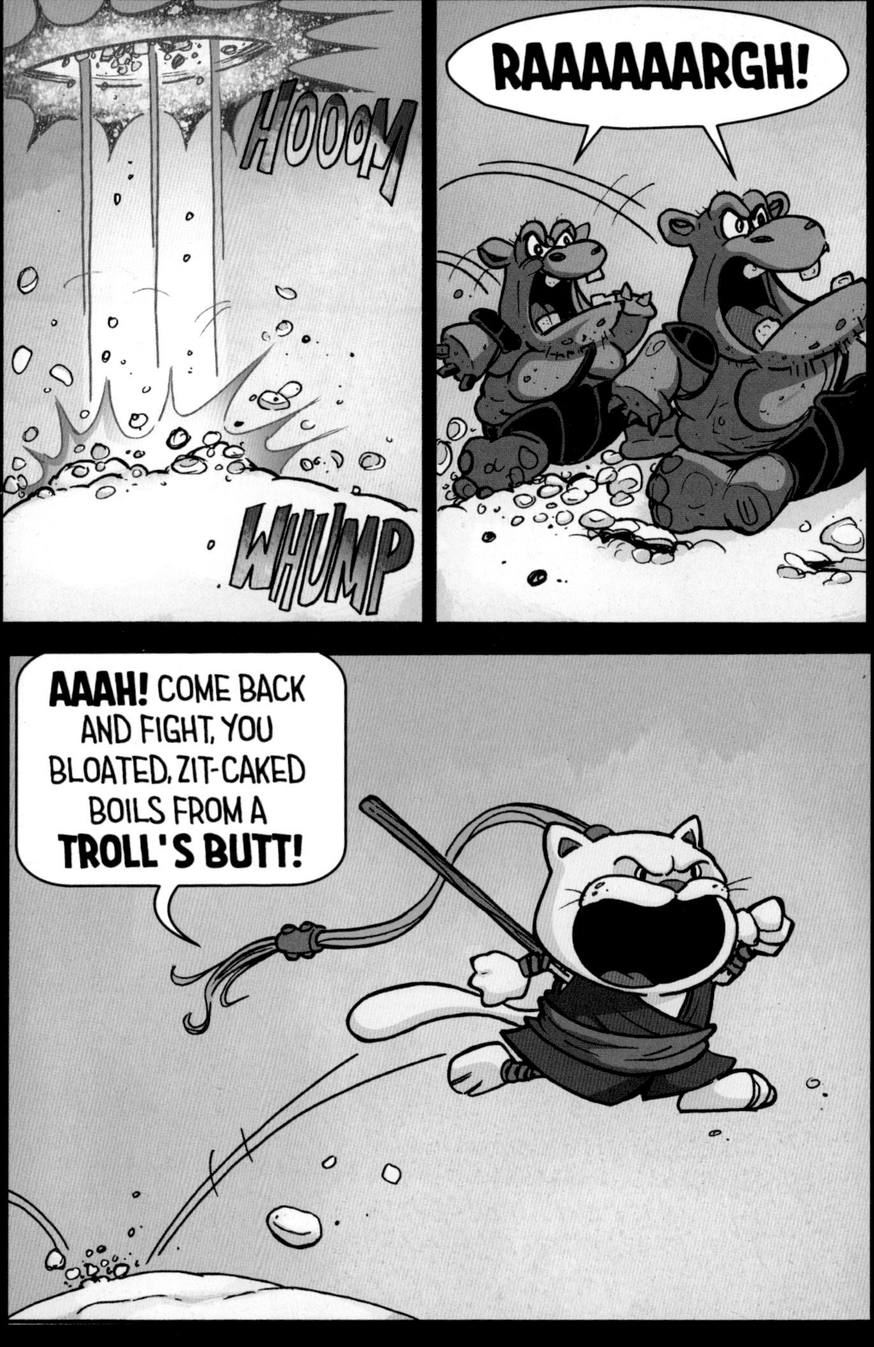
HOOOM
WHUMP
RAAAAAARGH!
AAAH! COME BACK AND FIGHT, YOU BLOATED, ZIT-CAKED BOILS FROM A TROLL'S BUTT!

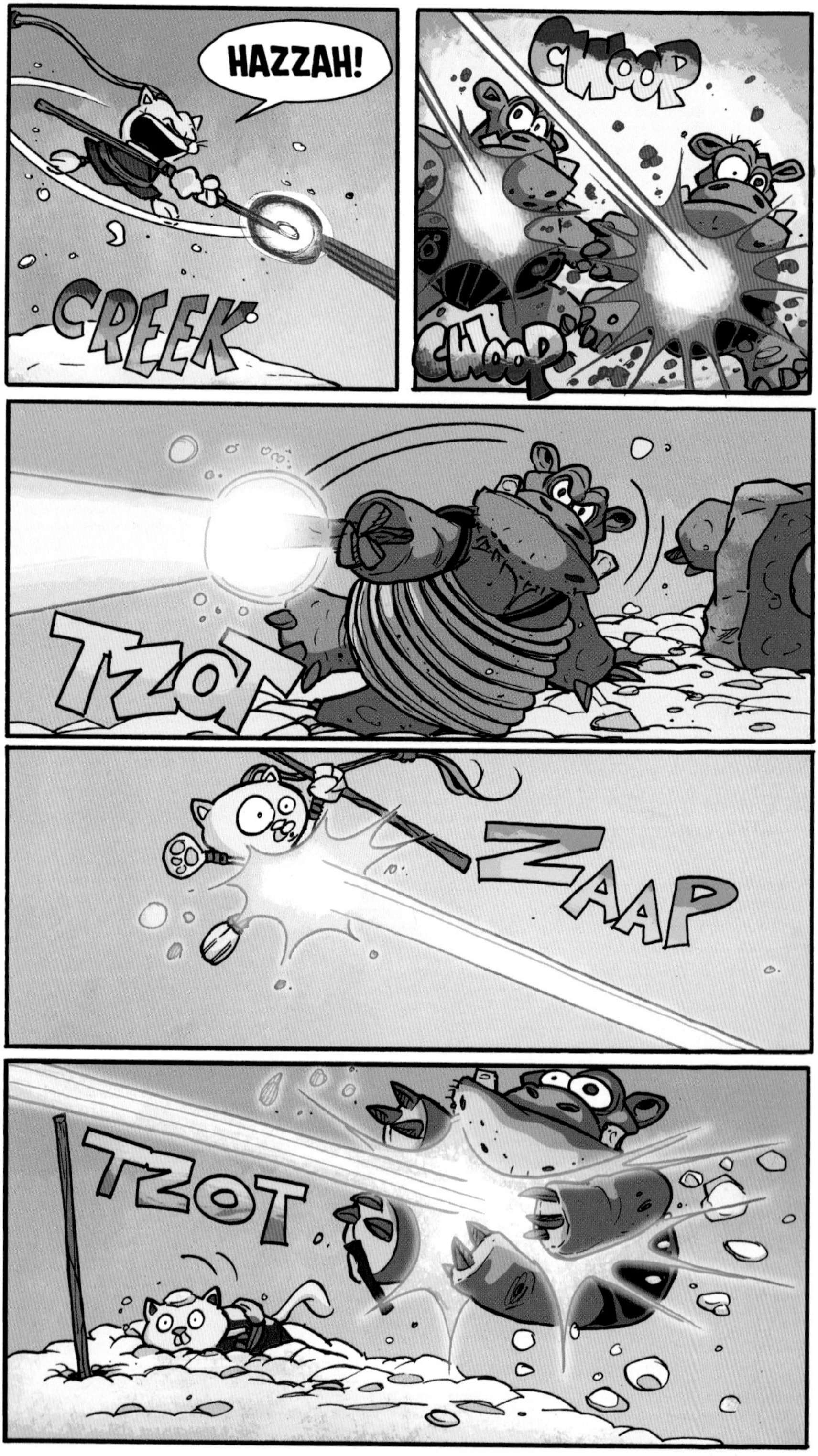

HAZZAH!
CREEK
CHOOP
CHOOP
TZOT
ZAAP
TZOT

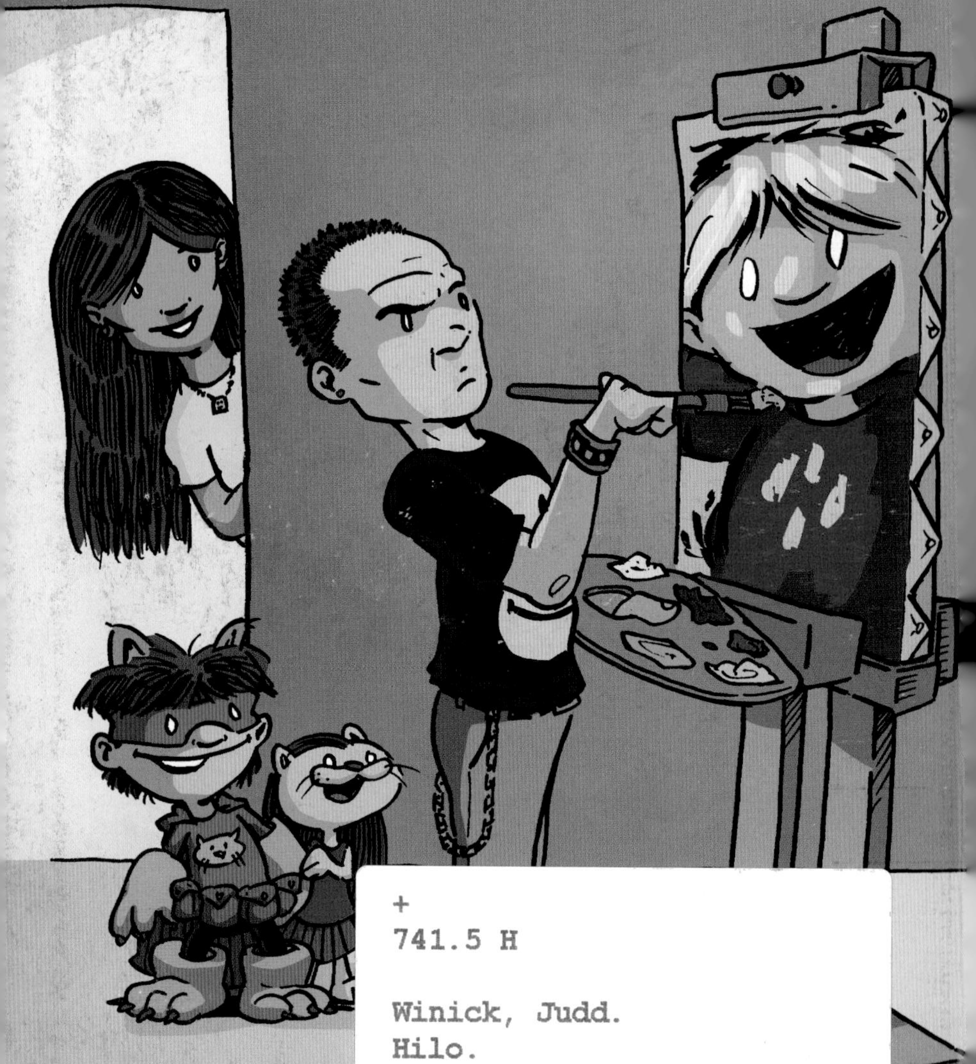